Remember the Butterfly

Rebecca L. Marsh

This is a work of fiction. All places, characters, and events in this novel are a product of the author's imagination or are used fictitiously.

All rights reserved. No part of this book may be reproduced in any form.

Visit the author's website: rebeccalmarsh.com

Cover design by Trim Ventures

www.TrimVentures.com

Cover photo by Patrick Foto at Shutterstock.com

Copyright © 2022 Rebecca L. Marsh

All rights reserved.

ISBN: 978-1-949498-07-3

1Samuel 1:27
"I prayed for this child, and the LORD has granted me what I asked of him."

For Maegan

Michelle,

May love fill your life

[signature]

Other books by Rebecca L. Marsh

Standalone novels
When the Storm Ends
The Rift Between Us

Princess Island series
Where Hope is Found

Part One

Chapter One

Jillian sat on her living room couch with her knees tucked under her chin and arms wrapped around her legs. She'd cried every tear she had. Her eyes were dry now, but her heart was broken, and her hope was shattered—again. It should get easier at some point, she thought, but it never did. She was devastated month after month, and today was the twenty-third month.

Wyatt kept telling her not to get her hopes up. Jillian knew he was trying to protect her, but she didn't know how to follow his advice. How was she supposed to stop hoping for the one thing she wanted most? Every month her shattered hope came to life again with the possibility that this could be *the* month. People always talked about the importance of hope, but hope could be painful. Hope could cause your heart to break over and over again, as Jillian's did every month when she realized that, once again, she was not pregnant.

When the phone rang, Jillian straightened up and glanced at the caller I.D.—JACKIE SWANSON. She answered, "Hi, Mom. Is everything okay? Do you need me at the store?"

"Hi, sweetheart. Everything is fine. Something just told me I should call you. How are you doing today?"

A sob burst from Jillian's lips, despite her efforts to hold it back.

"What's the matter?" her mother asked.

"I had the dream again," she cried. She couldn't talk to her mother about the lack of a baby in her womb. She and

Wyatt had agreed not to tell anyone they were trying until they had a success to talk about. The subject she brought up was no less painful, maybe even more so. But in her mind, the two things were inexplicably connected, and this was something she *could* speak about with her mother. She needed to release some of the emotion—had to—so she talked about the dream.

"Oh, Jillie, I'm sorry."

Jillian thought about the dream, the way it always ended with Natalie's head exploding in blood. New tears ran down her cheeks. "It's so awful, Mom. Every time I see it happen again in my head—and I'm sorry. I'm so sorry."

Her mother's voice came through strong now. "Jillian, it was *not* your fault. You know that."

"I know." She wasn't directly responsible, but she knew she was to blame. No one could convince her otherwise, even if she didn't fire the shot that killed her sister.

When Wyatt came home, Jillian was cooking dinner, her dog Dodger begging for scraps at her feet.

"Something's wrong," Wyatt said.

"I'm fine," Jillian said fighting to keep her emotions at bay and pretend this evening was like any other. She didn't want to cry again.

Wyatt moved in behind her and laid a hand on her shoulder.

At the warmth of his touch, her composure crumbled. She turned and buried her face in his chest, sobbing. Wyatt held her and rubbed her back while she cried.

When her tears were almost gone, she pulled back and looked into her husband's face. His warm, brown eyes met with hers, and he reached up and wiped tears from her cheeks.

"It's going to be okay, Jills. We'll have a baby. The doctor did all the tests and said nothing is wrong."

Jillian stepped back from him and clenched her jaw. She remembered the tests perfectly well as most of them had been on her. She knew that wasn't Wyatt's fault, so the anger was misplaced. Her emotions were just running so hot it was hard to keep them in check.

She gave him a tearful nod.

"You probably just need to relax. Remember, Dr. Melton said stress might be the problem," he said.

Now the anger flared out and she couldn't stop it. She pushed back from Wyatt, her green eyes flashing. "So, it's my fault? Is that what you're saying?"

At her tone, Wyatt stepped further back, a cautious look on his face. "No, of course not," he said, holding up his hands. "That's not what I'm saying. It isn't anyone's fault."

Jillian's body, rigid from the spike of anger suddenly wilted as tears flooded her eyes again. "Maybe it *is* my fault." *Just like Natalie was my fault!*

Wyatt moved back to her and wrapped his strong arms around her. "No, it isn't. ... God, I'm sorry. I think we both need to relax." He held her for a few more minutes, and when her sobs quieted, he lifted her chin and looked into her watery eyes. "Let me finish with dinner. Then I think we need to pick a movie and a bottle of wine. We both want a baby, Jills, but we need to remember we have each other. I don't want the stress of all this to tear us apart. I don't want to lose you, Jills. I don't want to lose *us*."

Jillian nodded and gave him a tentative smile. He was right. The pursuit of a baby was putting a lot of pressure on their relationship. Sometimes she forgot what it was like to be together with no goal except to love each other.

She let him finish the dinner preparations while she stared mindlessly at the TV. They ate together without mentioning their failure, the doctors, or their hopes for a baby. The wine eased Jillian's hurt in some minuscule way as she cuddled with Wyatt on the couch in front of a movie. They still had each other which, she kept reminding herself, was much more than many people had.

Chapter Two

The next morning, Jillian arrived at her family's shoe store just before eight o'clock. She stared up at the sign that read *Swan Shoes* and thought about her grandfather. The store was his great accomplishment. When Jillian and Natalie were little girls, Grandpa Mac would bring them to the store and point up at the sign. "Blood, sweat, and tears—that's what that is, girls. And someday it will be yours," he would say. He thought leaving the store to his descendants was the greatest gift, and most of them agreed.

Jillian loved the store. She couldn't think of anything she would rather do. She enjoyed working with her family. They didn't always agree—and they had their arguments, but they always worked it out. The only downfall was the memory of the family members no longer working with them. Grandpa Mac died the year before, and Grandma Elsie was in a nursing home now. But the most noticeable ghost in the store was Natalie. She shouldn't be gone. Her vibrant spirit should still fill this space, and Jillian felt the emptiness of her loss every day.

She walked to the store with her coffee cup in hand. Inside, her cousins were preparing to open.

"I'm sure it's not my turn again," Robbie said. "I just did it."

"Yeah, three weeks ago. So now it's your turn again," Layla retorted.

"Inventory argument?" Jillian asked, looking at her cousins. The two of them looked almost exactly alike. From their mother, they had both gotten curly hair but the auburn color came from the Swanson side. It was the same color as Jillian's father and their father. They also both had the same green eyes as Jillian. A trait shared by every child born into the Swanson family for the last four generations. The one difference in their appearance was the spray of freckles across Layla's nose and cheeks.

Robbie and Layla were only a year apart in age, and since Robbie had always been a little small for his age growing up and Layla had been on the tall side, people regularly mistook them for twins. Jillian was pretty sure Robbie still harbored sore feelings over that.

Layla glanced at Jillian. "No argument. I did it last week, you did it the week before last, so that means it's his turn this week."

Robbie threw up his hands in surrender. "Okay, fine. I just hate inventory."

"We all hate inventory," Layla said. "That's why our parents have passed the lovely job on to us."

"Hey, Jill, any chance you could talk Wyatt into leaving his illustrious career at the high school to come work here? Then we'd only have to do inventory once a month."

Jillian tensed at her cousin's words, and she could find none of her own. *If Natalie were alive, there would be four of them.* She knew Robbie wasn't trying to point that out, but it screamed through her mind anyway.

"Don't be an idiot!" Layla said, taking the pressure to answer off Jillian. "Do you think Kaitlyn is going to stop working as a paramedic and come sell shoes when she marries you?"

Robbie shrugged. "Maybe."

Layla threw an empty shoebox at his head.

"Hey! There's no need for violence," he protested.

"You're hopeless," Layla said, shaking her head.

"Who wouldn't want to work here? I mean, inventory sucks, but other than that, this place is great."

Layla raised her eyebrows in response. She wasn't planning to stick with working at the store, even though it meant she would not inherit a share of the business. Grandpa Mac stipulated in his will that all family members who worked in the store until retirement would, as an inheritance, continue to receive their share of the profits for life. Those who left the store for other ventures got nothing.

"It *is* great," Robbie insisted. "Jillian agrees."

Jillian smiled. "I do love the store."

"And why wouldn't you? You get to work with family, people who care about you. And you get to meet new people and help them. The schedule is flexible. Best of all, it isn't just a job, we own it."

"Well, let's see," Layla began. "Boring dead times and crazy customers that yell at you. Picking up after the customers who don't know what a trash can is—remember when Dad found a half-eaten banana rotting in a shoebox? Then there're stinky feet, and, oh yeah, *inventory*." She stopped for a moment and a sour look came over her face. "I don't even want to think about that one guy and what he was planning to do."

Layla was referring to a man Jillian's mother once discovered undressing in the lady's dress shoes section.

"And that's why he was banned from the store. But hey, way to find the negatives, sis," Robbie said.

"Don't get me wrong. I like the store most of the time, but it was Grandpa Mac's dream. It just isn't mine."

Layla was almost finished with her four-year degree and then she'd be on to veterinarian school next year to fulfill her dream of becoming a large animal vet.

"Yeah, I know," Robbie said. "And when you leave, Jillian and I will be stuck doing inventory every other week."

"It's not so bad. You two will get all the profits for yourselves."

Robbie rolled his eyes. "Not really. Since Wyatt and Kaitlyn aren't likely to work here, we'll have to hire employees once our parents retire."

Layla smiled. "Maybe not. If you guys all get busy having kids, maybe they'll be old enough to start working by then."

At the mention of having kids, Jillian's heart sank. There seemed to be nowhere she could go to escape the heartache. It always came up somehow or another.

Robbie sighed. "Kaitlyn wants to wait a couple of years."

Before anyone could say another word, Rose Swanson, Robbie and Layla's mother, breezed in. "Hi, kids," she said.

As Robbie, Layla, and Jillian returned her greeting, Rose glanced around at their faces. The brows over her dark eyes lifted. "Are we having a serious discussion this morning?"

Layla shrugged. "To sum it up, Robbie doesn't want to do inventory and he's sore about my choice to leave the store next year."

"I see," Rose said. She looked at her son. "Well, you could probably get your dad to help you with inventory once in a while if you offer it up as a chance for father-son bonding. He misses spending time with you."

Robbie grinned as Layla sidled up to her mother. With a smile, she threw an arm around her mother's shoulders. "And in a couple of weeks would you be interested in some mother-daughter bonding?"

"Sure sweetheart. We'll go shopping." Layla's smile wilted away. Rose turned to face her and put a hand under Layla's chin. "Sorry, darling, but you can't turn my own trick against me. Now, you have to leave for class in two hours, so I think you need to get some work done around here before you go. The men's sneaker section needs to be re-stocked."

After Layla stalked away to the men's section with the sullen demeanor of a punished child, Jillian went to the back room and began bringing out some of the inventory that needed to be put on the shelves. She dropped several boxes off with Layla and then headed to the children's section to stock shelves there. Robbie and Rose stayed in the front and opened the store.

Before long, the store was buzzing with customers on and off, keeping them all busy. Jillian was grateful for the activity and the relief it provided from the worries of her mind. In the moments when the store went quiet, she cleaned up and stocked the shelves, trying very hard not to think about her unfulfilled desire for a child or her recurring nightmare.

When lunchtime rolled around, Robbie left for the rest of the day and was replaced by Jillian's parents. She and Rose worked together with them until three o'clock, when Layla returned from school and her father, Danny, came in as well, allowing Jillian and Rose to leave.

That afternoon when Jillian went home, she resolved to push away last month's disappointing failure and not even think about the next month. She put on relaxing music, poured herself a glass of wine, and started cooking dinner. Wyatt, who taught high school math, was working late helping to coach the school's soccer team. By the time he came home, dinner was almost finished. He walked up behind her and hovered for a moment until she turned to him and smiled.

He returned her smile. "I'm glad to see you looking better today," he said. Though he didn't say so, she knew he'd held back from touching her until he was sure she wouldn't burst into tears. He always walked on eggshells around her for a few days after her period arrived.

She reached out and embraced him, holding on tight and breathing in his scent. "There's always next month, right?" It was hard to say those words because that statement would always be true, right up until she reached menopause. But she didn't want to say that anymore, didn't want to have to keep hoping that the next month would end with joy instead of heartbreak.

She pulled back and looked him in the eye. "And we have each other." Those words she meant with every ounce of her being.

"Always," he said, reaching out to run his fingers through her honey-blond hair that fell just past chin-length.

They sat down and ate together, talking about their day. She told him about the customer at the store who insisted she was a size seven and continued cramming her feet into shoes that were clearly too small. "Like Cinderella's sisters," he said with a laugh. Then he talked about one of his struggling students and how well the soccer team was shaping up.

When the conversation lulled, Wyatt changed the subject. "Did you get the birthday gift for Braylee?"

A wave of sadness fell over Jillian, not because she didn't love Wyatt's little niece—she did—but because it was so hard to spend time with his family these days. She'd once enjoyed Wyatt's family, maybe even more than her own. Wyatt had a brother and a sister, both of whom Jillian loved. She also loved their spouses. They were a family that laughed, joked, and played games together. Things her family used to do—before they lost Natalie. And, Jillian supposed, the main reason she'd loved spending time with Wyatt's family was because being with them didn't make her feel like she was drowning in guilt. She could be with them without thinking about Natalie, without feeling her sister's absence like an ever-present weight.

It was all different now, though. For the last two years, Wyatt's sister and sister-in-law had been taking turns having babies. Braylee, belonging to Wyatt's sister Courtney was the oldest. Then Anika, Wyatt's sister-in-law, was blessed with a son. After that, Courtney had another girl, and now Anika was pregnant again.

Jillian loved every one of those babies but spending time around them intensified her pain at not having one of her own. The fact that the only topics of conversation that went on between the women were those related to babies—pregnancy, feeding choices, babysitters, and sleepless nights—added insult to injury. Jillian had zero input on any of that. She was left to sit and listen to them talk about the thing she most wanted but didn't have.

In a couple of days, she'd have to deal with all the emotional turmoil being around his family dredged up for her when they got together for little Braylee's second birthday.

"Not yet," she said. "I'll run out tomorrow and get something."

Wyatt smiled. "I heard she likes to play with building blocks. She might be another mean, Green math-brain."

Jillian tried to smile back, though she was sure it looked as forced as it felt. "I guess we'll see."

Wyatt's smile fell away. He looked down and concentrated on his food.

"I'm sorry," Jillian said. They should be able to talk about his family without it making her sad, but she couldn't stop the sadness.

He reached out and took her hand, squeezing it. He was trying to reassure her that he understood or maybe that the sadness would end one day. Somehow the gesture made her heart break a little more.

Saturday morning, after sleeping in until nine o'clock, Jillian and Wyatt had a quiet breakfast together before preparing to head over to Courtney and Brent's house for the birthday party. Jillian wrapped the set of mega blocks she'd bought in shiny paper covered with balloons, then she called to Dodger, an old terrier mix she and Natalie had adopted when they were teenagers. He trotted into the kitchen, where Jillian and Wyatt were waiting for him, his tail wagging. Jillian smiled at his happy-go-lucky demeanor. She remembered the day she first saw him at the animal shelter. He'd jumped up the moment she and Natalie stepped in front of his cage, his tail wagging and his eyes full of life.

The memory was a good one, and Jillian loved remembering sweet Dodger as a puppy, but then she thought about how happy Natalie was that day. She remembered the smile on her sister's face, the sparkle in her mischievous eyes. She could see Natalie's young face with the dusting of freckles framed by strawberry-blond hair. The memory was a stab to Jillian's heart. Natalie's face should still be seen. Her laugh should still be heard. Instead, because of one wrong choice, she was gone.

Jillian shook the memory away. She'd have enough to deal with today.

"Wanna go to a party with the kids, Dodge?" Wyatt asked. Dodger pranced around in response. He loved the kids and they loved him. "Good. We're gonna have lots of fun." Wyatt clipped on the dog's leash and they all headed out the door.

An hour later, Jillian was sitting on Courtney's patio with Wyatt's older brother, L.J. and his wife Anika. L.J., or Lewis Junior, was named after their father, though he looked exactly like their mother. He had inherited wavy, black hair and dark hazel eyes. His wife, Anika, was a pale, blue-eyed blond. L.J. was very tall and Anika very short. Together they were an interesting contrast.

They all watched as the two children who could walk chased Dodger around the yard. The gentle spring breeze rustled the leaves, and the sky was nothing but blue. Birds chirped in the trees.

L.J. laughed. "That dog is one in a million. He actually fakes running in slow motion so the little tots can keep up. If I thought we could get one just like him, I'd run out right now. Tucker would be entertained all the time."

"Yeah," Anika responded, "and I'd be taking care of a dog plus two kids in another couple of months. I think the two kids will be quite enough, thank you."

"A dog like Dodger would make it easier for you," L.J. insisted. "Tucker would wear himself out chasing it all day."

Anika cut a sideways glance at her husband. "And I'd have to clean up after kids and dog. I'd have to worry about the baby chewing on dog toys and the dog chewing on baby toys." She shook her head. "And who knows what else."

"Fine, have it your way."

"Who's going to have their way about what?" Rhonda, Wyatt's mother, asked as she stepped out of the sliding glass door. Everyone turned and looked at her.

"Your son was just trying to talk me into getting a dog," Anika said.

Rhonda raised an eyebrow. "Because you don't have enough going on?"

"Exactly! Thank you, Rhonda."

"Sure, jump all over a guy for trying to make his kid happy," L.J. protested.

They dropped the subject and everyone returned to watching the kids toddle after Dodger. Rhonda stepped up behind Jillian and put a hand on her shoulder. "Soon there'll be two more out there chasing the dog. Could be three if you and Wyatt get started."

Jillian went still and stiff. She bit her lip to keep from tearing up. Hoping Rhonda didn't notice, Jillian stayed silent and kept her eyes on Dodger. He was licking the face of little Tucker, who'd lost his balance and plopped down on his butt in the grass. Tucker giggled, stood up, and began to chase the dog again.

Rhonda patted Jillian's shoulder and moved to the side for a better view of the kids. Jillian released a breath she hadn't even realized she was holding. Sometimes, at moments like this, she wanted to scream, "We're trying!" But if she did, she would have to deal with people tiptoeing around her, trying not to say things to upset her, going silent when she entered a room. Even worse, trying to console her and looking at her with pity. She didn't want any of that, so she kept her mouth shut.

Just before noon, Brent and Courtney came outside, along with Wyatt and his father, Lewis. Brent and Wyatt started the grill and Lewis sat down on the opposite side of the patio from Rhonda. They had been divorced since Wyatt was twelve but managed to come together civilly for events involving one of their children or grandchildren. Of course, they did so by avoiding conversation with one another as much as possible.

Lewis was a tall, stately man with thinning sandy-blond hair and light brown eyes. He looked like an older and slightly blonder version of Wyatt. Jillian enjoyed his company. He was a man of good humor and easy to be with. He never pushed Jillian about having kids the way everyone else did. With him, there were no questions and no subtle hints.

For a few minutes, all the adults talked while the kids continued to play in the yard. When a shrill scream erupted, everyone's attention turned to the yard where the birthday girl was lying face-down in the grass crying.

"It's okay, Braylee, mommy's coming!" Courtney called.

The next thing Jillian knew, Braylee's three-month-old sister was being shoved into her arms. "Hold Darcy for a minute, Jill."

Courtney dashed off toward her screaming toddler, leaving Jillian with the baby blinking up at her. She gazed at the infant. The baby's head was covered in fine, dark wisps of hair and her gray eyes were curious. Her little mouth formed an O as she looked at the face above her. Jillian ran a finger along the child's arm, feeling her silky-soft, delicate skin. Her heart ached for the moment when she would look into the face of her baby instead of someone else's. Darcy cooed, smacked her lips, and closed her eyes.

Jillian stared at the sleeping child, unable to look away. She didn't even see Courtney come back to the patio and was startled when her sister-in-law spoke. "You two are looking cozy. She's really comfortable with you." This was another subtle hint, Jillian believed, Courtney's way of telling her she should have one of her own.

"She's a good baby," Jillian said, keeping her eyes on the infant.

"She's an angel until she's crying at three in the morning and you can't figure out why."

Jillian didn't respond. What she wouldn't give to know how that felt. Even the parts of parenting everyone complained about were things she craved. Oh, she knew she'd complain too someday if she ever did find out what it was like. But now, she longed to know how it felt to stay up with a baby of her own.

"Well, since she's sleeping, I'm going to leave her in your capable hands. Bring her to me if she wakes up and needs something."

Jillian nodded, cradling the baby against her. She loved the feel of Darcy's warmth and the baby powder smell of her.

Enjoying every second of having a child in her arms, Jillian sat with Darcy until everyone else ate. The baby continued to sleep, and Jillian was content to let her. But when Courtney came over and insisted she go eat, Jillian reluctantly handed the baby over to her.

The party continued to the gift-opening phase, and by the time that was over everyone said goodbye so the toddlers could get their naps.

Jillian and Wyatt took Dodger and went home. All the way, Jillian thought of nothing but the feel of a baby in her arms.

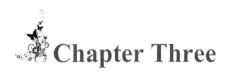

Chapter Three

"Ewww, that's gross," Layla said as she walked up behind Jillian.

"I know." Jillian used a plastic bag to pick up the used tissues someone had shoved into a shoebox. Then she sprayed the inside of the box with Lysol, properly arranged the shoes, and put the box back on the shelf. "Some people will leave their trash anywhere."

"That's the truth." Layla paused. "You mind if we have dinner and then drive to the beach … for our night out tonight?"

Jillian turned to look up at her cousin from where she knelt on the floor. Layla had been careful not to use the words *girls' night*. No one in her family ever said those words now. "Sure. Are we inviting our mothers this time?"

Twice a month Jillian and Layla, and sometimes their mothers, got together for an evening out, a tradition for the last several years. At one time, their outings had included Natalie, and they called it girls' night. Then one of those nights ended with Natalie's death, and they never used those two words together again.

For several months following Natalie's death, Jillian refused to go, and didn't think she ever would again. She hadn't even been able to think about such an evening without remembering the horror of what happened to her sister—and the choice she made that led to it. She couldn't think of going out with the ladies without remembering the moment her sister's life ended right before her eyes, without seeing the blood, without feeling the guilt.

Her therapist disagreed with her choice to stop going out with the women. He understood her resistance but felt continuing the outings would be beneficial in the long term.

After months of prodding, Jillian finally listened to him, mostly so he would stop pushing her. She was glad she did because he had been right. The time with her cousin, mother, and aunt was good for her. She was sad the tradition would have to be put aside again soon while Layla was away at vet school.

"Um, I'd rather it be just us this time," Layla said, tentatively, which was unusual for Layla. She was typically very open and opinionated. "I need to talk to you about something—just you."

Jillian smiled. "Okay. Do you want to get dinner around here or downtown?"

Layla shrugged, "Downtown. Seafood."

"In that case, I'll pick you up around five o'clock so we can get to the restaurant before the swarm. Then, we'll head to the beach and talk."

"Sounds perfect. I'll tell my mom that she and Aunt Jackie can do something of their own." Layla walked away, leaving Jillian alone, wondering what was on Layla's mind.

"So, it's Seth I want to talk about," Layla said, plopping down on the sandy beach. They'd already eaten dinner at a nice Wilmington seafood restaurant, where they talked about a movie they'd recently seen and the bride's maid dresses chosen for Robbie and Kaitlyn's upcoming wedding. When they arrived at the beach, they walked for about a half-mile into the wind before Layla was ready to talk.

"Seth? The guy you're dating?" Jillian avoided using the word *boyfriend* because Layla always bristled at the word.

"Yeah." Layla gazed out over the ocean where the setting sun was painting the sky with streaks of pink and orange.

"What about him?" Jillian asked since her cousin seemed to need prodding.

"I think I let it get too serious, Jill. I *really* tried not to."

Her cousin looked like she was in pain, but Jillian couldn't understand why. Falling in love with Wyatt was the best time of her life. So, why wouldn't Layla be happy? "What's wrong with getting serious?"

Layla turned to her, surprised by the question. "Everything is wrong with it. I'm going to vet school in a few months. He's staying here. It isn't a good idea."

Jillian sucked in a long breath of the salt air. She loved the beach—the air, the sound of the crashing waves, voices carrying in the wind—all of it. Whatever life was throwing at her, she felt encouraged in this place. Somehow the vastness and power of it made her feel like anything was possible. Different as they were, love of the beach was one thing she and Layla shared. "Maybe you're right—but maybe not. Sometimes long-distance works out. You could try."

"It doesn't usually work out. That's why I didn't want it to get serious."

The wind kicked up, making Jillian shiver. She pulled her light jacket tighter around her. "Then why don't you just end it?"

Layla's eyebrows knit together, deepening the look of pain in her expression. "That's what I was going to do. But I've been putting it off because … well, I like him … a lot. I might even—" She stopped seemingly unable to get the words out.

"Love him? You might even love him?"

Layla stared at her for a second, then nodded.

"Why does that upset you? Maybe he's the one for you."

"The timing is all wrong. I need to focus on school right now. I can't do this … but I can't seem to let go either."

Jillian rubbed Layla's back. "You can't choose when you fall in love or who with."

"Then what am I supposed to do?"

Jillian shrugged as the sun finally dipped below the horizon and darkness replaced the streaks of color. A seagull flew down in front of them, hoping for a handout. "What does your heart tell you?"

"That I can't let him go, but my brain says I need to concentrate on school."

"Layla, I know you, and you will make it work with school. You've never let anything stop you from reaching the goals you set for yourself. Becoming a vet is your dream, so I know you'll make it happen. Maybe you want to do that with Seth here waiting for you and maybe you don't. Only you can decide that. Just don't over analyze it."

A few seconds ticked by and the waves crashing against the shore were the only sound. "Maybe I wouldn't if he wasn't talking about marriage."

Jillian gaped at her cousin. "He's talking about marriage?"

"A little. I think he's trying to feel it out, see how I'll respond."

"And how have you responded?"

"So far I've been changing the subject, but that's not going to work forever."

Jillian raised her eyebrows. "It sure isn't."

"What should I do?" Layla sounded like a child begging for help.

"I think you have to tell him how you feel about it. What else can you do?"

Layla whimpered pitifully. "Why did I even start dating someone? I should have known better."

Jillian wrapped an arm around Layla. "Somehow, I don't think you mean that."

"Part of me does. Part of me says I should just break up with him now and concentrate on school." She stopped talking for a moment, and Jillian waited in silence for her to work through her thoughts. "But the other part of me can't stand the thought of letting him go, or the thought of him finding someone else. And that part seems to be stronger."

Jillian was doing her best to console and guide her cousin, but she and Layla were poles apart. Layla's dream had always been the most important thing to her, and Jillian always wanted love and a family above all else. They were two very different people. She looked out at the sea as she spoke. A few stars twinkled in the sky now. "I think the best you can do is talk to Seth and tell him how you feel. Tell him you aren't ready to talk about marriage, but you want to give the long-distance thing a try when you leave for vet school. He's probably just as worried about it as you are. That might even be the reason he's talking about marriage. He may just want you to know that he's serious about the relationship. Maybe he's worried that you *are* going to dump him before you go."

"Probably. I told him I would."

Jillian whipped around to look at Layla. "What? You told him that?"

Layla shrugged. "Yeah. When I started seeing him, that was my plan. I thought it was only fair to tell him. I thought we could just have fun, and no one would expect it to be anything more."

"I see." Jillian was stunned. She couldn't imagine starting a relationship under those circumstances.

"It isn't working out the way I planned."

"All the more reason to talk to him."

Layla sighed, then nodded. "I guess you're right."

Chapter Four

Jillian came home from work to the smell of gumbo cooking, one of the few dishes Wyatt was really good at making. Probably because the recipe was a family tradition, and his mother insisted all her children learn it well. She flatly refused to teach any of their spouses, because only Greens were allowed to know the secret recipe.

Jillian breathed in the scent as her mouth began to water. Smiling, she took in the sight of her tall, strong husband standing in the kitchen wearing her blue, frilly apron. Dodger sat near him hoping for a handout. She snuck in behind Wyatt and wrapped her arms around his waist. "That smells great," she said. "It's so nice coming home to my man in the kitchen after a long day at work."

He snickered. "I'm glad you're enjoying it. Maybe someday you'll see fit to buy a manlier apron."

Jillian stepped back and tapped her forefinger to her chin. "I don't know. This apron brings out your softer side."

He cut his eyes at her and went back to stirring his pot. Lifting the spoon with a small amount of the gumbo, he turned and offered her a taste.

She blew on it a couple of times and then allowed him to put the spoon to her lips. "Very good, Chef Wyatt. Might be your best yet."

"Glad to hear it. If you would set the table, I think we can eat now."

Jillian set bowls and spoons on the table along with a loaf of bread. When they'd filled their bowls, they discussed their days. Jillian didn't have a lot to say since her day at the shoe store had been uneventful.

"Hey, I want to talk to you about something," Wyatt said after he finished relaying his adventure at the golf course where he'd spent the day with his father. The story included a pair of nesting geese chasing golfers away from their balls.

Jillian looked up from her gumbo to meet his eyes. His expression was solemn and his voice unsure. Wyatt was a fairly self-confident person, so this got Jillian's attention. "Sure. What is it?"

He met her eyes for a second, then looked back down at his food. He seemed to be choosing his words carefully. "I was thinking ... and we don't have to do it if you don't like the idea ... but I was thinking we could—" He shrugged and met her eyes again. "Well, what if we became foster parents?"

Jillian was momentarily at a loss for words. She never expected him to suggest something like this, and she didn't know what to make of it. Did it mean he was giving up, that he didn't think they would ever succeed at having a baby? Or was he making the suggestion in an effort to appease her? Had he grown weary of her desperation for a baby and thought this would fix it?

She stared at him.

"You hate the idea, don't you? I said we don't have to do it. It's just an idea." He was speaking fast, like someone trying to erase a mistake. Maybe he thought she was angry at the suggestion.

She wasn't angry. She didn't know what she was feeling. A strange sense of loss washed over her as if the mere idea had removed any possibility of a baby in her womb. The smallest hint of hope followed it, then confusion.

"The doctor wants us to try the fertility drugs," she said.

He nodded. "We'll only be able to try that a few times. It's expensive and our insurance doesn't cover it."

That felt like a stab to her heart. Maybe he had given up. "I know," she murmured. "But I still want to try. Don't you?"

"Of course, I do, but ..." Wyatt met her eyes, silent for a moment. Then one side of his mouth twitched upward into a crooked smile. "It's not like we can't do both."

Why hadn't Jillian thought of that? He wasn't asking her to abandon hope in having a baby, he just wanted to give them something to pour their energy and love into in the meantime. And, as she thought about it, she realized it was a wonderful idea. It could make waiting for a baby far less demoralizing. They'd have someone around to love and maybe they would even want to adopt the child. Who knew?

"Can we? What would we have to do?"

He grinned at her. "I'm not sure what all we would have to do. We'll find out. But why couldn't we do it while we're doing the fertility stuff?"

She watched his face light up and the dimple in his left cheek flash. A surge of hope filled her soul. Yes, this was a good idea. She nodded. "You're right. Let's do it."

"We can start by fixing up the guest room for a child."

"Shouldn't we go to social services and get the information first?"

"We'll do that, but they might want to see what we have to offer. Right now, that room is just a double bed and a nightstand. It needs to look bright and lively. It needs some toys."

Wyatt was so happy and excited by her acceptance of his idea that Jillian felt it herself. It was lifting her up with a new hope that was different from any she'd felt before. This might be exactly what they both needed.

After filling her roller with soft green paint, Jillian moved back to the wall and began covering white paint. They chose the green since they wouldn't know if their foster child would be a boy or a girl. They had also decided to only take one child since they both had jobs and were still trying to have a baby. Besides, neither of them had much experience with kids. Starting small seemed wise.

"It's looking good," Jillian said as she stepped back again.

"Yeah. And it'll be even better once we get a few more things to put in here. L.J. says they have a dresser we can have. Then we'll get a colorful bedspread and a few toys."

"You talked to L.J. about this already?"

He shrugged. "Sure. Why not?"

She thought about that and she could see his point. "I guess you're right. No reason not to." She paused for a moment as something occurred to her. "What about your mom? Did you tell her yet?"

"Haven't talked to her yet. L.J. called me last night, so I told him."

Jillian didn't know why she felt relieved, but she did. It was silly. Rhonda was going to find out about their foster care plans. Jillian knew that, but for some reason the idea of her mother-in-law learning about this made her feel very anxious.

"Of course, it's possible she talked to L.J. since I did, and he told her. You know how it goes."

Jillian felt a sinking sensation in her stomach. Yes, she knew how it went.

She hadn't told her family about their plans yet, but she felt confident that they would all be excited about the idea. She wasn't so sure about Rhonda.

Brushing aside her anxious feeling, Jillian smiled. "Yeah, I know how it goes."

Wyatt furrowed his brow at her. "You're worried about what she thinks, aren't you?"

She looked down, away from his gaze. "I don't know."

He sighed. "Jills, she's going to love the idea."

"I hope so." Jillian was not convinced.

They painted in silence for a few minutes, then Wyatt said, "She was in foster care for a while, you know."

Jillian looked up in surprise. She just couldn't picture that. Rhonda had this self-confident, almost superior air about her. It didn't fit with her having once been a foster child. Jillian would have imagined the perfect, stable home for the foundation of Rhonda's life.

"Really?"

Wyatt nodded. "I guess it never came up, but her birth parents died in an accident when she was only two. She went into foster care and then the family adopted her." He paused for a moment. "So, I think she'll be pleased about us doing this. I mean, she doesn't even remember her birth parents, but she knows they died. And she knows she would have had a very different life had it not been for another couple who decided to love her."

"Wow! I had no idea she was adopted. No one has ever mentioned it."

"I guess we don't think about it most of the time. Grams and Pop are her parents. They raised her. But I think maybe it was the reason I thought of doing this in the first place."

Jillian let the new information sink in. She had to admit it made her see her mother-in-law in a whole new light. *Did that make sense?* Nothing had changed. The things she'd just learned had always been true. She just hadn't known them. Still, for some reason, her perception of Rhonda softened.

 **Chapter Five**

It would take the better part of a year to do everything they must do to become foster parents, and Jillian found she had mixed feelings about that. On the one hand, now that she and Wyatt had decided to do this, she was eager to get started. She often found herself daydreaming about playing with a sweet little girl or boy, teaching him or her the alphabet song, or cooking with the child standing next to her on a chair. She longed for the day when that daydream became a reality.

On the other hand, undergoing treatments with the fertility doctor was time-consuming with all the required appointments. And besides that, the medication was making her a little crazy. She felt anxious and agitated most of the time, almost as if she was filled with an energy she couldn't expend. Sometimes she thought she might jump right out of her own skin. It was hard enough keeping that under control around the other adults in her life. She was pretty sure some of them were on the verge of organizing an intervention as it was. And added to it, there was the emotional roller coaster they went through each month—the buildup of hope, the anticipation, and the fear of another heartbreak. So, it was probably best that no children were involved yet.

Jillian got down on her knees to look through a stack of shoe boxes in search of a particular shoe that needed re-stocking. As she looked, she thought about the first month with the fertility drugs. It began with a surge of hope unmatched by any other time during their journey, including the very first month they'd tried. Night after night, she prayed the drug was their answer. Then, when she realized the drug hadn't worked, the letdown for both of them was even more intense than ever before. She and Wyatt held each other and cried for a long time. For a few days after that, they lived like zombies—working, eating, sleeping—but nothing more. They barely spoke to each other or anyone else. When Layla noticed how quiet Jillian was at the store, Jillian told her she wasn't feeling well. To a point, that was true.

Then, she and Wyatt picked themselves up, grabbed onto hope once again, and prepared for the next try. They had to take a month off, but now that month had passed, and she was taking the Clomid again. She was also experiencing all the effects again.

She knit her brow in frustration as she looked for a shoe that seemed to be missing in action. It had to be here. The computer said there were still two more pairs back here. Unless, of course, Robbie had messed up on the inventory last week.

"Hey, Jill, there you are," Robbie said, breaking the silence as he pushed through the door.

Jillian jumped at the sudden sound, then turned and yelled at him. "What do you want, Robbie?"

A few seconds ticked by as Robbie stared at her wide-eyed. She had let it happen again—let the hormones racing through her, making her feel crazy—take over. She took a couple of deep breaths to calm herself down.

"I'm sorry. I can't seem to find the shoe I need."

"I see," Robbie said skeptically. "Want help looking?"

She was about to say no but stopped herself. "It's that chunky black work boot from the men's section. The one that's been so popular. The computer says there are two more pairs back here, but I can't find them." She wanted to call his ability to do inventory correctly into question but held her tongue and forced back the strange need to scream at someone.

Robbie started searching the boxes of shoes next to her. After only a couple of minutes, he said, "Here it is," and handed her two boxes.

Jillian looked at the spot from which he'd pulled the boxes. She shook her head. "Can't be. I just looked there."

Robbie shrugged. "You must have missed them. This is it, right?" He held an open shoebox out for her to inspect.

She looked and, sure enough, it was the shoe she was looking for. She ought to feel relieved and grateful for her cousin's help, but instead, she felt agitated with him for finding what she couldn't. She jerked the boxes from his hands, and he flinched at the sudden move. "I guess I can't do anything right. Not even find a stupid shoe," she huffed.

Robbie stared at her. She met his eyes for a split second, then turned on her heel and started to stalk out of the storeroom. Robbie's voice stopped her.

"Are you okay, Jill? It's just a shoe. I'm sure you would have found it."

Of course, he'd be confused by her comment. He didn't know that what was making her feel like a failure had nothing to do with shoes. And he had no idea about the drug rushing through her body, making her feel like she was possessed by an angry spirit. She sighed and, without turning around answered him, "I'm just having an aggravating day. I'm fine." She started to push through the door and stopped again. "I'm sorry, Robbie. Thanks for finding the shoe."

"Sure, anytime," Robbie said as Jillian went through the door and out to the sales floor.

She took the two shoeboxes to the proper shelf and put them in place. Then she stood still, closed her eyes, and took a couple of long, deep breaths. She would not let the drug take over again, she told herself.

"Jillian?"

Her eyes flew open, and she turned toward her father's voice, forcing a smile. "Yes, Dad?"

"Your mother wants to know if you and Wyatt are coming to dinner tonight."

She nodded. "We'll be there."

He smiled at her. "Good. Your mother is making chicken parmesan because she knows how much Wyatt likes it."

"Oh," Jillian started. Wyatt was not a huge fan of chicken parmesan. But Jillian didn't have the heart to remind either of her parents that it was Derek, Natalie's husband, who'd loved that dish. "That's nice." She felt a wave of sadness both at the thought of her sister and the need to keep anything back from her father. But she didn't want to bring up Derek in conversation. Jillian and her parents had reached out to him several times since Natalie's death, but he didn't want to be around them. He said it was just too much of a painful reminder, but Jillian wondered if he blamed them, blamed *her,* for what happened to Natalie.

She looked back up at her father. "That sounds great, Dad." She knew her voice didn't portray the same enthusiasm as her words, but that was nothing new. Almost three years had passed since they lost Natalie, but healing was a slow process. Their family had a hole in it, and they felt the missing piece every time they were all together.

Her father patted her on the shoulder, then strolled away toward the front of the store.

When Sunday rolled around, Jillian and Wyatt were with his family for a picnic at a local park where the kids could play. Jillian was having a good day. The effects of the fertility drugs were not as strong as they sometimes were.

She stood at the picnic table, setting out the plates and cups, and watched all of the interaction around her. Dodger chased a ball and brought it back to Braylee and Brent. Then Brent helped Braylee throw it to him again, and he ran off after it. Braylee giggled every time the dog ran for the ball. Tucker sat in a baby swing with Anika pushing him, and everyone else was either preparing the food or chatting with those who were while baby Darcy slept in her infant seat.

Everyone seemed happy, joyful to be together, and Jillian was reminded again how different it was from time with her family. When she and Wyatt had dinner with her parents a few nights before, the whole evening felt forced. They were supposed to be happy to spend time together, so they smiled. But the smiles were hollow as they tried their best to talk to each other and never mention who was missing.

Jillian was glad they had the store. When they were there, working together, it was different. There were moments, of course, like the one with her father when he'd thought Wyatt was the one who liked chicken parmesan. But most of the time, when they were working, they could be together without the dark cloud that hovered over them everywhere else.

It was all going to change soon. Whether the fertility drugs were successful, or they simply brought a child into the family through foster care (and hopefully adoption at some point), Jillian felt sure that having a child in their midst would help fix what was broken—it had to.

When she told her therapist her thoughts about that, Dr. Parks studied her with concern in his eyes. Then he warned her not to expect too much. "Healing is a process," he'd said. "There is no easy fix. It might feel like one at first, but if there are things that haven't been resolved, then it will be like sweeping dirt under a rug."

Jillian had recoiled at his words. Their pain being compared to dirt felt harsh and wrong somehow. She thought about not going back to see him again, but then she had to admit that he'd helped her. For the first month after Natalie's death, she had hardly done anything but cry. Her talks with Dr. Parks, even though she held some things back, helped see her through. She would just have to disagree with him on this. They were in pain, but what else was there to talk about or resolve?

She gritted her teeth as that question went through her mind. There was something, two things actually, that her parents didn't know. But those things were the reason she felt sure that a child coming into the family was the answer.

When a hand touched her shoulder, Jillian jumped.

"I'm sorry. I didn't mean to startle you," Rhonda said.

Jillian placed a hand over her heart and took a deep breath. "That's okay. I was just watching Dodger play ball, and I didn't notice you come up behind me."

Rhonda smiled. "Dodger is going to be a happy dog when you and Wyatt have a child to bring home."

For once, her mother-in-law's mention of them having a child didn't stab her in the heart. This time, she knew Rhonda was talking about the foster child they were preparing for. There was no pressure, and it didn't make her feel like a failure. Joy filled her heart instead of pain. Wyatt was right. His mother was pleased about their plans, and Jillian knew both sides of the family would warmly welcome the child they brought into their home.

"Dodger will be ecstatic. He's always happiest when he's got a child to play with."

Rhonda patted Jillian's cheek in a motherly gesture. "You and Wyatt are doing such a good thing. I'm so proud of you both." Tears stung Jillian's eyes as Rhonda pulled her into a hug. Her mother-in-law was beginning to see her in a whole new light, and Jillian felt the same way about her. They seemed to be embarking on a new and deeper relationship.

Pulling back, Rhonda offered her one more smile, then went over to the grill where L.J. and Wyatt were arguing about the correct way to cook. "Boys!" Rhonda interrupted them. "They're hamburgers. What's there to argue about?"

"He's doing it wrong," L.J. said. "He's going to burn them."

"I assure you, I know what I'm doing. Let's ask Anika who the better cook is," Wyatt responded.

"This isn't cooking. It's grilling. They're not the same."

"It's food getting cooked. That means it's pretty much the same."

"Do I have to call Brent over to handle the grill?" Rhonda asked in her stern motherly tone.

Jillian smiled when both men answered with a sheepish, "No, Mom."

Ten minutes later, the burgers were ready, and they all gathered around the table. They bowed their heads while Rhonda said a blessing. "Thank you, Lord, for this food before us. Thank you for family and time together. Lord, please bless and guide Wyatt and Jillian as they embark on this new journey. Send them a child who needs them and allow them to become a family. Amen." When she finished, she looked at Jillian, nodded slightly, and smiled again. Jillian felt warmth go through her with her mother-in-law's approval. She reached for Wyatt's left hand under the table and squeezed it. He responded by kissing her on the head before going back to his meal. Jillian smiled and ate her meal with a happy heart.

Chapter Six

As summer rushed in with heat and humidity, Jillian and Wyatt kept busy with the training required for becoming foster parents and visits to the fertility clinic. There were blood draws, ultrasounds, medications, and procedures. And there were letdowns when Jillian felt as if she were watching her hopes and dreams fade away. When the third attempt with the Clomid failed, they moved on to injectable medications. The shots were painful, and she didn't like letting Wyatt give them to her. She liked the idea of giving them to herself even less though, so Wyatt it was.

The new medication was also more expensive, taking a toll on their savings account. They did everything possible to scrimp and save money to cover the cost, but Jillian knew in her heart they could only afford a few tries.

The summer also came with the arrival of a new family member. L.J. and Anika's new little daughter, Callie, arrived the first week of July which earned her the nickname, Firecracker, from her father and grandfather. Each time they gathered with Wyatt's family, and Jillian held the baby, she felt the deep and painful longing for a child to call her own.

In mid-August, Layla left for veterinarian school, leaving Jillian and Robbie to handle inventory duty. Jillian didn't mind that so much as she missed her cousin. She was happy and grateful every time Layla came home for a visit, and they spent a little time together. She often longed to tell her cousin what she was going through. For that matter, she longed to tell her mother. But as much as she wanted to share her pain with someone other than Wyatt, she didn't like the idea of becoming the object of pity. She didn't want them giving her sad looks or asking her how it was going with the treatments, reminding her when she was trying not to let her thoughts dwell there.

With the end of summer, the preparations for Robbie and Kaitlyn's wedding went into full swing. Jillian attended the bridal shower, relieved that it wasn't another baby shower—those were hard for her to bear. In October, as the seasons began to change, the wedding day arrived.

"I can't go out there. This dress makes me look hideous!" Layla cried.

Jillian stood in the dressing room designated for bridesmaids, looking into a mirror at the same dress on her body. She moved side to side to view at different angles. "I think the dress is nice—tasteful and not too fluffy. Sleeveless might get a little chilly since it's October, but otherwise, I like it."

"Sure, it looks great on you."

Jillian turned from the mirror to look at her cousin's back. Layla was looking into a mirror of her own. Jillian was in awe looking at her cousin's beautiful frame. Layla in a dress or anything showing off her figure was a rare event. She looked amazing from Jillian's viewpoint. "And why doesn't it look good on you?"

"It's *pink!*"

Jillian furrowed her brow. "So?"

"I guess you wouldn't understand. You're blond and you have nice porcelain skin. Pink looks good on you. Natalie would have understood."

Jillian stepped back as if someone had slapped her. The mention of Natalie's name was something she wasn't prepared for today. She recovered quickly and didn't let on that Layla's mention of her lost sister felt like someone punching her in the gut. *Should it still hurt so much?* She remembered her sister's lovely strawberry blond hair and realized that Layla was probably right—Natalie would not have liked the choice of pink.

She waited for Layla to explain further. "It's just that you don't have the red in your hair. Of course, it isn't the hair that's the problem so much as the skin with the pink undertones. You don't notice until I wear something red … or *pink*."

Jillian stepped closer to Layla and lifted her chin with a finger. "We are all our own harshest critics. I think you look beautiful today—even in pink. Seth will think so too."

"He probably won't know what to think. He's never seen me in a dress." A tiny smile crept across Layla's face and her cheeks flushed.

Seth must be something special. Jillian had never seen her cousin get nervous or flustered over a guy. She smiled back. "I think my wedding was the last time I saw you in a dress. It's a special experience for all of us." She stepped back again and appraised Layla. Nodding she said, "He's a lucky guy, Seth."

Layla turned away. She'd always been uncomfortable with a lot of attention.

At that moment, the door opened and two of Kaitlyn's friends, also in pink dresses, ushered the bride and the bride's mother into the room. Kaitlyn was dressed in a gorgeous, pristine white wedding dress with a lacy, sleeveless bodice and a long satin train. Her light brown hair was swept up with just a few loose tendrils hanging around her face.

"You look so beautiful," Jillian said to Kaitlyn. "And so happy."

Layla, also admiring the bride's dress said, "I sure hope my brother knows how lucky he is."

Kaitlyn smiled at them radiantly. "I am happy—so happy. And I'm lucky to have found a great guy like Robbie."

Layla's eyebrows shot up, and Jillian could see she was preparing to make a snippy remark about her brother. Jillian grabbed her cousin's hand and squeezed hard to stop her. "Ouch," Layla said, scowling at her.

"I see your mind at work," Jillian whispered. "And now is not the time."

"Okay, okay." Layla pulled her hand away. "I'll behave."

Kaitlyn's friends attended to her—adjusting the dress, fixing her make-up. A few minutes later there was a knock at the door followed by the voice of Kaitlyn's father. "Sweetheart? Are you ready?"

Kaitlyn glanced around the room at all the ladies in pink and her mother, her face flushed with excitement. "Yes, Daddy," she called. "I'll be right out."

All the women filed out of the room and walked to the vestibule of the church. The groomsmen were there waiting, wearing their black tuxedos with pink bow ties. Robbie hadn't been any more excited about the choice of pink than Layla was, but it was a battle he'd quickly given up fighting.

The groomsmen paired up with the bridesmaids and the doors of the sanctuary were opened. Jillian was paired with one of Robbie's good friends and Layla, much to her disapproval, was paired with Josh, the one male cousin they had on their mother's side. Robbie didn't get along with Josh but felt obligated to have him in the wedding. Layla's disapproval was evident in the way she pushed at Josh the moment he tried to take her arm.

"You said you'd behave, remember," Jillian whispered, leaning forward so Layla could hear her.

Layla stopped elbowing Josh and scowled at Jillian. "Fine!" she said between clenched teeth.

Just then the music changed to the processional, and the adorable flower girl, Kaitlyn's niece, started down the aisle alongside the ring bearer, who was the son of one of Robbie's older friends. The first couple followed them and so on until Kaitlyn and her teary-eyed father came at the end of the line.

Jillian watched as Robbie and Kaitlyn vowed to love and care for one another for the rest of their lives. When the ceremony was over and the pictures taken, they moved on to the ballroom of a nice hotel for the reception.

After a lovely dinner and a couple of heartfelt toasts, the dancing began. Jillian sat at a table and watched as Wyatt danced with the flower girl. Watching them, she thought it would be nice to have a daughter. Wyatt would be so sweet with a little girl. They had been through four attempts with the fertility doctor and, so far, no luck. Between each try, they took a month off. This month was their break, and it was nice not to have the extra hormones coursing through her. Next month they would try again—probably for the last time. Wyatt's job as a teacher and hers at the store only went so far. Paying for the medication and the artificial insemination procedure each time was hitting their savings pretty hard. Jillian would be willing to keep going for as long as possible, but Wyatt would only deplete their savings so far. He was right. She knew he was, but it was hard to think of quitting.

Jillian looked up when Layla approached with Seth. Shaking away her thoughts, she smiled and stood up, reaching for Seth's hand.

"Jill, this is Seth," Layla said with uncharacteristic shyness. "Seth, this is my cousin Jillian."

"It's nice to finally meet you, Seth," Jillian said to the handsome young man at her cousin's side. His black hair was parted on the side and perfectly combed. His eyes were dark and warm. He took Jillian's hand and held it firmly for just a split second, then let go.

"I'm glad to meet you also," he said. "Layla talks about her family with so much affection. I've wanted to meet everyone for a while."

"But there hasn't been time since I've been away at school," Layla spat out.

That wasn't really true since Layla had come home on a few occasions already. Jillian knew the real reason they hadn't met Seth before was because the whole idea of a serious relationship scared Layla to death and she wasn't comfortable with the idea herself yet. This was the first time since Layla graduated high school that anyone in the family had been introduced to a boyfriend.

Jillian glanced at her cousin with a knowing smile. "Layla has been a busy girl," she said, going along with the excuse. "And what about you, Seth? What do you do?"

"I'm an electrician. I work for my family's business."

"Really? I'm sure Layla told you about our family's business."

Seth nodded. "The shoe store, yes, she did. You work there, right?"

"Yes. Layla is the first to go after other adventures."

Seth grinned. "She is a girl with her own mind. That's one of the things I love about her. Her love and compassion for animals is probably the only thing I love more."

Seth gazed at Layla with such affection it was almost tangible, and Jillian suspected she would have another wedding to attend down the road. Knowing Layla, it would be a few years. She was not the type of girl to jump in without looking at every angle first. Then again, Seth was already making waves in Layla's plans, so who knew what would happen.

Jillian continued to talk to Seth and Layla until Wyatt returned and took her to the dance floor. They danced until the cake was cut and the bouquet thrown, then they danced some more, and Jillian allowed her worries about the future to wash away with the music. Tonight, she would just hold onto her loving husband and celebrate with her family.

When the evening came to an end, a group of happy but tired guests sent Robbie and Kaitlyn off in a shower of bubbles before heading home.

"This has to be the last try, Jills," Wyatt said with sadness in his eyes.

"We still have some money. We could scrape up enough for one more try if this one doesn't work. And I'll get my Christmas bonus at the store …"

He knelt in front of her where she sat on the couch and took her hand in his. "Your Christmas bonus isn't enough to cover even half. What if something happens and we need some savings to fall back on? Plus, there are Christmas gifts to buy, and the new medication is very expensive."

A tear rolled down Jillian's cheek, and Wyatt wiped it away with a finger. "What if that next month is *the* month?" Jillian knew it was a fruitless argument, childish even, but her heart was breaking at the thought of giving up and the pressure of only having one more try was overwhelming. She wished they could try in vitro, but there was no way they could afford that.

"Honey, we could ask that question until the end of time. We have to decide without knowing." He spoke so sorrowfully that Jillian knew the choice was killing him as well. Someone had to be the responsible one and he was stepping up to the plate.

She wanted to tell him that she knew he was hurting too, but she couldn't speak through her own emotion at that moment. Tears flowed freely down her face, splashing on their joined hands.

"We'll have children," he said with conviction. "We'll be able to take in foster children in a few more months and we'll adopt. There are lots of kids who need good homes."

She nodded. "I know."

Wyatt looked helplessly at her for a few seconds. Then he pulled her into his arms and held her while she cried.

The following day, she pushed aside the worry and the sadness at their failed attempts, and began another month, their last, with the injectable medication. She cringed as

Wyatt gave her the first shot, then she told herself that it was going to work this time. It had to.

Chapter Seven

Thanksgiving Day began with Wyatt's family gathering at Rhonda's house for a noisy, joyful lunch that included passing around the two babies.

When lunch was over, Wyatt and Jillian headed to the home of Jillian's Aunt Rose and Uncle Danny to have dinner with Jillian's family.

When they arrived, everyone else was already there. Jillian and Wyatt went inside and greeted everyone. The mood was cheerful, and Jillian was happy they were all together. It was so much easier when her aunt, uncle, and cousins were with them. They were less apt to focus on missing Natalie.

"Hey Layla," Wyatt said once they were in the living room with the rest of the family. "Where's that boyfriend of yours? Isn't he coming today?"

"No, he isn't," she said curtly as if even asking was a sin. "He's spending the day with his own family."

Wyatt held up his hands. "Sorry I asked. It just seemed like you two were getting to that point."

"What point?" Layla asked defensively.

"The point where you spend holidays together."

"Well, we're not." Layla turned away trying to end the topic.

"You will be soon," Robbie spoke up. "That boy is really into you."

"Makes no difference," Layla insisted. "He won't be coming until I invite him."

"Sure. That's how it works," Robbie scoffed.

Kaitlyn's eyebrows shot up. "And what does that mean? Do you feel I pushed you into things?"

Robbie wrapped his arms around her. "Not at all. I didn't need any pushing. But whether my sister wants to admit it or not, she's just as into Seth as he is into her. She won't be able to keep holding him at arm's length for too long."

"I am not holding him at arm's length! I'm simply keeping our relationship at a slow pace. That's how it needs to be until I'm done with vet school, and he's just going to have to live with that."

"Yup, he sure is," Robbie said sarcastically.

Layla grumbled at him, folding her arms across her chest.

Jillian tapped her agitated cousin on the shoulder. "Let's go see if our moms need help with the food."

"Why not? At least the company is better in there." Layla got up from her chair and followed Jillian to the kitchen.

As soon as they walked in, the smells of turkey and yams and potatoes greeted them. "It sure smells good. Need any help?" Jillian asked.

"Sure, you can stir those pots on the stove, Jill. And I can put Layla to work whipping the potatoes," Rose said.

Jillian went to the stove and began to stir pots of green beans and peas and carrots. Her mother moved in behind her and gave her a little hug. Jillian smiled at the warmth in the room.

Thirty minutes later, the food went on the table and everyone gathered around. Jillian's father said the blessing, and Uncle Danny carved the turkey. They passed the food around and everyone dug in. Jillian didn't mind that it was her second time having turkey in one day. She was glad they could work things out in both families so that everyone could be together at some point in the day. She hoped it would always be that way.

When the meal was over and the kitchen cleaned up, the family settled down to watch a movie together. Jillian's mother suggested A Wonderful Life, but she was out voted and they ended up watching Die Hard. Jackie and Rose complained, but all the men insisted it was a Christmas movie. After a few minutes, Jillian slipped out to use the restroom.

A while later—Jillian wasn't sure how long—a knock sounded on the door. "Jillie? Are you okay in there?" Jackie asked in a soft voice.

All Jillian could manage in response was a sob as emotion clogged her throat.

"I'm coming in there," her mother announced as the doorknob turned.

As soon as Jackie entered, Jillian threw her arms around her and cried into her shoulder. Jackie held her and rubbed her back while whispering soothing words into her ear.

When the sobs lessened, Jackie pulled back and lifted Jillian's chin so she could look her in the eyes. "Sweetheart, what is going on?"

Jillian tried to look down and was about to tell her mother that she was just really missing her sister today. She *was* missing Natalie today, even more than usual, but that wasn't the cause of her outburst. Her mother lifted her chin again, and when Jillian looked into Jackie's eyes, she couldn't tell her anything but the truth.

"Mom," she looked pleadingly into her mother's face, searching for an answer she knew wasn't there. "I want to have a baby, but I don't think I can."

Jackie didn't respond right away, and the look on her face went from surprise to confusion to something between sorrow and hurt. After a few seconds to process what she had just been told, she said, "Tell me what you mean by that. Have you and Wyatt been trying for long?"

Jillian was surprised her mother didn't ask why she hadn't been told they were trying to have a baby. Swallowing her tears, she said, "We've been trying for over two years."

"I see." Again, the look on Jackie's face told Jillian that her mother was a little hurt because she hadn't been told before. She recovered quickly. "There's still hope, sweetie. There are doctors you can see. They do amazing things these days."

Jillian was shaking her head before Jackie stopped talking. "We've been to the doctors. They couldn't find a thing wrong, but they wanted us to try fertility drugs and artificial insemination and we did. We tried it several times. That's why I've been so edgy. The drugs mess with me."

Jackie took one of Jillian's hands and led her into a small room with a computer desk and a loveseat. They sat down together, and Jackie waited for Jillian to tell her the whole story. "This month was our last try and it didn't work."

"You're sure?"

Jillian nodded.

"You were doing all of this and the preparation to become foster parents at the same time?"

"Yes. Wyatt suggested becoming foster parents, and I thought it would be a good idea. I guess now it's the only idea."

"Why was this month the last try?"

"We don't have the money to keep going." She shrugged. "It probably wouldn't matter anyway. At some point, we have to accept that this isn't working."

Jillian wasn't sobbing now, but tears streamed down her cheeks. Jackie took a tissue from a box on the computer desk and pressed it into Jillian's hand. "I'm so sorry, baby. I wish you'd told me what you were going through sooner. I always want to be there for you."

Jillian looked down. She knew all the reasons they had decided to keep it to themselves, but now they all seemed foolish. Keeping it just between the two of them was killing them both. They needed their family and friends to help them. "We were hoping the secret would be short-lived. I should have told you sooner."

Jackie patted Jillian's hand. Any hurt she felt from being excluded was forgotten. Looking up at her mother again, Jillian said, "I guess adoption is the way we're going to become parents."

"Adoption is a lovely way to become parents. Your father and I will look forward to meeting any child who is going to become a member of our family. He or she will be welcomed with love."

Tears gathered in Jackie's eyes now too, making it hard for Jillian to keep from sobbing again. "I know you'll welcome any child we bring into the family. Wyatt's family will too. It's just hard to let go of the dream I had, the one where I got to know what it's like to have my child grow inside me, to have a little bit of me and a little bit of Wyatt make a whole new person."

"There will be beautiful things about adopting a child too, things that people who haven't adopted never experience."

Jillian nodded. "I know." She did know that and had already spent time thinking about what it would be like to have a child brought to them, or a baby placed in her arms. She had thought about what it would mean to provide a home and love to a child who truly needed it.

There was one other reason letting go of the idea of having a natural child was so hard, but she wasn't going to tell her mother about that.

Jackie stroked Jillian's hair. "It's hard to let go. I understand that."

"Yeah. I feel like I've failed at the one thing that all women are supposed to be able to do."

Jillian expected her mother to argue with her right away and tell her that it wasn't true. Instead, Jackie nodded. "I imagine that's how any woman in your situation would feel." She looked Jillian in the face. "Because we expect to be able to do this thing that women are supposed to do. And women have been struggling with that since the beginning of time. But it isn't a failure. If you aren't able to have a child this way, then it's because you were meant for something else. And it might be different, but it will be just as beautiful and wonderful."

"You really think so?"

Jackie smiled. "I'm sure of it."

Jillian smiled too, although tears were still running down her cheeks. "Okay, on to the new dream."

Jillian managed to clean herself up and get through the rest of Thanksgiving with her family without anyone but her mother knowing of her breakdown. Wyatt had been engrossed in the movie and never realized she was gone for so long. But when they got home that evening it was time to tell him that their dreams of having a baby of their own had been dashed. She'd also have to tell him that it wasn't just between them anymore.

Waiting until they were both comfortable in their pajamas and settled on the couch, Jillian finally brought it up. As she expected, Wyatt was saddened to hear that their efforts with the fertility doctor had once again failed. What Jillian didn't expect was his reaction to hearing that she'd confided in her mother. "I'm glad you told her," he said earnestly.

"You are?" Jillian studied him to see if he was sincere. "You don't mind that I didn't keep it between us?"

"Jills," he said with minor exasperation. "Keeping it between us was never my idea. I was only doing it because you wanted to."

She furrowed her brow at him and thought back. *Had it really been only my idea?* After searching her memory, she had to admit that he was right. She had been torturing herself all this time and it was her own stupid fault. "I guess you're right."

"I'm sure talking to your mom felt good. You need that. Keep talking to her." He looked at her seriously now. "About other things too." She knew what he meant but chose to ignore it.

"It did feel good, like opening a pressure valve. She was very supportive. When we get that foster child, he or she is going to have plenty of love waiting."

Wyatt grinned, his brown eyes almost dancing. "Yes. Love will be here and all around."

"And we only have a little more to do before that day can come."

"You're right! Maybe we should pick up a few more toys this weekend."

Jillian laughed at his enthusiasm. "I think we should wait on that. We don't know if we'll get a girl or a boy and we have no idea if it will be a baby or a five-year-old."

"Everyone loves blocks and if he's too young, he'll grow into them," Wyatt pleaded.

"I didn't love blocks as a kid. And we might get a kid like me, ya know."

"I know." He thought for a moment. "We could just get a couple of little things for both boys and girls. You know we'll probably get more than one foster child before we're able to adopt one. We should be prepared for anything."

Jillian decided to go along with the idea, and they spent the rest of that evening talking about all the possibilities for the child that would someday be theirs.

Chapter Eight

Three days after Thanksgiving, Jillian was on her way home from work. Suddenly, she realized that she was about to drive right past the one place she always avoided—the convenience store where she witnessed her sister's death. She had not driven home this way for almost three and a half years, choosing to take a longer ride rather than see the place that held her life's worst memory. She didn't know what had made her take this route now. Maybe some part of her was desperate for her sister, and so she was going to the last place where Natalie had been alive.

Jillian was trying to embrace the new dream of adoption. She was getting there but releasing the old dream that she would someday hold a baby of her own flesh was hard. Part of the reason it was difficult was because that baby would also be Natalie's own flesh. Over the past few years, she had often envisioned a little girl with strawberry-blond hair like her sister's. Besides that, she was the only one who could give her parents a natural grandchild because Natalie was gone.

As she drew closer to the convenience store, she decided to pull into the lot and park her car. Her hands were already trembling, so she needed time to get herself together. And besides that, some part of her had been drawn here. She might as well follow that through.

She parked in the same space she had that terrible night, where she could see into the front windows. It looked innocuous now. No one could guess the horror that had once happened right there on the other side of that window.

Closing her eyes, Jillian let her mind drift back to that night. She remembered Natalie jumping out of the car, sticking her tongue out at Jillian, then walking into the store.

Neither of them had noticed the man in the black jacket standing near the register. They hadn't realized that a madman was robbing the store. Less than five seconds after Natalie walked into the store, Jillian had watched in horror as he shot her sister in the head. Blood had splattered all over that window and Jillian had sat for several moments in total shock. Luckily for her, the man in the black jacket couldn't quite see her and thought Natalie was alone. When Jillian recovered enough from the shock, she had started the car, driven about a mile down the road, and called the police. She had never told them, or anyone, why it was her fault Natalie had been the one to die. Maybe she never would.

Jillian jumped when a knock sounded on her car window. Holding a hand to her heart, she looked over and saw her brother-in-law, Derek. She rolled down her window to talk to him.

"Derek, what are you doing here?"

"I was going to ask you the same thing, but I figured I'd say hello first."

Jillian nodded. "You're right. I'm sorry. I was just surprised to see you—especially here."

"Mind if I get in so we can talk?"

"Sure." Jillian hit the button to unlock the passenger door and waited until Derek was seated next to her.

"Actually, I think you being here is the bigger surprise. This place isn't the same for me as it is for you. I didn't see what you saw. By the time I found out what had happened, Nat was already in the morgue. I never came here that night. So, this place doesn't hold the same horror for me as for you." He stopped for a moment and let her absorb his words. "For me, it's the last place my wife was ever alive. I come here sometimes when I want to feel close to her."

Jillian studied him. "Even now, so long after?"

He shrugged. "Not often anymore. Just once in a while when I feel like I want to tell her something."

"What did you come here to tell her today?"

Derek looked down and Jillian felt sure she had gone too far in asking what she had. It was too personal. "I'm sorry," she said. "You don't need to answer that."

"That's okay." He looked up, made eye contact. "I came to tell her that I wouldn't be coming anymore. This is the last time."

"I see." But Jillian didn't see. *What did he mean?*

"Jill, do you think Nat would want me to move on?"

So that was it. She looked away, pained by the question. Derek moving on felt like putting Natalie in the past even more, which hurt, but she knew what Natalie would say to his question. She met his eyes. "Yes, she would."

He nodded and a tear ran down his cheek. "Thank you." He closed his eyes. Opening them again, he said, "I didn't even realize how much I needed to hear that from someone who really knew her."

"Natalie loved you. She would be happy if you're happy." Jillian stopped for a minute while Derek wiped the moisture from his face. "So … you met someone?"

A smile slowly crept across his face. "I did."

"What's she like?"

Derek gave her a probing glance. "Are you sure you want to hear about her?"

Jillian wasn't sure that she did, but she was sure Natalie would want her to support Derek, so she nodded.

"Her name is Maya and I met her about three months ago at a mutual friend's house when he was having a little get-together. She's a paralegal, very smart and kind. I think you'd like her."

"I'm sure I would. I know you have good taste in women. After all, you picked my sister."

Derek chuckled. "Thanks for listening, Jill. It means a lot."

Jillian thought about that and about the way Derek was talking with her. It didn't seem like he blamed her as she had thought he might.

"So, tell me," he said, "why are you here?"

"I don't know. I didn't even realize I was going this way until I was almost here."

He stared at her for a few seconds. "There must be some reason you came—something that brought you here."

She looked at him, wondering if she should be open. Then her lips began to move, and she didn't even think she'd given them permission. "I wanted to have a baby, but I can't. I needed Natalie, wanted to feel close to her."

Derek didn't respond right away. After a long moment of silence, he said, "I take it you and Wyatt have been trying for a while."

"Yes. We've been to the doctors. We've tried the drugs. It didn't work."

He reached over and squeezed her hand. "I'm sorry."

Jillian sniffed, holding back the torrent of emotions that threatened to break loose. "We're planning to adopt. I'm excited about it, but …"

"Yeah, I think I get it."

Jillian stared into his eyes and, feeling that talking to him was the closest thing to talking to her sister, she said what she would say to Natalie if she could. "Derek, I hope you know that I wish all the time that I'd been the one to go into the store that night. I should have been the one."

His forehead wrinkled as he studied her face. "Don't wish that, Jill. It wasn't your fault and Nat wouldn't want you thinking like that. She loved you."

Tears streamed down Jillian's face. She pulled her hand free and swiped at them. When she felt Derek's hand rubbing her shoulder, she began to cry harder. He pulled her into as much of an embrace as the car's seats would allow and held her until she stopped sobbing. She didn't realize until she lifted her head that he'd been crying right along with her.

Pulling tissues from a packet, Jillian handed one to Derek and they both dried their faces.

"I think maybe Natalie brought us here today at the same time. She probably knew we both needed this," Derek said.

Jillian nodded, then Derek kissed the side of her head and opened the car door. "Take care, Jill," he said getting out and going back to his car. She watched him look up at the store one last time, then climb into the vehicle and leave.

Jillian sat there for several more minutes trying to feel her sister's presence. She couldn't, but she believed that Derek might be right. Perhaps it had been Natalie who brought them both there at the same time.

Chapter Nine

Jillian carried a pair of black pumps, in the requested size seven, out to a customer and offered them. Her customer, a lady of about sixty-five with white hair and a kindly smile, took the box and began trying the shoes on her feet. Jillian watched, offering a genial smile, while her mind moved to other things.

It had taken a little over eight months to complete all the requirements to become foster parents, but she and Wyatt finally got it done just after Christmas. They were looking forward to accepting a placement, but Jillian hadn't been feeling very well and she was hoping to be in a better place when the call finally came. At the moment, she was feeling edgy, which she thought was odd since she was off all the fertility drugs. She had also been queasy and hated the thought of bringing a child into their home only to infect the poor kid with a stomach flu.

"This is pretty good," her customer said. "But I think I might like a six and a half better. Do you have that size?"

"I'm sure we do. I'll go and—" Suddenly Jillian was overcome by a wave of nausea. She clapped a hand over her mouth and ran for the bathroom.

After several minutes of retching, she began to feel a little better. She went to the sink and washed out her mouth. Then she splashed some cold water on her face and dried it with a paper towel. Looking in the mirror, Jillian was surprised by how pale she was. *Maybe I should go home for the rest of the day.* But her mother had an appointment today and her aunt and uncle were out of town for the weekend. That left only her father, Robbie, and her. That was barely enough to get by during the busy part of a Saturday. She'd have to be on her death bed before she could ask to leave.

She took a deep breath, deciding that she would have to suck it up and stay. At least the nausea was not as bad now.

By the time Jillian headed back to the ladies' dress-shoe aisle, Robbie had taken over with her customer. She could hear them talking before she made it all the way there. She stopped suddenly when she heard a snippet of their conversation.

"I'm sure she'll be okay," Robbie said. "She probably just ate something for lunch that upset her stomach."

"I sure hope so, dear. She's a nice girl." There was a brief pause then the woman added, "She's not pregnant, is she?"

Jillian's heart seized at the words. After so many failures, she hadn't even considered that possibility. *Was it a possibility?* She felt herself latching onto the idea. The thought made her breath quicken and her heart beat faster. *Could it be?*

No, it wasn't possible, and she'd be foolish to let herself believe it. If she did, she would have to face the heartbreak that came later when it turned out to be a stomach bug or food poisoning.

Forcing her feet to move and plastering a smile back on her face, Jillian continued forward and greeted Robbie and the customer as if she hadn't overheard the end of their conversation.

She looked at her cousin. "Did you find that six and a half for her?"

"Sure did," Robbie said. "Feeling better?"

Jillian nodded, finding it hard to answer him with words. She looked at the woman sitting on the stool. "How did that size work out for you?"

"Oh, just fine, dear. And I sure hope you're feeling better."

She decided to go with Robbie's thought on the matter. "Probably just something I ate. I'll be fine. If you're ready to check out, I can walk you to the front."

"Thank you. I am ready. I'm getting this pair and those nice tennis shoes you helped me find."

"Wonderful!" Jillian proceeded to walk the woman to the front where her father was manning the register.

She went on about her work and fortunately didn't have to run to the bathroom again, but the nice woman's words stayed with her and she couldn't stop her mind from drifting back to the idea that it could be possible.

By the time Jillian got home, she was feeling better, and she had put the idea of pregnancy out of her mind. She certainly didn't mention it to Wyatt. Instead, she chose just to be glad the nauseous feeling was gone and enjoy the evening with her husband.

It was a pretty evening, unseasonably warm, and they decided to take a picnic out to the beach. They spread a blanket on the sand, ate the cold chicken and fruit they brought, and talked about the children they were waiting for. As the sun went down, Jillian snuggled into Wyatt's arms and watched the sky turn pink.

They sat in the darkness for a while, listening to the waves crash on the beach and enjoying the warmth of their embrace. When the night began to grow cold, they packed up their picnic and headed home.

The next morning, Jillian woke up to the smell of bacon cooking. Wyatt was making her breakfast, but she knew she wouldn't be able to eat it. The smell was making her stomach roll as furiously as the ocean waves. She jumped out of bed and ran to the bathroom.

When she was fairly certain the retching had stopped, she wrapped herself up in a fuzzy, purple bathrobe and trekked out to the kitchen. Wyatt was at the stove flipping bacon. Once again, he wore the frilly apron, right over the t-shirt and boxer shorts he'd slept in. Dodger sat next to him, ready to snatch up any food that fell to the floor.

Jillian moved closer, enjoying the scene in front of her. But the closer she got to the sizzling bacon, the more her stomach churned. When it overtook her to the point of making a gagging sound, Wyatt turned and looked at her. Before he could say a word, she clapped a hand over her mouth and ran back to the bathroom.

As she reached the door, she heard Wyatt say, "Well, that isn't the reaction I was hoping for."

Several seconds later, Wyatt arrived in the bathroom doorway. She'd left the door open for expediency.

"Not feeling well today, huh?" Wyatt asked sympathetically.

Jillian didn't answer right away because her stomach was still in spasms and she didn't feel like she could speak. Understanding, Wyatt came in closer and pulled her hair back from her face for her.

When her stomach calmed down, she flushed the toilet and rinsed her mouth out in the sink. Then she looked at her husband. "I'm sorry, honey. It was really sweet of you to make breakfast for me, but I don't think I can eat it. I can't even seem to handle smelling it."

He rubbed her back. "That's okay. I'll make you some dry toast. And I guess there will be more bacon for Dodger and me."

Dodger, who was standing nearby, seemed to dance in celebration of the news that he'd be getting some bacon. Jillian smiled at his exuberance despite her unsettled stomach.

Managing to eat her toast while Wyatt shared bacon and eggs with their dog, Jillian thought again about the woman's words at the shoe store. It did seem odd that she would feel sick for a few hours the day before, then feel fine all evening but become ill again the next morning. That wasn't the way viruses typically worked, and certainly, it didn't fit the idea of food poisoning any longer.

She looked at Wyatt and said, "I was feeling sick for a while yesterday too."

"You seemed fine last night."

"I know. That's what seems weird about it."

Wyatt shrugged and tossed another small piece of bacon to Dodger. "Just a strange virus probably."

"Maybe." Jillian waited a few seconds, debating whether or not to bring up the words of the woman in the store. She was beginning to think the idea of her being pregnant might not be so impossible. Thinking about it brought both excitement and trepidation. Her desire was so strong, yet her heart was already so wounded from all the past disappointments.

Wyatt looked so content at the moment, while she was feeling such turbulent emotions. She decided that he didn't need to feel what she was feeling just yet. Still, she had to find out if this was just a weird virus or something else. She would go out and get a home pregnancy test later in the day and talk to Wyatt if and when there was anything to tell him.

Since it was Sunday, Jillian waited until the next day after Wyatt went to work before going to a pharmacy for the test kit. Again, she woke up feeling nauseous and unable to eat anything but dry toast. Even her attempt to add butter made her queasy.

When she got home from the drug store, she immediately took the test kit to the bathroom and followed the instructions. The three minutes she had to wait for the results felt like an eternity. She was sweating and her heart hammered as she listened to each second tick by. Dodger stared at her, his head cocked to one side. She rubbed his head and tried to think about something else, but that was futile. To distract herself, she pulled out the contents of the vanity drawer and reorganized them.

When her timer dinged, she jumped at the sound, snatched up the test stick with trembling fingers, and looked at the result.

Chapter Ten

When Wyatt arrived home, Jillian had dinner ready and waiting. She knew he would get home around six o'clock, after finishing with practice for the soccer team. The table was set with the dishes they were given when they got married and a bud vase sat in the middle holding a single rose. The smell of rosemary chicken wafted from the oven as Jillian opened the door to take it out.

Wyatt glanced around the room, a confused and somewhat concerned expression on his face. "What's all this?" he asked. "Did I forget a special occasion?"

Keeping her back to him as she spooned green beans into a bowl, Jillian said, "You didn't forget anything."

"Okay," he answered slowly, drawing out the vowels.

"Go wash up and have a seat."

Looking at her with one eyebrow raised, he said, "Sure. Be right back."

When he returned, all the food was on the table and Jillian sat waiting for him. He sat down, placed the cloth napkin (the ones they never used) in his lap, and turned his eyes on her.

"Soooo, are you going to tell me what's going on tonight?" Wyatt asked.

Trying to hold back the smile that wanted to come, she shrugged. "What makes you think anything is going on?"

Waving his hand over the table, he said, "I don't know. Maybe the rose or the dishes we never use."

"The only reason we never use them is because we didn't get the full set."

"It's usually only the two of us. We have enough for just us. You had enough for tonight. So, what's up?"

She answered by handing him a gift-wrapped box. He turned it over in his hands a couple of times, hearing something inside move around. "I know it's not my birthday," he said.

"Open it," Jillian prodded, barely containing her desire to bounce up and down.

Wyatt carefully unwrapped the baby blue paper, and took so long that Jillian wanted to scream, *just rip it open!* She held back and waited patiently, though she couldn't stop her foot from anxiously tapping the floor.

When the paper was off, he lifted the lid of the box and stared down at the contents. Curiously, he lifted it, then recognition dawned on him. "Is this ... does this mean what I think it does?"

Jillian's face broke into a wide, bright smile. When she tried to answer him, emotion clogged her throat, so she began to nod furiously. Tears welled in her eyes and began to slide down her cheeks.

"It really happened? Without the doctors and the medicine?" Wyatt asked.

Finding her voice, Jillian said, "It really happened. I can't believe it, but it really happened. I did four tests to make sure."

"Oh, honey!" Wyatt lunged from his chair and grabbed her up, holding her close and swinging her around. When he put her back on her feet, he wiped the tears from her face and kissed her with a fierce passion that was different than ever before. It was a kiss filled with promise for their future. "We're gonna have a baby," he said with wonderment in his voice. "You and me, Jills. We're gonna have a baby."

"We really are."

The following week, Jillian's pregnancy was confirmed by a doctor. "It's funny how this happens sometimes," he said. "You try everything you can, and nothing works. Then, you stop trying, and boom, it happens all by itself. But they never did find a reason why you weren't getting pregnant, did they?"

That was true, Jillian had to agree, but this still felt like a miracle to her. That was how she thought of the baby growing inside of her—a little miracle.

She and Wyatt decided not to tell anyone about the baby until the first trimester was over and there was less chance of miscarriage. It was a good plan, but it was challenging to keep the news from her mother. She felt as if she might burst with the happiness she was feeling and she wanted so badly to share some of it.

A more difficult decision was the one regarding their plan to become foster parents. Everything was done and they were ready for a placement; however, starting with a foster child now when they were expecting a baby soon seemed overwhelming. When Jillian told Wyatt how she felt about it, he was somewhat disappointed but agreed that the timing might not be the best.

"I was excited about getting a foster child too," Jillian had said. "But you remember all the warnings we were given about how difficult it might be at first. I don't know if we want to be in the middle of that when we bring home a new baby. We'll still do it … just a little later, when we get the hang of taking care of this baby."

Wyatt had nodded. His face showed sad resignation but also understanding. "I think you're probably right. It's funny, we've wanted this for so long and I'm thrilled it's finally happening, but I still feel sad that we have to put becoming foster parents on hold. I was looking forward to welcoming a child into our home that way too."

Jillian rubbed his back. "I know. I feel the same way. I just don't want us to bite off more than we can chew. We're new at all of this."

Jillian wasn't sure how they were going to give the news to her mother-in-law. She hoped the news of the baby growing inside her would be more powerful to Rhonda than the disappointment over not bringing a foster child into the family right away.

Humming as she stacked shoeboxes on the shelves of the store, Jillian thought about her little miracle. She didn't know why, but she felt certain it was a boy. She'd heard that some women have intuition about the sex of their unborn children, though she had never believed it before. Now, she supposed she did believe because she felt sure about this.

"Hey, Jill," Layla said slipping up next to her. "You sure are happy today."

Today and every day! No reason not to be. She smiled at her cousin. "I am."

"Good. Wanna go out to dinner with me tonight?"

Jillian raised her eyebrows at Layla. "Is Seth willing to give you up tonight? You're only here for the weekend."

"He'll be okay. It's not like he owns me. I mean, I need to spend time with my family too. Besides, I was with him last night."

Jillian was a little mystified by all the excuses Layla was giving. None of them were needed and it wasn't like her. "Okay. I'm up for dinner. Where do you want to go?"

Layla shrugged. "You choose and I'll drive. I'll pick you up at five-thirty."

Having already sent Wyatt off to spend an evening with his brother, Jillian was ready to go when Layla arrived promptly at five-thirty. She gave Dodger his dinner and a pat on the head before heading out the door.

Jillian jumped in Layla's car and said, "I feel like pizza tonight. Let's go to that new place—what's the name of it?"

"Dominic's?" Layla asked.

"Yeah, that's the one."

"Sure. Sounds good."

During the drive, they talked about the store and Layla's classes. When they arrived at the restaurant, they found a quiet table in the back corner and looked at the menu.

"We can share a pizza if you want," Layla suggested.

"Sure. It has to have pepperoni and sausage."

"Are green peppers okay? And maybe a little bacon?"

Jillian shrugged. "Why not?" She waited a beat, then added, "Let's put some black olives on it too."

"I thought you didn't like those on pizza."

Jillian considered that. "You're right, I usually don't. But tonight it sounds good."

Layla furrowed her brow at Jillian's ever-present smile. "You're acting a little weird lately."

Jillian's smile widened. "Am I? It's only olives."

Layla scowled at her. "Uh-huh."

The waiter came and they ordered their pizza. Then Jillian looked her cousin in the eye and asked, "What do you really want to talk about tonight?"

Layla tried a dismissive glance and said, "What makes you think there's something, in particular, I want to talk about? Maybe I just wanted to spend some time with you."

Instead of answering her, Jillian stayed quiet and just kept looking at her. Layla liked playing coy, but she wasn't very good at it.

"Okay—fine!" Layla began. "It's Seth. I want to talk about Seth."

"Go on," Jillian encouraged.

"This relationship is killing me, Jill!"

Jillian raised one eyebrow. "What do you mean?"

"I mean I've got to get some distance from him. It's all too much."

"He's too needy? Is that what you mean?"

Layla's face went from a look of certainty to one of misery. "I wish that *was* the problem. I could deal with that. I'd just tell him to back off."

Jillian could believe that.

"But it's me. I'm the problem." Layla said.

"How are you the problem?"

"I can't stop thinking about him. That's the problem." Layla cried.

Jillian tried not to smile, knowing it wouldn't be welcomed by her cousin just now. Layla was in love. All the signs were there. She just didn't want to admit it.

"I didn't want this. I wanted to go to school with a clear head so I could focus on my studies and my goals. I wanted to be at the top of my class."

"You can still do all that."

"I don't know. I got a seventy-eight on my last test."

Layla had rarely ever gotten a grade that wasn't an A. She had always been a great student with clear focus on her goals. Now, something else had come into her life that was also important and she was struggling to find balance.

Jillian reached out and took Layla's hand. "This thing with Seth is a new frontier for you and it might take a little time for you to figure out how to fit it into your life. You'll get there."

"He's all I can think about, Jill. That isn't normal. Not for me. I try to study and then he's in my head. It's messing me all up."

Now Jillian allowed a tiny smile to cross her lips. "It is normal … for people who have recently fallen in love."

"Love! You think that's what this is?" Layla's expression was one of distress.

Jillian nodded. "I'm sure of it. But don't worry, the obsession will calm down a bit as time goes on and you'll figure out how to be in this relationship and still be the vet student you want to be."

"I sure hope so."

"It had to happen to you sometime and at least you found a nice guy who feels the same way about you. Unrequited love would be even worse," Jillian assured her.

"I guess that's true. He is a great guy. And he's so good-looking too." Now Layla was smiling along with Jillian.

"Well, he's no Wyatt, but yeah, he's pretty easy on the eyes."

They both laughed just as the waiter came back with their pizza. They spent the rest of the evening talking about the men they loved and laughing over some of their shared memories.

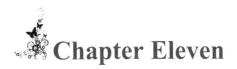# Chapter Eleven

Jillian woke up feeling elated. The moment her eyes fluttered open, she was smiling. Today was a big day. She gently shook the blanket-covered lump in bed next to her. Then she leaned down and whispered in Wyatt's ear, "Wake up sleepy-head. Today's the day. We can finally tell our families about the baby."

Wyatt groaned. "Can it wait five more minutes?"

"You can have fifteen while I'm in the shower but then I'm getting you out of this bed."

"Okay," he mumbled before falling back to sleep.

Jillian got her shower and, after waking Wyatt up again, she went into the kitchen to make breakfast. Dodger danced at her feet, hoping for a handout. She tossed him a piece of the scrambled egg she was cooking.

Watching as the dog gobbled up the egg, Jillian said, "You're going to have a brother soon, Dodge ...a human brother. I hope you're ready for that."

"A brother, huh?" Wyatt said as he came around the corner into the kitchen. "I thought we didn't know yet."

Jillian shrugged. "Officially, we don't. But I know it's a boy."

"Jills, you can't know that."

"I can't explain it, Wyatt, but I *do* know. I'm sure of it. We're gonna have a boy." She stopped for a moment and looked at him imploringly. "And I want to name him Nathan."

Wyatt smiled at her, understanding that it was her way of honoring Natalie. "That's a great name," he said, stepping closer to her and laying a kiss on the top of her head. "I guess the only thing to decide on is a middle name."

Jillian stared into his face, feeling more love than she knew how to express. Their eyes locked, then Wyatt sniffed, pointed toward the stove, and said, "I think breakfast is about to burn."

"Oh no!" Flustered, Jillian turned back to the pan of eggs and pulled it off the heat.

Wyatt moved in behind her. "I think we can still eat most of that. And Dodger will be happy to eat the part we don't. He never minds if they're a little overdone."

Jillian scooped out the eggs that were not burned and scraped the rest into Dodger's bowl. The dog pranced as he waited for her to finish, then dove into the bowl joyfully. Smiling at the dog, Jillian put the pan into the sink and pulled two Eggo waffles out of the toaster before joining Wyatt at the table.

As they ate, Wyatt talked about middle names for their baby, but Jillian was falling into her own thoughts and having a hard time listening.

"Jills? Are you okay?" Wyatt asked.

Jillian glanced up at him. "Huh?"

"You're not listening, and you stopped eating too. What's up? I thought we were happy today."

She forced a smile and put a bite of egg in her mouth. "We are happy today." She paused, trying to put her thoughts into words. "It's just that I wish I could tell Natalie about the baby. I wish I could celebrate this little miracle with my sister." That was the best she knew how to explain what she was feeling. Part of the reason having a child was so important to her was because Natalie never got the chance. But it felt like a bit of a hollow victory when she thought of not being able to share it with her sister.

She looked at her husband sadly. "Natalie would be so excited to have a nephew. But she isn't here to even know about it."

Wyatt reached across the table and took Jillian's hand. "Sweetheart, she knows. She's dancing in heaven for us."

The image of Natalie dressed in a white robe and dancing on a cloud filled Jillian's mind and she smiled. "I hope he looks like her."

"No matter what the baby looks like," Wyatt said, not quite willing to commit to the idea that it was a boy for sure, "there will be a piece of her in him—or her. You know that."

Jillian nodded. She did know, but she still hoped her son would resemble her lost sister in some way. Maybe he would have her strawberry hair and a spray of freckles across his nose. If he looked like Natalie, then it would feel like he was a little bit hers as well. And Jillian needed that because her sister had lost the chance to have a child, and Jillian didn't think she would ever stop feeling like that was her fault.

She gave Wyatt a weak smile, but her mind went back to that day when she lost her sister.

It had been an unusual Saturday. Jillian had the entire day off and she'd spent it with Wyatt. Around six o'clock, Natalie had called.

"I'm not interrupting you two lovebirds, am I?" Natalie asked.

Jillian grinned at her husband. If her sister had called a few minutes earlier, she might have interrupted something. "No. We're just watching a little TV."

"Yeah, I'm sure that's all you were doing," Natalie said with a snort. "Think you can break away to spend a little time with us girls?"

"Of course. What are we doing tonight?"

"Movie night at Aunt Rose's house. I'm on your way there, so you can come by and pick me up."

"Sounds good. I'll be over in thirty minutes," Jillian said.

"Perfect. Should give you time for another quickie."

"Very funny, Nat."

"Who's joking? I might even take my own advice."

They both chuckled, then Natalie said, "See ya in a few, sis."

Thirty-five minutes later, Jillian pulled up in front of her sister's house and honked her horn. Natalie walked out the front door and hurried to the car. It was chilly and she was wearing a blue coat and pulling it tightly around her body. "Hey, sis," she said as she scooted onto the passenger seat. "Mom called me and said we need to stop and pick up the popcorn."

Jillian nodded. "We can stop at a convenience store on the way." Jillian put the car in gear and started to drive toward her aunt's house.

Natalie glanced at Jillian and lifted an eyebrow. "I can tell by the pink glow of your cheeks that you and Wyatt had a great day."

"My cheeks are pink because it's cold out," Jillian protested.

"Sure they are. You know, you don't have to act so prim. You guys are still in the honeymoon phase. You *should* have that glow and you *should* enjoy every moment you have together—in the way that honeymooners do."

A smile spread across Jillian's face.

"I knew it!" Natalie said.

"We had a good day," Jillian responded.

"Glad to hear it. Derek and I need a few days like that." Natalie looked at Jillian for a moment. "Tell you a secret," she said in the conspiratorial tone she had always used when they were children.

Jillian glanced over at her sister's contagious smile. "Spill," she said.

"Derek and I are trying to have a baby."

The surprise of her announcement caused Jillian to swerve just a little. She regained composure and said, "Really?"

Natalie nodded.

"Mom and Dad are going to be so excited." Jillian pulled into the parking area in front of the convenience store. "I'll stay here and keep the car warm. You go get the popcorn."

"Come with me. It will only take a minute. The car will still be warm."

"We don't both need to go in. Just run in and I'll keep the heat running."

"Fine," Natalie said. "But don't tell Mom or Dad or anyone else what I told you. Derek and I want it to be a surprise when it happens." She hopped out of the car, stuck her tongue out at Jillian, and ran into the store.

Less than two minutes later, Natalie was dead.

Jillian and Wyatt spent most of the day shopping in the baby department and making a registry. That evening, when the shoe store finally closed, they went to Jillian's parents' house to have a late dinner with everyone. They had arranged the gathering a week before, but no one knew yet what it was all about.

Layla was the first to ask. "So, Jill, this isn't anyone's birthday and it's not a holiday. What's the big family meeting all about?"

Jillian gave her cousin a dismissive look. "Why do we need a special occasion to get together? We're family aren't we?"

Layla scrunched her face up in Jillian's direction. "Yeah, but we usually don't do that."

"Maybe we should start," Jillian said finding it hard to keep from smiling.

"Sounds like a good idea to me," Seth spoke up from where he stood behind Layla. "Every family should spend time together—often if they can."

Layla elbowed him just enough for him to feel. "Right, sure. Now, what's really going on, Jill?"

Jillian let go of the grin she'd been holding back and said, "Wyatt and I have some news."

Immediately Jackie threw a hand over her mouth and shrieked, startling her husband.

"Jillian, is this what I think it is?" asked Aunt Rose.

Jillian nodded. "We're going to have a baby!"

Jackie and Rose rushed over in unison and pulled Jillian and Wyatt into a group hug.

"I'm gonna be a grandfather," Richard said in wonderment.

Layla and Seth congratulated them followed by Robbie and Kaitlyn.

"So, when's the baby due?" Kaitlyn asked.

"The beginning of November," Wyatt replied.

"That soon?" Jackie said. "When did you find out?"

"We've known for about six weeks. We wanted to wait until the first trimester was over before we made the announcement," Jillian said.

Jackie nodded. "I guess I can understand that."

"Doesn't make a difference," Richard insisted. "We're gonna be grandparents, and this is going to be one spoiled baby."

"You got that right," Uncle Danny agreed. "This will be the first baby our family has seen since Layla was born. We'll all be looking forward to spoiling the little tyke."

"Maybe your baby will get Robbie and Kaitlyn thinking about children," Rose said, glancing in their direction.

Barely restraining herself from rolling her eyes, Kaitlyn said, "It will still be a while for us. We just got married a few months ago."

Rose gave Jillian a conspiratorial smile and said, "Well, you never know."

As they sat down to eat dinner, the chatter continued. Everyone was joyful and excited about the new member of their family. Jillian watched her parents talk with glowing faces about their soon-to-be grandbaby and all the plans they had. They were not the same people they had been for the past few years since losing Natalie. Their joy filled Jillian's heart. She could never bring Natalie back to them, but there was hope in this new life—for all of them.

Gathering with Wyatt's family to share the news needed no pretense. They were already getting together to celebrate Braylee's birthday. On the way to Courtney and Brent's house, Jillian thought about all the family gatherings of the past year. She really couldn't believe that a year had passed since Braylee had her second birthday and was now turning three. Over the course of that year, they had celebrated Tucker's second birthday, welcomed baby Callie into the family, and watched baby Darcy dig into her first birthday cake.

Several other changes had taken place in Jillian's life, from dealing with many disappointments with infertility to gearing up to become foster parents. And now they were going to have a baby of their own. For the past three-plus years, Jillian had felt the emptiness of her womb while her sisters-in-law were announcing one baby after another. Her turn had finally arrived, and she was excited. She was also a bit nervous about telling Rhonda that they were going to put off becoming foster parents.

"I'm sure she'll understand," Wyatt had assured her. "She knows what it's like to be a new parent."

Jillian had nodded and hoped he was right.

Arriving at the party, they let Dodger out of the car and gathered the gift and cookies they baked that morning. Brent let them in and led them to the backyard where the party was taking place.

Jillian smiled when Braylee and Tucker ran to greet Dodger. The dog pranced joyfully, basking in their attention. Wyatt handed a tennis ball to Braylee. "Birthday girl gets to make the first throw," he said.

She tossed the ball out into the yard a few feet, and Dodger took off after it. Both of the children laughed and ran after the dog. Darcy, sitting on Rhonda's lap, bounced up and down, straining to be freed. "You want to go chase the doggie too, do you?" Rhonda said. She gently placed the fifteen-month-old on her feet and the child slowly toddled into the yard making every effort to keep up with the older children.

Jillian watched as she sat down next to her mother-in-law. It was a perfect spring day. The sun was high in the sky and the birds were singing. A light breeze ruffled the leaves of the trees.

Idle chit-chat commenced while the food was cooked, and all the guests were arriving. When Brent finished at the grill, he called everyone together for a blessing. When he'd finished, Wyatt squeezed Jillian's hand and cleared his throat. "Everyone, Jillian and I have some news to share before we eat," he said.

Rhonda's face lit up. "You got a placement, didn't you?"

"Well, not exactly," Wyatt answered her. "Something else happened, something wonderful." He turned and gazed at Jillian with loving eyes. "Jillian and I are going to have a baby. She's pregnant."

For a moment there was a stunned silence. Then Courtney said, "That's wonderful news! We didn't even realize you were trying. We thought you just wanted to adopt."

Jillian blushed a little. They didn't know because she hadn't wanted to tell them. "We've been trying for a long time, actually," she said. "We even went to fertility doctors, but that didn't work. We gave up after our last fail in November." She shrugged. "Then, it just happened on its own."

"A little miracle," Anika said, clapping her hands together in excitement.

"Another baby in the family," Rhonda said with tears in her eyes.

Everyone gathered around them and congratulated them with slaps on the back and hugs. The entire family was happy and celebrating with them. Jillian felt elated as they sat down to eat, and everyone wanted to talk about their coming baby. *Their baby!*

"What we talking 'bout?" Braylee asked, looking quizzically at the adults around her.

Courtney leaned down to look her daughter in the face. "Uncle Wyatt and Aunt Jill are going to have a baby. Isn't that wonderful? You'll have another little cousin."

Braylee's little face lit up and she began to clap. "Yay!"

Tucker clapped with her, laughing as he did. Darcy and Callie stared at them in confusion, then Darcy joined in.

The moment was beautiful and blissful. Jillian didn't know if she had ever felt happier. Then Rhonda looked lovingly at her and Wyatt and said, "And when you do get a placement, we'll have even more to celebrate."

Wyatt cleared his throat again. "Actually, Mom, we've decided to put that off for a while. Jillian thinks it's best for us to adjust to the baby first ... and I agree with her."

Jillian sucked in her breath. She was sure he hadn't meant to, but it sure felt like Wyatt had just thrown her under the bus. The elation she felt a moment ago faded away.

Rhonda stared at them in silence for a few seconds, her face giving little away. "I see," she said, her disappointment evident.

"We're still going to be foster parents, Mom. We just don't want to take on too much at once. We've never been parents before. You can understand that."

Rhonda nodded, but sadness etched her face. "Of course, I can."

The subject was dropped, and the focus went back to the birthday girl. They finished eating, had cake, and watched Dodger help Braylee open her gifts. But underneath all the smiles, Jillian could feel her mother-in-law's disappointment.

During the ride home, Jillian stewed. She was upset that Wyatt told his mother about their decision the way he did. She wanted to let him know how she felt, but she didn't want to start a fight. As she tried to think of the right way to broach the subject with him, she gazed out the window barely noticing the wildflowers that were blooming on the side of the road or the strikingly blue, cloudless sky.

"What's wrong?" Wyatt finally asked after glancing in her direction several times.

"Nothing is wrong," she said in a clipped tone.

"Something certainly is wrong. It would be easier if you just tell me what it is."

Turning to look at him, she took a deep breath and tried to choose her words carefully. "It's just the way you told your mother that I wanted to wait on a placement for foster care. Now she's mad at me."

"She isn't mad at anyone and you did suggest waiting."

The last part was true, but she thought they had made the final decision together. Besides that, she believed he knew Rhonda *was* unhappy about it. "She is mad at me. I could tell. And I thought we agreed about waiting."

"We did. And I said that I agreed with you. Isn't that how it happened?" His tone was mildly defensive.

"That's true." She kept her voice calm even though she wanted to yell at him. "All of what you said was true. It's just that you didn't have to present it that way to her. Yes, I was the one to bring it up and you were the one to agree. But we did make the decision together and I hoped you would present it to her that way."

His brows drew together. "I thought I did."

She let out a sigh. He didn't seem to be getting her point. "You could have just said that *we* decided to wait. You didn't have to tell her that I was the one to suggest it first. She didn't need to know that. It's a lot easier for her to be mad at me than at you. You could have helped me out a little."

Wyatt didn't respond right away, so Jillian continued, "We were getting closer because she liked the idea of us doing foster care. We were growing a bond and I was hoping to keep it going. Now, she thinks I don't care about the kids that need homes."

Wyatt stayed quiet again and this time Jillian waited for him to answer her.

"I guess I can see your point," he said softly. "I want you and my mother to have a good relationship. I'm sorry I didn't think about how I worded what I said today. I'll make sure she knows that we made the decision together and that I feel the same way about it as you do."

Jillian was surprised that he didn't argue any further and relieved that he was able to understand where she was coming from. "Thank you," she said looking at him as he steered the car into their driveway.

He put the car in park, turned off the ignition, and looked at her. "You don't have to thank me. I love you, Jills. We're on this journey together."

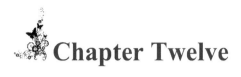
Chapter Twelve

Shortly after starting her second trimester, Jillian's morning sickness went away. With that gone, she truly enjoyed being pregnant. She loved watching the little bump form at her belly and knowing there was a tiny life growing inside of her. The wait had been so long. She frequently found herself talking to the baby, telling him everything she was doing. She told him about the store that he would one day have the option to be part owner of and all about their family members.

"You're going to love playing with your cousins," she said to the baby as she straightened the children's shoe section. "You'll have so much fun with little Callie and Darcy. And Tucker will be thrilled to have another boy around."

She picked up an adorable pair of cowboy boots for a baby and smiled. "I can't wait to see you in a pair of these, little one. You'll be so cute." She put the shoes back down on the shelf. "Your Aunt Natalie would have loved to see you in those." She stopped, feeling the familiar pain she always felt when she thought about her sister. Still, she wanted to make sure her child knew all about his namesake. Natalie would never be forgotten or pushed out of conversations no matter how painful they were.

"Oh look!" Jillian picked up a sweet little pair of blue slippers. "You'll have to have these as well."

"Who are you talking to?" Robbie asked as he came around the corner and into the aisle she was straightening.

She knew he wouldn't understand, but she didn't care. "The baby," she said.

"You know he probably doesn't even have ears yet, right?"

She shrugged. "They say that babies know their mother's voice when they're born. That means that at some point they begin to hear. Since I don't know exactly when that starts happening, I'm just going to talk to him all along the way. I want him to know how much I love him and how important he is to me."

To Jillian's surprise, Robbie smiled. "He'll know that, Jill."

Jillian nodded, her lips turning up. *Her baby would know.*

"What do you need, Robbie?"

"My dad needs you to take the register for a little while. There's some discrepancy between what we were supposed to receive in yesterday's shipment and the inventory that I took last night. He and I need to check it out."

"No problem. I'll head up there."

She started toward the front. When Robbie called out to her, she stopped and looked at him. "Yes?"

"Might be best if you don't talk to the baby while you're at the register. We don't want the customers to think you're crazy."

Jillian shook her head with a snicker. Now that sounded like the Robbie she knew.

When she reached the front, she began to straighten some of the items that were near the register since no one was waiting to check out. She stooped to pick up packages of shoelaces that had dropped from a display and put them back where they belonged. About the time she got all the shoelaces back in their proper place, her phone trilled. She looked at the screen and saw Wyatt's name. "Yes, darling?" she said.

"No practice after school today. Want to go out for dinner?" Wyatt responded.

"Sure. That would be nice."

"Where?"

Jillian tried to think of a good place but was overwhelmed by a craving for ice cream. "How about that new sandwich shop that opened last month?"

"Really? I offer to take you to dinner and that's your choice?"

"All I can think of is strawberry ice cream. I think the baby wants some." Jillian rubbed her belly.

"Oh, I see, the baby wants ice cream. I guess that means my desire for steak takes a back seat." Jillian could tell by the sound of his voice that he was smiling.

"If you want to make us both happy, then I suppose it does."

"Is there anything else our little guy wants?"

"A foot rub?" Jillian said. Her feet were aching terribly.

"I'll have to say no to that one for now. I can't get to his feet," Wyatt joked.

"Very funny, but he wants you to rub his mother's feet. Happy mom, happy baby," she said.

"Ice cream instead of steak *and* a foot rub? I'm starting to feel a little used."

Jillian grinned. "You know we both love you, honey."

"Yeah, I know. Put the phone on your belly. I want to talk to my son. He needs to know that steak is better than ice cream."

Jillian giggled. They still didn't officially know that the baby was a boy, but Wyatt had given up and gone along with Jillian's belief that it was.

She put the phone to her belly and let her husband talk to the baby for a few moments.

Then a voice surprised her. "Now you're getting really weird," Robbie said.

"Wyatt wants to talk to the baby," she defended herself. "I thought you and Uncle Danny were in the back."

"I need to get the list from the shipment." His voice sounded unhappy.

"Did you get something wrong on the inventory?"

"It looks like it. I guess I'm about to get chewed out," he said.

"Sorry," Jillian said as Robbie retrieved the list he was looking for and started back to the storeroom.

After her cousin walked away, Jillian realized she was still holding the phone to her belly. She lifted it to her ear. "Wyatt? Sorry about that. Robbie came up to the front and needed something."

"No problem. We got through our talk about the importance of red meat in a man's diet and moved on to baseball."

Jillian laughed. "Baseball?"

"We were discussing little league teams."

"I see."

"What time do you get off today?"

"Five-thirty," Jillian said as she began to rearrange some socks.

"Okay. I'll meet you at the sandwich shop at five forty-five then."

"See you then, darling. I can't wait for that foot rub after."

"Yes, ma'am." Jillian could imagine him shaking his head as he spoke. "The things I do for love."

"This is the day!" Wyatt's voice sang out.

Jillian cracked open her eyes. *Was it even morning yet?* She scrunched up her face and groaned. "What time is it?"

"Five-thirty," Wyatt answered.

"Why are you waking me up so early? I don't have to go to work until nine today." She rubbed her eyes, fluffed her pillow, and turned over with her back to him.

"It's an important day and I want to make sure I have everything right about times and all." He was leaning over her and talking into her ear.

"I'll message you later. Leave me alone." She used one hand to wave him away from her head.

"Sorry, honey, but this day is too important for messages. We're going to find out if you're right today."

"No big deal," she insisted. "I know I'm right. This is a boy. Now leave me alone."

"Come on! I need a kiss at least before I leave." He started making smooching sounds in her ear and she couldn't help but laugh.

"You don't want to kiss me with my morning breath. I'll kiss you later."

"You're right. Morning breath is terrible. You should brush your teeth first." He wasn't letting up.

When he shook her shoulder, she slapped at him. "Wyatt! Let me sleep! The baby doesn't want his mother to be tired all day."

"Weeell," He drew the word out and she knew he was close to giving up. "At least let me kiss my little guy goodbye before I leave."

She sighed. "Oh, all right." She rolled over on her back to allow him to kiss her slightly rounded belly.

First Wyatt rubbed the bump and said, "You have a great day in there, big fella. Be good and don't kick your mom too hard. Try not to give her any cravings that will make other people barf. That's just not nice. But I know you're a good boy ... or girl." He leaned down and kissed her belly.

As he got up from the bed, Jillian said, "It's a boy." Then she turned over and drifted back to sleep.

Her mind returned to the past and she saw Natalie. Her sister's face was alight with happiness and hope for the future. Natalie was talking, but Jillian couldn't hear the words. She was only able to understand the joy in them. She felt wrapped up in love and warmth.

In the next moment, she was watching as Natalie's head burst open and blood splattered. Her heart began to hammer, and she felt the need to flee but she was frozen in place. Then Natalie's voice filled her ears. "Today," was all it said.

Jillian jolted awake, gasping for breath. She was sweaty from head to toe and her heart was galloping. The dream was always disturbing, but it had never continued past Natalie's death. Hearing her sister's voice, feeling sure it meant something, and not knowing what that meaning was, made the dream even more disturbing.

Jillian went into work that morning still feeling uneasy. She had thrown up after getting out of bed and that hadn't happened in over a month. But the dream was so upsetting that it had made her sick. After the retching stopped, she took a shower and attempted to eat some dry toast. Jillian knew she should eat more for the baby's sake, but her stomach was still churning.

When she arrived at the store, Robbie was at the register. "Wow! You look like death warmed over," he said.

"Thanks. I love you too."

"You're seriously as pale as a sheet, Jill. Maybe you should just go home."

"I'm okay. I just had a rough start this morning." Going home was the last thing she wanted. If she did, she would spend the whole day with disturbing images running through her head. She needed a distraction.

Robbie shrugged and let it go.

Jillian went into the back room and put her purse in her locker. When she got out on the floor, her mother was waiting for her.

"Robbie says you look sick," Jackie said. She evaluated Jillian for a second. "You are really pale."

"I'm okay," Jillian insisted, keeping her eyes down.

"No, you're not. Tell me what's going on."

Jillian never could lie to her mother. Jackie always seemed to know. Jillian didn't know if that was because her mother knew her so well or because she was just a really bad liar. She sighed. "I had the dream again this morning before I got up."

"Oh, sweetie." Jackie rushed over and folded Jillian up in her arms.

Jillian didn't mean to start crying, but something about her mother's embrace brought it all to the surface. When she pulled back, tears were streaming down her cheeks.

"That bad?" Jackie asked.

"It was different this time. Natalie said something to me at the end of the dream—after I saw her die."

Jackie kept eye contact but didn't say anything.

"It's really bothering me. I feel like it means something, but I can't imagine what," Jillian said.

"What did she say?" The words came out of her mother's mouth slowly as if it were an effort. Jillian imagined it must be almost as hard for Jackie to hear about these dreams as it was for her to have them.

"Only one word. She said, 'Today.'"

Jackie thought for a moment. "I can't imagine what that could mean either."

Jillian shook her head. The dream felt ominous, and it was hard for her to dismiss that, but she didn't see how continuing this conversation would help either of them.

"Probably nothing. It was only a dream. I'm sure I'm reading too much into it."

She was sure that would be enough to end the topic, but Jackie still looked shaken. Then she said, "I wish she would talk to me."

Jillian didn't know what to say. She stood there silent for a few seconds as her mother stared at the floor with a sad expression. Then, Jackie looked up at her and forced a smile. "Oh well, today's the day we find out if I'm going to have a granddaughter or a grandson."

"It sure is," Jillian said, getting on board with the change of subject.

Moving on to her tasks at the store, Jillian worked until noon, then she stopped for a quick and desperately needed lunch before heading to her doctor's office for her one-thirty appointment. Just before arriving, she came to an intersection and continued forward without slowing down when she saw that the light was green. A split second after crossing into the intersection, she heard a loud boom and her world went black.

Chapter Thirteen

Jillian's eyelids fluttered but wouldn't stay open long enough to see anything. She could hear a rhythmic beep and her nose filled with the scent of antiseptics. She felt a dull, throbbing pain throughout her body—most of it anyway. She moaned and tried to get her lids to stay open for a couple of seconds so she could see where she was.

"Jillian," Wyatt's voice rang out. Then her hand was scooped up in his larger, warmer one.

She moaned again. Her lids stayed open long enough for her to get a blurry image of her husband's face. "Wh—what … ummm … what happened?"

She heard a sniffling sound but didn't try to force her eyes again yet. "You were in a car accident. You're in the hospital."

Her eyelids slowly opened, and she saw the distress on Wyatt's face. A tear dropped from his face and landed on her hand. *Can it really be that bad? Am I dying?*

She gave his hand a weak squeeze. "Wyatt? H—how bad is it?"

He shook his head. "You're okay. You will be," he said quickly in response to the worry in her voice.

"Everything … hurts."

"Yeah, I bet it does. It was a really bad accident."

Despite the pain, she thought about her little red Kia. She knew that should be the least of her worries. Still, she wanted to know how it had fared. "Is my car totaled?"

He nodded. "Definitely. Someone ran the light at an intersection when you were going forty-five miles an hour. He was going fast too. The front end of your car was completely crushed." He teared up again and took a minute to compose himself. "It took them so long to get you out of there ... it was almost too late."

She thought back and tried to remember what had happened. "The light was green." That was all she could remember.

"I know. Several witnesses confirmed that it was the other guy's fault."

"Is he okay?"

Wyatt's head dipped and he looked at the floor. Then his head began to move side to side. "No. I'm afraid he didn't make it. His car took the impact in the driver's side."

"Oh," she said. She felt sad for the man who was dead even if it was his fault. She also felt lucky to be alive.

Pain surged up through her and caused her to groan. "Wyatt, should it hurt this much?"

He looked at her with his brows drawn together. He was trying not to cry again, she realized. "You had to have surgery. That's why it hurts so much."

"Surgery?" Panic rose in her chest. *What kind of surgery? What did they cut open? ... What about the baby?*

She pulled her hand free and reached down to her belly, realizing that it hurt more than anything else. There was a large bandage. "Wyatt, what about the baby?"

He answered her with sobs that shook his whole body.

"No," Jillian said in disbelief. "No, it can't be." She shook her head, feeling as if she had just taken a sucker punch. She sucked in a painful breath. Her baby couldn't be gone. After all they had been through, she just couldn't believe that something so terrible could have happened. Tears welled in her eyes and spilled onto the pillow beneath her head.

Then her ominous dream came to mind, but she didn't want to believe that this was what it meant. This just couldn't be true. Maybe she was dreaming again. She prayed with all her might that it was just a dream.

"Wyatt, tell me it isn't true," she begged in a hoarse whisper.

Wyatt grabbed her hand once more and squeezed it to his chest. He didn't seem able to speak. This wasn't a dream. Her baby was gone.

Once Wyatt stopped sobbing and was able to speak, he explained to Jillian that the impact of the crash had killed their baby and caused trauma to her uterus. There was hemorrhaging, and the only thing they could do was perform a hysterectomy.

Jillian felt utter shock at this news. Not only had she lost her baby, but she had also lost any chance of ever having another one. She wasn't even sure how to process that. The news left her feeling hollow inside. And Wyatt's sadness and despair were almost harder to take than the emptiness she felt. She knew it wasn't her fault, and yet she felt as if she had failed them both; just as she had failed Natalie that night at the convenience store.

When the nurse came and gave her another dose of pain medication, Jillian was grateful as her eyes grew heavy. The oblivion she descended into was far better than the reality she was living.

Jillian spent the next two days in the hospital. She had so many visitors that the nurses had to come by occasionally and send them all away so she could rest.

Her parents came by twice a day. Her aunt and uncle came by once each day, as did Robbie and Kaitlyn. Layla was away at school and unable to come, so she called both morning and evening to check in on Jillian. She also sent Seth by once to check on her. On top of that, Wyatt's mother came once a day and his father, brother, sister, and their spouses all came at least once during her stay. She felt as if her room had a revolving door.

Jillian was grateful to have such a loving family, but the visits were difficult and strained. Everyone wanted to console her, make her feel better, but no one could. They all shared their sorrow for the loss she and Wyatt had endured, and they attempted to find other topics to discuss while offering weak smiles. There were no right words. Nothing they could say would lessen the blow and they all knew that.

With each visit, Jillian found it hard to decide which was worse: the attempts at consolation or the moment the visit ended, and she was left with only Wyatt (who stayed by her the entire time) and the pain of their loss.

When she went home, the visits continued. Jillian began to feel even more grateful for the distraction from her own thoughts. Wyatt had to go back to work, so for a few days, family members took turns staying with her during the day to help her. She wasn't allowed to lift more than a few pounds and it was difficult to manage certain tasks like dressing herself for the first few days. Until she was better able to do the basics of taking care of herself, one of the women in the family stayed with her.

Once she was able to handle her own basic needs, the visits tapered off and Jillian was left to spend more time on her own. The first day she was alone wasn't too bad. She was exhausted from all the time she'd spent with her visitors, and it was nice to have a quiet house to rest in.

On the second day, Jillian got up late in the morning. The silence of the house pressed in on her almost instantly. It felt like a void that waited for her grief to pour into it. Jillian didn't want to cry. She didn't want to face the loss at all, so she tried her best to push all of it out of her mind.

Getting out of bed, she went into the bathroom to shower. She carefully took her nightgown off, throwing it on the floor. When she looked up, the stitches across her belly seemed like a beacon. *Why did this have to come with a physical reminder that would never go away?*

For several long seconds, Jillian stared at the stitches. The wall she was trying so hard to build around her pain began to crumble. She looked up at her face. Her lips trembled and tears welled in her sad, green eyes. She touched the incision site gingerly, and tears fell down her cheeks.

Closing her eyes against the sight, she tried desperately to push the pain back, but the flood gates were open now and she couldn't get them closed. She grabbed the sink counter as her legs went weak and lowered herself to the lid of the toilet. Leaning back, she let the pain pour out of her until her tears were all used up.

After three weeks had passed and Jillian began to gain more strength, she started working at the store again, but only for two or three hours and only at the register. She was grateful for those hours. Every moment she was kept busy was a moment she wasn't thinking about her dead baby or her missing womb.

On her second week back at work, Layla showed up late in the afternoon on Friday. Jillian was just finishing up her short shift when her cousin walked in.

"Layla!" Jillian exclaimed. "I didn't know you were coming this weekend."

"I had to come spend some time with you," Layla said, making it sound as if she had come only for that reason. But Jillian could see that her cousin was upset about something and was trying to hide it.

Instead of asking directly what the problem was, a tactic she knew Layla wouldn't respond to, Jillian asked, "Want to go out for dinner? Wyatt has to stay late to do his coaching duties." Jillian wasn't happy that Layla had some kind of problem, but she was glad they'd have something to talk about other than her current situation.

Layla gave a wan smile and said, "That's exactly what I hoped you'd say."

"Great! I'm just finishing up here and we can leave. You'll have to drive. I'm not allowed to do that yet."

"Sure, I can drive. How are you getting here and back home if you can't drive yet?"

"Everyone helps. My mom brought me in this afternoon, and Robbie was supposed to take me home."

Jillian was certainly blessed by the family business. If she had any other job, she would probably have to take sick leave for her entire recovery time. Because her family owned and operated the store, they were able to allow her light-duty and help her get there and back.

"So," Layla said, "I'm getting my brother off the hook."

"I'm sure you'll make certain he knows it. Be nice, though. He's been really helpful, and it's put a lot of extra work on his plate."

Layla raised her eyebrows. "He's been doing inventory every week?"

"Just about. I think my dad did it last week so he could have a little extra time at home."

Layla nodded. "I'll try to play nice this weekend—for you. I can't keep that up for long, though, or he'll think I've gone soft."

Jillian giggled, wincing at the pain it caused in her belly, just as her mother walked up to the front of the store.

"Layla!" Jackie said. "It's good to see you."

Jackie closed the distance and hugged her niece.

"It's good to see you too. If you don't mind, I'm going to take Jillian out to dinner now."

Jackie smiled. "That sounds nice. You two have a good time and I'll tell Robbie he doesn't need to drive her home."

Jillian retrieved her purse from the back room and ambled out to her cousin's car, slowly sliding herself into the passenger seat and trying not to move in a way that would cause her pain. Layla watched her slow, careful movements, but didn't say anything. As they headed toward the restaurant, Jillian noticed that Layla was driving more carefully too, taking more time to speed up and slow to a stop. Jillian didn't comment on it, but she appreciated the care her cousin was taking with her. She also noticed that Layla seemed agitated about something and hardly said a word the whole drive.

When they were seated at their table in O'Charley's, Jillian said, "I think I'll just get chicken tenders. What about you?"

Layla was flipping through the menu as if it had done something to upset her. "I don't know. Maybe I'll just get chicken too."

Jillian furrowed her brow in her cousin's direction. "What's going on?"

Layla continued to look down at her menu. "Not a thing."

"That's a lie and we both know it." She hesitated until Layla looked up at her. "Come on, just tell me. You're terrible at hiding it."

"You have enough to worry about right now, Jill. You don't need me dumping on you," Layla said looking at her with an earnest expression.

Jillian's mind briefly flashed to thoughts of the baby she would never hold. "That's exactly what I need. Anything else but my problems to think about right now is a welcome change of pace. And it's what you need too. Let me help you, or at least let me listen."

Layla sighed, but before she could say anything, the waiter came and asked for their orders. When he was gone, she said, "Seth dumped me."

Jillian was truly taken aback. She was sure Seth was head over heels in love with Layla. "What?" she asked. "Why?"

"Because he's a jerk!"

Jillian raised her eyebrows, giving Layla a skeptical look. "If you're not going to be straight with me this is going to be a long and tedious conversation."

Layla blew out a breath and scrunched up her face in irritation. "Fine. It was all my fault. Does that make you happy?"

"No," Jillian said, crossing her arms across her chest. "I want to hear what happened. And we both know I'll get it out of you sooner or later."

Layla glared at her for several seconds while Jillian met her gaze with determination.

"He showed up at my school two days ago! On a Wednesday!" Layla spoke with exasperation as if everyone in the world should know better than to show up unexpectedly on a Wednesday.

"And?" Jillian prompted.

"And he wanted to take me to dinner. I needed every minute to study, Jill. It was finals week."

Jillian waited a moment and then motioned with her hand for Layla to continue.

She huffed out a breath. "He insisted that I had to take time to eat, so I decided to go out with him—just for dinner. That's all I agreed to."

"And what does that mean?"

Layla's nostrils flared. "He pulled out a ring, Jill."

"He proposed?" Jillian's eyes widened and the corners of her mouth turned up.

"Don't smile! I'm not smiling."

Jillian tried to keep her smile on the inside and said, "Then what happened?"

"I said no. I'm in school. He knows I'm not ready."

"So, you told him that," Jillian said in a matter-of-fact tone. "Then what happened?"

Layla's face reddened. "I said it pretty loudly and then I got up and stomped out of the restaurant. Just about everyone in there noticed."

Jillian's eyebrows went up as she thought about how mortifying that must have been for Seth. "Wow!"

"He started it!" Layla said defensively just as their waiter returned with plates of chicken tenders. When he was gone, Layla continued, "He made a big spectacle of it, getting down on one knee in front of me. *He* got everyone watching."

"Getting down on one knee is the traditional way," Jillian pointed out.

"But he chose to do it in a public place, and he knew I wasn't ready!" Layla stopped for a moment, her face turning from indignant to regretful. "Besides, it was Wednesday. There were only about twelve people in there anyway."

Jillian nodded, though not so much in agreement as in understanding. "I think I'm getting the picture. So, after you embarrassed him, he dumped you?"

Layla nodded. Her eyes were downcast, and her lips pursed tight. Jillian was pretty sure her cousin was holding back tears.

"Have you talked to him since then?" Jillian asked.

One tear escaping and running down her cheek, Layla shook her head.

Jillian gave Layla a moment while she took a bite of her chicken. Then she asked, "Did you ever consider that he might have just wanted to get engaged for now and wait until you finish school to get married?"

Layla looked at her curiously.

"Some people do that," Jillian said. "Besides, I think he knows getting married right now wouldn't work too well. He has a job here and you're away at school."

Layla furrowed her brow. "But why get engaged now?"

Jillian shrugged. "Just because the time isn't right yet for the actual wedding doesn't mean it can't be right for the commitment. Maybe he just wants you to know that he loves you that much and that he's waiting for you."

Another tear rolled down Layla's cheek. She swatted it away. "We don't need to have rings to promise that."

"I suppose not. But it's a gesture. He wants you to know he loves you and he wants other people to know it too." Jillian hesitated and ate another bite of her food. "At least that's what I think."

Layla's face went from sadness back to irritation. "You think he was trying to brand me so other guys will know I'm taken?"

"No. I don't think that's what he was doing. I think he was telling you in a grand way that he loves you." She lifted one brow at her cousin. "You don't really see getting engaged or married that way, do you?"

Layla sighed. "No. But it's easier than admitting I might have been a little bit wrong."

Jillian smiled at her. "A little bit?"

Looking annoyed, Layla said, "Maybe a lot. I don't know. We'll see what he says."

Jillian beamed at her. "You're going to talk to him then?"

"Yeah, I guess I need to." Layla munched on her chicken for a moment, then said, "Thanks, Jill. You always help me put things into perspective."

"I'm glad I could help."

# Chapter Fourteen

Jillian looked around the dinner table at her parents' house. Forks scraped the plates, but there was not much sound otherwise. Attempts were made at conversation, but little came of them. It was hard to avoid the one thing everyone was thinking about, but no one wanted to talk about. Jillian felt heartache every time she looked at her parents. They would never have a grandchild.

Even with the uneasy lack of conversation, Jillian was glad she and Wyatt had accepted the dinner invitation. Her mother's cooking was soothing, and it saved her from trying to cook something decent when her heart wasn't in it.

Her mood had been all over the place since the loss of the baby. She was snapping at people some days and barely talking on others. Sleep eluded her and when she did sleep her head was filled with nightmares. Being in her parents' presence was comforting, though, and she thought it might even lead to a better night.

Wyatt was enjoying the visit too, which was evidenced by the way he scooped bite after bite into his mouth, barely taking a breath. When his plate was empty, he looked up and said, "Thank you, Jackie. That was the best pork roast I've ever eaten."

Jackie beamed at him. "You're quite welcome, Wyatt. I'm really glad we could do this tonight. It's good to have both of you here."

Jillian let her mother's words sink in. Despite the difficulty they were all having now, it was good to be together. Things were hard right now, and they had been for a few years, since Natalie's death, but they were a family that loved one another. They could weather any storm as long as they held on to each other.

When everyone was finished eating, Richard and Wyatt went into the living room to see what they could find on TV. Jillian cleared the dishes from the table, and Jackie loaded them into the dishwasher. They worked in silence, Jackie giving her daughter worried glances every so often.

"Here's the last one," Jillian said, placing a final plate on the counter.

Jackie washed it and then turned to Jillian. "Come sit with me for a little while," she said.

Jillian complied, walking with her mother to the table where they sat down.

Jackie placed a hand on one of Jillian's. "How are you doing, sweetheart? Tell me the truth."

Jillian shrugged. "I'm healing."

Her mother looked saddened by this answer. "I meant, how are you doing emotionally?"

Jillian pulled her hand away and looked down at her lap. "Oh, Mom, I'll be okay. I just need time."

"Time heals all wounds, but It's hard—losing a child. I know. It's something we share now. I can understand better than anyone." She hesitated a moment, then pleaded, "Talk to me."

Jillian looked up into her mother's warm, sad eyes. "It's not really the same, is it? My baby was never here. I didn't hold him. I didn't even get to see him."

"Oh, sweetie." Jackie leaned forward and placed a hand on the middle of Jillian's chest. "He was here, in your heart. And he was very real in mine too. We lost him, and it hurts like crazy."

Jillian nodded as her throat grew thick with emotion, and tears brimmed in her eyes. She couldn't speak in answer to her mother's statement. As the sobs began, she fell into Jackie's arms.

Jackie rubbed Jillian's back and held her until she stopped crying. Then Jillian sat back up and wiped her eyes with a napkin.

"I'm going to get us some coffee," Jackie said. She walked over to the counter and turned on her Keurig. A few minutes later, she returned to the table with two cups of hot coffee. She retrieved a bottle of creamer and a bowl of sugar before sitting down again with Jillian.

They sipped the coffee quietly for a moment, then Jackie asked, "Are you sleeping okay, Jillian?"

Jillian sighed. "Sometimes."

Her mother didn't say anything in response. She just sipped her coffee quietly and watched Jillian's face.

"It's just … the nightmares make it hard some nights," Jillian said.

Jackie looked her in the eye. "You still have them?"

Jillian nodded. "About half the time, it's the dream about Nat. The other half of the time, I dream about the accident."

"I thought you didn't remember the accident," Jackie said cautiously.

Jillian furrowed her brow. "I don't. I only remember seeing the green light and starting into the intersection." She hesitated for a moment, trying not to cry again. "But when I'm asleep my mind conjures up its own version of what happened after that. I see my car moving forward and …" She stopped. It was hard to say what came next. She looked down into her lap and, fiddling with her fingers, went on. "In the dream, I see the car coming before it hits me. I see it in time to stop but I don't." She looked up and met her mother's eyes. "Do you think that's what happened? Is it possible that I could have stopped and didn't?"

"No. I don't think that's what happened," Jackie said adamantly. "Don't you think you'd remember if it did happen that way?"

"I don't know. I could be blocking it out, and my unconscious mind is trying to tell me." A tear trickled down her cheek again as she thought about this possibility.

Jackie grabbed her hand and squeezed. "Sweetheart, I know that isn't what happened. I know that because you would never have taken a risk like that with your baby. I also know because of what the witnesses said. It all happened too fast for you to have been able to stop it. I think, somewhere deep inside, you're just blaming yourself because you need to blame someone, and you don't like the idea of blaming a man who's dead. But it wasn't your fault."

Another tear dripped down Jillian's face. *Was she trying to blame herself?* Maybe it was tied to her guilt over what happened to Natalie. People she loved kept dying in her midst and she was always the survivor. "But I was driving," she said in a very small voice.

"That doesn't make it your fault. You know that."

"It was my job to keep him safe."

"Oh, Jillie, you did the best you could. You didn't have control over everything that was happening that day. None of us ever have that kind of control. And sometimes bad things just happen."

Jillian looked into her mother's face, searching the clear, blue eyes that looked back at her. "Why do they keep happening to me?"

Jackie shook her head, at a loss for an answer. Then she reached out and pulled Jillian into her arms again.

# Chapter Fifteen

Jillian awoke to Wyatt's voice calling her and his hand shaking her shoulder. She groaned and rolled to her side facing him. Keeping her eyes closed, she hoped she could quickly dispel his concern.

"I'm okay," she mumbled.

"You didn't sound okay," Wyatt said. "You were crying in your sleep."

"Just a dream."

"A really bad one, I'm guessing."

He wasn't letting up easily. Jillian cracked her eyes open and saw the worry in his face. "Part of it was bad. Not really all of it." She thought for a moment. She still remembered every bit of her dream with perfect clarity, and she wasn't sure how to explain to Wyatt the feelings it left her with. They were all mixed up. She shook her head against the pillow. "I don't know. I'll be okay. Let's go back to sleep."

Wyatt reached out a hand and wiped an errant tear from her cheek. "You sure?"

She grasped his hand and squeezed it for a second before letting it go. "I'm sure."

"All right. But if I wake up to the sound of you crying again, we're going to talk about it."

She nodded and closed her eyes hoping he'd do the same. Several seconds ticked by quietly. When Jillian opened her eyes again, Wyatt was asleep. She tried to fall asleep herself, but the images of her dream would not let her rest.

It had started the same way all her Natalie dreams did, in the car in front of the convenience store. Like always, Natalie got out of the car and looked back at her through the window. This time, however, her sister didn't stick her tongue out and head into the store. This time, the window was open, and Natalie stood there for several seconds smiling serenely.

Then Natalie spoke to her. "Don't worry about him," she said. "He's safe with me now."

Jillian knew Natalie was talking about the baby. She just wasn't sure how she felt about the message. Of course, it was comforting to think that Natalie and the baby were together in heaven. It made her feel as though she'd given her sister the baby she was never able to have. However, it also reminded Jillian that they were both gone. She would never see her sister's face again in this life, at least not outside of her dreams, and she wouldn't get to see the face of her baby until she died herself.

The jumble of feelings was disconcerting enough, but there was something more to it than that. The dream had also left her feeling a strange emptiness that was more acute than it had been in a while. Four months had passed since the accident that took her baby away and, while it still hurt like crazy, the immediacy and intensity of the feeling had dimmed a bit. Her dream brought it all back in vivid color. She felt like there was a black hole in her heart that couldn't stand to stay empty for one second longer.

When Wyatt got up for work, Jillian pretended to be asleep. She didn't want to talk about her dream anymore or why it had kept her awake for the last two hours.

She got out of bed once she heard him leave the house and got into the shower. She didn't have to work until that afternoon, but she wasn't going to stay home that whole time. The restlessness that had prevented her from getting back to sleep was still eating at her.

After her shower, she got dressed and went out to the kitchen to eat breakfast. Dodger was waiting for her at the back door. She let him out and went to the pantry to get a box of cereal. Usually, she ate Shredded Wheat or Raisin Bran, but today she pulled out the box of Fruit Loops that she'd bought at Wyatt's insistence. She wasn't in the mood for healthy.

When she finished her breakfast, she let Dodger back into the house and locked the back door. She patted the dog's furry head and smiled at his happily wagging tail. "I'll come back in a while to let you out again before I go to work. Until then, look after the house, okay?"

Dodger licked her hand in response, and she smiled despite her unnerving emotions.

When she got into her car, Jillian had no idea where she was headed. She just started driving and kept going for close to an hour. When she thought to look at where she was, she realized she had driven into a part of town that she didn't really know. Nothing was familiar.

She was about to tell her GPS to show her the way home when she noticed a church in front of her. It wasn't all that large, but it was a lovely building with a steeple that reached high into the sky and stained-glass windows all around. The sun was shining down on it and glinting off the cross at the top of the steeple. Jillian felt strangely drawn to the church. As if someone were nudging her forward, she pulled into the parking lot and got out of her car.

Walking up the steps, Jillian's mind went back to her dream and the deep feeling of loss and emptiness she felt upon waking. By the time she reached the door, tears were rolling down her cheeks. She pushed the door open, stumbling through as all of her pain began pouring out of her in deep sobs.

Jillian made her way forward to the altar and stood staring at the image of Christ depicted on the back wall. She thought about the horrible way he'd died and knew she should be grateful and know that he understands suffering, but she didn't know how to stop feeling like she was being punished.

"I would have rather died myself," she said in a near whisper. "But instead, I keep watching people I love die. Why did You let them get taken from me?" She fell onto her knees and let the rest of her tears fall.

When they were all used up, she sat in the first pew and continued to stare at the image on the wall behind the altar, trying hard to listen for any answers that might come. She was here for some reason; every part of her being told her so. But the church remained eerily quiet, and no messages came to her.

Then, after several long minutes in total silence, Jillian heard something. She turned at the sound, unsure of what it was. It didn't seem possible that it could be what it sounded like. The sound came again a few seconds later, and this time she was sure of what she heard—it was a baby beginning to fuss.

Jillian looked around. She didn't see any other people there, so where was the sound coming from? Listening intently when the sound came again, Jillian began to move in the direction it was coming from. When she reached the center of the church, she stood in the aisle and waited again for the baby's fuss. It was coming from the right side of the church. She turned it that direction and saw a bassinet-style basket sitting on a pew. Light from one of the stained-glass windows poured down over it. Jillian slid along the pew until she reached the basket and then she peered in. A tiny newborn infant lay wrapped up in a blanket, kicking its feet. The baby's face was scrunched up and reddening, ready to begin screaming.

By the time the first yell sounded from the infant's mouth, Jillian was sliding her hand under its little head and lifting it out of the basket. She noticed that two bottles full of milk had been left in the basket with the baby along with a few diapers and a travel pack of baby wipes.

She cradled the tiny bundle in her arms and the crying stopped as curious eyes tried to focus on her. "Where is your mother, little one?" She glanced around again but still didn't see a soul. "Who would leave you here like this?"

The baby began to fuss again, so Jillian picked up one of the bottles. She shook the milk up and put the nipple into the baby's mouth. The milk was gratefully received, so she sat back in the pew and allowed the infant to drink.

Still alone in the church when the feeding was done, Jillian picked up one of the diapers. "Maybe we should see if you need a change. Then I guess I'll have to call someone to tell them you're here."

She laid the baby down in the basket and carefully unsnapped the green sleeper between the baby's legs so she could get to the diaper. Sure enough, it was wet. She removed it and pulled out one of the wipes. "So, you're a little boy," she said as she put on the fresh diaper. "I bet you feel much better now."

She snapped his outfit up and wrapped his blanket around him. Then she pulled out her phone and called 911 to report the abandoned infant.

Moments later, the baby began to cry again. When Jillian picked him up, he stopped immediately. She felt a strange warmth go through her as she rocked him gently in her arms. *This was the reason.* The baby was why she had been drawn to the church. She was meant to find him.

When Wyatt showed up and tapped Jillian on the shoulder, she didn't even know how long she'd been sitting there. All she could do was stare at the beautiful little face of the baby in her arms.

Shortly after her phone call, the police had shown up. They talked to her for a while, asking lots of questions, and now they were checking the church from top to bottom, looking for anything that might lead them to the baby's mother.

By the time the police were done questioning Jillian, someone from child protective services showed up. Ilene, the woman they sent, was a middle-aged, black woman with concerned eyes and a gentle smile. She took the baby from Jillian to check him over and make sure there weren't any obvious health concerns. The moment the infant was pulled from Jillian's arms, he began to wail. He continued crying until Ilene handed him back to Jillian to hold for a moment while she called her boss to see about finding the child a foster home.

Surprised by the way the crying ended the moment the baby was placed back in Jillian's arms, Ilene said, "He seems very comfortable with you. Would you mind holding him for a little bit while I see about getting him a place to go for tonight?"

"I don't mind," Jillian said. She wasn't thinking about anything but the tiny boy in her arms and her certainty that she was meant to find him.

Pulling herself back to the moment, Jillian looked at Wyatt.

"The police called me and told me you were here. And that was after your mother called wondering if I knew where you were because you were late for work. She said you weren't answering your phone." He stopped and stared at her for a moment. It was clear he was looking for an explanation, but Jillian didn't respond.

"You didn't answer when I called either. The police officer who called me said you were in a daze and I should probably come get you. What's going on?"

She nodded to the infant in her embrace. "I found him. And I turned the sound off on my phone a while ago when he fell asleep."

Wyatt was silent for a moment as he watched Jillian cradle the child. Then he said, "Jills, we should probably go now. Your mother is worried about you, and they need you at the store."

"We can't go," Jillian said.

"Why not? The police are here. They'll make sure he's taken care of."

"I found him, Wyatt. And I think I was meant to."

Wyatt's face fell into a worried frown. "Jills, he isn't ours. They'll be looking for his mother. You need to let them take care of him."

"I know all that. I haven't lost my mind." She gave him an irritated look. "But I feel like I was led here for a reason." Her eyes pleaded with him for understanding.

He looked down and scratched his head. "Maybe you *were* led here for a reason, and I think you fulfilled that reason. You found him and now he will be okay."

The baby opened his eyes and smacked his lips. Jillian smiled at him. "He needs a home, Wyatt, and we're approved foster parents."

Wyatt sighed and sat down next to her on the pew. "We're not ready yet. We decided that together. We need time to heal."

Jillian glanced at him. "I know. But I think God has a different plan for us, and I believe this is it." She stopped, uncertain of how her husband would react to the next thing she had to say. "He's our Nathan, Wyatt. I feel sure that God is telling me that."

Wyatt's brows drew together over eyes filled with intense pain. "Oh, Jills, this baby isn't ours. You have to let him go. *Our* Nathan is dead."

Jillian waited a moment, trying to find her next words. "I know you think I'm not in my right mind right now, but I promise you that I am. Our baby died. But I think *this* baby is meant to be our Nathan."

He started to shake his head, but Jillian said, "Just listen to me for a minute, and open your mind to what I'm saying. Can you do that?"

He nodded.

"You believe in God, don't you?" Jillian asked.

"Yes, you know that."

"And this baby is going to need a foster home, right?"

"I suppose he is," Wyatt said.

"And we're approved foster parents, aren't we?"

"We are."

"Then why shouldn't it be us? Why can't you believe that God sent me to this baby?"

Wyatt put a hand on her knee. "I don't want you to be hurt again," he said. "I don't want you to believe that this baby is meant to be ours and then be crushed when he is taken away." He stopped and his eyes brimmed with tears. "And *I* don't want to be hurt again either."

Jillian nodded in understanding. Tears filled her eyes as the pain of all they had been through rushed back through her mind. She took a deep, steadying breath. "If we ever want to have a child, we'll have to take the chance sometime that we might get hurt. I don't want that to happen either. We've been hurt a lot already. But if we don't take the chance, we won't have a family."

Wyatt took a long look at the baby in Jillian's arms and stroked a finger along his round cheek. "Just because we're approved foster parents doesn't mean they'll let us take him home with us. There are other foster parents out there. It's a long shot, Jills."

Jillian nodded in the direction of the lady from child protective services. "That's Ilene," she said. "She's here from child services, and she put the baby back in my arms because he cried when she took him from me and wouldn't stop.

She's trying to find a place for him right now. If we tell her that we're approved foster parents, maybe she'll consider us for him."

Wyatt thought about it for a moment. "I guess it won't hurt to ask her."

Jillian called to Ilene, and the woman walked over to her and said into her phone, "Hold on a sec." Then she looked at Jillian and Wyatt. "What can I do for you?"

"Are you still looking for a place for him?" Jillian asked.

"Yes. All of our foster homes are pretty filled up right now, but I have a few more to call. I'm sure we can get an emergency placement for him that will get us through until we can find something more permanent."

"We could take him," Jillian said. Ilene raised her eyebrows and Jillian continued, "It just so happens that we're approved foster parents. We put off taking a placement because I was pregnant, but I lost the baby a few months ago." She paused, took a deep breath, and then went on, "We've had some time to heal. I think we're ready, and we'd like to help this little guy."

Ilene looked at Jillian and Wyatt for a long moment. Then she said in a tone wavering between skepticism and hopefulness, "I'll have to check that everything is still current with your approval."

Jillian smiled broadly. "I understand."

"Do you have what you'd need—a crib or bassinet?" Ilene asked.

Jillian looked at Wyatt. "We do have a crib, but we never got it put together. But Wyatt's sister already offered us a bassinet that they aren't using anymore. We could get her to bring it over."

"We have some other things too," Wyatt said, "but we'll need to go shopping for the rest."

Ilene nodded slowly. "He does seem to like you." She stared at them again, then she lifted her phone back to her ear and said, "Jim, I might have another option. Check the system for—" Stopping she looked at Jillian again. "I didn't get your last name or your husband's name."

"Jillian and Wyatt Green," Jillian said.

"Did you hear that, Jim? Check the system for Jillian and Wyatt Green." She waited while Jim checked for her. Then her face brightened. "They're up-to-date on everything? ... Yeah, I can do that. Thanks, Jim."

Ilene beamed at them. "You two must have been sent from above. Jim says you're up to date, but he wants me to take the baby to your home and give everything a quick check since you have been in the system for several months but haven't had a placement. I'm guessing you don't have an infant car seat anyway, right?"

"No, we don't. At least not here." They did have one at home that was still in the box. She and Wyatt had picked it out a month before the accident, and Jillian's heart swelled at the thought of finally getting to use it.

"Ma'am?" One of the police officers stepped up to Ilene.

She turned to him and said, "Yes, officer?"

"I just wanted to let you know that we're done here. We'll take all the evidence we collected and see if we can find out who left the little guy here. Are you almost ready to leave with the baby?" the officer asked.

"Yes, I am. Do you think you'll be able to track his mother down?"

The officer shrugged. "Hard to say." He glanced at the baby. "He looks to have some Asian background, but his hair is light brown, so his mother might be Asian and she might not. We've got plenty of fingerprints but that only helps if she's in the system."

Ilene sighed. "Well, I guess we'll just have to see what you can turn up." She looked at Jillian. "Bring the baby out to my car, and we'll get him in the car seat. We need to take him by the hospital and have him checked out, then you can lead the way and we'll get you all set up."

As Jillian laid the baby in the infant carrier, his eyes fluttered open. In just a quick moment, they seemed to take her in and close again. Jillian smiled at the trust he already seemed to have in her. She stroked the soft hair on his tiny head. "See you in just a little while. Be a good boy for Ilene."

She closed the door on Ilene's Ford Explorer and walked to her car. Wyatt's car was parked right next to hers and he waited for her there. "Are you sure you're up to driving right now? We can come back and get your car tomorrow," he said.

"There's no need for that," Jillian insisted. "I told you, I'm fine."

Wyatt nodded uncertainly. "All right. You follow me. And call your mom on the way to let her know you're okay and that you won't make it in to work today after all."

"I'll call her," Jillian said. She hoped her absence wasn't causing too much trouble at the store, but she was sure her mother would be excited to hear about the baby.

When they arrived at home, Wyatt and Jillian led Ilene inside. Jillian wanted desperately to take the baby out of the carrier and hold him. She wanted to keep him in her arms forever, but she resisted the urge and, instead, showed Ilene around the house while the child slept.

"Everything looks pretty good," Ilene said, "but you need to get that baby room finished up with a crib and changing table."

"We have those things. We're going to get the changing table up tonight, and we'll work on the crib this weekend," Wyatt said. Despite his efforts to keep it at bay, his excitement was beginning to show. "We also have the car seat to install in the car tonight. And my sister is going to bring the bassinet over along with some things that we will need right away like diapers and formula."

"Then I think you have things under control here," Ilene said.

Jillian nodded. It was already getting late since they had been at the hospital for a couple of hours, but she felt exhilarated.

The doctor at the hospital told them that everything was fine and when he filled out a birth certificate, Jillian asked what name would be given to him.

Ilene shrugged and said, "In cases like these, we usually just pick something to put in temporarily. If he ends up getting adopted, which is likely, the adoptive parents will choose a name."

"We want to adopt him," Wyatt said, surprising Jillian.

Ilene's eyebrows shot up. "Are you sure? There's no telling what will happen if his mother is found. Maybe you should take a little time to think it over."

Jillian shook her head. "No. We don't need any time," she said. If Wyatt was ready to jump in, she certainly was. "We want to adopt him. We understand that it might not work out the way we hope." She shrugged. "But you never know, maybe it will work out. He needs a home, and we want to be the ones to give him one."

Ilene smiled cautiously and nodded. "Okay. I'll get the ball rolling. Of course, it will be a while before adoption proceedings can even start. The police will be investigating—looking for his mother. In the meantime, you can pick a name for him."

Jillian beamed. "Nathan," she said.

Remember the Butterfly

Wyatt allowed the name "Nathan" to be put on the baby's birth certificate, but it was evident to Jillian that he was biting back a protest. When everything settled down that night, Jillian turned to him and coaxed him to tell her what was on his mind.

"I thought we already gave that name to *our* baby. I know we lost him, but does that change it?" Wyatt asked.

Jillian thought about the dream she had the night before and a shiver went up her spine. It seemed strange to her that it had been less than twenty-four hours since those images spilled through her consciousness. Yet, at the same time, the dream was still so fresh in her mind that she might have just had it seconds ago. She didn't want to share the dream with Wyatt. Somehow it felt like a true conversation with Natalie, which was meant for only the two of them to share.

She took Wyatt's hand in hers and looked into his eyes while her own eyes shimmered with forming tears. "Our baby will forever be in my heart. I'm not pushing him aside. I know he's in heaven, and I look forward to meeting him there someday. But I can't let Natalie's namesake be a child who never got to live." She looked at him pleadingly now, hoping he could understand. "Natalie is dead. Her name needs to carry on with someone who's alive. I need that."

Wyatt was quiet for several seconds. Then he nodded. "I think I understand. Are you sure you want to give that name to a baby we might not be able to keep?"

Jillian looked at the infant now sleeping in the bassinet Courtney had delivered. "I know you can't understand this, but I feel certain he was meant for us. He's our Nathan. I know he is."

Jillian felt a tear fall on her head as Wyatt leaned over to kiss her. "Nathan it is," he said.

When darkness fell that evening, Jillian found it impossible to sleep. Next to her, in the bassinet, was the child she'd been waiting years to have. Her heart was so full of love for the baby that she thought it could burst at any moment, and her mind swam with thoughts of the future. She could see Nathan a few years from now running around the yard with Dodger chasing after him. She could see Wyatt mowing the lawn while the young boy followed behind with a plastic mower. She imagined holding him in her lap and reading to him. They were a family now. It was finally happening.

Jillian sat up on the side of the bed and gazed into the bassinet, watching the baby's tiny chest rise and fall rhythmically. She knew he would wake in an hour or two and want to be fed. She should sleep while she had the chance. Instead, she gently stroked the silken hair on the top of Nathan's head.

"I know we just met," she whispered, "but I love you. I'll always be here for you, Nathan. You're my dream come true."

Chapter Sixteen

Nathan was accepted into both sides of the family with cautious joy and measured enthusiasm. Jillian couldn't blame them. They wanted to welcome him wholeheartedly. They were just afraid to. Their fear was the same monster that showed in Wyatt's eyes every time he had a quiet, unhurried moment to look at Nathan and think of something beyond the next feeding or diaper change. It was the same monster that, if Jillian was honest with herself, she had to admit lived deep inside her as well. She always stomped the monster down, reminding herself of the feeling she had sitting in that church when she knew without a doubt that God had sent her there.

But Wyatt, nor anyone else in their family, had the benefit of that moment of clarity. So, they were hesitant to let their hearts wrap around this child who came into their lives so suddenly.

Nathan's introduction happened in a whirlwind of visits. The day after Jillian and Wyatt brought him home, all four grandparents arrived to meet him. They each held him and gushed about how beautiful he was but none called him by name. It was as if they were afraid that if they used the name, he might be swiped away from them.

When the weekend arrived, Jillian bundled the baby into his car seat, packed a diaper bag, and she and Wyatt headed to Rhonda's house for a picnic.

When they got into the house, Anika was the first to meet them and take Nathan from his carrier. "Oh, look at him," she said. "He's adorable!"

"Didn't I tell you?" Courtney responded. She had been the first to see him when she brought them the bassinet and a few other things the first night.

"I wanna see," whined Braylee.

Anika stooped down and allowed the three-year-old to look at the baby.

"Don't touch his head," she said, mirroring the words of her mother when other new babies had come into the family. "It's soft."

Anika smiled. "It has a soft spot, Bray, you're right. You have to be careful with his head and I promise I will."

Braylee nodded with a serious expression before asking, "Where's Dodge?"

"He stayed home this time," Wyatt answered. "All this baby stuff is new to us and it was a lot to handle. We'll bring him the next time."

Braylee's face filled with disappointment. The dog was far more fun than the baby. Accepting the dog's absence, Braylee headed into the backyard to find her cousin and sister who could at least walk and play with her.

Courtney laughed as her daughter left. "She loves that dog. But she'll learn to love this little guy too."

L.J. was next to hold the baby, followed by Brent. As the food was cooked and served, they passed the child around just as they had done with every other baby in the family. Still, Jillian could feel the difference as if it were palpable in the air, a consensus of love somewhat withheld.

When the picnic was over and everyone was leaving to go home, Jillian found Nathan in Rhonda's arms. He was cooing up at her while she murmured to him words that Jillian could not quite make out. She could, however, understand the feeling. Unlike the rest of the family, and in contrast to the way she had responded to Nathan the first time she met him, Rhonda wasn't holding back anything. She was pouring her heart out to the baby in her arms.

As Jillian watched, her eyes filled with tears. She stopped still, barely breathing, in the doorway to the kitchen, not wanting to interrupt the moment.

When a hand rested on her shoulder, Jillian turned to see Wyatt standing just behind her. "She's in love," he said, watching his mother.

"She sure is," Jillian said. Rhonda had been ecstatic with every new baby that came into the family, but Nathan was different. He was like her—a child left behind and in need of love. Jillian knew they would have a special bond.

The following day, Jillian's family got together after the store closed. They closed at six o'clock on Sundays and came together about once a month to have dinner. This time they met at Richard and Jackie's house.

When Jillian and Wyatt arrived with Nathan, the house already smelled of garlic bread and tomato sauce. Wyatt sucked in a deep breath and sighed. "This is going to be a good dinner," he said.

Jillian giggled. "I guess a whole weekend of good food means more when neither of us has been able to get anything decent made at home lately."

Wyatt nodded with a smile. "Yes, but we've been busy in the best possible way."

Hearing those words melted Jillian's heart. She was constantly uncertain if Wyatt was fully on board with their fostering this baby in the hope they would eventually adopt him. She worried that he'd gone along with it at her insistence and maybe he wasn't so sure about it.

Before they had time to leave the doorway, Richard took Nathan from Jillian and sat down in the living room with him where he was watching college football with Robbie and Danny. "He'll be one of the guys before you know it," Richard said. "We'll teach him who to root for."

Wyatt joined the other men and Jillian went out to the kitchen to see how her mother was coming with dinner.

"Hi sweetie," Jackie said when Jillian walked in.

"Can I help?" Jillian asked.

"Certainly not! You've just had your first few nights of mom duty. You sit down and relax."

"I'm okay. I can still help," Jillian insisted.

"I'm helping," Aunt Rose said. "And you know what they say about too many cooks in the kitchen. You just sit down and talk to us."

"If you insist. The food smells great by the way."

Jackie beamed at her. "That's what I like to hear. Where's the baby?"

"Dad has him."

"Then I guess we get you all to ourselves for a while," Rose said.

Jillian sank onto one of the kitchen chairs. "Looks that way."

"How's it going with the baby?" Jackie asked. "Is he sleeping?"

"He's doing well. He sleeps for two to three hours at a time. Wyatt and I are adjusting. How are things going at the store?"

"Just fine," Jackie said. "Don't you worry about us. You're taking care of a new baby. You get six weeks off."

"Thanks, Mom. I guess I need to start looking for a good daycare. I'm not sure what to do about days I work the late shift, though, since Wyatt works late some days too."

"You know," Rose said, "we can probably work out a baby care schedule and keep the little guy out of daycare."

"I don't know," Jillian said. "That's a lot to ask of everyone."

Rose snapped a hand towel at her playfully. "Don't be silly. We'll all enjoy spending time with the baby. God knows Robbie and Kaitlyn are in no hurry to give me any grandchildren."

Jillian glanced around. "Where is Kaitlyn?"

"She's working tonight and can't make it," Rose said. "And don't get me wrong, I love that girl tremendously. But having children isn't at the top of her list right now."

"What do you think, Mom? Would it work to have a care schedule for Nathan or should I look for daycare?"

Jillian saw her mother flinch at the baby's name and tried not to feel hurt. She knew it was hard for her to hear that name and not know for sure if the baby it had been given to would be with them forever.

Jackie turned and looked at her. "I'm sure we can work it out so he doesn't need to go to daycare. Having us care for him would be better and it would save you and Wyatt a lot of money."

"That's true," Jillian said.

"Who's saving money?" Layla said, walking into the room.

"I guess Wyatt and I are thanks to your mom and mine," Jillian said.

"I see," Layla said.

Jillian smiled at her cousin. "I'm getting used to seeing you around here. It's going to be hard when you go back to school in a couple of weeks."

"It's been good for me too. I never thought I would say this, but I missed working in the store while I was gone." Layla looked around the room. "Where is the little one?"

"Didn't you see him in the living room with the guys?" Jillian asked.

"I didn't look. I thought he'd be back here with all the ladies, so I came straight back."

Jillian stood up. "Come on. We'll go get him."

When they got to the living room, Layla went straight over to Richard and said, "My turn, Uncle Richard. Let me hold my new cousin."

Richard smiled and lifted the baby gently into Layla's waiting arms.

"Look at you!" Layla said in a breathy voice. She gazed at the baby with open affection. "It's so good to meet you, little Nathan. You're going to do your namesake proud, aren't you?"

From across the room, Jillian beamed at the two of them.

"All right, little man, I think you've had enough football for your first time. Let's go see how dinner is coming." Layla carried Nathan into the kitchen and Jillian followed.

When they were both seated at the table, Layla looked at Jillian and said, "We didn't get any warning about this baby, but I think we still need to have a shower. Don't you think so, Mom?"

"Definitely," Rose answered.

Jackie smiled at the idea but didn't say anything.

"The police are still looking for his mother. We don't know if we'll get to keep him," Jillian warned.

Layla studied her. "Even if they find her, why would that change anything? If she'd wanted him, she wouldn't have left him in that church."

Jillian shrugged. "She could change her mind."

Layla scrunched up her face. "Would they really let her have him back after she abandoned him? Wouldn't she be facing charges?"

"I'm not sure," Jillian said. "I guess it might depend on what she has to say for herself … plus, there might be a father that wants him back."

Everyone was silent for a moment while that idea sank in. Then Layla said, "You obviously believe it's all going to work out. If you didn't, you wouldn't have named him after Natalie."

Jillian thought about the way she felt a few days before in the church. She did feel that things were going to work out, but she didn't think she could explain it to her family. Wyatt was barely able to wrap his head around her insistence that it was meant to be. She wasn't about to bring it up with her mother, her aunt, and her cousin.

"I want it to work out. I feel like it will, but there's no guarantee," Jillian said.

Layla looked down at Nathan. "I think it will work out too." She glanced back up and directly at Jillian. "But even if it doesn't, you'll have this baby with you for a while, right?"

Jillian nodded. "Probably."

"Then you'll need baby stuff."

Jillian smiled. "I guess we will. Thanks, Layla."

"Don't thank me," Layla said, "I'm just making the suggestion. I won't be around to plan it."

"You can leave that to us," Rose said, putting her arm around Jackie.

"Sounds like fun," Jackie said, "but it will have to wait until after dinner. Jillian, go tell all the boys that it's time to eat."

Dinner was filled with delicious food and light conversation. It was the closest Jillian's family had come to being joyful in a long time. Despite the underlying worry that Nathan could be snatched away from them, his presence was lifting them out of a long-lasting fog of sadness. In time, Jillian knew, the worry would fade away.

When dinner was over, Wyatt took Nathan back into the living room to hang out with the men. Rose and Jackie sent Jillian out of the room so they could plan the baby shower. "We need to make sure we have a surprise or two for you," Rose said.

"Come sit on the porch with me for a few minutes before I leave," Layla said to Jillian.

When they got outside, Layla pulled Jillian over to the rocking chairs on the front porch and they both sat down. Jillian waited for Layla to speak since it was obvious she had something to say.

"I went to see Seth yesterday," Layla said.

Despite their earlier conversation and the fact that Layla had been home for the summer break, she had been putting off talking to Seth.

"Did you?" Jillian asked and then waited for Layla to continue.

"We had a good talk." Layla reached into her purse and pulled something out. "He gave me this," she said holding out a ring. It was made of yellow gold and had a single purple stone.

"So, he proposed? And you have the ring. Does that mean you said yes?"

Layla smiled. "He didn't exactly propose. Apparently, that was never his intention. He knows I have school right now and I'm not ready."

Jillian furrowed her brow. "So … he got down on one knee in a public place to give you a ring that isn't an engagement ring?"

Layla giggled. "He sees the error in that now, believe me. And I see the error in making an assumption and storming out without letting him speak." She looked at Jillian earnestly. "I'm glad you talked some sense into me and got me to go see him."

Shaking her head, Jillian said, "I still don't understand. What is this ring for—it's not your birthday, and why did he do the one knee thing with it?"

"It's a promise ring," Layla said, putting the ring on her right hand. "He wanted to make a big show of letting me know that, when we're both ready, he intends to ask me to marry him. For now, it doesn't change anything."

"So, it was all just a big declaration of love."

Layla's cheeks turned pink as she gazed at the ring. "Yeah."

"That's sweet. You found a good one with Seth."

Layla looked up at Jillian. "I did, didn't I? I don't know how I did that when I wasn't even trying."

"I think people usually find real love when they aren't exactly looking. It comes when you're in a good place with yourself."

"Yeah, maybe you're right."

They sat quietly for a few minutes, rocking in their chairs. Then Layla said, "I guess I better get going. I told Seth we could meet up for a movie tonight. Thanks for being such a good friend, Jill. I couldn't ask for a better cousin."

"Neither could I," Jillian said.

They both stood up and Jillian reached out and pulled Layla into a hug. Pulling back, Layla said, "When I am ready for marriage, Nathan is going to make an adorable little ring bearer."

Jillian smiled as her heart tightened. She could see him, a little boy in a tiny tux walking down the aisle of a church with a pillow in his hands. "I can't wait to see that, and you in a wedding dress."

Layla gave her a wicked smile. "You never know, I might just get married in a pair of shorts and a white t-shirt."

"Over your mother's dead body," Jillian said without missing a beat.

Layla opened the driver's side door of her car and started to get in. "You're probably right. I'll have to wear a dress." In the car now, she pulled the door closed and started the engine. Jillian watched her drive off before going back into the house and rejoining the rest of her family.

A week and a half later, Jillian was just finishing up feeding Nathan a bottle when the doorbell rang. Cradling the baby in the crook of one arm, she went to the door and opened it to see Ilene standing on her porch.

"Ilene, come in," Jillian said opening the door wide enough for the other woman to move past her.

Jillian closed the door and led Ilene into the living room where they both sat down.

Ilene looked around the room at all the baby stuff strewn about and then she watched the baby sleep in Jillian's arms for a moment. "He's looking good," she said.

Jillian smiled. "He's a good baby."

"I wanted to come and let you know what's going on with Nathan's case," Ilene said.

Jillian sucked in a breath, fearing the news Ilene came to tell her. "Okay," she said cautiously, "did they find out who his mother is?"

"The police looked for video showing who left Nathan in the church, but the church doesn't have any cameras and there aren't any in the area that point in the right direction. They checked records at all the area hospitals, but they didn't find any indication that Nathan was born in any of them. They also used a sample of his DNA and checked to see if his mother could be found in any database. They didn't find anything."

"So, what does that mean?" Jillian asked.

Ilene smiled. "It means we can start forward with the adoption process."

Joy filled Jillian's heart so completely and so suddenly that she thought her chest might burst open. She sucked in a deep breath and placed her free hand over her heart. She didn't realize she was crying until her vision blurred and tears began to fall into her lap.

Ilene's face remained incredibly indifferent, and Jillian didn't know what to think of that.

"Don't get too excited yet," Ilene warned. "The process will take about a year to complete and there's no telling what may happen in that year. His mother could still show up … or even his father. Abandonment cases are filled with variables that are impossible to predict."

Jillian nodded, but her excitement did not abate. It was all going to work out. She felt sure of that. "I understand," she said.

Ilene allowed the hint of a smile now. "We'll get the ball rolling, and until the adoption completes, you and Wyatt will be his foster parents. It looks like he's in good hands."

Chapter Seventeen

Eleven months later

Jillian watched as Nathan slowly toddled after Dodger in the backyard, his chubby little legs stomping forward as he struggled to keep his balance. He'd only been walking for a week and he was already trying to keep up with the dog.

When the baby plopped down on his butt and looked at her, Jillian smiled at him. "It's okay. Hop back up."

Nathan ambled to his feet and started in pursuit of the dog once again. Jillian sat down in a chair on the patio and watched dog and boy play in the hot July sunshine. She was gladly enjoying the day with him since she didn't have to work. In the last eleven months, Nathan had filled her heart and home with joy.

Soon he'd officially be her son and she couldn't wait. As that time approached, however, Jillian found herself more and more nervous. She prayed nothing would happen to take him away from them. If that did happen, she didn't know if her heart could survive. She loved this little boy with every fiber of her being. And it wasn't just herself she was worried about. Losing Nathan would devastate the entire family.

Her worry that something might go wrong now when they were so close to adopting him was likely the reason Jillian was having the dreams again. Though they had never completely stopped, after bringing Nathan home, they had lessened. Then about a month ago, they returned with a vengeance. If Natalie was trying to tell her something, Jillian didn't think she wanted to hear it.

"Oggie!" Nathan yelled to Dodger as he picked up a stick and attempted to throw it. The stick landed just in front of Nathan's feet and the dog ran over and picked it up, then dropped it again in almost the same spot. The baby giggled and picked the stick up once again. Dodger pranced happily waiting for Nathan to attempt another throw, making Jillian laugh.

When Jillian's phone rang, she glanced at the screen. She saw Ilene's name and answered the call. "Hello?"

"Jillian, would it be possible for you and Wyatt to come into my office later today?" Ilene asked in a voice that sounded worried.

Jillian's brow furrowed. She looked again at Nathan playing in the yard and her stomach churned with worry. "We could probably come in around four o'clock when Wyatt gets off work. Is it okay to bring Nathan, or should I see if my mom can watch him?"

There was a long pause before Ilene's answer which increased Jillian's concern. She looked worriedly at the little boy who owned her heart. He was sitting in the grass now, patting Dodger on the head. *What would she do if she lost him?*

"Maybe it's better to let your mom take him for this meeting," Ilene finally said.

"What's this about, Ilene? Is there a problem?" Jillian asked.

"Something's come up, but I don't want to get into it over the phone, Jillian. It'll be best if I talk to you and Wyatt in person."

"Okay," Jillian said, frowning. "We'll be there as soon as we can."

At four o'clock, Jillian and Wyatt pulled up in front of the social services building. Wyatt turned to Jillian and said, "Did she give you any indication of what we're here to talk about?"

Jillian shook her head. "I asked, but she wouldn't say." She bit her lip, then said, "She sounded worried though."

Wyatt stared out the windshield for several seconds, his eyes fretful. Then he blinked it away, grabbed Jillian's hand, and squeezed it. "Maybe she was worried about something else. She deals with all kinds of hard stuff every day. Whatever she needs to talk to us about might not be so bad."

Jillian felt reasonably sure that Ilene's worry had everything to do with their case, but Wyatt was trying to stay positive, and she didn't want to trample that. She nodded and squeezed his hand in return.

When they got to Ilene's office, she was at her desk looking over some paperwork. She looked up at them with a grim expression and waved them over to the chairs in front of her desk.

"Something very unexpected has happened," Ilene said. She regarded them for a long moment with pursed lips as if trying to find words that would make what she had to tell them easier.

"What is it, Ilene?" Wyatt said, unable to wait any longer.

Ilene let out a long breath. "Remember when you first volunteered to adopt Nathan and I told you that abandonment cases can be very unpredictable?"

A tear rolled down Jillian's face as she and Wyatt both nodded. She was sure by the expression on Ilene's face that she didn't want to hear what was coming. Bracing herself, she felt every muscle in her body tighten.

Ilene continued, "It looked like everything was working out smoothly with Nathan's case. But this morning a call came in from a woman who claims to be his mother."

Jillian's heart began to thump wildly in her chest. Her worst nightmare was happening. Someone wanted to take her baby away from her. *This couldn't be happening. They were meant to be Nathan's parents.* She was sure of that—or at least she had been when she found him in the church that day.

As she thought about the day she'd found him, Jillian realized she was shaking her head and crying.

Wyatt grabbed her hand again. "How do you know if it's really his mother?" he asked.

With a furrowed brow, Ilene said, "She named the church where he was left, and she knew a few details that weren't ever reported to the public. Still, we'll do a DNA test to check it out."

After a few seconds of total silence, Wyatt asked, "What does she want?" His words came out in a near growl.

Jillian held her breath as she waited for the answer.

"She wants him back," Ilene said in a small, regretful voice.

Jillian began to sob, holding onto Wyatt's hand. *She was going to lose her baby.*

"No!" The word ripped from Wyatt's mouth with such fury that Jillian stopped crying and stared at him. "You can't let her do that!"

As she responded, Ilene's expression was sorrowful, but her voice was firm. "*I* won't be letting her do anything. A judge will decide that." Then Ilene's eyes dropped, and her tone softened. "But, for the record, I will do whatever I can to make sure Nathan stays with the two of you."

There was silence for several seconds. When Wyatt spoke again, the fury was gone and he sounded somber. "I'm sorry I snapped at you, Ilene. I know you're in our corner."

"Could she actually get him back?" Jillian asked, afraid of the answer but needing to know.

Ilene looked her in the eye and said, "Maybe."

"But she left him," Wyatt said, trying not to let his anger shoot out at Ilene again. "She left him in that church not knowing when he'd be found."

Ilene sighed. "One of the hardest parts of my job is dealing with this kind of thing. As unfair as it may be, the courts tend to prefer keeping children with their biological parents."

"Why now? She hasn't seen him for eleven months and now she wants him back? Why?" Jillian asked, wiping tears from her cheeks.

Ilene shrugged. "She says there are extenuating circumstances to why she left him in that church. She says she did it to protect him."

"Protect him?" Wyatt's voice rose again. "How is that protecting him?"

"I don't know. I haven't heard the story yet. I don't even know for sure that she's his mother yet," Ilene said.

Forcing back more tears, Jillian spoke up, "So, what do we do, Ilene? How do we fight this?"

Ilene looked at her with sadness and sympathy. "There isn't a lot you or Wyatt can do except continue as Nathan's foster parents. As for me, I'll work to convince the judge that Nathan's best interest would be served if you adopted him."

"I'm sure the judge will listen to you," Jillian said, trying to sound more confident than she felt.

"I hope so, but you should be prepared. There's no way to know what the judge will decide. And there's still a lot we don't know."

"Mama!" Nathan squealed as soon as Jillian walked through the door at her parent's house. The baby ambled into her arms as quickly as his unskilled legs would take him.

Scooping him up, Jillian buried her face in his silken baby hair and sobbed.

"My goodness, what's wrong," Jackie asked, rushing to put her arms around her daughter.

When Jillian didn't seem able to answer, Jackie looked up at Wyatt.

"It's—" Wyatt began then had to stop and gather control of his emotions. "A woman is claiming to be Nathan's birth mother. She says she wants him back."

Jackie gasped and threw a hand over her mouth. "Oh, no! They won't let her take him, will they?"

"Ilene doesn't know if they will. It's going to be up to a judge ... if she's really his mother," Wyatt said.

Jillian felt Nathan begin to struggle against her embrace, wanting to get down and play. She loosened her hold on him and pulled her head back from his. The baby looked up at her curiously and touched her cheek where a tear was sliding down. She sniffled, forced a smile for him, and kissed the top of his head before setting him back on his feet.

As Nathan padded off toward the scattering of toys on the floor, Jackie took both of Jillian's hands in her own. "It's going to be okay. We'll all start praying about it right away." She nodded for good measure, or maybe in an effort to convince herself. "It'll all work out."

Jillian knew her mother was no more certain of that than she was, but somehow, she felt just a tiny bit better hearing her mother's words of conviction. She returned her mother's nod and said, "I'm sure it will. Maybe she isn't even really his mother."

Jackie looked Jillian in the eye and said, "She isn't his mother. You are."

Jillian sighed. "Yeah, but you know what I mean, his birth mother."

"Look at me, Jillian," Jackie said when Jillian turned away. As Jillian turned back to her, Jackie said, "She walked away from him. You and Wyatt have been loving and caring for him for his entire life. No matter what happens, or what any judge decides, you *are* his mother."

Jillian hugged her mother, feeling the weight of those words flow over her. That was what was important now—for her to be his mother.

Chapter Eighteen

"You can't be serious!" Layla said with enough force to attract the attention of a few onlookers. She was sitting in a little diner named Carla's with Jillian. Nathan was in a highchair at the end of their table, eating Cheerios while waiting for their order.

Layla looked at the baby lovingly and ran a hand over his hair. "They're actually going to consider giving Nathan back to her?"

Jillian looked down at the table, trying not to let her emotions get the better of her. Every time she had to talk about this, it was a struggle not to burst into tears. "They're going to have a hearing to decide about visitation for now. If they grant her that, and she does everything they ask her to do, then they might give her custody."

"I can't believe they would even think about it," Layla fumed.

"She is his biological mother." The DNA test had proved that much, and she wanted him back. That fact weighed on Jillian's heart heavily. Every day she tried to just continue as normal and be Nathan's mother. But now, when the baby called her Mama, she found herself wondering how much longer she would be that for him. Soon, he might be calling Keeley Chan mama. And, if that happened, his memory of her would fade and soon he wouldn't even know who she was.

"Some mother," Layla scoffed.

Jillian studied her cousin. She appreciated and understood what Layla was saying, yet she had this strange desire to defend Keeley. She had no idea why. Whatever the extenuating circumstances were, she had still left a baby alone in a church when she could have taken him to a hospital or fire station. Surely, there wasn't any reason not to at least do that. The hearing was going to happen, though, so her story must have seemed good enough to the powers that be.

Jillian shrugged somberly. "Maybe she really did have a good reason."

There were several minutes of silence, during which time their food was delivered. Jillian cut some of her food into small pieces and put them on a plate in front of Nathan. Then she picked up a French fry and took a bite.

"Whatever her reason," Layla said, picking up her sandwich. "It isn't right for her to do this. Nathan's happy ... and you're finally happy." Her voice was full of hurt. "Why does she get to tear that apart?"

Despite her best efforts, a tear escaped and ran down Jillian's cheek. "Wyatt and I are foster parents. We knew going in that we might not get to keep him. That's how it works."

Layla shook her head. "Doesn't make it right. Everyone has to suffer so she can get what she wants just because of the biological connection? He doesn't even know her. You're the only mother he knows. That should count for something."

Another tear rolled down Jillian's face as Nathan picked up a piece of food and tossed it to the floor. "More!" he called out.

Jillian cut a few more bites and placed them on his plate. He smiled at her and popped a little bite of ham in his mouth. "Num," he said.

"Yum, yum," Jillian echoed, her heart breaking a little each time she looked at him and thought that she could lose him.

She glanced at Layla. "I wish the system worked differently. I wish they cared more about emotional connections and the bonds that have already been formed. But they don't care what I think." She paused, then said, "Let's talk about something else, okay?"

Layla nodded and took another bite of her sandwich. After several minutes of silence, she said, "Seth invited me to his grandparents' anniversary party."

Jillian smiled weakly, grateful for the new topic. "That's nice. How long have they been married?"

"Fifty-five years," Layla answered. "Seth says his grandmother has been threatening to get a divorce for as long as he can remember."

Jillian raised an eyebrow.

"I think it's just a joke. Seth laughed when he told me about it," Layla said.

"I guess it might be an interesting party," Jillian said.

Nathan grunted and pushed his plate away. "All done, buddy?" Jillian said. She cleaned his hands and face before getting out a book for him to look at while she and Layla finished eating.

"I'll get to meet the rest of Seth's family," Layla said in a voice that sounded a little nervous. "So far, I've only met his parents."

"Seth is a great guy. I'm sure the rest of his family will be nice too."

"I just hope they like me."

Jillian studied her cousin. This relationship with Seth had brought out a whole new Layla. The girl who had always been bold and brazen was nervous and self-conscious.

"Of course, they will. Don't worry so much," Jillian assured her. "You make Seth happy and that will make them happy."

"I hope you're right," Layla said, throwing her napkin on her plate. She took Nathan out of his highchair and sat him on her lap. "I need some baby snuggles before I go to the store and help out."

Nathan bounced happily in Layla's lap, grinning from ear to ear. Jillian watched and smiled at him. He was her little boy ... but for how long?

Jillian wiped her face with a tissue and continued stocking the men's department with a new boot they had just received. She tried to concentrate on her work, but it was impossible to stop worrying about the changes that were on the horizon. The day before, she'd gotten a call from Ilene, who reported in a solemn voice that Keeley had been granted visitation rights. She would get an hour a week with Nathan and that time might increase if things went well.

Jillian sniffed and blew her nose, then rubbed on some hand sanitizer. She felt as if her whole world was getting pulled out from under her. If the judge was granting visitation, then he was considering letting Keeley regain custody.

"Excuse me, do you work here?" came a male voice.

Jillian looked up at a large man in his fifties with a bushy mustache. "Yes, sir, I do," she said.

"Could you help me find this shoe in my size?" he asked, holding up a white sneaker.

"Sure," Jillian got up and wiped her face again. The customer eyed her curiously as she walked with him back to the sneaker aisle. "What size do you need?"

"Ten and a half," he replied.

Jillian began to search the boxes on the shelves for the correct shoe in that size. She tried hard to keep her emotions at bay while she looked for the shoe. The customers didn't need to see her losing it. But despite her best efforts, another tear ran down her cheek.

Before she could swipe the offending moisture from her face, the man asked, "Honey, are you okay?"

Jillian wiped the tear away with her sleeve, then smiled at the customer. "I'm fine. Just allergies," she lied.

With one last glance at the shelves, she said, "It looks like I'll need to check the storeroom for that shoe. I'll be right back."

She went to the storeroom and returned with the shoe the man wanted. He thanked her and took the shoes to the counter for purchase.

A few minutes later, as she went back to stocking the boot section, she found herself quietly crying once again.

"Jill," Uncle Danny said stepping up to her.

She looked up at him with flushed, wet cheeks.

Danny moved in closer and put an arm around her. She laid her head on his shoulder for a moment.

"Your shift is almost over," Danny said. "And it's not that busy right now. Why don't you go on home?"

"Are you sure? You could get a surge," Jillian said.

"Robbie will be here in less than half an hour. I think I can handle it. I've been doing this for a little while."

Jillian nodded. "Thanks, Uncle Danny."

"Don't you worry about it. We all need to be given a break once in a while." He squeezed her before pulling his arm back. "Give Nathan a hug for me and remember that we're all in your corner."

"I know you are." She offered him a weak smile before going to retrieve her purse from the back room.

Jillian got into her car and drove to her parents' house, where her mother was looking after Nathan.

When she knocked on the front door, there was no answer, so she walked around to the backyard. Nathan, who was getting a bit steadier on his feet, toddled across the yard and picked up a brightly colored ball. Jillian watched him, loving everything about the sweet little boy that she longed to call her own.

Two weeks earlier, they had celebrated his first birthday with a big family party. They had all laughed as they watched the baby eat his own little cake by the handful, getting frosting all over his face, clothes, and hair. They had smiled while he opened his gifts, but underneath all the smiles there was a sense of worry and uncertainty from all of them. Nathan had stolen their hearts and soon he might be yanked away from them.

Nathan tossed the ball a foot in front of him, then he looked up and saw her standing there. "Mama!" he yelled and ran toward her as fast as his little legs could carry him.

Jillian swept him up in her arms and hugged him, then sat him on her hip. "Hey there, little man. Did you have a good day with Grandma?" Jillian choked back a sob with her words. She didn't just hurt for herself, but for her parents who could lose their only grandchild.

Nathan nodded and pointed to Jackie. "Gran!" he said.

Jillian walked over to where her mother sat on the patio. She put Nathan down on his feet and watched him hurry back to the ball. Then she sat down in the chair next to Jackie.

For a moment they watched the little boy play in silence. Then Jackie said, "You're early."

"Yeah, it was slow, and Uncle Danny sent me home," Jillian responded.

Jackie turned in her chair and regarded Jillian, then she turned back to watch the baby again. "I've been crying all day too."

Jillian didn't try to argue with her mother. She knew her face showed the signs of her emotional status. And her heart ached to know her mother was hurting just as much.

"I didn't sleep much last night," Jillian said.

"The dream again?"

Jillian sighed as she thought about the images that had gone through her head the night before. "A version of it," she answered.

"Mama, ook," Nathan called, pointing toward the large oak tree near the back of the yard. A squirrel was hanging onto the tree's trunk.

"I see," Jillian said with a smile. "A squirrel."

"skir," Nathan tried to repeat the word. When the animal darted up the tree, the baby laughed. "Bye, bye, skir."

With the squirrel gone, Nathan went to the little sandbox Jackie had in the yard for him and sat down with a shovel and bucket to play.

"Why don't you tell me about it," Jackie said.

Jillian furrowed her brow at her mother. "Tell you about what?"

"The dream you had last night."

Jillian wasn't sure she wanted to talk about it, but Jackie probably wouldn't let it go. "It started with the accident. I watched as my car hit that other car and I saw …" She sniffed as the emotion got the best of her. "I saw the baby I was carrying float right out of my belly and up into the sky. Then I was back in my car in front of that convenience store the night …" She couldn't bring herself to say the rest, but she knew she didn't have to. Her mother knew which night she was talking about. She swiped a tear from her face and continued, "Natalie stood there staring at me through the window like she needed to tell me something." That wasn't quite the right way to put it. Jillian thought for a moment about what she felt at that moment in the dream and what Natalie's face was telling her. "Or more like she wanted me to do something … something I knew I wouldn't want to do. I begged her not to tell me anything. Then she shook her head at me, walked away, and then … then it ended the way it usually does." Jillian broke into sobs.

Jackie got out of her chair, knelt in front of Jillian's, and held her.

Once she let all the emotion out, Jillian suddenly found herself thinking about what Dr. Parks had said to her every time she had insisted that having a child in the family would fix what had been broken when Natalie died. And at that moment, she thought she knew what her sister had wanted to tell her in the dream. She looked at her mother and said, "Mom, I think I need to talk to you about a couple of things."

Jackie gave her a quizzical look before moving back to her chair. "Okay."

"The night we lost Natalie … it was my fault."

"No, Jillian, it wasn't. Don't you know that by now?"

"She wanted me to go into the store with her. I insisted that she go alone so I could keep the car running and the heat going." The words spilled from Jillian's lips in a rush, and once they were out, she felt as if a weight had dropped from her.

"Sweetheart," Jackie said, looking Jillian in the eye. "Is that what you've been holding onto all this time?"

Jillian nodded, her lips tight in an effort to keep from crying again.

"I'm sorry it's had you feeling guilty, but I'm glad you made the choice you did. If you had gone into that store with your sister, I would have lost both of you. Don't you realize that?"

She did, but her guilt defied logic.

Jackie looked at her sternly. "Let go of the guilt. It was the kind of choice we all make every day. You had no way of knowing what was about to happen." Tears flooded Jackie's eyes. "And thank God I didn't lose you too."

Jillian kept her lips tightly closed until she had her emotions under control, then she said, "I know, Mom. I sometimes think it should have been me, though, instead of her."

When her mother began to shake her head furiously, Jillian stopped her with a hand to her shoulder. "There's more I need to tell you," Jillian said. She took a deep breath and looked away. She didn't think she could say the next words with her mother's eyes on her. "Natalie was trying to get pregnant. She and Derek wanted to have a baby. She told me about it right before she went into the store."

As Jillian's last words were spoken, Jackie began to weep, her head dropping into her hands. Jillian sat watching as shallow breaths forced their way out of her lungs. She thought telling her mother all of this would help her, free her somehow, but instead, she found herself consumed with new pain. Each tear that dropped from her mother's eyes stabbed at her heart. She *should* have been the one to die.

After several long moments, Jackie's tears began to wane. Her head drew back up and she looked at Jillian.

"I'm sorry," Jillian said desperately.

Jackie reached out and took Jillian's hand. "Jillian, do you believe I had a favorite daughter? Do you think I loved your sister more than you?"

Jillian began to shake her head, though she wasn't sure what she believed at the moment. "No ... I don't know. I just thought ..."

"Never, Jillian," Jackie said with a firm voice. "I never loved either of you more than the other."

"But if she had lived you would have grandchildren by now. And you wouldn't have to worry about seeing them taken away. And ... the way you just cried ..."

Jackie nodded. "I cried because I miss your sister with every fiber of my being. I cried because I'm heartbroken for the life she never got to live and the children she never got to have." Jackie stopped and squeezed Jillian's hand tighter. "But those children are dreams that never came to be. Nathan is more than that. He's here, he's real, and he's the grandson I want. I could never want a dream over him."

"But we might lose him," Jillian sobbed.

Jackie let go of Jillian's hand and lifted her chin. "That would break my heart. But it doesn't make me want to trade even one second with him for a dream, for anything else. And, though I miss Natalie with every bit of my heart, I would never trade your life for hers."

Tears flooded Jillian's eyes and she found herself wrapped up in her mother's arms.

"That's it," Jackie said. "Let it all out. And let go of all that guilt you've been holding onto."

As she cried, Jillian felt the guilt and pain she'd been keeping inside since Natalie's death drain out of her. With each tear, her soul was set free.

When the tears were gone, she felt the tickle of a touch on her knee. She pulled back from her mother to see Nathan standing in front of them looking up at her.

He furrowed his brow and asked, "Mama kay?"

Jillian wiped her face and smiled at him. "Mama is okay, buddy."

She kissed the top of his head, and he returned her smile before toddling back out into the yard.

Chapter Nineteen

Jillian tapped her foot nervously as she and Wyatt waited for Ilene to come by and pick Nathan up. He was about to meet his birth mother for the first time. The judge had ordered that Keeley have supervised visits once a week for at least an hour each time.

Watching Nathan sit in the middle of the living room floor and play with his dump truck, Jillian wished she could wait as calmly as he was. But Nathan didn't know what was happening. He didn't know that everything might change. He didn't know that in a few short months, he might be living in a different home—a home that didn't include the mother and father he'd always known.

Wyatt took Jillian's hand and pulled it away from her mouth. The nervousness was making her chew her fingernails. She looked at her husband with desperation in her eyes. "What if we lose him?" she asked.

"We won't. We're gonna fight for him." Wyatt's words were confident, but his tone fell short.

"How? The judge is listening to her. He granted visitation."

"Calm down. He's going to listen to Ilene too, and she's on our side." Wyatt rubbed her hand with one finger. "She left him all alone in a church. I don't see how the judge could give her custody."

Jillian wanted with every fiber of her being to believe him, to trust that he was right, but she'd seen the uncertainty in Ilene's eyes when she told them about the judge granting visitation. Ilene saw these kinds of cases day in and day out and she wasn't convinced it would go their way.

Nathan laughed as Dodger trotted up to him and licked his cheek. "Love oggie," he said.

"Doggie loves you too, buddy," Jillian said. A tear ran down her cheek. This house was a home with all of them in it. What would it be without Nathan? How could they go on without his laughter, without his sweet face, and the warmth of his hugs? Her heart constricted as she thought of how empty that would feel.

Wyatt wiped the tear from her face. "We won't lose him," he said again with a firmer tone.

"We can't," Jillian responded.

Moments later the doorbell rang, and Wyatt let Ilene into the house. Jillian picked Nathan up, hugged him, and handed him to Ilene along with a diaper bag that was packed and ready.

"Ilene's going to take you for a little ride," Jillian said to Nathan. "You'll have a good time and then she'll bring you back home." She forced a smile for the baby's sake.

Ilene looked from Jillian to Wyatt, and seeing their somber faces, told them that she would have Nathan back home in a couple of hours. Jillian nodded, but a lump had formed in her throat and she couldn't get any more words out. She felt like a dam about to burst, but she forced back the tears until Ilene and Nathan were out the door. It wouldn't help for the baby to see how upsetting this was for her.

"Ilene, I don't understand. I thought you wanted Nathan to stay with us. I thought you were fighting for us," Jillian said, her voice full of hurt.

A month had gone by since Nathan's visits with his birth mother had begun and, not only were they going to continue, they were also going to increase. Jillian felt sick at the thought. Her sweet baby was getting taken from her one step at a time and it felt like her heart was getting the life squeezed out of it.

Jillian and Wyatt were seated in Ilene's office. Nathan was in the corner of the room, playing with the toys Ilene had there.

"I do want him to stay with you and I am fighting for you, but Solomon cases are never simple. It's a complicated situation," Ilene said, looking at them earnestly. "Remember I warned you about the complications that can come up in abandonment cases."

"Solomon cases?" Wyatt asked.

"Oh, I'm sorry," Ilene said. "It's a term I picked up from one of the other social workers."

"What does it mean?" Jillian asked.

Ilene met her eyes. "You know the story of King Solomon in the Bible?"

"Seems like there's more than one of those. Maybe you can refresh my memory about the one you mean," Jillian said.

"Solomon was known as the wise king," Ilene said. "And he had a case brought before him involving two women fighting over one baby. Both women claimed to be the baby's mother. Solomon, in his wisdom, figured the true mother would give the baby up rather than see any harm come to him. So, he told the women that the baby would be cut in half and they could share him. Of course, the baby's true mother was aghast and said she would rather the child go to the other woman than be harmed. Because she cared more about the baby's well-being than winning, Solomon knew she was the true mother."

Ilene paused to let the story sink in. Then she said, "Obviously, the judge, in this case, isn't going to threaten to split Nathan in two to find out who will give him up first." She stopped again and looked down at her desk. "And in this case, I think he'd still be lost if he did."

Jillian scrunched up her face. "I don't understand, Ilene. What does that mean?"

Ilene looked back up. "I know you love Nathan with every bit of your heart, both of you," she said, letting her gaze go from Jillian to Wyatt. "But I think Keeley does too. That's what makes it complicated."

There was a pause and Jillian felt her heart drumming against her ribs. It sounded like they might be losing Ilene's support too. If she stopped fighting for them, she had no doubt they'd lose.

"I've watched her," Ilene said. "I see the love in her eyes. And ... I know her story now." She shrugged, her eyes full of sadness. "It's complicated."

"She walked out on him. How much more complicated can it be," Wyatt demanded.

"I can't discuss it, but she did have reasons and they're understandable," said Ilene.

"Reasons that prevented her from taking him to a fire station or a hospital?" Wyatt asked, his voice rising just a bit.

"Whether or not that was necessary is impossible to know. But I can understand where she was coming from."

Jillian could sense Wyatt's agitation increasing. She put a hand on his arm to stop him from continuing the argument. When he looked at her questioningly, she tipped her head toward Nathan. Wyatt nodded reluctantly.

"Ilene," Jillian said. "It sounds like you've changed your mind. It sounds like you're not on our side anymore."

"Jillian, it's my job to be on Nathan's side." She sighed. "And what is best for him is a little less clearcut than I thought at first." She paused in thought. "One thing that hasn't changed is the fact that Nathan has been with you his whole life. You're the parents he knows. That matters to me."

"He's everything to us," Jillian said. It was true and it was the only thing she could think of to say. She didn't know what they would do without him, but she had met Keeley during the child and family team meetings that were now a part of their life, and she knew Ilene was right about one thing. She saw the love in Keeley's eyes too.

Jillian watched as Nathan ran through the yard at Rhonda's house. He was moving as fast as his little legs would go trying to keep up with the other children as they chased Dodger. When Nathan lost his balance and plopped down on his bottom, Callie, who was only a year older, stopped to help him up.

Jillian smiled at them and how sweet they all were together. She wanted to believe that it would always be this way, that for years to come, she would be able to watch her little boy playing with his cousins. But legally, he wasn't her little boy, not yet, and her nieces and nephew weren't his cousins.

That thought brought tears to her eyes. This was his family, the people who loved him. Yet, every time she had that thought now, she couldn't stop herself from thinking about what Ilene had said about Keeley. She couldn't stop thinking about what she saw herself when she looked into the other woman's eyes. She and Wyatt loved Nathan with all of their hearts. But if Keeley's love was just as deep, if she did have a good reason for leaving him, then what did that mean?

Jillian jumped when a hand touched her shoulder.

"Sorry," said Rhonda. "I didn't mean to startle you."

She and Rhonda were looking after all the children while Wyatt, L.J., and Brent played golf with Wyatt's father. Courtney had taken Anika out shopping to help her pick out a birthday gift for Brent.

"That's okay," Jillian said. "I was just wrapped up in my thoughts."

Rhonda let out a heavy breath. "I'm sure you were."

There was silence between them for a few minutes as they watched the kids. Braylee brought Dodger's ball to Nathan and told him to throw it for the dog. Nathan tossed the ball about two feet in front of him and giggled as Dodger snatched it up, ran across the yard, then returned and dropped it in front of the group of children.

"Good job, Nathan!" Braylee said.

"Throw it again," Tucker said.

"I wanna throw it," whined Darcy. "It's my turn."

Braylee, as the oldest, took charge and gave Darcy and Callie both turns before handing the ball to Nathan again.

"It hurts a little every time I watch them together now," Rhonda said. "I can't stand to think that—" She stopped short, not able to say the words. When Jillian looked at her, there were tears on her cheeks.

"I know," Jillian said. "But the way things are going." She shook her head, trying not to break down. "I'm not even sure if Ilene is going to stay on our side."

Rhonda rubbed Jillian's back soothingly. "We'll keep praying about it."

Jillian nodded and stayed silent for a moment as thoughts began to tumble through her mind again. Finally, she spoke. "Rhonda, how do we know what to pray?"

Rhonda gave her a questioning look but didn't answer.

"You were adopted. I mean, you were an orphan and I know your adoptive parents were the only parents you knew, but what if it had turned out that one of your birth parents wasn't dead? Or if another relative from your birth family had come forward wanting you? Would you still have wanted to end up where you did, or would you have wanted to be with your blood relatives?"

Rhonda studied Jillian's face. "Let's go sit down," she said, leading Jillian to the nearby patio chairs. "You're asking some hard questions. I'm not sure I know how to answer them."

"I guess I'm just wondering if we're doing the right thing trying to keep Nathan. Maybe we're just being selfish."

Rhonda raised her eyebrows. "Well, I don't know if I can give you an answer to what you asked me. I was loved and cared for so well by my adoptive family. I can't imagine a life without them in it." She sighed. "But I can't honestly tell you that I never thought about the parents I lost. I *have* wondered what my life would have been if they had lived. Now you're asking what I think would have been the better outcome." She shrugged. "I don't know. I know how my life turned out with the family I had. I can never know what would have been if my birth parents hadn't died."

Jillian considered what her mother-in-law said, but it didn't help her.

"What's got you asking all these questions?" Rhonda asked.

"Ilene seems to think Keeley did have good reasons for leaving Nathan in that church. She believes Keeley truly does love him … and I think she might be right." Jillian stopped talking and chewed her fingernail. "So, if Wyatt and I truly love him, don't we need to think about that? What if going back to her is what's best for him?"

Rhonda stared at her for several seconds and the voices of the children playing filled her ears.

"Well," Rhonda finally said. "The fact that you are even thinking that way shows how much you love him."

Jillian's face scrunched up as she tried to control her emotions. "It would kill me to lose him. But his needs have to matter more than mine."

Rhonda reached out and took one of Jillian's hands. "You are a true mother. That's a fact whatever the outcome of this." She paused, then said, "I believe with all my heart that Nathan is where he belongs. I can't look out and see what I'm seeing in front of me today without feeling certain of that. But … maybe we should just pray that things work out in whatever way is best for Nathan."

Jillian looked into Rhonda's eyes, seeing the sadness. She knew losing Nathan would hurt Rhonda nearly as much as it would hurt her and Wyatt. Slowly Jillian nodded. She would pray that prayer. She would do it for Nathan.

Jillian flew up in bed, gasping, cold sweat on her skin. She glanced at the clock on her nightstand. It was three-thirty in the morning. She needed to go back to sleep but she wasn't sure she could.

She looked over at Wyatt and saw that he was sleeping soundly, and she was glad she hadn't disturbed him. Easing back, she laid her head down on the pillow again and pulled the covers up to her chin. The dream that had awakened her played through her mind even as she tried to push it away.

She was in the car with Natalie again. They were talking but she didn't know what they were talking about. It had played through her subconscious like a silent movie. She was watching rather than participating.

She watched the conversation end, and Natalie got out of the car. Then, instead of sticking her tongue out and walking directly into the store, Natalie knocked on the window and dream Jillian rolled it down. Then, Natalie lifted a basket like the one Nathan was left in at the church and placed it on the passenger seat. Natalie smiled and said something that the Jillian watching the dream couldn't hear. When the usual end of the dream came about, the part where Natalie walks into the store and gets shot, Jillian didn't see it because she was staring at the basket on the seat. Her dream counterpart didn't look up until the silence was broken by the sound of the gunshot. When she looked back at the seat, the basket was gone.

The dream was strange, and she didn't understand it. Yet, it left her feeling lost and empty.

Unable to fall back to sleep, Jillian got out of bed and walked down the hall to Nathan's room. She peeked into the crib and watched the little boy's chest rise and fall rhythmically. Reaching a hand down to his head, she stroked his soft brown hair as she breathed in the baby powder scent of him.

Stepping back from the crib, she looked around Nathan's room. The nightlight glowed against the soft green walls, giving just enough illumination to see the forest mural Kaitlyn had painted. Jillian's eyes moved over the depiction of leafy trees and the faces of woodland animals peeking out. Nathan loved the mural.

Then her eyes locked on the closet door and she found herself moving toward it as if it were calling to her. She opened the door, careful not to make any noise, and looked down at what lay on the floor in the back right corner. She knelt and reached for the basket, pulling it out. It had been right there in the corner of the closet since the day they brought Nathan home. She had never looked at it again. Now, after the dream she had, she needed to see it.

There was nothing special about it. It was a long oval-shaped basket with a cloth lining and a thin pad in the bottom. Jillian ran her hand over the pad, and when she did, she had an overwhelming desire to look underneath. She lifted the edge of the pad and saw something under it ... an envelope.

Picking it up, Jillian saw the name Ollie scrawled across the front. *Was that the name Keeley had wanted for Nathan?*

The envelope was stuffed so thick, Jillian was amazed it hadn't been noticeable even through the little pad. Turning it over in her hands, she wondered if she should open it. Maybe it was only meant for Nathan's eyes, something Keeley had left for him to read when he was older. It did, presumably, have his name on it.

Still, there was something inside Jillian telling her to open it and she couldn't seem to tamp it down. Gingerly, she lifted the flap on the envelope, careful not to tear it. She pulled the stack of folded paper out, opened it up, and began to read.

Dear Ollie,

I know you probably think I left you because I didn't want you. Nothing could be further from the truth. I want you more than I've ever wanted anything, but I can't keep you. If I do, your life will be in danger. It tears me apart, but I have to let you go. I wish it didn't have to be this way. You are the only person I have loved in such a perfect and complete way and I want you to feel that love.

There has only been one person in my life that ever loved me with such a perfect love as I feel for you. That person was my father, your grandfather. He was a good and kind man, and I have missed him every day since I lost him.

From the first moments of my life that I can remember, my father was the one person I could count on, the one person I knew would always take care of me. He showed me his love every day. There was never a problem too big or too small for me to take to him. He enjoyed spending time with me and teaching me things. He was my rock, and I looked up to him with total adoration.

After his death, the thing I wanted more than anything else was to find that kind of love again. My heart longed for someone who would make me the center of his life and love me with his whole heart. Unfortunately, it was my search for that kind of complete love that led to my having to let you go. So, in an odd way, it is my father's love that is now breaking my heart.

Part Two
Keeley's story

Chapter Twenty

While I have many memories of my father, I only have a few of my mother. The first clear memory I have of my mother, the only one that was truly happy, was on a spring day when she drove me to a meadow so we could have a picnic. I was filled with excitement from the moment her car stopped. It was a beautiful day with a cloudless sky and brilliant sunshine and the meadow was full of wildflowers: pink, yellow, and purple.

"Get me out, Mommy," I said, impatiently waiting for her to open my door.

"Just a second, sweetie," she said with a laugh. "I have to get myself out first."

She opened my door and unbuckled my seatbelt. "I know you're excited, but you need to stay right here until I get the picnic basket out. Then you can run around and pick all the flowers you want."

I nodded and waited for her. When she retrieved the basket, we took it into the meadow and set it down. Then she walked behind me as I ran through the tall grass and flowers.

"I like the purple flowers, Mommy. Which ones do you like?" I asked joyfully.

I looked back at her, and she smiled at me. She was beautiful with long, golden-brown hair that fell all around her shoulders and hazel eyes.

"I think they're all lovely, but the pink ones are my favorite," she said.

A few minutes later, my hands full of the flowers I'd picked, my mother called to me, "Look, Keeley, there's a blue butterfly."

I turned and looked to see her pointing toward the butterfly perched on a yellow flower, his wings still moving slowly. I tip-toed up to it and reached my hand out. The butterfly fluttered into the air and landed on my hand. I gasped in response. "Look, Mommy. He likes me," I said with awe in my voice.

"Of course, he does. You're the sweetest girl."

"I want to keep him," I said, looking at her hopefully.

"Butterflies aren't pets. We can't keep him," she said.

"But I want him," I said with a pouty expression.

She knelt in front of me. "He likes you, but he needs to be free."

"I'll take care of him. I'll bring him flowers every day, so he isn't hungry."

"Sweetheart, that might make you happy, but he would be sad. He needs to fly through the sky. That's what he was made for." She looked me in the eye. "Love is caring more about someone else's needs than your own. And sometimes, it means letting go. If you love this little guy, you have to let him go."

My chin dropped at her words and I stared at the butterfly's blue wings with black spots on them. "Okay. I want him to be happy."

As if waiting for my permission, the butterfly flapped his wings and left my hand. I watched as he danced haphazardly in the sky, then landed on a pink wildflower.

My mother smiled at me. "You're a big girl, Keeley. You did what was best for him."

We continued to play in the meadow until it was time for lunch, then my mother spread the blanket out and we sat down to eat peanut butter sandwiches and grapes.

"Help me fold the blanket, Keeley," said my mother when we were done eating.

Remember the Butterfly

I grabbed two corners and walked them to her. We packed up the blanket and the picnic basket and got in the car to leave. As we drove away, the blue butterfly fluttered past my window. I waved to him. "Goodbye, pretty butterfly."

Halfway home, my mother took an unexpected turn down a road I didn't know. "Mommy needs to make a quick stop, okay?"

I nodded to her as she glanced at me in the rear-view mirror.

"Whose house is this?" I asked when we stopped in front of a little brick home.

"It belongs to an old friend of mine, and I need to see him about something today."

"Okay. Get me out," I said.

She turned to me and smiled, but something about the smile seemed wrong, almost sad. "Not this time, sweetie. You wait here and I'll be back in just a couple of minutes."

I frowned at her. "Promise?"

"I promise." She got out of the car and I watched her approach the house and knock on the door.

A man with shaggy blond hair and scruff on his face opened the door. He glanced around cautiously as if he were expecting trouble, letting his gaze rest for a moment on the car. Then he ushered my mother inside and shut the door.

I watched the door, counting seconds the way my father had taught me to do during a thunderstorm. When two minutes passed and the door remained shut, I began to feel nervous, though I didn't know why.

By the time my mother returned to the car, I was close to tears. She looked at me when her door was opened. "Keeley, why are you upset, baby? I told you I'd be right back."

"You said a couple of minutes," I said between gulping breaths. "That means two. You promised! And it was a lot more than two minutes. I counted."

She got into the car and placed a paper bag on the seat next to her. Then she turned to me and said, "Oh, sweetheart,

I didn't mean it that literally. I'm sorry. But there was no need to worry."

For reasons I couldn't explain, I felt a strong sense that there was reason to worry. I searched her face for reassurance that what she said was true. I wanted to believe her. She was smiling at me in the way she always did, but something in her eyes didn't hold the same tone.

I nodded at her slowly, but the uneasy feeling in my gut remained.

For several weeks after our day in the meadow, my mother was either jumpy and on edge or overly mellow. The mellow times were almost like depression except for the strange wistfulness about her. She would stare out the window and talk endlessly about how wonderful it would be to fly.

"Keeley," she said to me one day, "do you remember the butterfly we saw in the meadow?"

I nodded.

"Don't you think it would be wonderful to fly like he did?" she asked.

"I guess so," I said with a shrug.

"It is wonderful, you know. I know just how it feels." She called me over to her and pulled me onto her lap.

"How do you know, Mommy?"

She held me close to her and I could smell the faint scent of her perfume. "I want to fly just like the butterfly," she said, ignoring my question.

She ran her hand down my long, black hair, pulling strands of it away from my face. "I'm not sure how much longer I can stay on the ground, Keeley. My soul needs to be free. I need to fly."

I didn't understand what she was talking about, so I sat with her quietly until she kissed my cheek and set me back on my feet. She spent the rest of that afternoon pacing the living room until my father got home. Then, she left me with him and went to her room, not coming out again until the next day.

The day everything changed started as a good one. For the first time since our picnic, my mother was happy. She came to my room that morning smiling and woke me up.

"What shall we have for breakfast?" she asked.

"Waffles?" I said hopefully.

"Hum," she began, tapping a finger to her chin. "I don't think we can have waffles."

I frowned and my shoulders sagged.

"Not without eggs anyway," she said, grinning at me.

My eyes brightening, I beamed back at her. "Yay!" I sang, clapping my hands.

She lifted me up on a stool and I helped her prepare the meal. We laughed and talked, and for once, she didn't seem preoccupied with the idea of flying.

When we were finished with our breakfast, she drove me to school. I waved at her as I got out of the car and she promised me she would be back to pick me up.

I was joyful all through the day. My mother was back. She was herself again.

Just before the bell rang for the end of the school day, a lady from the office came and spoke to my teacher. When she left, the teacher, Ms. Bolinski, came to me. "Keeley, your mother called the office and said she isn't feeling well. She needs you to ride the bus home today."

Panic immediately flooded through me. "I don't ride the bus. I don't know which bus it is," I cried.

"It's going to be okay, Keeley," she said, taking my hands in hers and looking at me with warm, brown eyes. "I'll help you find the right bus and I'll make sure the driver knows where you need to get off."

She smiled at me and I nodded, but my stomach rolled with anxiety. Something about this felt very wrong.

I held onto Ms. Bolinski's hand as she walked me to the bus line and when she tried to let go of me, I gripped tighter.

She looked down at me, and I expected her to reassure me and insist I let her hand go. Instead, she wrapped her fingers back around mine and stood with me until the bus arrived. When all the children in front of me were on the bus, Ms. Bolinski stepped up to the door with me and spoke to the bus driver.

"Mr. Taylor, this is Keeley. She has never ridden the bus before and needs to today. I have her address written down for you." She handed him a piece of paper. "Could you please make sure she gets off at the right stop?"

Mr. Taylor glanced at the paper, then looked at me with a smile. "I sure can. Come on up here, Keeley. You can sit right here in the seat behind me, and we'll make sure you get home safe and sound." He was an older man with gray hair that was thinning on top and blue-gray eyes that made me feel a little safer.

I looked at Ms. Bolinski, who smiled and nodded at me. The feeling of unease lessened. Mr. Taylor seemed nice, and I believed he would get me home safely. But there was still a sense of dread running through me as I let go of my teacher's hand and climbed the steps onto the bus. It coursed through me the whole ride home, and when Mr. Taylor turned to me and said, "This is your stop, young lady," it was still there.

I stepped down off the bus and waved to the driver. My house was only a short walk down the street and I didn't know whether to drag my feet the whole way or run. Something wasn't right, and I was worried about my mother, but a little voice inside me told me to stay away.

When I got to my house, everything looked fine. The front door was unlocked, so I walked in and called to my mother. Silence answered me and the dread I felt grew stronger.

I dropped my backpack and hurried up the stairs to my parents' room. "Mommy?" I called. There was no response. I looked around and didn't see her, but the open window drew my attention. I walked over to it and looked out. The roof over the front porch was right under the window and my mother was sitting on the roof.

"Mommy?" I said in a quiet and worried voice. "What are you doing?"

She turned and looked at me with wild eyes. I took a step back.

"I'm flying, Keeley. Just like the butterfly," she said, looking back out at the sky.

"Ms. Bolinski said you were sick. I had to ride the bus."

"I'm not sick anymore. I can fly now." She looked at me again, and I felt a cold chill run through me. Her cheeks were flushed, and her voice sounded funny like her words were blending together.

"Come out here with me, Keeley," she said, reaching for me.

I shook my head and backed up.

"You can't fly in there."

"I can't fly, and you can't either." My brow furrowed in worry as I looked at her wild eyes. "I think you *are* sick. I'm going to call Daddy."

"No!" My mother's shout startled me, and I jumped.

"He won't understand. He doesn't know what it's like to fly," she insisted.

I stared at her for a moment, squeezing my lips together. My heart raced, and I wanted to cry. I ran to the door and pulled it shut behind me. Then I hurried downstairs and grabbed the phone in the kitchen. Fumbling with the buttons, I dialed my father's work number.

"Oliver Chan," he said when he answered.

"Daddy, you have to come home right now. Something's wrong with Mommy." The words spewed from my lips.

"Slow down, baby. What's going on?"

"She didn't come to get me at school. And now she's on the roof."

"Wait, if she didn't pick you up from school, how did you get home?" he asked.

"Mommy called and told someone in the office that she was sick. They put me on the bus. Mommy says she feels better now, but something is wrong." My words continued to spill out of my mouth quickly as my heart galloped in my chest. "She didn't want me to call you. But I need you, Daddy." A sob escaped, and I forced back the urge to cry again.

"Don't worry, sweetie, I'm coming home as fast as I can."

"Hurry, Daddy," I whimpered. "I'm scared. Mommy thinks she can fly. She might fall." Tears streaked down my cheeks as I pleaded for his help.

"I'm going to hurry. I promise," he assured me. "I need you to do something for me while I'm on my way."

Forgetting he couldn't see me, I nodded. "What do you want me to do, Daddy?"

"Go keep an eye on Mommy and talk to her. Keep her occupied until I get there. And try to get her to come back inside."

I didn't want to go back to my mother. The very idea filled me with fear, but if that was what my father needed me to do, then I would do it. "Okay, Daddy," I said in a shaky voice.

"It'll be okay. I'll get home fast."

I put the phone back on the cradle and climbed the steps again. The feeling of trepidation grew with every step, but I forced my feet to move. My father was the center of my world and I trusted that he knew the right thing to do.

When I reached my parent's room, I sucked in a deep breath and cautiously opened the door. My mother was not there, and the window stood open just as before. I tip-toed over and peeked out. She was squatting on the roof just outside the window.

"Mommy?" I said in a small voice.

She didn't look at me, so I continued, "Daddy's coming home to help. He wants you to come inside."

"I can't fly inside, Keeley," she said.

"You can't fly at all," I pleaded. "You're scaring me, Mommy! You might fall." I sniffled and dragged my sleeve across my face to wipe away the tears.

She turned and looked at my tear-stained face.

"Please, Mommy, come back inside."

"Okay," she said, but her face showed no emotion. "Help me." She reached her hand out to me, and I moved closer so I could help her through the window. My heart slowed down a bit as relief flooded through me. *Daddy will be proud of me.*

I got as close as I could to the window and grabbed her outstretched hand. Her fingers curled around mine and then I screamed as she yanked me toward her. She took hold of my arm with her other hand and pulled me forward. Tightening all my muscles, I pulled against her. She let my arm go and used that hand to push my head down, then pulled my hand hard, forcing me halfway out the window.

"Mommy, no! Let me go!"

"Not until you fly." She kept pulling, using the hand that wasn't holding mine to grab my waist, pulling hard until I had no choice but to go out on the roof with her.

I fell out the window, landing hard on my knees. Tears flooded my eyes as fear seized my heart. "I don't want to fly! Please, Mommy, let me go back inside. I'm scared."

"You're a beautiful butterfly, Keeley. You have to spread your wings and fly," she said in a wistful voice, unaffected by my fear.

"I don't have wings. I'm not a butterfly." I started sobbing. "I want to go inside."

She pulled me up to her side and held me tightly. "We'll do it together, baby."

"No, Mommy. We'll fall."

If I hadn't been crying, if I hadn't been so scared, I might have heard my father's car pull up next to the house. But tears blurred my vision and my heart pounded in my ears.

I was surprised when he shouted out the window to my mother. "Greta, what are you doing?"

She turned and looked at him, and for a split second there was regret in her eyes, but it faded quickly. "I tried, Oliver," she said. "But I couldn't stand it any longer. I can't stay locked in a cage. I need to soar." With her last words, the wistful expression came back over her face. "Keeley's going to fly with me." She started to push me away from her side and toward the edge of the roof. I cried out and fought against her.

"Just like the butterfly, baby. Fly away," she said.

In one quick and unexpected motion, my father lunged out the window, grabbed me, and tugged me from my mother's grasp. My butt bumped along the rough shingles as he pulled me back to the window. Protecting my head with his hand, he maneuvered me back inside the house and held me tightly in his arms, kissing the top of my head. "I got you, angel. You're okay," he said against my ear.

When he tried to release me, I gripped him tighter and cried into his shoulder. "Daddy, I'm scared."

"I know, but I need to get your mother back in here before she hurts herself. You'll be okay. You're safe now."

He pulled back from me enough to look me in the face. His dark brown, almond-shaped eyes that were just like mine looked at me with compassion. Wiping my tears away with a finger, he said, "I won't let anything bad happen to you, Keeley. Do you trust me?"

Biting my lip against the fear, I nodded and let him go. He was the one person in the world I trusted completely.

He smiled at me, saying, "That's my big girl." Then he climbed out the window.

I cautiously stepped closer to the window and peered out. Daddy edged close to my mother and sat down with her, wrapping his arms around her. He began to speak to her in hushed words that I couldn't hear. At first, she fought him, but eventually, she collapsed into his arms and sobbed. He let her cry for a while, then he gently scooted back toward the window, pulling her with him. When they were close enough, he helped her through the window first and then followed, closing and locking the window behind them.

Chapter Twenty-one

I didn't see my mother again for two days. She stayed closed up in her room and Daddy took care of us both. He started by nailing every window in the house shut.

Daddy spent a lot of time in the bedroom with Mommy, but I was not allowed inside. Sometimes I heard her moaning or crying. Sometimes she screamed at Daddy and begged him to let her fly again. He patiently tended to her.

When he wasn't with her, he was caring for me.

"Daddy," I asked him the day following my mother's episode, "why did Mommy think she could fly? What happened to her?"

He scooted me over on the couch and sat next to me, putting an arm around my shoulders. "Keeley, your mother took some medicine that wasn't good for her and it made her believe in things that aren't real."

"Why did she take that medicine? Was she sick? Did the doctor give her the wrong thing?" I looked up at him with a furrowed brow, trying to understand.

He sighed and pushed strands of black hair away from my face. "She does have a sickness, but it isn't like a cold or anything."

"Is it like what I had last year when I had to stay home from school?" I asked.

"No, it isn't like that either." He studied my face for a few long seconds. "You know how when you were sick, you needed medicine to get better?"

I nodded.

"Well, Mommy's sickness makes her want to take medicine that's bad for her."

My face scrunched up as I tried to make sense of this. "Why do they make medicine that's bad for people?"

"Hum, that's a hard question." He tapped his chin in thought. "Some medicines can be good when you need them, but bad when you don't. For your mommy, it started with medicine she needed. She hurt her back when you were a baby, and she needed some medicine to help her feel better. The thing is, that medicine can make people want to keep taking it even when they don't need it anymore." He looked me in the eye. "That's called addiction, and that's what happened to your mommy. After a while, she went from that medicine to something else, something that didn't come from a doctor. But she wanted to get better and for a while she did, but addiction is a sickness that never goes away. Mommy continued to want that medicine, and then yesterday she took some."

"Oh," I said. I looked down into my lap and tried to sort through what he'd told me. "Why did the medicine make her think she could fly?" I wanted to ask why it made her think I could fly, but even talking to my father about that overwhelmed me with fear.

"Some medicines are very strong and affect the way you think. They can make you believe things that aren't real and do things you would never do otherwise." He took my hand and rubbed it with his thumb. "Mommy would never hurt you when she's herself," he said, addressing my unasked question. "When she takes that bad medicine, it's like she's someone else."

"I still love her," I said, feeling my father needed to know that. But I was greatly relieved that he'd nailed the windows shut, and I didn't trust my mother the way I had before. I was still afraid of her.

When my mother finally came out of her room, she was quiet and sullen. She gave me weak smiles and kisses on the top of my head. It felt as if she were trying to say *I'm sorry,* without actually saying it.

I tried to be the best daughter I could be for her, helpful and obedient. I didn't want to upset her and cause her to take the bad medicine again. But no matter how good I was, she always seemed unhappy and a little lost.

She spent hours staring out the window, and I wondered if she was watching butterflies and wishing to be one of them. Sometimes I wished I could turn into one so she would look at me again and really see me. When she did look at me, it felt as though she was looking through me.

Two weeks after her first episode, she sent me to school one day and didn't pick me up. At the end of the day, I waited in the car rider line for her, but she never showed up. I was taken to the principal's office, and Mr. Lewis, the principal, looked at me with sympathy while he dialed our home phone number.

When he put the receiver down, his warm, brown eyes met mine and he asked, "Keeley, is there any other number I can call to reach your mother?"

I gave him her cell phone number, but she didn't answer that call either.

He smiled at me wanly and scratched his bald head. "Maybe she had an appointment that ran long. I guess we'll have to try calling your dad at work."

He tried another smile as he picked up the phone again. Despite his reassurances, my stomach rolled with worry. *Where is my mother?* I didn't even want to contemplate the answer, but I was glad Mr. Lewis was calling my father. He would come for me, and I'd be safe.

The features of the principal's brown face lifted, and he said into the phone, "Yes, Mr. Chan, this is Darrell Lewis, the principal at Keeley's school." He waited a couple of seconds. "No, there isn't anything to worry about. Keeley is fine. But your wife didn't come to pick her up this afternoon." He was quiet again, and his brow furrowed as he listened. "I tried calling your wife at home, but there was no answer." Silence again. "Yes, I'll keep her here with me until you arrive. Thank you, Mr. Chan."

Mr. Lewis looked up at me and smiled. "Your father will be here in about ten minutes, Keeley. Until then, you can wait here with me."

I forced a smile back at him even as worry for my mother filled me. My daddy was coming, and he'd make everything okay, I told myself.

"I have a deck of cards. Would you like to play a game of go fish?" asked Mr. Lewis.

"Okay," I said.

He pulled out his cards and shuffled them. I watched as the cards fanned quickly from his fingers back into the deck.

"How do you do that?" I asked.

He glanced up. "What, shuffle the cards? It's not that hard. You just have to practice." He split the deck in two and held the cards with his thumbs at the top of each stack, his forefingers pressing into the middle of the back of the stacks and the rest of his fingers at the bottom end. "You hold them like this," he said, then began to fan them back together. "See? You want to try?"

I nodded and he handed me the deck. I split the cards and tried to hold them the way he had, but my hands were not big enough, and all the cards simply fell into a pile on the desk.

"Looks like you might need to try again when you get a little bigger," Mr. Lewis said. He gathered the cards, shuffled one more time, and dealt them.

"Now," he said, "you go first."

I looked my cards over. "Do you have any 3s?"

He raised one eyebrow at me. "How did you know?" He handed me a card and I smiled as I took it.

"Do you have any 5s?" I asked.

"Not this time. Go fish." Tapping his chin, Mr. Lewis asked, "Do you have any 6s?"

Grinning, I shook my head and said, "Go fish."

He picked up a card and looked at me.

"Do you have any kings?" I asked.

He scratched his head, then handed me a card. "You're good at this game."

For the next several minutes, I sat with the principal playing cards. He made me laugh and, for a short while, I didn't think about why my mother didn't come to pick me up.

When my father showed up, I was surprised that the time had passed so quickly.

"Well," Mr. Lewis said when my father came through the door, "You've got more cards than I do, Keeley. Looks like you're the winner."

I smiled at him, grateful for the distraction he'd given me.

My father thanked Mr. Lewis, nodding to him respectfully, before taking me home.

Pulling up to our house, I saw my mother standing on the roof over the porch. She had her arms out to the sides and her head back with her hair blowing all around her.

"Daddy!" I yelled. I felt a surge of panic run through my veins.

"I know, baby. I see her." He parked the car and turned in his seat to look at me. "It'll be okay. I'm going to get her back in the house."

I squeezed my lips together and nodded. I was terrified, but there was no one I trusted more than my father.

Daddy jumped out of the car and opened my door so I could get out. He took my hand and strode to the front door.

Once we were inside, he knelt in front of me and took my hands in his. "Keeley, I know you're scared."

I nodded.

"It's going to be okay. I need you to stay here while I go get your mother."

Tears springing to my eyes, I shook my head furiously and gripped his hand. I couldn't wait alone. I needed to know what was happening.

He sighed with a nod. "All right, you can come with me to the bedroom. But I have to go out there to get her and I need you to stay in the house where you'll be safe."

I sniffled and nodded my agreement. The last thing I wanted was to be back out on that roof with my mother.

When we reached the bedroom, we found the window broken and blood on the edges of the broken glass.

"She's hurt!" I cried.

"It looks like she cut herself." He looked me in the eye. "It's probably not that bad. But I need to go get her before she hurts herself anymore." He tugged gently at the hand I was still holding. Reluctantly, I let it go.

Daddy went into the bathroom and came out with a bath towel. He wrapped his hand up in the towel and knocked the rest of the glass out of the window frame so there were no more sharp edges.

He climbed out the window, and I inched forward until I could see him and my mother.

"Greta," he called to her, but she didn't react.

Daddy stepped forward carefully until he was behind her. "Greta, look at me," he said. She was close to the edge, making my heart race in fear.

She didn't turn when Daddy called her, but she did acknowledge him. "Leave me alone, Oliver. I'm ready to soar." Then she did turn with a hopeful gleam in her eyes. "You can come with me."

"No, Greta, you need to come with me." He nodded to her hands and legs that were bleeding. "You've hurt yourself. Come inside and let me clean you up."

She looked at the blood but seemed unaffected by it. "I'm going to fly, and it will all be better then."

Turning her head away from Daddy, she took another step toward the edge of the roof. I gasped. "Mommy!" I yelled out to her.

She whirled around to look at me, and Daddy used her moment of distraction to grab her arm and pull her hard toward the house. She fell to her bottom on the roof, and he quickly lunged toward her and grabbed her around the waist.

"Oliver, stop! I have to fly!" she protested and fought as he dragged her toward the window.

I ran to the other side of the room and cowered by the dresser. Watching, I saw my mother's head come through the window, then her body as my father maneuvered her. She was still fighting him and fell to the floor once her weight was mostly on the interior side of the window.

Daddy climbed inside carefully, trying not to step on my mother as she lay sobbing in a ball on the floor. He glanced at me and saw my fear and distress.

"It'll be okay, baby. I've got to get her into the shower now and clean her up."

I nodded but couldn't seem to move from the dresser. My knees were shaking, so I let myself slide to the floor.

Daddy looked at me with hurt in his eyes. I knew he wanted to come to me and comfort me, but he had to take care of Mommy.

He bent down and slid his arms under her knees and back, then lifted her and carried her into the bathroom.

A moment later, the shower started, and Mommy cried out. "It's cold, Oliver!"

"I'll warm it up just as soon as you stop fighting me," he said.

She continued to scream at him for a few minutes and I curled up on the floor and cried.

Finally, the screaming stopped and all I heard was Daddy talking to her in a soft, soothing tone.

Swallowing hard, I picked myself up off the floor and waited for my parents to come out of the bathroom. The door opened and Daddy helped Mommy out. Her hands and legs were wrapped up in bandages.

Daddy looked at me. "Keeley, I'm going to take her to the guest room to rest while I get this window sealed up."

He walked her out the bedroom door, and I opened the guest room door for him. Laying her on the bed, Daddy said, "Greta, stay here and sleep for a while." He pushed the hair back from her face and kissed her forehead.

When he came back out into the hallway, he knelt down to me and spoke quietly. "Keeley, I need to go out to the shed and get a few things to close up that window. I want you to stay here in the hallway, and if your mother leaves the guest room, you come for me and yell as loud as you can, okay?"

My face scrunched up as I tried not to cry, and my breath came in short bursts. I wanted to help him. I wanted to help my mother. But I was only a little girl, and this was more than I knew how to handle.

Daddy wrapped me up in his arms. "I'm so sorry, baby. This is so hard, I know. And so scary."

I sobbed against his shoulder, my arms tight around his neck. He let me cry and when my sobs slowed down, he pulled me back and looked at me. "You're so strong and such a good girl." He wiped my tears away. "I promise I'll be really fast, but I have to get that window closed up."

"I'll yell if she comes out here," I whispered between hiccupping breaths.

"That's a good girl—such a good girl."

Daddy hurried away to get the things he needed, and I anxiously watched the guest room door. A few minutes later, Daddy came back with boards, nails, and a hammer.

"You did a great job, baby," he said. "Now I need to go close up the window, and I need you to keep watching that door. If she comes out, you call me."

Feeling stronger and more assured now that he was back in the house and would only be across the hall, I nodded.

I watched the guest room door while Daddy hammered boards over the broken window. Then he brought in a broom and cleaned up the glass that had fallen on the floor. Most of the glass was outside on the roof.

"Keeley," he said when he was done. "You did a great job, sweetheart. I'm going to go in and check on her now, okay?"

"Okay, Daddy."

He went into the guest room and spoke to my mother in hushed tones. She was calm now, and the house was quiet. I tiptoed into my room, curled up on my bed, and fell asleep.

I didn't awaken until late that night. I hadn't eaten any dinner and my stomach rumbled. Sitting up, I stretched and was about to get up and head to the kitchen for something to eat when my father's voice stopped me. It was muffled, coming from the other side of the wall in my parent's room. I sat still on my bed and tried to hear what he was saying.

"You have to go, Greta. You're a danger to Keeley right now," Daddy said.

"I won't do it again, Oliver. I promise," Mommy pleaded.

"You said that the last time."

There was a pause.

"I'd never hurt Keeley," Mommy insisted in a pouty voice.

"You'd never hurt her?" My father's voice rose a bit. "You had her on the roof. You nearly threw her off."

Silence. I pushed my ear against the wall.

"You're an addict, Greta. I can't trust you around Keeley," Daddy said.

I heard Mommy sobbing. "I won't do it again."

"You have to get treatment, and until you do, you have to go. You can't be around Keeley like this." Daddy's voice was sad but determined.

I wasn't sure what he was saying. *Where did he want Mommy to go?*

My stomach began to roll with anxiety, and I wasn't hungry anymore. I pulled my covers over me and curled back up.

The next thing I knew, I was waking up to see my mother's face close to mine.

"Keeley, wake up, baby," she said.

My eyes fluttered a few times, then I opened them fully. "What is it, Mommy? Are you okay?"

"I'm fine," she said with a smile, but a tear trickled down her cheek. "I need to tell you goodbye."

I shot up in bed as the conversation I'd heard earlier filled my mind. "Where are you going?"

Her eyes brimmed with fresh tears. "I'm sick, baby. I need to go get better."

"Dr. Barnes can help you," I said.

She shook her head. "He can't. Not with this."

My lips trembled, and I grabbed for her hand. As much as I'd been afraid of her earlier that day, I didn't want her to go away. "Why not?"

She squeezed her lips together. "It's not that kind of sickness."

"But somebody can help?"

She nodded. "I have to go to a special place for the help I need. I'll be there for a while."

I sobbed. "Who's going to take care of me?"

"Your Daddy will take very good care of you."

"But who's going to pick me up from school?"

She brushed my black hair back from my face. "Daddy will make a plan for that. You don't need to worry. You have a great Daddy, and he's going to take good care of you."

My chest heaved as tears fell from my eyes. I held tight to my mother's hand. "I don't want you to leave me."

She pulled me in close and we both cried. Then she peeled me back from her and laid me down on my pillow.

"Do one thing for me, baby," she said.

I nodded.

"When you think of me, remember the butterfly—the one we saw in the meadow."

I furrowed my brow at her, not understanding her words. But before I could ask her to explain, she was out the door and gone.

For a while, I asked my father every day when my mother would be home. At first, he answered by telling me that it would happen soon, when her treatment was done. After a few weeks, he began to answer by telling me he didn't know.

As time went on, I asked less and less. I began to adjust to life with just my father. He made sure I had everything I needed, and on the weekends, he took me to the park or to a nearby pond where he taught me to fish. I also spent time with our neighbor, Mrs. Hall, who taught me to bake cookies and plant flowers.

A few months went by before I asked about my mother again. When I did, my father's face drooped with sadness.

"Come sit with me, Keeley," he said, patting the couch cushion.

I sat down and he put his arm around me. It took him several long seconds to speak again.

"I don't know when your mother will come home," he said with a sigh. "The treatment center called me after the third week and said she wasn't there anymore."

"Then where is she?" I asked with dismay.

He shook his head. "I don't know where she is." He looked at me. "Do you remember when we talked about addiction and the bad medicine?"

I nodded.

"For people with addiction, it's very hard to get better. They want the bad medicine so much that it takes over their lives. They want that more than they want to get better."

I thought about what my father had said. "She wants it more than me?" I sniffled, feeling rejected.

"Oh, sweetheart," Daddy said, wrapping me in his arms. "It isn't quite like that. It's a sickness and it's really hard to fight. She loves you."

I lay against my father's side, tears in my eyes. "Doesn't she love me enough to get better?"

"I know this is hard to understand, Keeley. But it isn't a lack of love that makes it so hard for her to decide to get better." He scooted away from me enough to turn toward me and lift my face to look at him. "She loved you enough to walk away. I know that doesn't seem like love to you right now, but she was a danger to you, and even though it was very hard for her, she went away so that you would be safe."

Looking at my father with tears welled in my eyes, I thought of Mommy's last words to me—*when you think of me, remember the butterfly*. I thought back to that day in the meadow when the butterfly landed on my finger. I wanted to keep him, but Mommy said that loving him meant letting him go. She had chosen to let me go.

Now my father was telling me she left because she loved me and I understood that she had tried to tell me the same thing, but it didn't feel like love. It felt like abandonment.

# Chapter Twenty-two

Four years later

"I wanna do it, Daddy," I said, lying on the ground next to him, under his car.

"I think you need to watch this time. Maybe next time," he said.

"I watched the last two times. I can do it," I pleaded.

He sighed and glanced at me. "Okay, you do it this time." He handed me the ratchet and socket so I could remove the oil drain plug.

Taking the tools, I attached the ratchet to the socket, then placed the socket around the drain plug. I pulled hard, feeling my face heat up with the effort.

"You're almost there. A little harder," Daddy encouraged.

I continued to pull the ratchet.

"Quick, move your—" Daddy said, but he was too late. Before he could get the last word out, the drain plug broke free and oil poured over my hand.

I moved my hand out of the flow of oil, looking at it with a grimace.

"Scoot out and get that rag I left on my toolbox. You can clean your hand with that."

I worked my way out from under the car, and while I was wiping my hands on the rag, Daddy's cell phone rang.

"Keeley, my phone is next to the toolbox. Answer it for me, would you?"

I picked up his phone and flipped it open. "Hello?" I listened to the person on the other end as they asked to speak to my father. "Just a minute," I said. Then I held the phone to my chest and called Daddy. "They want to talk to you."

"Who is it?" he asked.

"I don't know, but he sounds serious."

Daddy began to scoot out from under the car. "Ouch!" He shouted when he sat up too soon and banged his head on the car's bumper. Rubbing his head with one hand, he reached for the phone with the other. I handed it to him.

"This is Oliver Chan," he said.

I watched him pace a few steps as he listened.

"Yes, I'm her husband."

A moment later, Daddy's face went pale, and he stumbled. I ran to him and grabbed his arm to steady him.

"What is it, Daddy?" I asked. He didn't answer.

His voice was thick with emotion when he spoke again. "Yes, I understand. I'll make the arrangements." He flipped the phone shut and covered his face with his hands.

"Daddy, what happened? What did that man say?" I looked up at him, concern tightening my chest.

A loud sob erupted from his mouth as he grabbed the car to keep from falling. I watched in horror, wondering what could be so bad. I'd never seen my father look so upset.

Wrapping my arms around his waist and laying my head against his chest, I waited for him to stop crying. When I thought he might be ready to speak, I asked again, "What's going on?"

Moving his hand from his face, he looked at me. "I don't know how to tell you this."

"Just tell me, Daddy. What happened?"

"Let's go in the house first."

I motioned to the car. "What about the oil change?"

"We can finish it later." It was not like my father to let a job sit half done.

I kept my arm around him as we walked into the house, just in case his knees grew weak again. Then we sat down on the couch in the living room, and I turned to him, waiting expectantly.

"Keeley, it's about your mother," Daddy said.

My jaw clenched. We hadn't talked about Mommy for a long time. I didn't know if I wanted to hear anything about her. "She still isn't better?" I asked cynically. "Did she do something crazy?"

His face scrunched and a tear ran down his cheek. This was more serious than Mommy acting crazy.

"Your mother ... she's ... dead. She's dead, Keeley." He broke down in sobs again.

I sat there staring at the wall. I didn't know what to feel. I hadn't seen my mother in four years. Now I knew I never would again.

I dragged my feet as Daddy and I walked up the steps of the funeral home. The visitation for my mother would last an hour, then the funeral would start. I was glad Daddy had decided to do it all in one day. It was strange having a funeral for someone we hadn't seen in years. And yet, deep inside, I knew I needed it. I needed to say goodbye to her.

A warm summer breeze blew against us as we reached the door, catching my attention. I looked up and saw a blue butterfly flutter by the door. Instinctively, as if I were six years old again and back in that meadow, I held out my hand. The butterfly landed on my finger, gave two slow flaps of its wings, then flew away.

My eyes welled with tears as I watched the butterfly flap its way back into the sky. *Maybe that's Mommy*, I thought. Perhaps her soul flew free now, the way she'd always wanted.

Inside the funeral home, Daddy led me up to the casket. But as we neared, I pulled my hand from him and shook my head.

"It's okay. If you're not ready to see her, we can sit a while first. No one will be here for about twenty minutes," Daddy said.

Breathing heavily, I nodded and backed up to a row of chairs against the wall.

Daddy and I sat for a while, listening to a grandfather clock ticking in the next room. My breathing slowed, and I was calm. I stood up and inched my way across the room to the casket.

Peering in, I saw her golden-brown hair arranged neatly around her head. Her eyes were closed in a peaceful sleep-like way. She looked the same as I remembered, and yet, different. Her hair looked the same but duller and her cheeks appeared a little more sunken than I remembered. *Had she been that thin before?*

I wanted to touch her, but fear filled my heart, though I couldn't be sure what I was afraid of.

When a tear fell from my face and landed on the satin lining of the casket, I swiped at my face. Then a sob burst forth from somewhere deep inside of me.

I felt my father's arms wrap around me, but I resisted when he started to move me away.

"No," I said. Controlling the emotion, I stared at my mother's body. "Why did you leave us? Why didn't you love me enough?"

"She loved you enough, darlin'. This was your daddy's doing." The words came from a person whose voice I didn't recognize.

I turned and saw a woman who looked a lot like my mother but older and with lighter hair.

"Lois," Daddy said. "I'm glad you made it." Daddy's words were polite, but his voice was pinched. He turned to me. "Keeley, you probably don't remember, but this is your Aunt Lois. She's your mother's sister."

Lois studied me. "I thought I'd see something of your mother in you. It's like she isn't even a part of you." She glanced at my father in disgust as if he'd done something to ensure I'd look like him.

My gaze dropped to the floor. I couldn't explain it, but she'd made me feel guilty for not looking like my mother.

Sometimes the fact that I couldn't see any of my mother in my own face bothered me as much as it upset Lois. Once, a year or so earlier, I'd voiced those feelings to Daddy. He explained to me about dominant and recessive traits, then he stood me in front of a mirror and pointed out all the features I did have from Mommy.

"See," He'd said, "You have your mother's nose and smile."

Under Lois's scrutiny, her nose and smile hardly seemed like enough.

The clock ticked a few times, filling the otherwise silent room. Then Lois made a hiss-like sound and breezed off to another room.

I wanted to ask Daddy why Lois blamed him for what happened to Mommy, or maybe it was her leaving that she blamed him for. I couldn't understand it either way.

Before I could ask him anything, he led me over to a chair. "People are starting to come in. I'm going to stay near your mother. If you don't want to be that close to the casket, you can stay here."

I dropped into the chair. I didn't think I wanted to look at Mommy's body anymore, and my legs felt strangely weak.

Inside me, emotions played tug-of-war. My eyes teared up at the thought that Mommy was gone, and I'd never feel her arms around me again. When I thought about the way she left and never returned, choosing drugs over Daddy and me, rage filled my chest like a fire. *Why didn't she choose me?*

People trickled in and out, some I knew and some I didn't. Daddy came and retrieved me before the service began and took me to the front row of chairs. Only a few people stayed for the service, mostly friends of my father. On the other end of the front row, staring steely-eyed at the casket, sat Lois.

# Chapter Twenty-three

Three years later

"Grab the tackle box, Keeley," Daddy said, stepping out of the garage with two fishing poles in hand.

"Sure, Dad." I scooped up the tackle box and hurried behind him. "Are we going to the pond or the stream?"

He took the tackle box from me, placing it in the bed of his pickup truck. "Which do you like better?"

"The pond. I like the little dock. You can see the fish swimming by." I smiled at him.

My friends didn't understand why I still liked to go fishing with my father. They preferred to go shopping or practice with make-up. But I didn't have a mother to shop or do make-up with. Daddy was all I had, and I loved every minute we spent together.

"The pond it is," Daddy said. "Hop in. I think we've got everything."

Arriving at the little pond, we unloaded the fishing gear and the cooler we brought, carrying it all down to the dock.

"You got the worms, Dad?" I asked, picking up my fishing pole.

"Sure do. You want me to get one on your hook?" He opened the container of worms we'd bought at the bait shop.

I shook my head. "I'm not afraid anymore. I'll do it."

He held the container out to me, and I peeked into it. I wanted to do everything myself and show him that I could, but I still didn't like the idea of picking up a wiggly worm.

I slowly reached into the container, closing my eyes as I wrapped my fingers around one of the worms. Lifting it out, I cracked open one eye then the other. It wriggled, and I had to fight the desire to drop it. Gritting my teeth, I pushed the worm onto the hook.

Looking up at Daddy, I saw he was smiling at me. "You did well, Keeley."

Heat rushed to my face with the compliment. "I didn't like doing it," I admitted.

"Because the worm is slimy or because you have to hurt him with the hook?"

"Both. And because he squirms." I tossed my line into the pond and waited for a fish to bite.

"You want to know a secret?" Daddy leaned close in a conspiratorial gesture even though we were the only people there.

"Sure."

"I don't like putting the worm on the hook either." He pulled back on his pole as a fish took a bite on his bait.

"Really?" I watched him while he reeled in his line and found an empty hook.

"Really," he said, taking another worm out of the cup.

"You don't act like it bothers you."

"Practice. You get used to it."

The worm fell to the dock before I saw the look on my father's face change. His eyes filled with shock and pain as he grabbed his chest.

My eyes went wide, and I reached out to him, but before my hands touched him, he fell to his knees.

"Daddy!" I dropped to a squat in front of him, grabbing him as he began to fall forward. Crying, I eased him down to the dock as his weight leaned into me.

"Daddy, what do I do?" I rolled him over so he was on his back.

"Call ... help," he said before he passed out.

I fumbled to get his phone from his belt, my hands shaking. Tapping in nine-one-one, I waited for an answer while my heart hammered. I thought it might explode right out of my chest.

"Nine-one-one, what is your emergency?" A female voice spoke in my ear.

"My dad ... he needs help ... please," I said between sobs.

"Okay, we'll send help. What's your name?"

"Keeley. Please, I don't know if he's breathing."

"Keeley, I'm Linda. Can you get close to his mouth and nose to see if you feel him breathing?"

I leaned down over his face and barely felt his breath on my cheek. "He's breathing, but only a little."

"Good. Can you tell me your location?"

"The pond." I spat the words.

"Do you know an address?" Linda asked.

I looked around as if that would help somehow. "No. I don't think it has a name. It's small, but there's a dock." The words spilled out quickly.

"Calm down, Keeley. I'm trying to track your phone's signal right now. We'll find you. But maybe you can help me by telling me something that's close to the pond." Her voice stayed completely calm and soothing.

"It isn't far from our house. It only takes ten minutes to get here." Trying to think of how to help the lady on the phone took some of my focus off my fear.

"What's the address at your house?"

I rattled off my address.

"Keeley, I think I have your location and I've dispatched an ambulance. I'll stay on the phone with you until they get there."

I nodded gratefully, tears dripping down my cheeks. "Okay."

"Can you tell me about what happened to your dad? That way, I can give the information to the paramedics before they arrive."

"We were fishing, and he grabbed his chest and started falling. He told me to call for help and then he passed out." I glanced around but didn't see or hear the ambulance. "Are they going to be here soon? He needs help fast."

"I know, Keeley. They should be there in just a minute. I know you're scared. Try to stay calm. I'm with you." Linda's calm tone washed over me and eased my panic.

I grabbed my father's hand. I couldn't lose him.

Please, God, please, I chanted inside my head. Then the scream of a siren filled the air. I breathed a sigh of relief. They would help him. They had to.

The paramedics rushed to the dock with a stretcher. They quickly started to work on Daddy.

"The ambulance is there?" I was surprised by the voice in my ear. In the sudden flurry of activity, I'd forgotten I still had Linda on the phone.

"Yes, they're here," I said.

"Good. They'll take care of him now." She paused. "Keeley, can I call your mother or someone else who can meet you at the hospital?"

"My mother is dead. I only have Daddy."

"Oh, I'm sorry, sweetheart. Go with the paramedics to the hospital. Make sure they know you'll be alone."

"Okay, thanks, Linda." I watched the paramedics get Daddy on the stretcher and put a plastic mask on him.

"You're welcome, Keeley," Linda said.

I ended the call and pushed the phone into my pocket.

"Is he going to be okay?" I asked one of the paramedics as the two of them lifted the stretcher.

He looked at me with sympathetic, brown eyes. "I hope so. It looks like he had a heart attack."

I followed as they carried the stretcher up the little hill toward the road and the waiting ambulance. "The lady on the phone said I should tell you that I'm alone with him."

"Can you call someone to meet you at the hospital?" he asked.

They pushed the stretcher into the back of the ambulance and the man I was talking to jumped into the back with him. "Come on up," he said.

I climbed into the back, and the other paramedic closed the doors. "Our next-door neighbor will come if she can. She's the only one I can think of."

He nodded. "Call your neighbor."

I made the call and spoke to Mrs. Hall, our neighbor.

"Oh, you poor thing," she said. "I'll get there as fast as I can."

Just before we got to the hospital one of the machines in the ambulance began to emit a shrill sound.

The paramedic in the back with us snapped into action. "Tom, he just stopped breathing!" He yelled to the guy in the front. "I'm starting CPR."

"Is he going to be okay?" I demanded, terror flooding through me.

The paramedic, busy trying to help Daddy, ignored my question. He was still trying to resuscitate my father when the ambulance bumped to a stop.

The doors were flung open and several people in scrubs helped get the stretcher out. One of them grabbed my arm and held me back after we were inside the building.

"You can't go with him right now," said the woman holding my arm.

I jerked my arm, trying to free it. Her hold was gentle but firm.

"I have to. That's my father," I pleaded, tears filling my eyes. "He wasn't breathing."

"They're going to do everything they can to help him." Her eyes were compassionate. "But you'll have to wait here."

My chest began to heave. I needed to be with Daddy and make sure he woke up.

"What about your mom? Can I call her for you?"

"No!" I cried. "She's dead."

"I'm sorry, sweetie. Who can we call?" she said in a gentle voice.

I stared at her, my mind screaming in fear. Then I remembered that Mrs. Hall was on her way. "My neighbor is coming."

She nodded and led me to a waiting area. "Good. I'll sit with you until she gets here."

I sat with the nurse feeling each second tick by in slow motion. I needed my father. I didn't have anyone else. Who would take care of me if he didn't start breathing again?

When I felt a hand wrap around mine, I looked over at the nurse. "Can they make him better?"

Her eyes dropped for a second, then came up to meet mine. "I don't know. They'll do all they can."

I began to gulp in short, fast breaths as I tried to hold myself together. When the nurse pulled me into her arms, I fell apart, sobbing into her shoulder. She held me and rubbed my back.

When my tears stopped, she handed me a tissue.

"Keeley," Mrs. Hall said, rushing up to me. "How's he doing? Have you heard anything?"

The nurse stood up and spoke to Mrs. Hall. "You're her neighbor?"

"Yes," Mrs. Hall said.

"I've been sitting with Keeley since she came in with her father. They're still working on him and there hasn't been any news yet," the nurse said. "I'll leave her with you now."

"Okay, thank you," Mrs. Hall said. She dropped into the seat next to me and grabbed my hand. "He's strong, and I've been praying the whole way here."

I didn't say anything. I didn't need to. Mrs. Hall had known me for the last eight years since she and her husband moved in next door. She often spent time with me, teaching me to bake. In some ways, she was the mother I wished I'd had. I leaned into her, drawing comfort from her presence.

I looked up when a doctor came into the waiting room and glanced around at the people there. When he saw me, he headed in my direction. The look on his face told me everything before he reached me.

"No!" I shook my head furiously. "No, you have to save him. You have to!"

"I'm so sorry," the doctor said. "We did everything we could."

Mrs. Hall had me wrapped in her arms before the doctor finished talking. I wrestled against her hold. "No! He's not dead!" I twisted and tried to wrench free of her arms. I wanted to run to my father. *It wasn't true. It couldn't be.*

"Keeley, you can't go back there. There's nothing you can do," Mrs. Hall said, her voice soft.

When I continued to fight, she held me by both arms and got close to my face. "Keeley, stop!"

At her sharp tone, I froze, stared at her a moment, then crumpled back into her arms.

She held me while my grief spilled out in a torrent.

"You'll come home with me," Mrs. Hall said when my tears subsided into hiccupping breaths. "Everything will be okay, sweetie."

I allowed her to pull me up from the chair and guide me to her car. I stared numbly out the window on the way to her house. Everything looked the same and yet different as if the world had been drained of all its color. For me, it had.

Chapter Twenty-four

I stayed with the Halls for a couple of weeks. Then child services told me I'd be going to live with my only remaining relative—Aunt Lois. For several days, I'd been mostly numb after crying until I couldn't cry anymore. When I heard the news, I found more tears. I didn't want to leave Mr. and Mrs. Hall. They'd been so kind to me. I didn't want to leave the only town I'd ever lived in. And, most of all, I didn't want to live with Aunt Lois.

"I know you don't want to," Mrs. Hall said when I refused to pack my things. "I wish you could stay with us, but you can't." She pushed my hair back from my face. Her voice held all the sadness I felt. "Refusing to cooperate will only make it harder."

Tightening my lips, I nodded and began to shove my clothes into a suitcase.

When I felt a tear land on my hand, I turned. Mrs. Hall wiped her eyes, trying to hide them from me. I grabbed her and held on tight while we cried together. "I'm going to miss you so much."

"I'll miss you too, Keeley." She pulled back and smiled sadly. "You write to me and call me anytime you want."

"I will." It was a promise I intended to keep, but I knew nothing would ever be the same.

"I guess we're stuck with each other now, kid," Aunt Lois said after the social worker left me at her apartment. She looked me over with a scowl.

"If you don't want me," I said, "Then tell the social worker."

Her scowl deepened. "I didn't say that."

We stared at each other, and silence filled the space between us.

"You're all I have left of Greta." She paused. "Even if you do look like your father." Her lips curled into a sneer when she mentioned my father. But I wouldn't let her make me feel bad about looking like him. Daddy was the best father in the world. She blamed him for my mother's death, but I knew better than that. I'd been there when my mother was out of her mind on drugs. I'd been there when Daddy wept over her death.

I raised my chin, glad I looked like him. At least when I looked in the mirror, a part of him looked back at me.

She pointed toward the hall to my left. "The bedroom at the end of the hall will be yours. You can put your stuff in there."

I nodded and picked up my suitcase.

The small bedroom was more welcoming than I'd expected. The walls were painted pale blue and the single bed in the corner had a colorful quilt.

Intending to make the room feel more like my own, I began to unpack my suitcase. I placed my clothes in the dresser drawers, lined my shoes up in the closet, and set pictures of my mother and father on the desk.

Once I'd unpacked the few possessions I had, I looked around the room. *This is my new home.* The thought made tears spring up in my eyes. Virtually everything had been ripped away from me. The mother I'd hoped would someday return to me, recovered from her addiction, was dead and I'd never see her again. The father I'd loved with every bit of my soul had died. The only home I'd known was no longer mine.

I went to the little bed and curled up on top of the quilt as tears flowed. Not wanting Aunt Lois to hear me, I mashed my face into the pillow.

When the sobs subsided, I fell asleep.

A knock on the door awakened me and, as I opened my eyes, I was surprised to see that it was nearly sunset.

"What is it?" I called.

"Time for dinner, that's what it is. Get on out here and eat," Aunt Lois answered.

Sitting up, I rubbed my eyes before pulling myself up from the bed. I shuffled down the hall to the kitchen, hoping my eyes weren't too red and puffy from crying. I didn't want Lois to notice. The thought of her sharing any part of my pain turned my stomach.

When I reached the table, it was set for two with dishes of food laid out. I sucked in the scent and was surprised again by how scrumptious it smelled. I couldn't say why, but I hadn't expected Lois to be a good cook.

I sat down in one of the chairs as Lois walked over with another dish. She set it down and looked me over.

Gritting my teeth, I waited for her to say something about my puffy eyes. She didn't.

"I hope you like meatloaf," she said, sitting in front of the other place setting.

I shrugged. "It smells good."

"Never had meatloaf?" She gave me a sideways glance.

I shook my head.

"Huh," was all she said, but the look on her face told me she was holding something back.

I sat still, not sure if I needed to wait for a blessing or anything else.

"What are you waiting for? Dig in before it gets cold," Lois said.

I reached for the dish that was closest to me and scooped mashed potatoes onto my plate.

"Here," Lois said, passing me the plate of meatloaf. "I think you'll like it. This was my mother's recipe."

I took the dish and forked a slice of the meat onto my plate. "Your mother?"

She met my eyes. "That's right. Your grandmother." She sighed. "Don't suppose you ever met her?"

"No. I thought she was dead."

"She is now. She died the year before …" she paused, and her lips tightened. "The year before Greta."

I scrunched up my face. "I thought she was dead before that." I'd always felt a loss at never having a grandmother. My father's parents had both died when I was a toddler. I didn't remember them. And I'd always been told my mother's parents were dead.

Lois took a bite of her food and chewed before responding. "I'm not surprised they told you that. Mama disowned Greta 'cause of her drug habit."

I put a forkful of meatloaf into my mouth, enjoying the new flavor. "But Mom was off the drugs for years. Why didn't her mother want to see her then?" Underneath that question, there was another one: *why didn't my grandmother want to meet me?*

Lois tilted her head. "Didn't matter to Mama. She said, 'Once a druggie, always a druggie.' She didn't believe in addiction recovery. I guess she was right in Greta's case." Lois's face darkened and a tear slipped down her cheek.

She glanced at me as I scooped a bite of peas into my mouth.

"Mama didn't believe in second chances. That's why she kicked our old man out the minute she found out he'd cheated on her," Lois said.

That explained why I didn't know my grandfather.

"She was right about him." Lois made eye contact with me. "Men ain't nothing but scum. You remember that." She sighed. "I really wanted to believe in Greta though."

I swallowed, the meatloaf going down my throat like a rock. "Daddy wasn't scum," I whispered.

Lois's head whipped around toward me, her eyes flashing with anger. "He threw Greta out instead of helping her, didn't he?"

I wanted to defend my father. I wanted to tell her about the day my mother had almost tossed me off a roof, but I found myself withering under her rage-filled gaze. She blamed Daddy—hated him for what my mother did to herself.

Turning away from her stare, I focused on finishing my meal, though it had lost its taste for me.

Lois turned back to her meal as well, and we finished eating in silence.

Chapter Twenty-five

"Keeley, shake a leg! We need to leave, or you'll be late," Lois called.

"I'm coming," I called back to her. Throwing my backpack over one shoulder, I took a last look in the mirror over my dresser, frowning at the face that looked back at me. I wasn't usually so worried about my appearance, but I was about to go to a new school, and I worried about what the other kids would think of me.

The breakfast I'd eaten gurgled in my stomach as I forced my legs to carry me down the hall. I'd gone to school with the same kids since kindergarten. On top of everything else I was dealing with, I hated the idea of being the new kid.

"There you are. It's about time," Lois grumbled.

"Sorry." I looked at the floor, not wanting her to see my fear.

She saw it anyway. "You'll make new friends. I always did." Her voice was unexpectedly compassionate.

Glancing up at her, I asked, "You had to change schools when you were a kid?"

"A few times. My old man moved us around a lot 'cause he was always losing jobs. Then we moved again when Mama left his sorry butt."

She waited for me to respond. When I didn't, she said, "I guess Greta didn't tell you about us moving around. It's never easy at first, but we always made new friends. You will too."

I still felt like throwing up, but her assurance helped a little. I nodded to her, and we headed to her car.

As we pulled up in front of the school, I stared at the ominous brick building. "You want me to park and walk you in?" Lois asked.

I was surprised at her concern for me, but I didn't think walking in with her was the best idea. Seventh graders didn't usually think walking into school with a parent, or aunt in this case, was very cool. I also had my concerns about what Lois might say or do. There was a lot I still didn't know about her.

I looked her in the eye. "Thank you, Aunt Lois. I'll be fine by myself."

"It's fine if you just call me Lois."

I nodded and grabbed my backpack. As I opened the car door, Lois stopped me.

"Keeley, stay away from the boys." Her eyes locked on mine, carrying genuine concern. "They ain't nothing but trouble."

I held her gaze for what seemed like an eternity. I disagreed with her about members of the opposite sex, but I didn't want to brush off her concern for me.

When she turned her eyes back to the windshield, I jumped out of the car and headed toward the school. I stopped by the school office first, and the lady at the front desk ushered me to the counselor's office.

A tall, thin man with dark hair greeted me when I knocked on the door. "Come on in."

"I'm Keeley Chan. It's my first day here," I told him.

"I see. It's nice to meet you, Keeley. I'm Mr. Masters. Let's find your schedule and I'll walk you to your first class. Sound good?" His voice was upbeat and friendly.

I nodded, my lips turning up slightly.

"Looks like you have math first. Mrs. Danbury is a very good teacher. I think you'll like her," he said.

I followed him down the long corridor, and he led me into a classroom. The teacher stepped over to us, and Mr. Masters introduced me.

"It's nice to meet you, Keeley. Would you like me to introduce you to the class, or are you more comfortable without the introduction?" Mrs. Danbury asked.

I shrugged, looking down at my shoes.

"How about if you take this empty seat near the front." She pointed to an empty desk. "And I'll give you a quick introduction. Will that work?"

I peeked up at her. "Okay."

She smiled at me. "Go ahead and take that seat."

I sat down and watched while my new math teacher spoke to the counselor in hushed tones before he left. *Were they talking about me? Was he telling her that I was an orphan who'd just moved in with her aunt? Did he know all that?*

The bell rang seconds after Mr. Masters left the room. The other kids in the class stopped talking and looked at the teacher.

"Good morning, class," Mrs. Danbury said. "Before we get started, I want to introduce you to our new student." She walked to my desk and put a hand on the writing surface. "This is Keeley Chan. I hope you will all welcome her and help her transition to our school."

I glanced around the room nervously. Most of the kids looked uninterested, but there was one girl to my left and one row behind who was looking right at me. She smiled, then looked away. I turned my attention back to the teacher and did my best to focus.

When the class ended, I looked at the printed schedule Mr. Masters gave me, hoping I'd be able to find the next class.

When a hand touched my shoulder, I jumped.

"I'm sorry, Keeley. I didn't mean to startle you," Mrs. Danbury said. "Would you like some help finding your next class?"

I nodded, and the teacher called to another student. "Ellis, would you come here a moment?"

I was surprised when the girl who'd smiled at me walked over, pushing blond hair behind her ears. "I know," she said. "You were expecting a boy. That's the curse of my name."

Mrs. Danbury patted Ellis's back. "Ellis, would you please help Keeley find her next class?"

Ellis grinned. "Sure. Come on, Keeley."

I gathered my things and threw my backpack over my shoulder. Then Ellis led me to the hallway.

"Let me see your schedule," she said.

I handed her the paper.

"You have social studies next with Mr. Brennan." She closed her eyes and made a sound like she was snoring.

I laughed. "Is he that bad?"

"He's nice, but he talks slow, and his voice is monotone." She looked at the schedule again. "But after that you have Ms. Lowe for science. She's fun. Everyone likes her."

Ellis stopped in front of a doorway. "This is your next class. When it's over, you need to go to the room at the end of the hall on the right." She pointed to the door.

I nodded. "Thanks."

"After science, you have lunch. I have lunch then too. I'll find you and help you find the next class after lunch."

"That's nice of you. I could probably find it myself if you don't want to worry about it," I said.

She smiled again and her blue eyes sparkled. "I'll find you. Good luck until then."

Ellis headed back down the hall to her class, and with a deep breath, I walked into mine and found a seat.

With my lunch tray in my hands, I found myself searching the lunchroom for Ellis. When I didn't see her, I hunted for an empty table. The closest thing I found was a spot at the end of one table that had empty seats all around it. With a sigh, I sat down and looked at the food on my tray—a chicken sandwich, an apple, and a small salad. None of it enticed me. My stomach was knotted with anxiety.

"There you are."

I looked up, startled, and saw Ellis smiling at me.

"Looks like you found a good spot," Ellis said, sitting down across from me.

I was grateful to have someone to sit with, but I didn't want her to do it out of pity.

"You don't have to sit with me," I said. "I'm sure you'd rather sit with your friends."

Ellis laughed. "If I had any real friends at this school, I would sit with them and invite you to join us. I only moved here myself a couple of months ago, and I don't make friends easily."

I stared at her. It was hard for me to believe what she was saying. She didn't seem shy. I couldn't imagine someone like her having trouble making friends.

"My dad says it's because I talk too much and don't let anyone else get a word in edgewise. My mom says it's because I have a strong personality and it scares people." Ellis picked up her sandwich and took a bite. I watched her and tried to think of something to say. She scrunched her nose up at me. "Aren't you going to eat anything?"

I looked at my tray with a grimace and picked up the apple. I brought the fruit to my mouth, and before I could take a bite, Ellis was talking again.

"I used to live in Tennessee. Where did you move here from?" she asked.

"Not far away. A few towns over," I said, wanting to avoid conversation about the past.

She accepted my vague answer and moved on. "Did your dad get transferred or something? That's what happened for me."

I shook my head and took a bite of my apple in the hope that she'd move on and pick a new topic. Instead, she waited patiently for me to finish chewing.

I swallowed hard and let out a breath. Then I looked down as I said, "My dad died, and I had to move in with my aunt."

"Oh, I'm sorry." Ellis went silent and we both focused on our food. I was halfway through my sandwich—forcing it down—when she spoke again.

"I love your hair. I wish mine was that straight and silky." She held a lock of her blond hair out for me to inspect. "You have really pretty skin too. I bet you can stay outside for hours. I get sunburned looking out the window."

I laughed and looked at her. She *was* very pale. "I think you're pretty," I said.

She smiled. "I knew you would make a good friend."

I took another bite of my sandwich, and this time, it didn't feel like a lump in my stomach.

"Let me look at your schedule again and we'll see where you need to go next," Ellis said.

I handed her the paper, and she studied it.

"Perfect!" She grinned at me. "You're in my English class next. Then you have art class with Ms. Long. I'll point you in the right direction after English class is over."

I was about to thank her but didn't get the chance.

"Want to come over to my house after school?" Ellis asked with a hopeful look.

"I can't. My aunt told me to ride the bus home and stay in the apartment until she gets home," I said.

Ellis furrowed her brow. "Bummer. So, your aunt isn't going to be home when you get there?"

I shook my head.

"What time does she get home?"

I picked up my fork and pushed the salad around on my tray. "She gets done working at the salon at six."

"Then you'll be home alone for at least two hours." Ellis cocked her head to one side. "What about tomorrow? Will she be working after school again?"

I shrugged. "I don't know. Probably."

"It's not good for you to be alone every day after school. Give me your phone number and I'll have my mom call your aunt and talk to her about it. Maybe she'll let you come home with me after school on the days she works so you won't be alone." Ellis gave me a self-satisfied smile.

I was less optimistic about her plan. "I don't think she'll let me."

"You might be surprised. My mom is very persuasive. She has a strong personality too." She picked up the banana on her tray and peeled it, taking a large bite.

I reached into my backpack and pulled out a piece of paper. Writing my phone number on the paper, I handed it to her.

"This is the beginning of a great friendship, Keeley. You just wait and see." She put the paper in her bag, tossed her banana peel on her tray, and grinned at me. "Let's go. It's almost time for English class."

I rode the bus home smashed up against the inside wall, staring out the window. A chubby boy sat next to me, and neither of us talked. He seemed just as alone as I. Later, when I was home, I decided that I should have been brave enough to talk to him. I wished that I could be more like Ellis.

While I waited for Lois to come home, I took out my homework and began to work on it. By the time the front door opened, I was finishing the last math problem.

Stepping into the apartment, Lois tossed her keys down on the table next to the door. She glanced up and saw me at the kitchen table. The look that crossed her face was one of momentary surprise as if she'd forgotten I lived with her now. "What a day," she said. "I didn't get a chance to sit down all day. How about you? How was your day?"

"It was okay. I'm done with my homework." I closed my notebook and put it in my backpack.

"Well, aren't you industrious? It's okay to take a break, you know." Her tone was almost accusatory.

"I know. I wanted to get it done. I didn't have anything else to do anyway." I stood up. "Do you want me to help you make dinner?"

She narrowed her eyes at me. "Is there something you want?"

"No." I looked down and sighed. "Well, maybe."

"You're not sure?" Lois scoffed.

Her pushy manner rattled me. Talking to her was nothing like talking to Daddy. "It's just ... I mean, I made a friend and ..." I looked up at her with hopeful eyes. To my surprise, she was smiling.

"You made a friend. See, I told you. That's good, Keeley."

"Yeah. Her name is Ellis, and she's really nice. She helped me find all my classes today."

"Ellis? This is a girl?"

I shrugged. "Yep. And that's her name."

"Are you telling me the truth that this kid is a girl?" She wrinkled her forehead as her eyes bore into me. "I told you to stay away from the boys."

"Ellis is a girl, Lois. I promise."

"Okay. So, what do you want? To invite her over?" Lois asked, walking into the kitchen.

I scurried behind her like a puppy looking for attention. "Actually, she wants me to come to her house. Her mom is going to call you."

"Go to her house when?" Lois got out a pan and put it on the stove.

"Tomorrow?"

Lois looked at me. "Her mom is going to call me?"

I nodded, a hopeful smile on my face. This was going better than I'd thought.

"All right, I'll talk to her, and we'll see."

Happy with her willingness to consider my request, I went to the refrigerator and brought a package of chicken to her, a smile on my face.

I helped Lois cook dinner and we ate quietly together. The phone rang as we were carrying our dishes to the sink. Lois turned to me and placed her plate on top of mine. "You take these and wash the dishes," she said. "I'll get the phone."

I readily agreed and began washing the dishes. Once finished, I peeked out the kitchen door to see that Lois was still on the phone, and I decided to wait in the kitchen.

"Keeley, are you still in here," she asked when she returned. "It doesn't take this long to wash the dishes."

"I was waiting till you got off the phone. I didn't want to interrupt," I said.

She wrinkled her face up at me again. "We weren't talking about state secrets."

"I know, I just ..." I let the thought trail off.

Lois stared at me while I waited for her to tell me about the call and if I could go to Ellis's house.

When I couldn't stand the wait any longer, I asked, "So, can I go?"

"No." Her response was deadpan and came with no explanation.

"But ... why?" I had just met Ellis and shouldn't be so upset about this, but strangely I was.

"Because I'm not working till six tomorrow. I get off at three and I want you to come home since I'll be here." Lois turned from me and strolled into the living room. She sat on the couch and put her feet up on the ottoman.

I followed her. "Then do I get to go the next day?"

She looked at me thoughtfully. "Depends."

"On what?" I furrowed my brow at her.

"On whether or not I think this Ellis is a good friend for you to be spending time with."

I clasped my hands together and squeezed my fingers. "But how will you know that?"

"I'll find out tomorrow when I meet her. She's coming home with you." Lois said, picking up the remote control for the TV and switching it on. "Her mother seems nice enough, but since I have the time tomorrow, I want to meet Ellis before I allow you over to her house."

Lois's concern about who I was friends with confused me. It was hard for me to believe she cared that much about me, and I wondered if her concern was genuine. I also felt uncertain about the idea of her meeting Ellis. How would Lois behave in front of her? Would she make Ellis feel as uncomfortable as she sometimes made me feel? Would she say unkind things about my father?

That last question made my cheeks burn as I remembered Lois's previous comments about Daddy. However, I wanted Ellis for a friend and that meant she'd meet Lois sooner or later.

"Thank you, Lois," I said, deciding to accept this as a good thing.

Her attention was on the TV, but she glanced at me again. "No need to thank me, kid. I'm supposed to take care of you, right?"

"Yeah, I guess so." I looked away. Her statement brought tears to my eyes as I thought about the fact that Daddy was gone. He was the one who'd always taken care of me.

I jumped in surprise when Lois grabbed my hand. Trying to hide my emotion, I turned back to her.

"I know this isn't what you want, to be living with me, but I'm all the family you got left. And you're all I got left." She squeezed my hand and then let go.

I stood staring at her as she turned back to the TV. I didn't know what to make of Lois. One moment she'd try to make me believe my father was evil, and the next, she was looking out for me.

# Chapter Twenty-six

"It's very nice to meet you, Ms.—" Ellis began, smiling brightly at Lois.

"You just call me Lois. No need to be formal," Lois said.

"Okay. Nice to meet you, Lois." Ellis grinned.

Lois studied her with a skeptical eye.

I cringed, waiting to see what Lois would say next.

"Keeley says you helped her find her way around school. I'm glad she's got someone making things easier for her," Lois said.

"I was glad to help. I like Keeley and I think we're going to be great friends." Ellis rocked back and forth on the balls of her feet.

"Good," Lois said. "Keeley needs a friend."

"So do I," Ellis said. "I usually scare kids away by talking too much."

Lois looked at me. "Keeley doesn't scare easily."

"I guess not, 'cause I've been talking her ear off," Ellis said.

Lois chuckled. "So, how'd you get a name like Ellis anyway?"

I held my breath, hoping Ellis wouldn't be offended by the personal question.

"My parents were sure I'd be a boy. They picked out the name Ellis Richard, and when I ended up being a girl, they decided to keep the name—well, the first name, that is. They were kind enough to change the middle name," Ellis said.

Lois cocked her head to the side. "To what, Rhonda?"

Ellis snorted with laughter. "No, thank goodness. My middle name is Lynnette. It was my great-grandmother's name. I don't think it suits me. Every time I hear it, I think of a girl sitting quietly in a library."

Lois nodded with a smile. "You're quite a character, Ellis. I think we'll get along fine. Now, why don't you and Keeley spend some time together? I'll order pizza in a little while. After dinner, we'll take you home."

"Come on," I spoke up for the first time. "Let's go to my room." I was grateful for the opportunity to get Ellis away from Lois. The conversation had gone well, and I didn't want to take the chance that it would turn in another direction.

Ellis followed me down the hall. "Your aunt seems nice," she said after we'd closed my bedroom door.

I shrugged. "Sometimes she is."

Ellis glanced around my little room and then plopped down on the bed. "How come you don't look like her?"

I tightened my lips at the question, not sure I wanted to talk about that.

"I mean, I expected her to be Asian, like you," Ellis clarified.

"Well, I'm half white. My mother was Lois's sister. But my dad was Asian," I said.

Ellis nodded. "You definitely got his looks."

"Yeah." I dropped down on the bed, and Ellis jumped up and walked to my desk. She picked up the photos on top.

"These are your parents?" She asked holding the framed pictures up.

"Yes."

She studied the photos. "Your mom was beautiful. She looked a little like Lois but different at the same time. And your dad was handsome. No wonder you're so pretty." She put the pictures down and looked at me.

I sniffed and wiped a tear from my eye.

"I'm sorry," Ellis said rushing over to me. "I messed up, didn't I? Now *you* won't want to be my friend either."

I shook my head to let her know I wasn't mad at her. "I just miss them, especially my dad. I still want to be your friend," I assured her.

"I bet you do miss them. I can't imagine not having my parents around." She sat back down on the bed and regarded me. "What was your dad like?"

I met her eyes. "He was the best dad in the world." I sighed. "Lois hated him."

Ellis's forehead wrinkled. "Why?"

I shrugged and looked away.

"I'm sorry," Ellis said. "I'm being pushy again. Let's talk about something else."

"Like what?"

She grinned and leaned toward me, then whispered in a conspiratorial gesture. "There's a boy that likes you."

I looked at her skeptically. "I've only been at school for two days."

"I told you," she said, "you're really pretty."

"Who is it?"

Her eyes twinkled. "Johnny Turner."

I furrowed my brow, trying to remember who that was.

"He sits behind you in math class," Ellis said.

I thought about Lois's warnings to stay away from the boys and decided to ignore them. "He's kinda cute."

"I know!" Ellis pulled her legs up and sat Indian-style on the bed. "You know who I like?"

I shook my head.

"Matt Connor. He's in our English class. I'll point him out tomorrow. He has dark hair like yours and amazing green eyes." Ellis's eyes twinkled.

When Lois called us for dinner, Ellis and I were still talking about boys. And by the time we dropped her off at her house, I knew we were going to be great friends.

I spent the next few afternoons at Ellis's house. We talked about boys, and she told me everything she had learned about the school, the teachers, and the other students.

When Lois got off work at six o'clock, she picked me up and we fixed dinner together. I enjoyed spending time with Ellis and her parents, and surprisingly I was beginning to enjoy my time with Lois. The routine was helping me settle into my new life, which I decided might not be as terrible as I first believed. As long as Lois and I could avoid talking about Daddy, everything went fine.

On Saturday morning, Lois and I slept in until late morning and went out for brunch at a nearby diner.

"What will you have, young lady," the waiter asked me with a smile.

"Pancakes and bacon," I responded, handing him the menu.

"Good choice. That's my favorite." He grinned at me, and dimples flashed in his cheeks.

I looked down as heat rushed to my face.

"And what about you?" The waiter turned to Lois.

"I'll have the western omelet." Lois tilted her head to one side, tossing her hair back, as she handed him her menu.

"Coming right up." The waiter smiled. "So, are you her big sister?" He motioned toward me.

"I'm her aunt," Lois said, her voice taking on an alluring tone.

"Her very young, beautiful aunt," the waiter said.

I rolled my eyes as they stared at each other.

When the waiter walked away, I scowled at Lois. "I thought you said men were nothing but trouble."

She met my eyes. "They are, honey, but that doesn't mean you can't have fun with them as long as you're smart about it."

"You said I should stay away from the boys," I said flatly.

"I did, and you better be listening. Girls your age don't know how to be smart about it." She regarded me. "I know you think I'm being unfair, but I know what I'm talking about, Keeley."

She blew out a breath. "Teenage boys are like walking hormones. And girls, well, you're full of hormones too, but unlike the boys, you girls have your heads full of romantic dreams. You all think you're going to be Cinderella and find a prince. But there ain't no prince out there for you." She looked down, then turned her face to glance out the window next to us. "All that's out there is heartbreak." She faced me and met my eyes. "I'm trying to spare you from that."

"I can worry about my own heart," I said defiantly, glaring at her.

Her eyes turned dark, and when she spoke again, her voice held an edge. "You wouldn't say that if you knew anything about it."

My defiance fizzled away in the face of her steely resolve. I looked down at my hands on the table and twisted my fingers together.

"You don't have to understand. Just listen to me and do as I say." Her voice had softened, and when I looked back up at her, her eyes pleaded with me.

I nodded and looked away, letting my gaze drift around the diner. The sound of the other patrons filled my ears as we waited for our food in silence.

"Pancakes and bacon for the young lady." The waiter set a plate on the table in front of me.

"Thank you," I said, picking up a slice of bacon and taking a bite.

"And a western omelet for her lovely aunt," said the waiter, putting Lois's plate down.

Lois smiled at him, and I picked up my fork, ready to dig into my pancakes.

"You wouldn't be free tonight, would you?" the waiter asked.

Lois flipped her hair again. "I might be."

As I watched Lois flirt with the handsome waiter, the bacon in my mouth began to lose its taste. I dropped my fork on the table and slouched against the back of my booth seat.

The waiter picked up a napkin and wrote on it, then handed it to Lois. "Here's my number. Give me a call sometime after four if you want to get together."

Lois took the napkin and shoved it in her purse. "I'll do that."

When the waiter was gone, Lois met my eyes. I stared at her with my lips tight, angry that she would act that way with a total stranger after insisting all men were worthless.

"What?" she said indignantly.

I let my eyes drop to the plate in front of me. "Nothing," I answered, deciding it wouldn't do any good to start the argument with her again.

"Good. Eat that plate of food I'm paying for."

"Keeley, come out here!" Lois hollered.

I put down the book I'd been reading and got up from my bed, stretching my arms and legs, before walking down the hall to find Lois in the living room with another woman.

Lois and the other woman were talking as I walked into the room and didn't notice me right away.

"You're lucky I don't have to work tonight," the woman said. "You should probably ask before making a date from now on."

"I know, I know. I'm not used to this having a kid thing," Lois said. "But I'd've just called him and canceled it if you weren't available. There'll be other guys. It ain't like I need him or anything."

I cleared my throat to let my aunt know I was standing there listening.

"Oh, Keeley, there you are," she said. "This is my friend, Jean. She's going to stay with you for a while tonight while I'm out."

I glanced at Jean, then glared at Lois defiantly. "I'm thirteen. I don't *need* a babysitter."

"Of course, you don't," Jean said. "But no one should be alone on a Saturday night. Plus, I'm Lois's best friend, so I need to get to know you now that you're living here." She stepped closer to me and held up a DVD. "I got a movie, and we'll have pizza and popcorn, maybe even ice cream sundaes."

"You won't even miss me with Jean here," Lois said. "She's the best company in the world."

I crossed my arms over my chest and turned my head away. *I wouldn't miss you anyway*, I thought.

"I don't know what she's so sour about. Teenage mood swing, I guess," Lois said, waving my behavior away.

Out of the corner of my eye, I saw Jean looking me over sympathetically. "No worries. I'm sure we'll have fun once we have a chance to get to know each other."

Lois shrugged. "I guess she'll either have fun or she won't. Her choice. Anyway, thanks for coming over on short notice, Jean. I better get going. How do I look?"

"Perfect. Mr. hot waiter won't know what hit him," Jean said.

"You better believe he won't." Lois laughed. Then she grabbed her purse and looked at me. "Have a good evening, Keeley. I know you will if you let yourself."

I scowled at her as she walked out the door.

Determined not to have a good time with the babysitter I didn't need, I went to my room and tried to read my book. But I didn't get very far because thoughts about Lois and the man we'd just met kept swirling in my head. Anger surged inside me at her insistence that all men, including Daddy, were worthless, while she went out with a man she didn't even know. And, even though I knew I was still young for dating, I hated the way she would behave so foolishly with a man while insisting I stay away from all boys. I tossed the book on the bed, deciding to simply stew in irritation.

When the smell of pizza filled my nose, and my stomach began to growl, I decided it wouldn't hurt to go out and eat with Jean.

I made my way out to the living room and saw Jean sitting on the couch with a plate in her lap.

"I'm just getting some Pizza," I said.

"Sure. It's on the table." She smiled. "And Keeley?"

I was already walking toward the kitchen, but I stopped and looked at her.

"It's fine if you don't want to hang out with me. You can take your pizza to your room if you want. But I really would love to get to know you if you're willing," she said.

She seemed genuine, and I decided it wasn't her fault Lois behaved the way she did, though she didn't seem opposed to it. I nodded slowly, before taking the last few steps into the kitchen.

There was a large pepperoni pizza on the table. I grabbed a plate and put two big slices on it before returning to the living room and sitting down across from Jean.

I ate a few bites silently, then eyed Jean and said, "You told Lois it was a good thing you didn't have to work tonight. Where do you work?"

"The hospital. I'm an ER nurse." She took another bite of her pizza.

Somehow, I hadn't expected that, though I didn't know what I did expect. I tilted my head, regarding her. "That must be interesting."

"It can be. I have some stories."

I nodded. "Have you known Lois a long time?"

"Since high school," Jean said.

Silence filled the room again as I went back to my food.

"Don't be too hard on her for calling me over. It's a good thing, you know, that she didn't want to leave you home alone." Jean chewed another bite, then said, "Besides, she'll be out late most likely. You don't really want to be alone all that time, do you?"

I met her eyes. She seemed nice and I didn't have any reason not to like her. "It's not actually you coming that made me mad."

"I see," Jean said.

She didn't press me to tell her the real cause of my anger, but for some reason that made me want to tell her.

"She just met that guy today," I said, angrily.

Jean nodded and waited for me to continue.

"But she hates men and tells me to stay away from boys."

The hint of a smile flickered on Jean's face, then disappeared. "She doesn't hate men. She distrusts them."

This time, I stayed silent and waited for Jean to say more.

She sighed. "Do you know what happened with her father?"

I shrugged. "I know he cheated and got kicked out."

"That's the PG version." She stopped and watched me. "Maybe I shouldn't say any more."

I scowled. "You can't say that and not explain."

"If I tell you, it stays between you and me." She raised her eyebrows at me.

I nodded, liking the idea.

Jean sucked in a deep breath. "He didn't just cheat. He assaulted one of Lois's friends." She eyed me. "Not me, another friend. She was there to meet up with Lois, but Lois wasn't home from her job at the grocery store yet. Lois's mom got home before it went very far and caught him ... then Lois walked in on the scene. Her friend was crying, her mom was screaming." Jean shook her head. "Her dad left that night and she never saw him again. And she lost a friend for good."

I took another bite of my pizza and chewed. "So that was it for men. She never thought there might be some out there that weren't like her dad?"

"No. She was like most young women after the dust settled. She dated, and she dreamed about finding Mr. Right."

"So, then what happened?"

Jean set her empty plate aside and stretched her legs out. "She found Greg. He was the one who convinced her men were scum."

"What'd he do?" I asked, leaning forward.

"Broke her heart. They were together for a couple of years, and Lois wanted to marry him. Then, she found him in a parked car with another girl. She confronted him and he just laughed at her." Jean shrugged. "That was when she decided all men were scum and that it's better to use them instead of letting them use her."

"My dad wasn't scum, but she hates him too," I said solemnly.

"Not as much as you think."

I scrunched my nose up at her.

She snickered at my reaction. "I know that might be hard for you to believe, but it's true."

"She's always saying bad stuff about him and blaming him for what happened to my mom. But it wasn't his fault. I was there. Lois wasn't. It was the drugs. Daddy loved her. He wanted her to get better."

Jean nodded. "Yeah, I'm sure he did. Lois blames him because she needs someone to blame besides herself."

I shook my head. "Why would she blame herself?"

Jean sighed. "Keeley, I don't know that I should tell you this. I believe your dad tried to help your mom all he could, and even if he didn't, it isn't his fault she had an addiction. It isn't Lois's fault either. I don't want to give you a reason to be angry with her."

I tightened my lips. "No one could help my mother except her. And she didn't want it bad enough."

Jean nodded. "Lois blames herself because she turned Greta away." She looked down, finding her words. "Greta came to Lois after she left you and your dad. Lois offered to take her to a treatment center but wouldn't let her stay unless she agreed to that. Greta wouldn't agree. Then she came back and tried again, and Lois turned her away. Two days after that second time, Greta died."

Anger surged through me—a gut reaction. I closed my eyes and swallowed hard. After a few deep breaths, I opened my eyes and turned them to Jean again. "It wasn't Lois's fault. My mother didn't want to get better, not enough anyway."

I thought about the day on the roof and about the night my mother left when she came to my room. She hadn't loved me enough to conquer her addiction. Certainly, nothing Lois might have done would have helped.

Jean watched me sympathetically but didn't offer the customary apology. Instead, she lifted the DVD box off the couch and held it up. "I think we've talked about serious stuff enough. How 'bout some *Top Gun*?"

I nodded.

"Good. You can ogle the attractive young men all you want, and I won't say a word about it to Lois."

Grinning, I set my plate aside and curled up in my chair.

Chapter Twenty-seven

Four years later

"Come on, Keeley, Cody is super cute," Ellis pleaded.

I gave her a sideways glance. "I know he is. That's not the point and you know it."

"It's not really a date if other people are going. Just tell her you're going out with a group of friends." She leaned in across the lunchroom table. "It isn't a lie."

I rolled my eyes at her and set my sandwich down on my napkin. "It's never that easy with Lois. Keeping me away from boys is her passion. She'll want to know who's going."

"So, tell her about the girls and leave out the boys." Ellis picked up a potato chip and crammed it into her mouth.

"She'll know I'm not telling her everything. She always knows."

Ellis scowled at me. "You can't even omit stuff without giving yourself away?"

We both knew I couldn't, so instead of answering her, I took a bite of my sandwich.

She munched on her food for a bit, then perked up saying, "I'll do it. I'll tell her about the movie outing. My face doesn't give everything away."

I stared at her, considering the offer. She could pull off the half-truth. I didn't doubt that. But it didn't mean it would work. Lois was relentless in her mission to keep me safe from the threat of the opposite sex.

With a sigh, I dropped my sandwich and dusted off my hands. "I guess we can try. Don't be surprised if it doesn't work."

Ellis raised her eyebrows at me. "Somehow, we'll make this work. I've been pining for Matt for the last five years. But if Cody doesn't have a date, he isn't gonna go."

I nodded, knowing how badly she wanted a date with Matt Conner.

"Good. This will work out. You'll see," Ellis said with a grin.

"What are you girls whispering about over there?" Lois asked, glancing at us from the opening in the wall between the kitchen and the living room.

Ellis sat up straight on the couch and met Lois's eyes. "I'm trying to convince Keeley to go out to a movie with me and a few other girls from school. Don't you think she ought to get out and have some fun?"

"What movie are you going to see?" Lois asked, ignoring the question Ellis asked.

"Oh, I don't know yet. Probably a romantic comedy or maybe an action flick. We'll see what the group decides."

"Who's in the group?" Lois asked without looking up from the food she was preparing at the kitchen counter.

"Well, so far Leah, Robin, and Tessa. Caroline might go. And Keeley if I can talk her into it," Ellis said, poking me in the ribs with her elbow. Her voice sounded so open and normal, I almost believed the girls she listed were the only ones going on the outing.

"And which boys are going?" Lois asked, looking up and meeting Ellis's eyes.

My heart pounded against my ribs and adrenaline filled my veins in the split second it took for Ellis to answer.

She scrunched up her nose. "It's a girls' trip to the movies."

Her lie sounded convincing, but Lois turned her eyes on me, and I immediately looked down to avoid them.

"No, it ain't," Lois said with conviction. She turned back to Ellis. "Why don't you tell me the truth now?"

Faced with this direct challenge, Ellis sighed. "Okay, you're right. A few boys are going, but we'd only be with them at the movie theater. We're going to meet them there and then leave after, separately."

"That might be what you're doing, Ellis, if your parents let you, but not Keeley," Lois said.

Ellis wilted into the couch cushions and remained silent until I got up and pulled her by the arm to my room.

When the door was closed behind us, I said, "I told you it wouldn't work."

"That's all you have to say?" she asked sullenly. "I'm losing my chance for a date with Matt. I've been waiting years for this."

I shrugged. "Sorry."

Her eyes darted up and fixed me in a steely glare. "She figured it out because of *you*. Can't you even look her in the eye when someone else is telling the lie?"

"I guess not." My shoulders slumped, and I slunk to the bed and dropped down.

Silence filled the room as Ellis sat with her arms crossed over her chest and her lips tight. I pushed back against the wall and stayed quiet, fearing Ellis might hate me now.

I startled when Ellis jumped up and turned to me. "What about Jean?"

I scrunched my face up. "What about her?"

"It'd be easy to go out to a movie if she were here that night. Lois would never have to know."

I shook my head, not able to follow her train of thought. "Lois only calls Jean over when she goes out on a date. There's no way to make sure she goes out on a date that night."

A mischievous grin spread across Ellis's face. "What if there is a way?"

I exhaled loudly. "Ellis, would you just tell me what you mean?"

"My uncle Ben will be in town visiting us that weekend." She met my eyes and hers danced with excitement. "He's a player. Every time he comes to visit, he finds some woman to go out with. Lois is exactly his type. I could arrange for them to meet the day of the outing or maybe the day before. He's a smooth talker. She'll be eating out of his hands."

"That doesn't seal the deal," I insisted. "If Jean is working the night of the outing, Lois won't go out. She'd never trust me to stay here alone—especially now."

"We still have a week. Call her and tell her that you want to introduce Lois to my uncle and want to make sure they'd be able to go out that night if they hit it off."

I mulled that over. Jean wouldn't insist on knowing my reasons even if she thought I was up to something. She might even be willing to help out if she did know what was going on.

I nodded. "It *could* work. But there's no guarantee."

"Any chance is better than no chance. I'll tell Matt we're in to go to the movie and if it doesn't work out, then I'll tell him you couldn't make it and maybe he'll still go even if Cody has to go without a date."

I wasn't thrilled about the fact that Ellis was willing to leave me behind if the plan went south, but I did understand. "Okay. I'll call Jean tomorrow."

"Everything is set up, Keeley. Now all you have to do is play it cool and act the way you normally would when Jean comes over and Lois heads out," Ellis said over the phone.

"I know. I can do that," I said. I chewed my pinky nail, worrying that Lois would ask a question that would cause me to give the whole thing away.

"Play it cool, Keeley. This night is super important to me."

"I know. I'll tell Jean about going to the movie after Lois leaves. I'll say you just called and asked. Then you can come pick me up." I swiveled in my desk chair and looked at the picture of my father on the desk, wondering what he'd think of what I was doing. A surge of doubt erupted in my gut and made me queasy. I pushed it away. I had to do this. Ellis was counting on me.

"Well, technically, Matt will be picking you up. He's going to drive us and Cody. But Jean won't have to know that. I'll come up to the apartment to get you alone and I'll make sure he parks the car where Jean won't be able to see it."

"Ellis! You said you were going to drive, and we would only be with the boys at the movie," I protested.

"I know, but Matt offered to drive, and it'll be more fun to ride with him. You'll have a chance to get to know Cody. You might like him." Her voice tried to brush away my protest but also held the tiniest bit of pleading. "What difference does it make?"

I sighed. It made a difference, but I could see arguing wasn't going to help. "Fine. I better go. Jean will be here any minute."

"This is going to work, Keeley. I told you it would. Lois was falling all over Ben. She can't wait to go out with him. She won't even remember about the movie plans," Ellis said excitedly.

I wasn't so sure about that. "I hope she doesn't. See you in a little while."

"Sure, bye," Ellis said.

I returned the salutation and hung up the phone before wandering out to the living room. Throwing myself into the couch cushions, I picked up the remote and switched on the TV.

By the time Lois sauntered out of her room, I'd found an episode of *Boy Meets World* and was pretending to be engrossed in the storyline.

"What do you think, Keeley?" Lois asked. "Will Ellis's gorgeous uncle lose his mind when he sees me in this?"

Normally, I'd argue with her about her frivolous behavior with men while I wasn't even allowed to study with a boy, but that might get her mind onto topics I'd prefer we stayed away from. I settled on hitting her with a glare, turning my nose up at the very short, very tight, black dress she wore and only saying, "His name is Ben."

She chuckled at my disgusted glance and said, "Whatever. He'll definitely love the dress." Then she spun around as best she could on her four-inch heels and adjusted the dress once more.

The usual irritation I felt when Lois went out on her "dates" swirled inside me, making me want to rant. Instead, I turned back to the TV, ignoring her chatter about Ben and how she'd have him wrapped around her little finger.

The doorbell rang and Lois let Jean in. I looked up and smiled at her.

"Hey, girly! How about nachos and a sappy romance movie tonight?" Jean said to me.

"That sounds good." I worked to keep my voice from wavering with the deceit I had planned.

"I'm glad you two have your plans all set," Lois said. "Now I've got to get going. Ben will be waiting."

"I thought you *liked* to keep a man waiting," Jean said.

"I do, but not so long he gives up and leaves," Lois returned.

"Have fun. I know Keeley and I will." Jean grinned at me, and I felt guilty that I was using her and planning to ditch her.

"No worries. This one is hot. I'll have fun." Lois started for the door, then turned back. "Don't wait up for me."

I rolled my eyes. We never waited up for her.

Five minutes after Lois left, I excused myself, saying I was going to my room to read a little before dinner. I sat in my room for another ten minutes, feeling each one tick by with the anxiety of my upcoming deception.

Walking back into the living room, I found Jean watching a game show. She looked up at me with a smile. "Ready for nachos now?"

"Actually, Ellis called while I was in my room, and she invited me to go to a movie with her. Lois probably wouldn't want me to go, but I thought ... well, I thought maybe you'd let me go and we could just keep it between us." I looked down at the seat of the couch, hoping Jean would think I was afraid to meet her eyes because I was asking her to deceive Lois and not realize I was trying to trick her as well.

There was a brief pause before she spoke, and I feared she was on to me.

"I was looking forward to the girl time with you, but every girl needs to get out and have some fun with her friends once in a while. I guess it'll just be me and the nachos tonight." Jean looked at me, and I met her with a grin.

"Thank you, Jean! You're the best!"

"Yeah, I know. But if I'm going to let you do this, you gotta be back on time. Deal?" She raised her eyebrows at me.

"I promise. Ellis is going to pick me up in a little while. She can tell you the movie time."

Jean nodded and patted the couch next to her. "Come sit with me while you wait for her. Tell me how school is going."

I sat down and talked to her about all my classes and the activities I was involved in until the doorbell rang.

"There's Ellis," I said, jumping up from my seat. I hurried to the door and let a grinning Ellis inside.

"Hi, Jean," Ellis said, pushing her blond hair behind her ears.

"Hey, Ellis. It's good to see you again. I hear you have a hot uncle," Jean replied.

Ellis shrugged. "Women do seem to like him."

"Lois sure does," I said.

"Thanks for letting Keeley go out to the movie," Ellis said.

"No problem, but we need to get the details worked out. What time is the movie starting?" Jean asked.

"Seven o'clock," Ellis answered.

"Okay, then I'll expect Keeley back here no later than ten."

Ellis nodded. "She will be."

"Good," Jean said, getting up from the couch. "You two have fun." She walked over to me and shoved a twenty-dollar bill in my hand.

"You don't have to do this, Jean. I have some money from babysitting," I told her.

"Tonight's fun is on me. I insist," she said when I tried to give the money back to her.

I launched myself into her arms. "Thank you."

"No problem, kiddo. You girls get going now and I'm going to go get those nachos and start my movie."

"The boys are waiting over here." Ellis pulled me by one arm toward a black Ford Taurus in the parking lot. When we reached the car, she guided me to the back door on the passenger side and let go of my arm. "Cody is super excited to hang out with you." She turned to face me and pushed at her hair. "Do I look okay, Keeley?"

I smiled, taking in her pink lipstick and perfectly arranged blond locks. "You look gorgeous. Matt is going to wonder why he waited so long to ask you out."

Ellis grinned. "Thanks, Keeley. Thanks for doing this."

I shrugged. "Anything for my best friend."

The passenger window rolled down and Matt's voice boomed out, "You girls coming or what?"

Ellis gave me a quick hug, then pulled the car door open. "We're coming."

I slid into the backseat next to Cody. "Hi," I said.

Cody's mouth tightened for a moment as he looked me over. "Hey," he said before turning to look out his window as if there was something to see other than a dark parking lot.

I sighed and pulled on my seat belt. *Yeah, he's super excited to hang out with me.*

As Matt drove us toward the movie theater, Ellis's chatter filled the car. I sat quietly next to a boy who didn't seem interested in looking at me and hoped Ellis wasn't killing her chance with Matt by talking too much.

"I mean, seriously, the yearbook staff acts like half the clubs in the school don't even exist. I'm in three clubs, yet the only place you see me in the yearbook is the individual picture we all get. You'd think they would get some pictures of club meetings, but they don't pay attention to them at all," Ellis went on.

"I don't know much about what's going on outside of football," Matt said in a disinterested tone. "They got me in the yearbook four times last year."

"That's exactly what I mean," Ellis said, not appearing to notice Matt's lack of interest. "All the clubs and activities should get space in the yearbook, not just football and cheerleading."

"Football and cheerleading are what people care about," Matt asserted.

"That's not true. There are seventy people in the French club," argued Ellis.

"Maybe, but nobody pays to see them speak French. They pay to see football—and the cheerleaders, I guess" Matt said with a snicker as he pulled into the theater parking lot.

I was beginning to dislike Matt, but Ellis was still looking at him with lustful eyes.

"Let's go watch the movie. We can discuss this more later," Ellis said, hopping out of the car.

At the ticket counter, Matt suggested we see an action movie instead of the romantic comedy Ellis had chosen.

"We can't do that," Ellis protested. "If we do, the rest of the group will go to the wrong one when they get here."

Cody snickered, and Matt said, "There is no rest of the group."

Ellis furrowed her brow. "What do you mean? You said they were coming in Jack's car."

Matt shrugged. "The group thing was what you wanted. But they were never coming. Jack and Tessa are hanging out at his house while his parents are gone."

For some reason, Cody laughed again.

"The others are partying at Ellen's house tonight," Matt said.

Ellis recovered from this news quickly and straightened up, facing Matt. "We have to go to the movie I picked. The other one starts too late, and Keeley has to be home by ten."

Matt looked at Cody and something passed between them as both their faces held knowing looks. Their smirks sent a shiver up my spine.

"Fine," Matt said, "we'll go to the girly movie."

We all paid for our tickets and filed into the seats at the back of the room. Ellis began talking about her plans for the summer, and I frowned at the way Matt ignored her and focused on throwing kernels of popcorn at Cody.

I sighed gratefully when the lights went down. At least now I didn't have to watch Ellis's hopes of true love with Matt washing down the drain. It was obvious to me that his reasons for going out with her were something other than what she imagined. Ellis was having a harder time seeing it.

For an hour, I enjoyed the movie, then Cody blurted, "I'm sick of this crappy movie. Let's go to Jack's house now."

Matt gave him a sharp look. But Cody didn't let up. "Come on. This is boring. You said you'd get her to go to the other movie."

"I tried," Matt hissed. "Shut up or you're going to ruin everything."

Ellis watched but didn't say anything.

"I can't sit through any more of this girly junk. Let's just go," Cody persisted.

Matt elbowed him and turned to Ellis. "This isn't my kind of movie. And since Keeley has to be home by ten, how about we go over to Jack's house for a while?"

Tightening her lips, Ellis looked at me. Her eyes showed conflicting emotions. "You never said anything about going to anyone's house. We can't do that."

"I promised I'd be home right after the movie," I said, trying to help Ellis.

"We'll get you home on time, but let's have some fun first. Jack's parents are out of town. His older brother bought him some beer." Matt scooted closer to Ellis in his seat and caressed her cheek with a fingertip. "And we could get some privacy."

My heart began to pound and my stomach turned at the prospect of the private party he wanted to take us to. I didn't want my friend to get taken advantage of, and I wondered if Cody had the same thing in mind for me.

"Is that all you want?" Ellis asked, hurt in her voice.

Matt shrugged. "Isn't it what you want? You've been staring at me in class for years."

Ellis's face wrinkled up. "I actually liked you, Matt, and I wanted to get to know you. I thought maybe ..." She shook her head rather than finishing her sentence. "Never mind. I see you're not the person I thought you were. Just drive us home now, please. We aren't going to Jack's house." She held her ground and glared at Matt with steely eyes, but I could see her lips trembling. My heart ached for her.

Matt stood up and Cody followed suit. "You don't wanna come? That's fine. You can find your own ride home," Matt spat the words. He and Cody pushed past me and stomped out of the theater.

I stared in shock at the boys leaving, then I looked at Ellis. She was sobbing. I rushed to her side and wrapped my arms around her.

"I'm sorry," I said.

She looked up at me. "I thought he was a nice guy."

"Yeah, I know."

Her eyes grew large as she looked around the room. "How are we going to get home?"

"I don't know."

Ellis brought her eyes back to me and her face crumpled up. "Oh, Keeley, I'm sorry. You set all this up for me and now we're in this mess. I should've known Matt was only interested in one thing."

I was worried about getting home too, and about the chance that Lois could find out. Strangely, though, I was more worried about Jean finding out that I'd lied to her. I really liked and respected Jean. I didn't want to lose her trust. Still, I didn't want to kick Ellis while she was down.

"How could you have known?" I asked.

She looked at the floor. "I guess I could've listened to Amber Watkins when she warned me about him." She met my eyes again with a pleading look. "I thought she was just jealous because he dumped her."

For a moment, I felt like I'd been punched in the stomach. Ellis never mentioned this tidbit when I agreed to sneak out for her sake.

A loud sniffle from my friend brought me out of my thoughts, and my heart melted for her. "I probably would have thought the same thing. That doesn't matter now. We need to think about how we're going to get home."

"We could call Jean. She'd be cool about it," Ellis suggested.

A picture of Jean's face, eyes filled with hurt because I had lied, filled my mind. I shook my head. "Not Jean. Not if we can help it. I don't want her to know I lied to her."

Ellis nodded her understanding, then with a hard swallow said, "I guess it's probably too far to walk."

"We'd never make it on time," I agreed.

"We'll have to call my parents then. They know we went out with the boys. They just don't know Lois wasn't cool with it. I think they'd come, and we'd be okay."

I nodded. "Let's go ahead out and call them."

We walked to the lobby and Ellis made the call, telling her parents how the boys had left without us. I chewed my pinky nail and hoped they'd never mention this call to Lois.

Hanging up her phone, Ellis turned to me. "They'll leave in a minute and come get us."

We walked up to the glass door and watched for one of her parents' cars. Silence stretched between us and hung heavy with the sorrow and regret we both felt.

The silence was broken when Ellis's hand flew up to her mouth as she gasped. "Oh no!"

"What?" I asked with alarm.

She pointed to a red car pulling up in front of the theater. "That's Uncle Ben's car."

Every ounce of color drained from my face as I stood staring at the flashy car. If Ben was picking us up, then surely Lois was with him.

I turned to Ellis with wide eyes. "You said your parents were coming."

"I know. That's what my dad said." She shook her head. "I'm so sorry, Keeley. He must have called Uncle Ben and asked him to do it. I don't know why he'd do that. I never thought that would happen."

I put a hand on Ellis's shoulder to stop her from rambling on with more apologies.

My heart pounded against my ribs as Lois stepped from the car. "I should have called Jean." Now she and Lois would both know what I'd done.

Lois's eyes turned on me with fire in them. She pointed at the car.

Biting the inside of my cheek, I pulled Ellis by the arm and walked out to the car.

"What in the hell did you get yourself into?" Lois hissed.

"It was all my fault, Lois," Ellis tried to take the heat for me. I squeezed Ellis's hand to silence her, knowing there was no point in saying anything to defend ourselves right now.

"Get in the car," Lois said forcefully. Ellis and I complied.

"Way to ruin your uncle's date, Sassy," Ben said to Ellis. His voice sounded more amused than angry.

"Sorry," she mumbled.

Ben laughed and shook his head, but Lois was fuming through the silent journey to our apartment. When the car stopped, she turned to Ben. "The date can go on," she said sweetly. "Just let me walk Keeley inside and then we can drop Ellis off."

Ben shrugged. "Sorry darlin', but the mood is gone. Maybe we can try again the next time I'm in town."

Lois held her gaze on him, then sighed. "Sure. Give me a call." She opened the car door and we both got out, Ellis staring apologetically after me.

When Ben's car was out of sight, Lois turned on me. "This is how you thank me for taking care of you all these years?" The anger in her eyes bore into me. "You lie and sneak around. You betray my trust and Jean's."

The mention of Jean was the only part that truly hurt. "I didn't betray your trust. You don't give me any trust to betray. That's why Jean is here," I spat the words at her.

"No, Jean is here because I knew you'd get stupid and try something like this sooner or later. You're just like every other teenage girl." She pushed hair back from her face roughly as the breeze blew it right back out of place.

"I'm seventeen! I shouldn't have to lie and sneak around just to go out on a date. I think I've earned some trust from you by now." Tears pricked the backs of my eyes, and I fought to hold them back. "I never get into trouble, and I get really good grades."

"Don't you get it, Keeley? You're on a good track, and those boys you want to go out with could ruin it all. They're not worth your time." Her expression softened a bit, but that didn't matter much to me.

Fiery anger rolled through me. "You're such a hypocrite! You go out on dates and stay gone half the night. I just wanted to go to a movie." I scrunched my face up to keep the tears from spilling, but one escaped and trailed down my cheek. I wiped it away impatiently.

Her expression hardened again. "When I go out with men, I'm in control. I make sure they never hurt me. Look how your date ended."

Her point that Ellis and I had picked the wrong boys was undeniable. I pushed on anyway, ignoring that part. "You use them, so they won't use you. Yeah, that's a really good strategy. Here's a news flash: I don't want to be like you! I don't want to use people or get used. And right now, I just want to go out on a date once in a while. Nothing more than that."

Her voice a low rumble, Lois said, "I know exactly what you want. And the first time you try a simple date, you get yourself dumped at a movie theater."

I stared into the face of my aunt and saw a bitter woman who was so afraid of getting hurt that she'd rather be lonely. My anger mixed with pity and rolled through me. The last thing I ever wanted was to end up like her. I stomped one foot against the sidewalk and threw my arms up. "Yes, Lois, those boys were jerks. That doesn't mean they all are."

She raised one eyebrow. "Trust me, they are."

"No, they're not! And you can't hold me hostage forever. Next year I'll be eighteen and done with high school. I'll be able to make my own choices." I glared at her. "And you won't be stuck taking care of me anymore."

The wind whipped around us in a gust as I waited for her to respond.

"I suppose you'll go out looking for prince charming just like every other foolish girl." She put her hands on her hips and looked at me with disdain.

I wiped another tear from my face. "I don't expect to find a prince. But there are good guys out there. There's real love, and I'm going to find that." Memories of my father and the way he loved my mother—the way he loved me—filled my mind. I'd find someone who loved me again. Someday, I'd find that.

 # Chapter Twenty-eight

Five years later

"It's the coil packs, isn't it?" I said, walking toward my old, beat-up Toyota Camry and the mechanic studying its engine.

The man shot up at the sound of my voice and banged his head on the car's open hood. "Ouch!" He said, rubbing the spot that was bumped.

He turned and focused his blue eyes on me. "You know cars?" he smiled, making my legs wobble. He was very handsome even with grease smudged on his face.

I shrugged. "My dad and I used to fiddle with engines some. He taught me what he knew."

The mechanic's smile brightened. "Sounds like a great dad!"

My eyes turned from his gaze. "He was."

His smile fell away. "Oh, I'm sorry."

Pushing away the memories of my father, I shook my head. "It's okay. He died years ago."

Silence passed between us as the mechanic scuffed his shoe against the concrete.

"But he did teach me a few things, so don't try to swindle me," I said, forcing a smile back to my lips.

He grinned and placed a hand over his heart as if wounded. "I would never do that." He reached out a dirty hand. "I'm Devin, by the way."

I took his hand and shook it. "Nice to meet you, Devin. I'm Keeley."

He looked at my hand as he released it and noticed the grease that had transferred from his hand. "Oh, I'm sorry. Let me get you something to wipe that off."

He went to a nearby shelf and grabbed a rag for me. "It's nice to have a customer who knows something about their car. You're right. It's the coil packs. I can get it fixed in an hour or so."

I nodded. "Mind if I hang out and watch?"

He smiled nervously.

"I won't get in your way," I said. "But I'll need to leave for work as soon as you're finished."

"Sure." He pushed his greasy hand through messy blond hair. "I guess you can hang out here."

My pulse quickened as I watched his handsome face. "I'll just sit over there." I pointed to a metal folding chair in the corner.

I sat in the chair and picked up a car magazine from the shelf next to me. Listening to the sound of Devin working on my car, I flipped through the pages, thinking about my father as I looked at the pictures.

"So what do you do?" Devin's voice said from under the hood of my car about thirty minutes into the repair.

"Huh?"

"You said you had to get to work. What is it you do?" he asked.

"Nothing exciting. I'm a hairdresser." I said the words with a sigh, thinking about the grief Lois would likely give me for showing up late again. Finishing high school hadn't been the end of my attachment to my aunt. Though I would never have considered it possible when I was seventeen, I'd begun to spend a lot of time at the salon during my senior year, doing anything they asked in order to make some money. In the process, I developed an interest in learning the trade. A year after leaving high school, I began to work at the salon as a trained hairdresser.

Devin looked at me from around the car. "There's nothing wrong with that, you know."

"Oh, I know that. I like my job. But I work with my aunt and I don't always love that." I put the magazine back on the shelf.

Devin ducked back under the hood. "Can't you go to another salon?"

"Yeah." I sighed. "But I like the other ladies there and, well, I guess I'm a little reluctant to change."

"I see. What hair salon do you work at? I might need a haircut soon."

"Topnotch Cuts. It's not that far from here," I said.

"Oh, yeah. I know that place."

When my phone trilled, I looked at the screen. "Sorry, it's my aunt."

"No problem. You can tell her that I'll have your car ready in about ten minutes," Devin said.

"Thanks, I will."

I accepted the call on my phone and said, "Hi Lois ... yes, I know I'm late." I tapped my foot on the floor while she complained about the customers that were waiting for me. "I know. I'm sorry. My car wouldn't start, and I had to have it towed to a garage."

Lois complained about my poor excuse for a car and told me that I should get a new one. I didn't bother to counter her by saying that I was saving up my money so I could move to a nicer apartment. That would only get her started complaining about the rat trap I lived in.

"The mechanic says it'll be ready in about ten minutes ... Yeah, I'll get there as soon as I can. Tell Mrs. Jarvis I'm sorry for her wait."

I ended the call and sat back down on the metal chair.

A few minutes later Devin closed the hood of my car. "All finished. You'll have to go around to the office and settle up with Josh at the front desk."

"Great! Thanks, Devin." I stood up and stepped forward to shake his hand again. This time he wiped it off on a rag first.

When he released my hand, I headed to the door that would take me to the office, but Devin's voice stopped me. "You want to go out sometime, Keeley?"

A smile spread across my face. I turned around slowly and met his eyes. "Sure."

Little did I know that I was stepping into a nightmare.

"I'm so sorry, Mrs. Jarvis! Come on over and I'll get started on your haircut right away," I said as soon as I got into the salon and put my things in the back.

Mrs. Jarvis smiled as she sat in the chair. "Car trouble, I hear."

I sighed. "Afraid so. But it's all fixed now."

I draped a smock over her and began preparing her hair for cutting.

"You want it the same as last time?" I asked.

"Maybe just a tiny bit shorter. I'm feeling spunky," Mrs. Jarvis replied.

I smiled. "No problem. You want me to spike it up for you?"

I watched her face show surprise in the mirror. "Oh dear, no! I'm not trying to give my husband a heart attack."

I chuckled and Mrs. Jarvis joined me.

Patting her on the shoulder, I said, "Just a tiny bit shorter, then."

I began the haircut, but my mind kept drifting back to Devin and his smile. There was something about him that made my heart beat faster. For reasons I couldn't explain, I wanted to impress him. I thought about our dinner plans for the weekend and considered what I might wear and how I'd fix my hair.

"So," Amber, the stylist in the next cubicle said, "who's the lucky guy?"

I turned toward her in surprise. *Was she a mind reader?* "What?"

"You've had a stupid grin on your face since you walked in and your cheeks are all flushed." She raised her eyebrows at me. "So, who is he?"

"No one."

"Come on, girl, who do you think you're trying to fool?"

I glanced toward the front of the shop where Lois was sweeping up her station. Then I spoke to Amber in a hushed voice. "The mechanic who fixed my car. He's really cute."

Amber threw a glance at Lois, then looked at me. "Secret date?"

I rolled my eyes. "It isn't a secret. But you know how Lois is about men. It's easier if she doesn't know."

"Doesn't that mean it *is* a secret?" Mrs. Jarvis spoke up.

"I suppose," I grudgingly agreed. "But it's not that big a deal if she does find out. It isn't like she has a say. I'm just trying to avoid having the same argument with her that we've had a thousand times."

"In that case," Amber said, "you better start thinking about something else before your face gives you away. No one looks that happy after having to get their car fixed."

When my doorbell rang Saturday night, I was still fiddling with my hair. I shoved a silver comb into one side and hurried toward my front door.

Devin stood in the hall holding a single red rose. His hair was combed perfectly and he wore khakis and a neatly pressed, blue button-up shirt. He grinned at me, and my stomach filled with butterflies.

"You look amazing," he said, handing me the rose.

I smiled as heat shot up to my face. "So do you."

"I clean up okay," he said.

He most certainly did, but I decided to move the conversation forward from that topic. "Let me get my purse and we can go."

"Sure." Devin's voice was pleasant, but for a split second his face seemed to darken. *Was he irritated with me for not being ready to walk out the second he rang my doorbell?* No, surely not. I pushed the thought away as I grabbed my purse from the couch in my tiny living room.

"Ready to go," I said as I returned to the door.

Devin drove us to a small Italian restaurant, and we were seated in a booth near the back.

"So," I said, "what's good here?"

"I love the chicken parm. But really, everything is good here. If it wasn't, I wouldn't have brought you," he said, smiling disarmingly.

"Have you ever had their alfredo sauce? I love a good plate of fettuccini alfredo, but some restaurants don't make very good alfredo—at least in my opinion." I glanced at the menu as I spoke.

"I don't like alfredo sauce," Devin responded.

"Okay. I guess I'll just have to take a chance on it."

Once we'd ordered, I asked Devin about his family.

"I'm the middle child," he said. "But I'm the only boy. My dad is a mechanic too. He taught me everything I know. He tried to teach my sisters, but they weren't like you. No interest."

"So what do they do?" I asked.

Devin shrugged and answered in a disinterested tone. "Lena is a receptionist at a hotel, Alicia is a nurse."

"My aunt's best friend is a nurse," I said, trying to tie our common threads.

"I don't know much about all that. Cars are more fun if you ask me." Devin smiled and launched into the story of how he'd started helping his dad with car repairs when he was still in elementary school.

"So, you like cars too. I haven't met a lot of women who have that interest," Devin said.

"I like to fiddle once in a while. I don't know all that much. My dad and I used to work on an old car he was trying to fix up." My gaze dropped from Devin's eyes to the tablecloth. "But he died when I was thirteen. I haven't done a lot with cars since then ... well, other than trying to keep my old clunker running."

Devin reached out and grasped one of my hands. "Sorry about your dad. He sounds great."

I nodded and met his eyes again. "He was. I miss him."

"Yeah, I know I'd miss my dad if he was gone."

Something about the way he said it made me feel cold inside, but I couldn't make any sense of that. His tone was sincere, and his eyes didn't betray that. I figured it must be me. "Let's talk about something else."

Devin accepted my suggestion, and the conversation moved on to his interest in basketball and my precarious relationship with Lois.

"I should meet your aunt," he said. "I'm sure I could change her mind and convince her I'm a good guy."

Forcing back an eye roll at the idea, I said, "Trust me, you couldn't."

He gave me a hurt expression and placed a hand over his heart.

"It has nothing to do with you, Devin. No one could change her mind. Trust me," I assured him.

"And what about yours?" he asked.

I scrunched up my face in confusion. "What do you mean?"

"I don't think you trust me either." He picked up his glass of soda and took a sip.

I fiddled with the napkin on my lap, uncomfortable with the direction this conversation was taking. "I don't *distrust* you. I just met you."

He put his elbows on the table and leaned closer to me. "Are you sure that's all there is to it? Maybe your aunt's ideas about men have rubbed off on you."

I pushed back against my chair's back, unnerved by his closeness and the implication he was making. I raised an eyebrow at him. "They certainly have *not*. I know there are good men in the world. My father was a great one. I have every hope that you are too, but I won't know that for sure until I get to know you better."

He smiled, his bright blue eyes flashing. "So, you want to go out with me again."

The corners of my lips tugged upward and my body relaxed. "Yes, I think I would like that."

# Chapter Twenty-nine

"So what do you think? Isn't he great?" I asked Ellis as soon as Devin dropped us off at my apartment and left.

"He's handsome, just like you said," she answered, tossing her purse on the table by the door.

"That's not what I'm asking and you know it." I put my purse down too and headed to the couch where Ellis had already sat down.

Ellis picked at the worn fabric on my old sofa which I'd gotten from Lois when she bought a new one. It wasn't much to look at anymore, and it wasn't all that comfortable either, but it was free. She frowned. "He's nice."

My brow furrowed. "You don't really think so. Why not? What did he do to deserve that?"

She met my eyes. "Nothing. He *is* nice."

Her words were pretty convincing, and she was looking me right in the eyes, but I knew Ellis well enough to know when she was just saying what I wanted to hear. I stared at her with a raised eyebrow until she fessed up.

"He was perfectly nice but … it felt artificial to me. And …" She looked at me imploringly.

"And?" I prompted impatiently. I wanted her to say it already so I could argue with whatever she said.

"Did you notice the look on his face when I said something about your past boyfriends?"

Was that all? I shrugged. "So he's a little jealous. So what?"

"Are you sure it's just a little jealousy? Everyone has a past and most have other relationships in their past. That shouldn't make him jealous. It's normal." My cat, Smoky, jumped up on the couch and Ellis petted him.

"I think it's cute that he gets a little jealous of my past boyfriends. It means he really cares about me." I smiled. "I think he might even love me. He might even be the one."

Ellis's lips tightened. "Maybe. But the way he acted sort of reminded me of Luke Tillman. It worries me, Keeley."

Luke Tillman was a guy that used to work with Ellis. She never dated him, but he became obsessed with her and started stalking her. She had to get a restraining order on him. When he got busted for violating the order, he finally decided to leave her alone.

I scowled at her. "He's nothing like Luke! I can't believe you're making that comparison!"

Ellis moved the cat out of the way and scooted closer to me. She grabbed my hands. "Keeley, we've been best friends for close to ten years now. You know I love you. I just want you to be safe."

I squeezed her hands. "I love you too, Ellis. I know you care about me. But I'm a big girl and I like Devin. You're wrong about him, you'll see."

She nodded. "I hope so. I want to be wrong this time. It's just ..."

"Just what?" I frowned. *Why couldn't she just like him?*

"It wasn't just the mention of past boyfriends that seemed to bother him. He didn't like the waiter talking to you either." She looked down and fiddled with the fringe on a blanket that was draped over the arm of the couch. "He seems a little possessive."

I smiled. "Is that so bad?"

She shrugged, but I could tell she was still worried. I brushed that away and moved on.

"You just need to get to know him better. We'll go out again next weekend and maybe Steven will be able to come with us."

Ellis blushed and looked down at her left hand where a beautiful engagement ring adorned her ring finger. "He's been really busy with school and work, but we might be able to work it out."

Steven, a few years older than us, was working part-time while going to school to get a law degree.

"Good. I'm sure he and Devin will get along great," I said. "How are the wedding plans coming anyway? Did you guys at least pick a date?"

"I told you we weren't worried about that yet. We'll plan it when he's done with school."

I sighed. "I think I'd at least have to pick a date. And I can't wait to plan a shower for you."

She laughed. "Steven will be finished with school soon. We can plan then. There's no reason to rush. And don't worry, you'll get your chance to plan a shower."

"And someday you'll get to plan mine," I said. "Maybe soon even."

Ellis's face darkened at those words. Her reaction to Devin made my heart sink, but it wouldn't change anything. I was falling in love with him, and I wasn't going to let anyone's objections stop me.

"If you liked the outfit that much, you should have bought it," Devin said, taking a bite of his taco.

I frowned. "I think it's more important for me to pay my electric bill this month."

Devin glanced up at me and met my eyes. "I thought you were getting more regular clients at the salon these days."

"I am, but I had to take Smoky to the vet this month and buy Lois a birthday gift," I said. "There's always something."

He scowled at me. "The way Lois treats you, I don't know why you bother with the pretense of gifts."

I sighed and pushed my food away. Lois was far from perfect and I hated the way she felt about my father, but she was still my aunt and the only family I had. "She still raised me. She loves me in her own way and she's my family."

Devin let that drop with a shake of his head. He picked up his cup and sipped. I went back to eating my burrito and let silence drift between us for a while as I enjoyed the sounds of the people around us in the fast-food Mexican restaurant.

"You should just move in with me," Devin said offhandedly.

My head flew up. "What?"

He met my gaze. "It just makes sense, Kee. We're together most of the time anyway and if you moved in with me, you'd live in a nicer apartment and have more money to spend on other things."

I couldn't deny his logic, but it felt too soon for such a move. Plus, I'd always believed in getting married first. I told him that.

"Come on, Keeley. No one does that anymore."

"Some people do," I said defensively.

He raised his eyebrows at me. "I think you're holding onto little girl princess fantasies and not seeing reality."

I scowled at him.

"Besides, if you did this, we could save up some money. It might come in handy down the road." He looked me in the eyes. "Might make some of the fantasies come true."

My heart fluttered. He didn't say marriage, but what else could he mean? A smile crept across my lips. "Maybe. But what about Smoky? Pets aren't allowed in your building."

"Ellis could take him."

I shook my head. "No, Steven is allergic."

"Lois?" He said before taking another bite of his taco.

I sighed. "Doubtful. She never let me have a pet as a kid."

Devin searched my face. "Is this really going to be what stops us? If it's a problem for us now to move in together, then it'd be a problem if we got married too."

I tried not to notice the fact that he said *if* we got married rather than *when*.

It was hard to think of giving Smoky away. I loved him and didn't want to simply toss him aside. Still, Devin had a point. My cat was only four years old. Was I going to wait for ten years or more to take our relationship to the next level because of the cat?

"What if we both moved and found a place where we could move in together and keep Smoky?" I tried hopefully.

He made a face at me that walked the line between frustration and disgust. "Keeley, we'd never find a place as good as the one I've already got for a reasonable price. You know that's true."

I was disheartened by the fact that he didn't seem to have any concern for my cat. But I supposed I shouldn't be surprised. He'd never shown any interest in Smoky when he was at my place. *Is his lack of concern for my cat enough to stop me from moving our relationship forward?*

No, I couldn't make that a deciding issue. Some people didn't like cats. That didn't make them bad people. And Devin meant too much to me to let him go over this. I knew one more possibility for a home for Smoky, and I hoped it would work out.

"I could ask Jean to take him. She likes animals and she has a house of her own, so there're no rules against it," I said.

Devin flashed a brilliant smile. "Great! Ask her."

"It's a good possibility for the future, but I'm still not sure I'm ready for it yet."

He sighed, and somehow it was enough to make me feel guilty.

"I'll think about it," I said.

Lois stood at the front counter of the salon during a mid-day lull, working on the schedule for the upcoming week. I was nearby tidying up my workstation.

"I think I'll have you and Amber open up this Saturday," Lois said.

"Actually, I was going to ask for Saturday off. I'm moving that day," I said casually.

"Moving? Did you finally save up enough to get a nicer place?"

My chest tightened, both with the excitement of the decision I'd made and with the worry of how Lois was going to react. "No, I'm moving in with Devin."

Dead silence filled the room, and I found myself holding my breath as I waited for her to say something.

"I thought I taught you better than that," she finally said, without turning from the front desk.

"You know I don't share your feelings about men." I put the broom I'd been holding down, leaning it against the wall.

Lois turned to me and her eyes seemed a bit moist. "Yes, I know. But I didn't think you'd be this foolish. You've only been seeing him for a couple of months."

I moved closer to her and looked at her pleadingly. "He's the one, Lois. I'm sure he is."

Instead of softening, her expression went steely. "If you take Saturday off, you'll work full weekends for the next two weeks to make up for it."

"Lois, that's not fair," I begin. "Janet took last Saturday off, and you didn't—"

"That boy ain't no different than any other man. He's scum. He'll break your heart. And don't you come crying to me when he does," Lois cut me off, her voice loud and full of venom. "If you're going to do this, I won't be there to pick up the pieces when it's over. You don't want to listen to me then you're on your own."

She stomped out of the salon and promptly lit a cigarette. I watched her pace the sidewalk as she puffed on it, and my heart sank. Maybe I shouldn't care, but I did. Lois was far from perfect as an aunt and stand-in parent, but she was the only family I had.

I knew she wouldn't be happy with my decision, but I hadn't expected her to be this angry. No matter what had happened between us in the past, she'd never told me not to come to her.

"She was so angry, Jean. She told me she wouldn't be there when he broke my heart," I said, putting some of my clothes in a box. I looked Jean in the eyes. "I mean, I'm sure Devin and I will be happy together, but I can't believe she would push me out like that."

"She's upset about you doing this, but she doesn't mean it, Keeley. If you really need her, she'll be there."

"You didn't see her." I swallowed hard, thinking about the look in Lois's eyes. "I think she meant it."

Jean dropped the pair of jeans she was folding into the box in front of her. Then she scooted over to me and draped an arm around my shoulders. "She's never been good at showing it, but she loves you more than you know. I've been her friend for ages. Trust me on this. She didn't mean it."

I studied Jean's face. "I hope you're right. Our relationship has never been great, but she's the only family I have." I sighed. "I love Devin, and I have to give it a try with him, but I don't want to lose Lois."

"Lois has been suffering the hurt of losing your mother since the day she turned her away. She would never have let Greta go if it hadn't been for the drugs. She knew Greta needed a kind of help she wasn't equipped to offer. But she's been drowning in guilt ever since that night. And it's different with you. She'd never turn you away if you truly needed her."

I nodded reluctantly, deciding to trust Jean's word on this. We went back to packing silently.

Smoky walked up and rubbed against me. I picked him up and nuzzled him. "I'll miss you too, buddy."

"You come by and see him whenever you want," Jean said. "But don't worry about him. He's in good hands."

I smiled. "That I know. Thanks for taking him, Jean. I don't know what I would have done otherwise. I couldn't stand the idea of taking him to the shelter or giving him to someone I don't know."

"No need to thank me. I'm looking forward to having this guy in my life. It'll be nice to have someone to come home to … even if it is a cat rather than a man."

I chuckled. "He's good company. And he loves to curl up in your lap for a romantic comedy."

"Perfect!" Jean grinned. "I've got plenty of those." She taped the flaps of the box she'd just packed and looked at me. "Let's get these boxes to the cars and move on out. We'll come back and collect the little fur-ball once we have you all moved into your new place."

Remember the Butterfly

I grinned. *My new place.* The next chapter of my life was about to start and I was sure it was going to be wonderful.

Chapter Thirty

The first few weeks of living with Devin were as wonderful as I'd expected. We ate breakfast together every morning, took turns cooking dinner, and fell asleep every night curled up in each other's arms. I was happy and my heart felt full. I was sure I'd found what I'd been searching for since the day my father died, someone to love me—someone I could give my love to.

Each day I went to work at the salon smiling, and I made sure Lois saw. I wanted her to know she was wrong. Devin loved me, we were happy, and he wasn't going to break my heart.

I daydreamed about our future. Soon, when we'd saved up some money, we would get married. Then we'd have children, two or three of them. They would be beautiful—how could they not be? I saw them in my mind every night when I closed my eyes with Devin's arms around me. I only wished my father were still around so my children would have a grandparent on my side of the family. Instead, they'd only have Lois, and I didn't know how she would react when that day came. I hoped her opinion of Devin and our being together would soften. I hoped she'd come to see it as a good thing, and I hoped she would love the children I planned to have. If she didn't, at least they would have grandparents, as well as aunts and uncles, on Devin's side.

I smiled to myself with the thought of those future children as I walked toward the garage where Devin worked. I was there to surprise him for lunch.

I glanced around the garage but didn't see Devin. Another mechanic was under a Toyota, so I called out to him. "Hey, is Devin around?"

The man came sliding out quickly on the wheels beneath him. He smiled up at me. "Hey, Keeley. Devin's out on a supply run. He should be back soon if you want to wait."

I smiled back. "Hey, Jimmy. I wanted to surprise him by taking him to lunch. I'll wait for a few minutes and see if he gets back here in time."

"Sure thing. I'll just be under this car if you need anything," Jimmy said.

"All right. What's wrong with the Toyota?" I asked.

"Gas tank is leakin'. I've got to replace it."

"I guess I should have guessed that from the smell," I said.

"Yeah, it's been drippin' all over me. Don't toss any matches this way," Jimmy laughed.

I giggled. "No worries, Jimmy. I don't smoke."

"Keeley?" Devin said, walking into the garage. "What are you doing here?"

I turned toward his voice and grinned. "I came to take you to lunch."

"You didn't tell me you were coming by for lunch today." His voice sounded irritated, which baffled me. Maybe he didn't like surprises.

"I know. I wanted to surprise you," I said brightly.

A scowl stayed etched on his face.

"If today isn't good for you, I'll just go to lunch by myself and we can do it another time."

After a brief hesitation, he said, "We can go today. Just let me go take care of something in the office."

I smiled even though he still didn't look happy about my visit. "Sure. I'll wait."

"No more flirting with my girl, Jimmy," Devin said before walking through the door to the office.

Is that what he thought Jimmy had been doing—flirting with me? I was baffled. I wanted to think he was joking, but the tone in his voice made it clear he wasn't.

Jimmy started to slide back under the car, then stopped, looked at me as though he wanted to say something, then shook his head and continued to slide back in place for his work.

An unsettled feeling washed through me and left my stomach heavy as if I'd swallowed a rock. I hated that feeling. It brought back memories of the time before my mother left when she'd been out of her mind on drugs.

I closed my eyes, took a deep breath, and pushed the feeling back. I *would not* let any momentary feeling mess up even one day of my new life with Devin.

I opened my eyes just in time to watch Devin walk back into the garage. He was still scowling. "Come on, let's go if we're going," he said, walking past me and heading to his car without waiting for me.

I stood still for a moment, watching him. Then I hurried behind him. I suggested we go to a restaurant that he liked. He didn't respond but drove to the place I'd suggested.

We ate in total silence, his agitation never fading, then promptly drove back to the garage.

Once we arrived in the parking lot, Devin turned off the car and said, "Don't stop by anymore without checking with me first. I don't like surprises." Then he got out of the car and walked away.

I sat in his car for several minutes, bewildered again by his reaction. Then I numbly went to my car and drove back to the salon.

When Devin came home that evening, I had dinner ready for him. I met him at the door with a smile and forced it to stay in place even when he didn't return it.

"I've got dinner ready for you. I made your favorite—tacos," I said brightly.

He turned a steely gaze on me. "You think you can make this all better with food—like I'll just forget?"

I shook my head. *Is everything I do going to upset him?* "Forget what? There's nothing to forget. I just wanted to make up for surprising you when I guess you don't like that."

"It wasn't only that and you know it. Don't play stupid."

What is he talking about?

"I'm not playing stupid, Devin. I really don't know what you're talking about." I took a step back from him, trying to get some distance from the anger emanating from him.

"You want to act like you don't know—fine. I'll remind you about the way you were acting with Jimmy before I got there today," he said in a pinched voice.

I furrowed my brow. "I don't know what you mean. I was just talking to him while I waited for you. I'd only been there for about two minutes before you got there.

Devin stomped forward so quickly it made me gasp. Then he grabbed me and pushed me up against the wall. "Do you think I didn't see the way you two were looking at each other? Or that I didn't hear you giggling?"

I stared at him wide-eyed, mouth agape. *What is happening?*

"Devin, I ..." I stammered, struggling to get my breath back and to understand what was going on. "I was just laughing because he said something funny, a joke about the leaky gas tank he was working on. That's all."

I cried out as his fingers dug into my shoulders. "Devin, you're hurting me!"

He kept his hands tight, his eyes flashing at me. "You don't need to be talking to him about anything. He's a player, after one thing with every girl. You're a fool if you don't see it."

My shoulders screaming in pain, I pleaded, "I'm sorry, Devin. Please, let go."

A tear ran down my cheek and Devin's face changed. It was almost like someone waking up from a dream. He released my shoulders and stepped back. "I'll go wash up for dinner. It smells great," he said before walking off toward the bathroom.

I stood still, trembling as tears slid down my face. *Am I supposed to act like nothing happened when he comes back?* I realized I didn't want him to come back.

Looking at the door, I contemplated grabbing my purse and running to my car. *Where would I go?* I couldn't go to Lois. She'd made that more than clear. I could go to Ellis's apartment or Jean's house.

I started forward, swiping at my tears, but before I took two steps, Devin appeared.

"The tacos smell great, Kee. Let's go eat, and you can tell me all about your day at the salon," He said, walking to the table as if nothing had happened between us.

I stood staring for a moment, crossing my arms and rubbing both shoulders where his fingers had just dug in. The sore spots screamed under my fingers. *Yes, it had really happened.* But Devin was acting like he had no memory of it. *Did he expect me to do the same?*

Sniffling to regain control as best I could, I ambled to the table and sat down across from Devin. I didn't scoot my chair up to the table. I wanted to stay as far away from him as I could.

He smiled at me and a shiver ran up my spine.

"How was work?" he asked.

I tried to swallow, but my mouth was dry. "Fine," I squeaked.

Devin began to load a taco shell and paid no mind to my hesitancy.

With wooden movements, I picked up a shell and dumped some meat, cheese, and lettuce into it. Then I took a shaky bite, but I couldn't taste it and my stomach rolled in response. I managed a few more bites before I gave up entirely.

When he was done eating, Devin glanced at my plate. "Not hungry?"

I shook my head.

"Are you feeling okay?"

Am I feeling okay? No, I'm not. You just assaulted me! Real words wouldn't come out of my mouth. I only stared at him, disbelieving.

He stood up and came to my side. I flinched when he reached up and put his hand on my head. "Well, you don't feel hot. But it could be a stomach bug. You better sleep in the guest room tonight. I don't want to get sick."

I looked up at him, surprise on my face. It was not because he suggested I sleep in the guest room, but because I hadn't even thought about how I'd be able to lay in bed next to him after the way he had grabbed me—after the way he acted like it didn't happen.

"I'd take the guest room and let you have ours, but that bed gives me a backache," he said in response to the surprise on my face.

I looked back down at the table, then nodded. He could think I was sick, and I'd sleep alone. I only wished I had Smoky there for comfort.

I awoke the next morning disoriented. After a few seconds, I remembered where I was—the guest room. My eyes were swollen from crying myself to sleep the previous night. And my head hurt, but not as much as my shoulders did.

Reluctantly, I pushed back the covers and got out of bed. Opening the door as quietly as I could, I peered out into the hall. The master bedroom door was wide open, and the apartment was quiet. Devin had already left.

I sighed in relief and padded down the hall to the bathroom.

Looking in the mirror, I was dismayed by my puffy, red-rimmed eyes. I looked terrible. I'd have to try a cold pack on my eyes. But first, I needed a shower. That would make me feel a little better.

I stepped into the spray of the water and winced when it pelted against the sore and torn skin on my shoulders. Glancing slowly to my right side, I saw the purple, swollen finger marks—thumb mark on the front and four fingers down the outside.

I didn't want to cry again but looking at the angry marks on my skin brought a torrent of emotion I couldn't control. I crumpled onto the floor of the shower and let my tears mix with the water spraying down on me. It wasn't until the water began to cool that I forced myself to stand up, stop crying, and finish showering.

After drying off and wrapping my hair in a towel, I walked into the master bedroom and pulled out some clothes to put on. As I dressed, I looked around the room. The day before, it had felt like my room. I was happy there. But it didn't feel like mine anymore. And, though I never thought I would, I wished I could be back in my old room in Lois's apartment.

Of course, that couldn't happen. Lois wouldn't take me back. But that didn't mean I had to stay where I was. Glancing around again, I decided to come home after work and pack all my stuff before Devin left work. I'd go to Ellis.

She'd let me stay with her until I found another apartment of my own.

With that decision made, I felt better.

Work went better that day than I'd expected. The ice packs I put on my eyes took the swelling away and the redness faded before I got to the salon. Of course, I thought my face would still give me away. I'd never been any good at keeping secrets from Lois. But, somehow, I managed to act normally all day despite the way I felt. Lois didn't notice a thing, or if she did, she didn't say anything. Neither did any of the other stylists.

When the workday came to an end, I headed back home to pack my things. But when I opened the front door, there was a large bouquet of roses and carnations on the table by the door.

I eyed it, unsure whether or not I wanted to take a closer look. The certainty of my decision that morning made me feel better. I didn't want to back track.

Curiosity got the better of me, and I stepped forward and found a card attached. Plucking it from the holder, I opened it and read the message.

Keeley, I'm so sorry for the way I treated you last night. I shouldn't have let my temper get the better of me. I hope you're feeling better. Relax and I'll do the cooking tonight. –Devin.

I stood for a long time, staring at the note. *If he's sorry, shouldn't I forgive him?*

My eyes traveled to the nearby wall where Devin had pinned me the previous evening. *What if he does it again? What if it's worse next time?*

Then I looked at the flowers again and the note in my hand. He'd gone out of his way to let me know he was sorry. He meant it and, I decided, he deserved a second chance. *Hadn't he been good to me every other day since I'd met him?* Yes, he had. He loved me. Everyone loses their temper once in a while. I couldn't give up on our relationship so easily.

Dropping my keys on the table next to the flowers, I decided to do exactly what Devin suggested. I turned on the TV and dropped into the couch cushions.

When Devin came home, he was sweet and accommodating. He doted on me and cooked a wonderful steak dinner. We watched a movie together, and he didn't complain when I chose a romantic comedy.

After the movie, we got ready for bed. I changed into a tank top and shorts to sleep in and walked to my side of the bed.

"Are you serious?" The edge in Devin's voice surprised me.

I turned and gawked at him. "About what?"

"You know I feel terrible about what happened. Do you have to throw it in my face like that?" He directed his gaze to my bare shoulders and the ugly marks on them.

I was flabbergasted. "Wh … what do you want me to do?"

He looked away with a pained expression. "Just cover your shoulders up until the marks go away. It hurts me to see them and know what I did to you." He looked at me again with watery eyes. "Unless you want to keep punishing me."

It was strange to have his actions thrown out as something I needed to protect him from. I was the one feeling the pain of those marks, and I'd feel them until they healed. Why should he be protected from even seeing them when it was his fault?

Still, was he that upset by what he'd done? If he was, that was good, wasn't it?

"I ... okay, I'll get a different shirt," I said.

He smiled. "Thank you. I love you, Keeley."

Still uncertain what to think of his reaction to the marks on my skin, I searched his eyes, but they didn't give anything away.

"I love you, too, Devin," I said hesitantly before changing my top and climbing into bed.

Chapter Thirty-one

My shoulders healed and life went on quietly for several weeks. Devin and I settled into a routine that worked well for us. I was sure the incident when he'd lost his temper was a one-time thing. He'd been so contrite. Surely, he wouldn't let it happen again.

It was Tuesday and I was in the kitchen making dinner as I always did because that was my day off. I sniffed the pot of tomato sauce on the stove and tossed in some chopped onion, garlic, and oregano. After stirring the pot, I tasted it and decided it was just right. I hadn't ever made spaghetti for Devin before and I wanted it to be perfect.

I put noodles in a pot of boiling water and sliced some French bread. All that was left was making the salad.

Once everything was ready, I checked my make-up and brushed my hair, so I'd look nice when Devin came in.

Just before the noodles were finished cooking, he walked in the door. The pinched look on his face disturbed me. Since our bad night, I found myself getting nervous anytime he was less than happy.

I cautiously walked into the living room and smiled at him. "How was your day?"

He glared at me. "I don't want to talk about it."

"Okay." I stepped back. His agitated tone made me want to keep my distance.

Devin sighed and said, "I'm glad to be home. I'll try to leave the day behind."

I tried another smile but kept the space between us. "Well, dinner is about ready. Maybe that will make you feel better. I made spaghetti."

"Sounds good. I'm sure that will help me feel a little better." He tossed his keys down and walked to the table.

I hurried into the kitchen, drained the water from the noodles, and dumped them into a large bowl. I carried that and the sauce to the table. The bread and salad were already there.

"Go ahead and get yours," I said, sitting down.

Devin piled his plate with noodles and sauce, then smiled at me before fixing his salad and starting with that.

I filled my plate and salad bowl and began to eat. I was halfway through my salad when Devin took a bite of the spaghetti and immediately stared at me.

"What's wrong?" I asked.

"You put onions in this, didn't you?" His words came out in an accusatory, biting tone.

I pressed my back into my chair, anxiety coursing through me. "Yes."

Devin swept his arm across the table and sent his plate flying into the wall.

I jumped in shock and stared at him while my heart hammered against my chest.

"You know I don't eat onions," he roared. "I told you what they do to me. Are you trying to make me sick?"

My heart racing, I gaped at him. Then, finding my voice, I said, "I don't remember you telling me that. I'm sorry."

Before he said another word, I hopped up and began cleaning up the mess he'd made. "I have some more sauce left in the jar that doesn't have any onions. I'll heat some up for you."

As I stood up and turned to go toward the kitchen, Devin grabbed my arm and pulled me to the table. I struggled to keep hold of the plate and spaghetti I'd cleaned up from the floor but lost my hold when Devin tightened his grip and dug into my skin.

Gasping, I cried, "Devin, you're hurting me!"

He glared at me without concern for the pain he was causing. "I *know* I told you about the onions. Don't pretend you didn't know." His voice was a growl.

"If you did, I don't remember. I'm not pretending."

He began twisting my arm until I cried out in pain. Tears sprung from my eyes. "Devin, you're going to break my arm!"

He loosened his grip on my arm by only a minute degree, then used his other hand to take hold of my face. "Your tears are pathetic." He stood up and pushed me back until I was against the wall again.

"Please let me go, Devin. It was just a mistake. You don't want to hurt me. You said you'd never do it again," I begged as fear rushed through me.

"Was it a mistake?" He narrowed his eyes at me. "Or did you want to make me sick?"

"Why would I want to make you sick?" I tried to reason with him. I couldn't imagine why he'd think I did it on purpose.

His breath was hot on my face, and I tried to turn my head away. He held it firm and seemed incensed by my effort. "Don't play innocent. You *did* do it on purpose. That's why you don't want to look me in the eye. You probably thought if I was sick, you could sneak out and see Jimmy."

"What?" I was stunned. *Was he serious?* "Devin, I don't have any interest in seeing Jimmy. I told you that last time." My arm was burning now, and I couldn't stop the tears that continued to course down my cheeks.

"Then why does he keep talking about you and asking if you're going to come by the garage again?"

"I ... I don't—" My attempt to answer his accusation stopped when he let go of my face and punched me hard in the stomach. For a moment, I couldn't get any breath and white flashes exploded in my vision.

Devin let go of my arm and stepped back just before I threw up and crumpled to the floor. He looked down on me in disgust. "You're pathetic, Keeley." He turned and began to walk off toward the bedroom. "Clean the mess up," he called out before slamming the bedroom door.

I'm not sure how long I sat on the floor sobbing before I pulled myself up and cleaned up the mess. Devin didn't come back out of the bedroom that evening and I was glad he didn't. Still, I jumped at every little sound I heard and tried hard not to make any sound myself.

When the mess was cleaned up, I went to the guest room and curled up on the bed, pulling the covers over my head. I thought about leaving right away and going to Ellis, but I didn't want to leave and have to come back to get my things. When I left, I didn't want to ever come back, and most of what I needed was in the master bedroom and bathroom. I'd go in there in the morning after Devin left for work and pack all my things. Then, when I'd finished my workday, I'd head to Ellis's place and tell her what had happened. I could stay with her until I got a new place of my own.

When morning came, I set about doing exactly what I had planned. No way was I going to come back and be swayed by a pretty bouquet or any other gift like last time. I was done with Devin. I wouldn't let him hurt me again.

I packed everything that truly mattered to me and stuffed it all in my car. Anything I'd left behind, Devin could keep. Then I drove to work hoping I'd done a good enough job with my makeup to cover the marks on my chin. I was pretty sure they weren't visible, but my arm still hurt with every movement and it was hard to walk with my back all the way straight because of the pain in my belly from Devin's punch.

It was all over now, though, and I didn't need anyone other than Ellis to know what Devin had done to me. Their pity would only make it worse. I'd hide the pain.

"Keeley, bring me that hairdryer from Margo's station, would you? Mine is on the fritz," Lois said about halfway through the day.

"Sure." I reached around to Margo's station, right next to mine, and grabbed the hairdryer with my good arm. Then, walking across the room, I held it out for Lois to take.

She reached out, taking the hairdryer with one hand and patting my badly bruised arm with the other.

I inhaled sharply, resisting the urge to cry out. The pain was searing.

Lois furrowed her brow at me in alarm. She laid the hairdryer down on her counter and then, taking my hand gently, pushed my sleeve up. She was careful and gentle, but even the brush of fabric was painful. The tear that rolled down my face, however, was not because of the physical pain, but because of the shame I felt watching Lois discover the bruises. But, strangely, I felt unable to pull away from her. It was almost as if I was a kid again and she was in charge. But once she saw the purple marks, there was a certain relief in having her know.

She looked up at my face. "He did this to you, that man you moved in with?" Her voice was low, almost a growl.

Tears flooded my eyes and my throat was clogged with emotion. I tried to answer her, but couldn't speak, so I nodded.

To my surprise, Lois eased me forward into her arms and held me while I cried. "He won't do it again. You're coming back home with me tonight."

I melted into her and cried even harder with the unexpected love and support. My fingers curled into the fabric of her shirt as I let my misery out. Lois's arms around me gave comfort like I hadn't known since my father died.

Everyone in the salon was surely watching, but I couldn't stop the tears. I didn't even think I wanted to.

Moving back into my old room was like wrapping up in a warm blanket on a cold night. The smallness of the room was comforting rather than confining. The old colorful quilt relaxed me. And seeing pictures of my mother and my father still sitting on the desk warmed my heart. The distance that had always been between Lois and me fizzled away. She really did care.

"Keeley," Lois's voice called softly after a quick knock on my door.

"Come on in," I answered.

She opened the door and stepped inside. We studied each other, neither sure what to say.

"I wanted to be wrong, you know," Lois said. "I wanted it to work out and for you to be happy." She paused, looking down at the worn carpet. "I'm wary of all men, so I hoped the way I felt about that fella you ran off with was wrong."

"Ellis got some bad vibes from him too. I didn't listen to her. I wanted him to love me. I needed to believe that he did." I twisted a loose thread on the quilt around my finger. Saying the next words was hard. "I missed being loved. I wanted to feel that again."

Lois's head snapped up. She stared into my eyes and hers were filled with sadness. "I know I'm not good at showin' it, but I always loved you. That's why I wanted to protect you."

I nodded. What else could I do? She had been right.

"But I tried too hard. I pushed my fears on you too much. It overpowered everything else," she said.

"I wanted to find someone like my father. I wanted love like that again. And you ..." I couldn't say the words. Here she was giving me refuge after I'd been so foolish. I couldn't condemn her. My eyes turned away.

"I put him down. Is that what you wanted to say?"

My eyes made their way back to hers. I was torn between the anger that still simmered inside me when I thought about her ugly words against my father and contrition for still feeling that anger when she was rescuing me. "It wasn't just that. It was the way you treated all men. You wanted me to believe they were all bad, but ... my father was a good man." I shrugged and let my eyes fall back to the quilt, expecting the same response from her that I'd always gotten before. When she didn't respond right away, I added, "I know you don't agree, but he was and he loved me."

There was a long silence and this time, I resisted the urge to fill it.

"I know he was," Lois said.

My eyes darted back to hers in surprise. "But you always argued with me. You wouldn't let me talk about him."

She pursed her lips, then said, "Men like him are rare in my experience. I didn't want you all starry-eyed about boys and ending up with a broken heart ... or worse." Her gaze fell on my arm, and I instinctively pulled it close to my body.

I took a deep breath and pressed on with the knowledge I'd gained years ago from Jean. "It was more than that. You could have just told me that not all men were like him. Instead, you hated him and said terrible things about him." My brows knit together as I tried not to cry. "You tried to ruin my memory of him, make me think he wasn't what I remembered."

"Ah hell," she muttered and sat on the end of my bed.

I wrapped the string around my finger again waiting for her to say more.

"I was mad at him, okay?" She waited, but I stayed silent. "And I was even madder at him because it was easier than being mad at myself."

I looked at her, my eyes asking her to continue.

"Greta died because I didn't help her. It was easier to blame your father. But he didn't do anything different than what I did. We both sent her away. Maybe if we hadn't—if he had tried harder, if I had tried harder—she might still be alive."

I reached out and took Lois's hand. "Daddy probably would have kept trying if he wasn't worried about her hurting me when she was out of her head. But I don't think that matters. She needed to help herself. She couldn't get better because she didn't want to bad enough ... even for me she didn't." As those words crossed my lips, sadness filled my chest bringing tears to my eyes.

Lois put a hand on my cheek. "I miss her every day. But having you with me always helped."

"It did?"

She let her hand drop and studied me with watery eyes. "Was I so harsh that you didn't see that at all?"

Not knowing how to answer without adding to the pain she was feeling, I shrugged again.

"I'm sorry. Guess I was never cut out for the job of raisin' a kid. I wish I'd done better by you," she said.

I took her hand again and squeezed it. "Let's start new today."

When she met my eyes again, the look in hers was gratitude. She smiled and nodded. "Let's do that." She let go of my hand and stood up. "There's something I need to tell you about."

She left the room, and I sat there wondering if she had intended for me to follow. I stood up to do that, but she came back into my room before I could take the first step.

Lois held a piece of paper out to me. My brow knit with curiosity, I took it from her and looked at it.

"This is a bank statement," I said, confused.

"It's your bank statement," she said.

I frowned at her, still confused. "What are you talking about? This isn't mine."

"Yes, it is. I started this account when you first came here, and I put money in it every paycheck. I figured I'd need it for school or your wedding …"

"Wedding? You would have paid for a wedding for me?" I was beyond shocked.

"Under the right circumstances." She paused. "I just figured it'd be needed for something. Now's the right time. You can use this money for whatever you need."

I glanced at the statement and saw the amount. The account had over thirty thousand dollars in it. "Lois, this is too much. How did you even save this much?"

"I managed my money carefully. And only I get to decide how much is too much. You ain't gonna tell me what to do with my money. If I say it's yours, then it's yours." She met my eyes with determination. "There's just one thing I'll ask."

I swallowed and nodded.

"My one condition is that you keep this account secret. Just between you and me. You never ever tell that," she shook her head and grimaced with the next word, "Devin about it."

"Of course, I won't. I don't plan to see him again."

She looked away. "Yeah, well, men like him don't usually disappear that easy. Just keep this to yourself." She handed me a debit card and another slip of paper. "Make sure you keep all this in a place where he'll never find it."

I shivered at her words. *Would Devin refuse to let me go?*

I looked at what was in my hand. The slip of paper had a PIN on it. "I will."

Chapter Thirty-two

The following day when I arrived at work, flowers were delivered to me. I threw them in the trash without even looking at the card. When I glanced at Lois, she nodded her approval, and I felt strengthened by her support.

The next day a man showed up from an expensive candy store with a box of chocolates and insisted on reading the card to me aloud. I tried to refuse the delivery, but he read on anyway.

Keeley, you are mine and always will be.

A shiver went up my spine as he read the words. To someone who didn't know what had happened, it sounded like a declaration of love. I knew it was, instead, a declaration of ownership. He wouldn't just let me go.

I grabbed the box of chocolates from the man, threw them in the trash, and pushed him out the door.

A few days went by with no word from Devin, and I hoped he'd decided to give up. Then, at the end of the day on Friday, a week and a half after I'd walked out on him, I slid into the driver's seat of my car and felt a hand wrap around my face, covering my mouth.

His lips beside my ear, Devin's voice came in a harsh whisper, "I told you: you're mine and you're coming home with me."

Tears slipped down my cheeks as fear sliced through me. I shook my head furiously.

Devin's other hand swung forward and took hold of my throat. I reached up and tried to pry his hands away, but he was too strong. He laughed as I continued to fight. Then the hand on my throat tightened, making it hard to breathe and harder to fight.

"I know you think you can get away from me. You'll file for a restraining order or try to hide. Don't bother. I'll always find you and no piece of paper will stop me. And if you try to stay with someone so they can protect you, then I'll hurt them too."

I whimpered, and Devin loosened his grip on my neck a tiny bit. I sucked in a lungful of air.

"You listen to me and you listen good," he said. "When I let go of you, you're going to go back to Lois's place and pack up your stuff. You'll convince her you want to come back to me. Then you'll come home, and you won't ever try to leave me again. If you do, I'll make you pay like you can't imagine. I'll break that pretty little face, so no one even wants to look at it again. And every time you look in the mirror, you'll know you're mine."

He pulled his hands away so fast I fell forward against the steering wheel. Feeling beaten and hopeless, I laid there and sobbed for several minutes. Then, sitting up slowly, I glanced around. He was gone and I didn't see his car anywhere. I thought about driving to the police station, but I'd heard the stories of other women who found themselves in situations like this. I knew Devin was probably right. They'd tell me to file for an order of protection and I'd have a piece of paper. What good would that do? And what if Devin did go after Lois or Ellis? I couldn't let that happen. I'd gotten myself into this mess and I wouldn't let them suffer for it.

When I arrived at Lois's apartment, I covered the marks on my neck with a scarf I'd left in my car a few days before. It didn't go with what I was wearing, but that didn't matter. I needed to convince Lois I was doing this of my own free will.

Before leaving my car, I took several deep breaths and prepared myself for the acting job I needed to pull off. I'd never been good at lying, but this time I had to lie. When I felt sufficiently distanced from my emotions, I slipped out of the car and headed into the building.

"There you are," Lois said when I walked in. "I thought you got off at four today."

I turned to her with an impassive look. "I did. I … was talking to Devin."

She jumped up from her seat on the couch. "Did he hurt you?"

I swallowed and felt the bruises forming on my neck as if they were on fire. I forced the feelings back and answered Lois without emotion. "No. We talked. And … I'm moving back in with him."

"Keeley, no! Whatever he said, you can't fall for it. If he could brutalize you once, he'll do it again." Lois rushed over to me and took hold of the arm that wasn't injured. Her eyes pleaded with me. "You deserve better than the likes of him."

It made my heart ache to lie to her. We'd finally formed a real bond, and I was ruining that. I wanted more than anything to tell her the truth and show her my neck. I wanted to wrap my arms around her and feel the safety of her embrace, but I couldn't do that. I wouldn't.

"He loves me. And I love him." The words went acrid in my mouth. I forced them to come out with enough sincerity for her to believe it, at least I thought so.

She searched my eyes, and I tried with all my might to keep them from giving me away. But she'd always been able to see through me.

"I don't believe you. He's making you do this," Lois said.

I turned my eyes away from hers. "I'm going to pack my things now. I'm doing this," I said without addressing her assertion. These words I could make believable because they were the truth. I was going to do what I had to so that no one else suffered Devin's wrath.

"If I can't change your mind, then at least make sure he never knows about the bank account. Promise me that, Keeley."

I looked into her eyes. "I promise." I'd already hidden the debit card and information in an out-of-sight compartment at my station in the salon. Devin wouldn't find it there.

Unpacking my things at Devin's apartment was a painful process. I took each item out of my toiletry bag and placed it back in the bathroom—hairbrush on the vanity, toothbrush in the holder next to Devin's. I stared at those toothbrushes, his blue one and my purple one, and my mind screamed, *No! They shouldn't be together! We shouldn't be together! I want to go home!*

Then I thought of Lois and Ellis and Jean. They were the people I loved, the ones who would help me if I asked because they loved me. And they were the people who would pay for it if I didn't stay with Devin. How could I put their safety at risk? They didn't choose Devin. Why should they pay for my mistake? I couldn't ask them to.

Forcing my eyes away from the toothbrushes, I went into the bedroom and began unpacking my clothes. Nothing had changed. The drawers I'd emptied when I left, remained empty. The space I'd left in the closet was still open space.

Devin had left them this way because he knew he'd make me come back.

I put my clothes back in the empty spaces and my stomach began to roll, but I didn't let any tears come. If I was going to do this, I couldn't cry all the time. I had to find a way to be numb.

Numb is what I forced myself to be when the unpacking was done, and I went to the kitchen to make Devin's dinner. I wouldn't eat. Though I was working to be numb, my stomach wasn't listening yet. If I ate, I knew I'd throw up.

When Devin came to the table, he ate his dinner and talked to me about his day at work, everything that had happened that day before he broke into my car. He acted like I'd never left, and he didn't seem concerned about the fact that I wasn't eating. Why should he be? I was his now the same way any other object in the apartment was his. What I felt was irrelevant, and if he did ask me, it wasn't because he cared, nor did he want to hear how I really felt. I understood that now. I was there to accommodate him, to make him happy. And we both knew what would happen if I failed in any way.

When dinner was finished and I'd washed all the dishes, I sat on the couch with Devin and we watched the TV shows he liked. He put his arm around me and pulled me close to him. I reminded myself to be numb. *Just watch the show*, I told myself, *focus on that.*

It worked for a while. Then Devin turned off the TV.

"Come on, time for bed," he said with a hungry look that made my stomach drop.

No, no, no! I can't do this!

I had to. The sore spots on my neck and the arm that still throbbed reminded me what the alternative was. And he still might take what he wanted.

I swallowed hard and forced the bile down as I stood up.

Devin didn't wait for me. He was already in the bedroom by the time I reached the hall and had turned off the living room lights as he went.

I stared down the dark hallway to the lighted bedroom at the end. My legs felt like rubber as I urged them to move. *No, no, no!—Yes, you must.*

I tried to remember what it felt like when I had first moved into this apartment—when I'd been madly in love with Devin and wanted to be with him. Maybe if I could remember what that was like I could force myself to feel it again. It wasn't so long ago, only a matter of a few months. But, no, I couldn't do it. Those feelings seemed like a distant memory. Recapturing them was like trying to make a hummingbird stay still. It didn't work.

When I reached the bedroom, I walked through to the bathroom. Devin was almost finished brushing his teeth, the blue toothbrush in his hand. I picked up the purple one and squeezed some toothpaste on with shaky hands. I brushed my teeth slowly and thoroughly. Then I slowly flossed and slowly brushed my hair.

Devin had already left the bathroom and was waiting for me in bed.

If I went slow enough, maybe he would fall asleep before I got to bed. As I washed my face and put on moisturizer, I prayed he would fall asleep.

When I walked into the bedroom, Devin was wide awake. My stomach twisted. I turned my back to him as I undressed, squeezing my eyes shut and willing myself not to cry.

I slid into the bed and Devin's hands were on me, all over me. I told myself to be numb.

Chapter Thirty-three

Two months after moving back in with Devin, I found myself kneeling over the toilet, my breakfast leaving my stomach almost as soon as it had gotten there. When the retching stopped, I stood up and rinsed my mouth out. I swished with a little Listerine and brushed my hair back into place. Then my stomach clenched, and I was on my knees again.

After cleaning myself up, I called in sick to work. *Maybe it's the flu.*

I spent the day on the couch while Devin was at work. By the time he came home, I was feeling fine and had started dinner. In fact, I was more than fine. I was ravenous. I ate everything on my plate and then got a second helping.

"Careful there," Devin said. "You don't want to ruin the figure I love."

My back turned to him, I grimaced at his words. "I'm just hungry because I didn't eat lunch," I told him, turning to glance at him with a forced smile.

When I found myself back on the bathroom floor, hanging my head over the toilet the next morning, I knew it wasn't the flu. *But I was so careful. How could this have happened?*

It shouldn't have happened. I'd always taken my pills. But it did happen—somehow. A pregnancy test confirmed that. I stared at the test stick in my hand in disbelief, willing it to change its answer. It couldn't be true. I'd been so careful. Yet, I knew deep inside that it was true.

I should have been happy and celebrating. After all, I'd always wanted a baby. *But not now, not like this.* My heart filled with dread, worry, and sadness. But above all, I felt ice-cold fear.

I wrapped the pregnancy test, box and all, in some toilet paper and then stuffed that in the plastic bag from the store before shoving it in the trash can. Sinking to the floor, I covered my face with my hands and cried. Moving one hand to my belly, I pressed down, trying to, in some way, reach the life inside that couldn't yet be seen or felt. Even invisible as it was, I felt a love for it that was unexplainable, and that made me weep all the more. *What would happen when Devin found out?*

Casting a pained glance at the trash can and hoping Devin wouldn't find the pregnancy test, I picked myself up off the bathroom floor. I didn't know what I was going to do now, but somehow, someway, I had to get away from Devin before the baby came. I wouldn't let my child grow up here in this toxic place.

I walked out of the bathroom and paced the living room for a while. My mind filled with thoughts about the life within me. Touching my still-flat stomach, I imagined the baby I couldn't see. *Was it a boy or a girl? What would it look like?* For some reason, the image my mind conjured up looked a lot like my mother, a thought that brought tears to my eyes.

Thinking again about the possibility that Devin would find the pregnancy test, I went back to the bathroom and pulled the bag out of the little trash can. I'd take it to the dumpster outside. I needed some time to think things through before Devin found out about the baby. Maybe he wouldn't even have to find out. I'd find a way out. I had to. Someone else was counting on me now.

"Keeley, what in the world are you doing?" Lois asked.

I glanced up at her. "What do you mean? I'm sweeping."

She raised one eyebrow. "You've been sweeping that same spot for the last five minutes. How clean do you think you can get it?"

I looked down at the little pile of hair on the floor. She was right. All I needed to do now was get the dustpan and be done with it. I'd been lost in my thoughts. I needed to figure out the right plan of escape. Devin was mean but he wasn't stupid. If I got it wrong, I'd pay a high price for the mistake.

"Sorry," I said to Lois. "I guess my mind was somewhere else. I'll get the dustpan and finish this."

"Mr. Hanson will be glad. He's been waiting on you."

I nodded and went to the corner for the dustpan.

"Your mind has been somewhere else a lot lately," Lois quipped when I was emptying the hair into the trash.

I cast her a sheepish glance. "Sorry. I guess it has."

"Just make sure it doesn't wander when you're cutting someone's hair."

"I will." I called Mr. Hanson over and prepped him for his haircut, then began my work, making sure to keep my head in the game.

When the workday ended and the salon had been cleaned up, Lois sidled up to me and put an arm around my shoulders. "What's going on?" She asked.

"Nothing. Why would you think something is going on?" I worked hard to keep my voice light.

I saw her scowl in my peripheral vision. "I know you better than that. Something has got your mind in another place nearly all the time lately. So, what's up?"

Emotion rising in me, I shrugged out from under her arm. "Did I mess up anyone's hair?" Agitation filled my voice. I wasn't really mad at her, but I was constantly on edge and only a little prodding caused some of it to spew out.

Lois's eyebrows lifted. "And you're touchy."

"I'm not touchy. But I'm not a child either. I did my job. I don't have to explain why my mind wanders sometimes as long as I do my job." I stared at her in a challenging way. Even though I knew my reactions were overblown, having her think I was touchy was better than letting her see what was actually going on. I didn't want to tell anyone about the baby. If anyone knew, there was that much more chance Devin would find out.

Still, a part of me wanted her to know. Holding this inside was tearing me apart.

After a long silence, she put her hands on her hips. "Fine, you're right. You're a big girl. If you don't want to tell me what's going on, then I guess you don't have to." Her words were reasonable, and her voice was even, but hurt filled her eyes. They screamed at me that she wanted to hold onto the progress we'd made. She wanted to be close to me.

I wanted that too, but I couldn't put her in a position where she might become a target for Devin's wrath.

I reached out and took her hand. Then, in a softer voice, I said, "I'm sorry. I didn't mean to snap at you. It's not a big deal. I'm okay."

She nodded, but her eyes remained skeptical. She pulled me into a hug, which surprised me because it was something she'd seldom done when I was a kid. As the shock wore off, I let my arms wrap around her.

"Please," she whispered in my ear, "tell me if you need me. Tell me if you're in trouble. I'll help you."

I squeezed my eyes shut as they burned from the tears that wanted to come. I held them back, and as I pulled away, I forced a weak smile. "I'm okay. Devin and I have been doing fine."

She nodded slowly. Then, before she had a chance to ask any questions, I said, "I need to go. I've got to stop at the store on the way home. I'll see you tomorrow." As soon as the words were out of my mouth, I turned and walked to my car.

 Chapter Thirty-four

After a month of thinking through all the possible ways I might get away from Devin, I decided to drive to a motel. I left after my shift at work on a Saturday. I wasn't scheduled to work for the next two days, so Lois wouldn't worry about me until then.

I took only what I needed, so it wouldn't be obvious to Devin that I'd left—at least not right away. I'd probably get an extra hour or two before he started looking for me. I drove to the next town and found a cheap motel. Trying to be careful, I registered under a fake name and paid with cash I'd taken from the account Lois gave me.

Once checked in, I took my small suitcase and let myself into my room. It was shabby but at least it looked clean. I ambled across the beige carpet and lifted my suitcase onto the rack in the corner. Glancing at the chipped wooden dresser, I decided it was better to leave everything in my suitcase. There was no way to know how long I'd be able to stay here.

I took my toiletries out and decided to take a shower. Moving into the bathroom, I let my eyes roam over the room. Several cracks were visible in the tile floor and there was a sink with a very small vanity and a mirror hanging above it that was also cracked. The toilet and shower looked pretty normal and everything was reasonably clean. I undressed and started the water.

Stepping into the shower, I relished the hot water running over me, easing the tension in my muscles. Washing away the dirty way I'd felt ever since I went back to live with Devin. I hoped I'd never have to feel his hands on me again. I hoped my baby would never have the misfortune of meeting his or her father. I realized now that Devin didn't know how to love another person. He only loved himself.

Finished with my shower, I put on a set of purple pajamas and climbed onto the queen-sized bed. I turned on the TV and tried to pay attention. It was the first time in nearly three months that I'd been able to watch what I wanted. But I couldn't focus on it. My eyes kept darting to the door to make sure it was closed and locked tight. It was—every time—yet I couldn't stop checking.

Then I started to think about Lois. When Tuesday rolled around and I didn't show up for work, Lois was going to worry. Of course, that was assuming Devin didn't go to the salon or Lois's apartment looking for me before then. *What if he hurt her trying to find out where I'd gone?*

Ellis would worry too. We always got together for lunch on Thursdays. If not sooner, Ellis would know by then. Sometimes she called me in the evening to talk about plans for her wedding. Even though Ellis said she didn't want to make plans until Steven finished school, she couldn't help looking at wedding magazines. When she saw something she liked, she'd call me and send photos to get my opinions.

My phone! I hadn't thought about it, but it was still turned on. Devin might call. I had no desire to talk to him ever again. I pulled my phone out of my purse and turned it off. Throwing it down on the bed next to me, I looked around the room once more. Emotions swirled inside me—relief at being somewhere away from Devin, loneliness because I couldn't talk to anyone about why I was doing this, worry for the people I loved who might get hurt because I'd run away, and love for the baby who grew inside me. Whatever else happened, I had to protect the baby.

On Tuesday, when I was supposed to be at work, I struggled with whether or not to call Lois. It seemed safer not to, but I hated the idea of simply disappearing and letting her worry about what had happened to me.

Maybe she would know without me telling her. She'd given me the debit card for the account, but she still had access to it. If she looked, she'd see the expenditures. She'd know where I was, and I was sure, she would know exactly why I was there. Still, what harm could calling her do? She and Devin didn't share a phone plan. How could he possibly know?

After picking up breakfast at a nearby diner, and bringing it back to my room, I decided to make the call.

"Keeley, where are you?" Lois asked when she answered. "You're thirty minutes late. Ms. Johnson is waiting on you and she's getting pretty upset."

"Yeah, I know. I'm not going to be able to come in though," I said, chewing my pinky nail.

"You sick?"

"No, I'm not sick," I said even as my stomach rolled a little. *I might have to save my breakfast till later.* "I ... I left Devin."

"What? Why didn't you come home then? Where are you? Did he hit you?" The last question came out like a growl.

"No, but I had to leave. He made me come back the last time. That's why I can't come home. He'd just come for me there." I closed the lid on my boxed breakfast, deciding I wasn't ready to eat.

"I knew you didn't really want to go back to him. Why didn't you tell me? I could help you." Her voice broke. "I'd do anything to keep you safe."

"I know you would. But he'd just hurt you too. I can't let that happen. I don't want him to hurt anyone I love. Devin was my mistake. No one else should pay for it."

"I'm willing to take that chance. I know some guys that could help." She sniffed.

A tear rolled down my cheek. "I'm not willing to let you take that chance. I don't want him to hurt anyone I love. But I had to get away."

"Where are you? I'll come see you."

"I'm in a motel outside of town, but I can't tell you exactly where and you can't come here. Devin might be watching you. He'll try to get me back. He did it before." My hand went to my throat where the bruises had faded away. The memory was as clear as ever.

"You can't just stay in a motel forever."

"I know. But I've got to figure out what to do next. I'll let you know what I decide to do if I can." I hesitated for a moment, then said, "Devin will come to you eventually. He'll want to know where I went. That's another reason I don't want to tell you exactly where I am."

"I'm a tough old girl. I won't tell him a thing." The determination in her voice filled my ears, but everyone had a breaking point.

"I know you're tough. I haven't forgotten that." I avoided her other statement. I was already overwhelmed with worry about what Devin might do to the people I love in order to find me. "I should go, Lois. I'm sorry to leave you in the lurch at the salon."

"Don't you worry about that. Just keep yourself safe."

I swiped at another tear. "I will. I love you." Saying those words to Lois was simultaneously strange and wonderful. I wished we'd had a better relationship when I was growing up and I was glad we'd made such progress. That was the one good thing to come from my relationship with Devin—that and the baby.

"I love you, too, Keeley."

Two more days passed quietly. I spent my time thinking through possibilities for what to do next. The plan I favored was moving to another town, further away, and making a new life for myself and my baby. But ... what if Devin found us? Once he knew about the baby, the baby wouldn't be safe. And what about Lois, Ellis, and Jean? Did I just cut ties with them? Would I need a new name? Was there any way to be safe?

The child inside me was still invisible to everyone but me and I hadn't told a soul. Soon, though, the baby would grow, and I wouldn't be able to hide the pregnancy any longer. Before that happened, I had to have a plan. Just how could I hide this from Devin? Would he ever stop looking for me? I knew I couldn't count on that.

I touched my belly as I walked back toward the motel with a grocery bag in the other hand. Unseen, my child was in there. The love that filled my heart with that thought was overwhelming. "I'll protect you," I said in a whisper. But there was only one way I could think of to be sure the baby was protected. My eyes filled with tears at the thought of what that one way was.

I gasped when my arm was grabbed from behind. The bag I was carrying dropped to the ground and its contents scattered. A second later, my arm was being twisted against my back. "You better get your ass in the car," came a vicious hiss in my ear. Devin had found me.

My arm hurt too much to ask questions. With a whimper, I moved along in front of him and got in his car when he opened the door and shoved me. I quickly cradled my throbbing arm in front of me. Tears burned my eyes.

Devin slid into the driver's side and glared at me without speaking.

"How did you find me?" I asked.

He snorted. "You think you can run anywhere I won't find you? I told you that you're mine."

I stared at his seat, trying to avoid meeting his eyes, while he seemed to struggle with whether or not to tell me exactly how he'd found me.

"Lois told me you left town. And that ugly green car of yours is easy to spot," he said in a self-satisfied tone.

My eyes darted up to his. "What did you do to Lois?"

"Not much. Didn't have to. She didn't think about how much your car stands out either. She seemed to think she was telling me I'd never find you. But I figured you wouldn't go too far, and you'd have to find a place to stay." He shrugged. "Wasn't hard from there.

"But now you're going to have to pay for what you did." He turned the car on and drove up to the motel, parking next to my car.

"Let's go," he said. "You're going to pack your stuff and check out of this hole-in-the-wall."

Not seeing any escape at the moment, I eased out of his car. He followed me to the motel room door and stood behind me while I fumbled with the key, my hands trembling.

As soon as we were both through the door, his arm struck me in the back and knocked me to the floor. I pulled my legs up and curled into a ball, trying to protect my belly. Devin kicked me once, then grabbed me by one arm and dragged me to the bed. He threw me down and reared back with his hand fisted.

I tried to move my hands to cover my stomach and screamed, "No, Devin, please! I'm pregnant."

His hand stopped just before making contact. He stood still and stared at me for several seconds. Then his eyes narrowed. "That's why you ran away?"

Terrified of what might be going through his mind, I slowly nodded.

"So, you want to keep it?" he asked.

"Yes." I croaked.

"And you want to protect it."

"Of course." I wanted to curl back up and shield the baby, but I was afraid to move.

When Devin started laughing, I stared at him.

"This is perfect." He reached down and patted my belly. For a moment, I wasn't sure what to think. Did he like the idea of a baby or was he being sarcastic? Then he leaned down close to my face and said, "If you ever try to leave me again, I'll kill that little bastard."

Horrified, my breath stopped in my throat. As he pulled back from me, the look in his eyes told me he meant what he said. If I ever planned to leave him again, I'd have to make very sure he didn't find me. My baby's life depended on it.

After packing my things, I got into my car, and in a daze, followed Devin back to his apartment. There was no need for Devin to force me. I'd go back to the life I'd tried to leave willingly, and he knew it. The baby I already loved with all my heart was at risk, and I would do anything to protect it.

Again, I unpacked, but all the while, I worked my brain to come up with a plan to keep my child safe. One way or another, I'd make sure my child never met his father. I'd keep him from becoming a pawn in Devin's sick game.

I went back to the salon the next day, and other than Lois, no one had any idea why I'd been gone. Since Devin knew about the baby, I told everyone at the salon as well. It worked well as an excuse for why I'd been out. *The morning sickness has been terrible*, I told them, *I was so sick.*

All the girls at the salon excitedly congratulated me on the baby and discussed names, but Lois hung back and stayed quiet. If one of the other ladies spoke to her directly about my pregnancy, she smiled and put on a façade. She wasn't fooling me. Worry hung over her like a dark cloud.

When I went to the back-room for a short break, Lois followed me. "This baby ... that's why you left, isn't it?"

I looked at her with sad resignation and nodded.

She pulled a chair up close to the one I'd collapsed into and sat. Then, taking my hands in hers, she looked into my eyes. "He knows about the baby now?"

Pursing my lips, I nodded again.

"What happened, Keeley? Did he hurt you?"

I shrugged as the memory of the day Devin found me played through my mind and a tear slid down my cheek. "Only a little."

Lois searched my eyes. "But there's more. I can see that in your face."

"I told him about the baby so he wouldn't punch my stomach." Tears filled my eyes and spilled over. I sniffed and tried to speak with trembling lips. "He said he'd kill the baby if I ever tried to leave him again."

Lois's eyes flashed with anger as her grip on my hands tightened. "We'll figure something out. We'll go to the police."

My tears stopped, but sadness filled my eyes as I answered Lois. "And fight him with a piece of paper? I can't take the chance of going to the police. If it didn't work ..."

She nodded. "You're right. We need another plan, a better plan. I know this guy. I think I could convince him to teach Devin a lesson."

"And what if that doesn't work, or backfires? Whatever I do next, it can't go wrong. My baby's life depends on it."

Trying to think of another answer, Lois's eyes darted around the room as if she might find it floating in the air.

"Lois," I said, drawing her attention back to my face. "I've been working out a plan already. But it has to be really good. I have to take some time and try to think of everything. If I leave again and he finds me ..." my voice trailed off at the thought of what Devin might do. "I can't let that happen."

"Yes, you're right. Don't rush into anything. And Keeley," she drew even closer to me and lowered her voice, though no one was near, "when you leave again, don't call. Don't call me, don't call Ellis, and don't call anyone else. Just disappear."

Tears filled my eyes again at the thought, but I knew she was right. I threw my arms around her, and she held me close.

As the summer sun heated up the days, my belly began to grow, and my child's presence became more and more evident. Devin paid little attention to my growing size and never went with me to the doctor's appointments. He primarily went on as he had before I tried to run away. Once in a while, he looked at my belly and smiled in a way that sent a shiver up my spine. He had no love for our child—his child—he only thought of the baby as an object that gave him control over me. My love was his weapon.

But as my baby grew, so did my plan. I would make sure my child was kept safe, even if it meant breaking my own heart in the process.

 # Chapter Thirty-five

I didn't make my move until I reached the eight-month mark in my pregnancy. By then, Devin was convinced he had me for good. After all, where would I go in that condition, with no doctor, no help? Scary as that truth was, my motivation for taking the chances I was taking was bigger.

My plan was timed to coincide with a weekend trip Devin had planned with his father. That would give me a little time to make my first moves.

Once he left that Friday night, I hurried off to a drug store, choosing one far enough away to make it unlikely Devin would ask any questions about me there. I went back to the apartment and cut my hair, adding bangs that fell a bit long, obscuring my eyes somewhat. I held back tears as I watched long locks of my dark hair fall to the floor. It wasn't my hair that brought tears to my eyes so much as what the haircut represented. My plan called for sacrifices that were overwhelming to think about.

When I finished cutting my hair, I dyed it a caramel color and added some red streaks. I hated it, but that didn't matter. What mattered was that it changed the way I looked.

When my hair was done, I once again packed up only the things I absolutely needed. Taking my bag to my car, I threw it in the backseat and took off. I drove two hours west and found a used car dealership.

Pulling my car up to the building, I eased out and walked inside. Almost as soon as I'd gotten through the door, a man in a polo shirt with the dealership's logo approached me. He smiled and ran a hand through his dark hair.

"Can I help you?" He asked.

Ignoring the churning of my stomach, I smiled back and accepted the hand he extended to me. "I'd like to trade my car."

He nodded. "Let's take a look at what you've brought."

"It's nothing fancy," I said.

"But you're looking for something fancy in return?" He asked jovially.

I shook my head as I led him outside to my car. "No, I just want something small and dependable."

He looked at my belly. "Dependable for sure. We'll make certain of that, but don't you think you'll want something with some growing room?"

Instinctively, I put my hands on my stomach. "Oh, this is just a car for running around town. My husband has an SUV."

"I see." He walked around my car. His attempts not to grimace were obvious. "I'm sure we can work something suitable out for you. Is it an even trade you're looking for, or are you trading up?" He turned his attention to me, clearly hoping that I'd pick the trading up option.

"Even if possible," I said with an apologetic look.

He cocked his head to the side. "Well, as long as you aren't expecting it to be pretty, I think we can still make dependable happen."

"Pretty isn't what matters."

Surprise registered on his face for a split second. "Okay, then. Let me show you what I've got."

I nodded and followed him.

An hour and a half later, I drove off in an old, faded black Chevy Cobalt. It was dented all over and the seats had tears in them, but the engine seemed strong and it didn't stand out.

With my newly bought car, I drove to a motel where I'd already made a reservation and paid over the phone. I walked into the lobby and checked in as quickly as I could, keeping my head low and my new bangs uncomfortably in my face.

When I got to my room, I threw my bag on the bed and made sure the door was locked. Then I collapsed on the bed, curled into a ball, and cried myself to sleep.

I spent two nights in that motel room before starting back toward home. When I reached the outskirts of town, the urge to run to Lois overwhelmed me. But that couldn't happen. Instead, I sniffed, wiped at my eyes, and drove on to another motel. I paid to have a room there for four days, and for those days, I only left my room to buy food and other necessities. Devin would be looking for me, and even though I looked different and had a different car, he might spot me. After all, I was eight months pregnant, and there was nothing I could do to make my belly less noticeable.

I watched TV a lot and spent time talking to the baby that kicked and stretched inside me. I told my child that I loved him and tried to explain why I was going to do the unthinkable soon. Of course, he wouldn't remember what I was telling him—he couldn't even understand—but explaining it to him reminded me why I was doing all this, why I had to go through with it.

When my four days at that motel elapsed, I drove to another one and stayed there for a few days. Then I went on to another. I would continue this routine until the time came to have the baby.

The pain hit me early one morning, waking me. I shot up in bed and grabbed my belly, holding it until the pain passed. Then I got up and went into the bathroom. I knew false labor pains could happen, and it was important that I didn't make any moves until I knew for sure this was the real thing. I washed my face and brushed my teeth before the next pain hit. Looking at the time, I saw that seven minutes had passed. *Not yet.*

As I brushed my hair, a rush of fluid ran down my leg and another pain hit. *Five minutes and my water broke—time to go.* I grabbed a small bag I had ready and hurried out to my car. This time, I drove to Jean's house.

When I got there, I was relieved to see her car in the driveway. I knew there was as much chance of her not being home as there was that she would be, but it was a risk I had to take. Since there wasn't a good backup plan, I was grateful beyond words to see she was there.

Hurrying to her door, I rang the bell and waited for her to answer. As I waited, another contraction seized me, making me double over.

"Keeley," said Jean, clearly confused, "is that you?"

Closing my eyes against the pain, I nodded and forced out an "Uh-huh."

"Oh, my word, are you in labor?"

As the pain subsided, I straightened and met Jean's eyes. "Yes, and I need your help."

"Honey, you need a hospital. I'll drive you," she said, grabbing her purse from a hook by the door.

I threw out a hand to stop her from moving through the door. "I can't go to a hospital."

"What do you mean? You have to," she insisted.

Tears burst from my eyes and I couldn't stop them this time. "No, Jean, I can't. I need you to help me. This baby's life depends on it."

She stared at me in confusion, then put her purse back on the hook, grabbed my arm, and tugged. "Get in here and tell me what's going on."

Once we were in the house, she raised her eyebrows at me and put her hands on her hips. "Lois said you ran away. She said you two had a terrible fight, that you had quit working at the salon, and that she didn't even know you'd left town until your boyfriend told her."

So, Lois had gone so far as to convince her best friend that she didn't know why I'd left. Good for her. She'd need that poker face if Devin pressed her for information.

"That's not exactly true, Jean, but when I tell you what's going on, you have to keep it all secret."

Her face was filled with concern and confusion. "The baby's life depends on it?"

I nodded as another pain overtook me.

Jean sighed. "Let's get you comfortable and you can tell me everything right after I call Lois."

"No! You can't call Lois." The words came out as a near yell while the last of that contraction held onto me. When it was over, I said in a more measured voice, "Knowing any of this could put her in danger. I'm only involving you because I need to."

"Danger? Keeley, what on earth is going on?" Jean demanded.

"I'll tell you everything, I promise."

Jean put me in her guest room, settling me in the bed. "Did your water break yet?"

"Yes."

"I don't want to put Lois in danger either but having her help could make a lot of difference since you won't go to the hospital. I'm not even an obstetrics nurse, you know."

"I know that." I was about to argue but thought better of it when I remembered how convincing Lois had apparently been with Jean and her false story. "Okay, call her."

After Jean called Lois, she went to the kitchen to boil water. When she returned to the bedroom, she sat down next to the bed and turned her eyes on me. "Now, what is going on and why am I delivering a baby in my house instead of driving you to a hospital?"

"I ran away because my boyfriend ..." I stopped as emotion clogged my throat and made it hard to speak. I could almost feel Devin's hand around my neck. "Because he's abusive."

Before I could say any more, Jean spoke up. "He beat you?" Her voice was angry and hurt at the same time.

Tears running down my face, I nodded.

"Then you'll stay here, and we'll call the police," she insisted.

The conversation stopped while I breathed through a contraction. When it subsided, I continued, "I can't take the chance that it wouldn't work." My voice was thick with emotion as I tried to explain everything to Jean. "I ran away once before when I first got pregnant because Devin threatened to hurt anyone who helped me." I looked at her imploringly. "I think he would do it."

"He'd be behind bars in a heartbeat if he did that."

"And what if he did damage that couldn't be undone ... what if ..." Fear of what Devin might do overtook me, making it hard to finish my thought. I swallowed hard. "Jean, what if he killed someone I love? I can't take that chance. And now..." I stopped for another contraction. The pain that surged through my body reminded me of what was at stake. I needed to make Jean understand.

The pain ended and I continued, "When Devin found me the last time, I had to tell him about the baby." Tears burst forth, running down my face and falling on the pale blue sheets. "He said if I ever left him again, he'd kill my baby."

Jean stared at me, taking it all in. "He'd really kill his own child? Is he some kind of psycho?"

I thought back to the look on Devin's face when he'd first made the threat. "Yes, I think he would. There's no love in him for anyone but himself."

She nodded slowly. "So, what's your plan?"

I squeezed my eyes shut and sobbed.

Jean took my hand and held it tightly. "Oh, sweetheart, I'm so sorry."

My tears were followed by another contraction. Then the doorbell rang. Jean left the room and returned with Lois.

Two hours after Lois's arrival, my baby's cries rang out into the room. As I panted in exhaustion and waited for Jean to clean him up, tears ran down my face again—tears of joy and also of heartbreak.

"Oh my, he's beautiful," Lois said, her voice filled with awe.

"He sure is," Jean agreed. "Take a look, Mama." She walked to the side of the bed and put my son in my arms.

"Welcome to the world little Ollie," I whispered, trying not to sob.

Lois sat on the side of the bed and pushed my hair back from my face. "Don't do it, Keeley. We'll find another way. I'll leave with you and we'll go far away. We'll make sure that slime doesn't find you, and we'll keep this little one safe." Her voice broke at the end, and I realized my plan was going to take her back to being alone in the world—just like I'd be alone. I wanted to nod and do just what she suggested, but when I looked at the baby in my arms, I knew I couldn't.

This tiny, defenseless person was counting on me to make certain he was safe. I only knew one sure way to do that.

I squeezed my eyes shut and fought for control before shaking my head. "No Lois. I have to make sure Ollie is safe." I looked at her with watery eyes and reached out for her hand. "I want to though. If I knew for sure it would be safe …"

Lois nodded slowly and ran a finger along the baby's head of silken hair. A tear dropped from her eyes. "That's what matters most."

I stayed at Jean's house until sundown, then ignoring her protests, I wrapped the baby up and headed back to my motel room. I stayed there for one night, drinking in every moment with my son. The following day, I packed my things, bundled the baby into a car seat I'd bought, and headed east toward the coast.

I drove for an hour or two at a time, and took breaks in between, stopping at rest stops to care for the baby and take short naps. By the end of the day, I'd made it to a town near the North Carolina coast. I found another motel and checked in for the night.

After taking a fast shower while the baby slept, I brushed my teeth and got into bed. I put Ollie in a bassinet-style basket I'd found the week before at a secondhand shop and it sat next to me on the bed. I spent the night stroking his soft hair and skin, trying to memorize every part of him. I tried to sleep, but how could I? Tomorrow was going to be the worst day of my life.

Chapter Thirty-six

When morning dawned, I opened my eyes and looked at my sleeping son. He was the most gorgeous sight I'd ever seen. He had my eyes, but lighter hair that was more like Devin's. He sucked his tiny thumb and looked completely content. I wished with all of my heart for that moment to stretch on forever, but the clock continued to tick forward defying my will.

Dragging myself out of bed, I went to the bathroom. I washed my face and brushed my teeth and hair.

By the time I'd finished, Ollie was starting to fuss. I went to him, changed him, and fed him. Then dressed him in a soft green sleeper and wrapped him up in a blanket. I let him lie in the basket while I packed. It was a task that should have taken only a few minutes, but my feet dragged in unison with the heaviness of my heart. The longer it took to pack up, the longer I'd have with Ollie.

Eventually, I did what had to be done. I put the baby in the car seat and locked it into my car. Then I slid into the driver's seat and started to drive. I didn't know where I was headed, so I just started to drive aimlessly around the town. I hadn't eaten anything, and I thought about going to a drive-through. But the way my stomach felt, I didn't know if I'd be able to hold anything down.

After thirty minutes of driving around, something caught my eye. Up ahead was a beautiful white church with a tall steeple and stained-glass windows. I found myself turning off the road into the church's parking lot without making a conscious decision to do so. It was as if I was being pulled there.

I parked the car, and for several minutes, stared at the building. Then I wiped the moisture from my face where tears had flowed and looked back at Ollie. He was sound asleep, his face serene. I took a deep, ragged breath and forced myself to get out of the car. Opening the back door, I took Ollie out of the car seat and put him in the basket. Then I grabbed the formula I'd bought and prepared a couple of bottles, placing them in the basket with him. After adding some diapers and a small pack of wipes, I reluctantly lifted the basket out of the car and headed into the church.

Once I got inside, the first thing I did was walk to the altar and place the basket on the kneeler. I knelt next to it and began to pray.

"Lord, you know why I'm here, why I'm doing this. Please, have mercy on me and protect my baby. Send someone to find him who will love him the way I love him." I broke into sobs at the thought of losing my child who I loved more fiercely than I'd ever loved anyone in my life. Yet, strangely, warmth spread through my chest and I knew Ollie would be safe. God would answer my prayer.

When my cries subsided into hiccups, I picked up the basket and carried it to a pew at the center of the church. I set it down and picked up the baby. I carefully changed his diaper and breastfed him for the last time. Then I sat for a long while and stared down at the little face of my son. As I looked at him, the last words my mother ever spoke to me came into my mind like a whisper in my ear, 'When you think of me, remember the butterfly.'

I thought back to the day I'd spent with her in the meadow. I remembered the butterfly on my finger and my mother explaining to me why I had to let him go.

Tears filled my eyes again because, for the first time, I really understood what my mother had been telling me that night, so long ago, when she'd left and never come back. I wondered if she had loved me as much as I loved Ollie. *Had it hurt her this much to leave that night?* I'd never thought of it that way. I'd always just thought she loved the drugs more than me. But maybe she did love me and was doing the only thing she could to make sure *I* was safe. Maybe the drugs had such a hold on her that she couldn't believe she'd ever truly be free of them, and she didn't want to risk hurting me the way she almost had that day on the roof.

I slipped an envelope under the lining of the basket before placing Ollie back inside. Leaning down, I kissed my son on his forehead. "I love you, Ollie. I always will," I said before turning and running out of the church, hand clasped over my mouth to keep myself from sobbing again.

Part Three

Chapter Thirty-seven

By the time Jillian finished reading Keeley's letter, a steady stream of tears ran down her face. She wiped at them and sniffled. Rising up on her knees, she looked into Nathan's crib and watched him sleep. His face was serene as his little chest rose and fell.

Trying to hold back another sob, Jillian's lips tightened. The story of King Solomon and the two mothers filled her mind. The true mother wanted to do what was best for the baby even if it meant giving him up. With that in mind, she knew what she had to do next, but everything in her screamed against it.

When the door to Nathan's room creaked, Jillian turned to see Wyatt. He wiped at sleepy eyes as he stepped into the room.

"What are you doing?" He asked.

Jillian's eyes turned back to the letter in her hand. She sank back down to the floor. "I couldn't sleep. I had a dream."

Wyatt came to her side and knelt next to her. "The Natalie dream again?"

"A version of it."

Wyatt put his hand under her elbow, trying to help her up, but she pulled her arm away and spoke again. "It was about Nathan too. And it felt like it was telling me something, but I didn't know what."

Accepting that she wasn't ready to leave the floor of Nathan's room yet, Wyatt moved his legs to a more comfortable position and settled in to listen.

"I didn't think I could sleep again, so I came in here. This basket," she said, tapping the side of the basket, "was in my dream, and when I came in here, I felt drawn to it. I found a letter under the cushion."

"A letter?" Wyatt prompted when Jillian fell silent.

She glanced at him with tears glistening in her eyes. "We have to give him back, Wyatt. We have to give Nathan back to Keeley."

"What? Because of a letter?" Trying to keep his voice low, Wyatt shook his head in utter disbelief. "What are you talking about?"

Jillian sobbed, trying to stay quiet as well and not wake the baby. She looked at Nathan. He still slept peacefully. He was a sound sleeper.

"She loves him. She left him in that church to protect him. She never wanted to abandon him," Jillian said.

"But *we* love him. We've been his parents all this time, the only parents he knows. We have to fight for him," Wyatt pleaded.

Jillian turned her tearful gaze on him. "If we fight for him knowing his birth mother really does love him, are we doing what's best for him or what's best for us?"

Wyatt shook his head. "Jills ... he's our son."

She nodded. There was no way she'd deny that. No matter what happened, he would always be her son. Maybe it would never be true on paper, but it was certainly true in her heart. "But he's her son too." She held the letter up. "If you read this, you won't be able to say otherwise."

Wyatt stared at the letter in her hand for a long time. "So, we just give him up? Just like that?" He sobbed and wiped his face. "What about us and our family? We'll be broken without him."

"I know." Jillian's voice cracked and she squeezed her eyes shut.

When she could speak again, she said, "If we did fight for him, and we won, what would we tell him when he found out that his birth mother wanted him, and we kept him from her?"

Wyatt shook his head again. "I don't know. I only know that I don't want to lose him."

Jillian handed the letter to Wyatt, and he pushed back from it as if it were something dangerous. *Perhaps it is.*

She pressed it into his hand. "No decisions tonight. You read this and think it through. Then we'll talk about it."

When he shook his head again, she insisted. "You have to at least read it. I won't go forward either way until you do."

For two days, Wyatt refused to read the letter. He and Jillian barely spoke. They went about their routines in tandem yet worlds apart.

On day three, when they were sitting at the table eating dinner, Jillian said, "We have a meeting with Ilene in a couple of days." She looked at him and waited till he met her eyes. "Please read the letter."

Wyatt sighed and didn't offer a response, but that evening when Jillian returned to the living room after putting Nathan to bed, Wyatt was sitting on the couch with the letter in hand.

Jillian went to their bedroom to read a book and allow Wyatt time alone to absorb Keeley's story.

A couple of hours passed, and Wyatt didn't come to bed. With a sigh, Jillian turned off the light and went to sleep alone.

When she awoke the following morning, Wyatt's side of the bed remained empty. Getting up, Jillian ambled out to the living room and found her husband in the recliner with Nathan asleep on his chest. As she drew closer, she heard Wyatt's soft sobs.

He looked up and met her eyes, then closing his, he nodded.

Ilene looked at Jillian and Wyatt over the top of her glasses. "Am I hearing you right?" she asked.

There was a lump in Jillian's throat, making it hard to speak. She nodded.

Turning his eyes away and wiping a tear from his cheek, Wyatt did the same. He was angry with her, Jillian knew, because she'd found the letter and read it. Then she'd insisted he read it, and once he knew what the letter said, he couldn't turn away from it any more than she could. She wondered if he'd ever forgive her—if they'd ever be okay again.

After a moment's hesitation, Ilene spoke again, "Well, I never expected this. But there's a fair chance it would have happened anyway. After considering all the facts, I was prepared to keep fighting to keep Nathan with you. He's happy and well cared for with you, but Keeley's claims have been checked and it appears that everything she said was true. Nathan's father was abusive. Witnesses testified to having seen the marks he left on Keeley. Her aunt and a friend—the ones who were there when the baby was born—also claimed that she was under great duress when the baby came because her boyfriend had threatened to kill the child. She felt it was important that there were no records or any evidence of her giving birth or leaving the baby behind—

even if it was only in someone's memory. Right or wrong, she made the choice because she felt it was in his best interest." Ilene stopped, studied Jillian and Wyatt, then went on, "I guess you know all that from the letter you told me about.

"Here's what you don't know," Ilene stopped and took a sip of water from the cup on her desk. "Keeley tried to move on with her life in another town, but Nathan's father, Devin, found her again when she made the mistake of contacting a friend and showing up at the friend's wedding. She told him the baby had been born dead and it seems he believed her. However, he forced her back into her old life with him. Then, one night when he was beating her, she got hold of a kitchen knife and put it in his chest." Ilene let out a heavy breath. "When the cops got to the scene, they determined easily that she'd acted in self-defense." Her brow drew together, and her eyes were filled with pain. "She had two broken bones and fingerprint bruises all around her neck."

Jillian began to weep. She wept for the baby she was letting go and she wept for Keeley and the hell she'd lived through.

"I can't say if leaving Nathan in that church rather than taking him to an emergency room or fire station was best, but I sure am glad she didn't let that monster get his hands on him. Most likely, a judge would have agreed and sent Nathan back to her, regardless of any argument I made. It'd be safe now that Devin is dead. That's why Keeley came back," Ilene said.

Jillian agreed wholeheartedly about Keeley keeping Nathan away from his birth father. The only thing that hurt more than the thought of losing the child she loved with all her heart was the thought of him being abused and maybe worse.

Once Ilene changed her recommendation from keeping Nathan with Jillian and Wyatt to sending him back to Keeley, everything happened quickly. Keeley had already had a few supervised visits with Nathan, so it was decided to give her one unsupervised overnight visit before sending Nathan back to her.

The overnight visit with Keeley was set to take place two weeks after Jillian and Wyatt urged Ilene to make the new recommendation. Jillian carefully packed the things Nathan would need for the night. His toothbrush, the blanket he liked, and his stuffed dog all went into a duffle bag while Nathan watched curiously.

When the stuffed dog went in, Nathan reached up toward it. "Oggie. Mine," he said. It was a new favorite, a gift from Layla for his first birthday. Looking at the toy, Jillian knew she and Wyatt were not alone in their brokenness over losing Nathan. Everyone in both their families was suffering.

Jillian turned sad eyes to the baby. "Yes, this is your doggie, Nathan. I'm just putting him in your bag, so he'll be with you tonight."

Unconvinced, Nathan kept his arms up and grunted until Jillian put the stuffed animal in his hands. Then he smiled, hugged the dog, and went back to playing. When the stuffed animal was abandoned on the floor, and Nathan's back was turned, Jillian picked it up and quietly placed it in the duffle.

An hour and a half later, Ilene came and picked up Nathan. Once he was gone, Jillian fell into Wyatt's arms and they both cried until their tears were used up.

 Chapter Thirty-eight

Keeley's heart was filled with joy when Ilene arrived with Ollie. She hurried to the door of the tiny apartment she'd rented shortly after coming to town and threw it open with tears of joy coursing down her cheeks. Her baby was going to be with her again, and soon it would be for good.

Ilene was smiling too, but hers was restrained, uncertain. "He's all ready for his overnight visit," she said, putting the baby in Keeley's arms and walking inside with his bag when Keeley opened it wide for her.

"I'm ready too," Keeley said. She kissed Ollie's cheek and he gave her a shy smile.

"I need to see where he'll be sleeping," Ilene said. "The last time I came by you didn't have a bed for him yet."

"Oh, sure. I have it all set up. Since he's a year old, I got him a crib that turns into a toddler bed." She went on hesitantly, "It came from a thrift shop. I couldn't afford a new one. But once I get a job here …"

Ilene smiled. "It's okay, Keeley. There's no rule against shopping at a thrift store."

Keeley nodded, relief flooding through her. She wanted everything to be right. She was so close to having Ollie back with her for good. The last thing she wanted to do was mess it up.

She led Ilene down the narrow hall to a bedroom that was even smaller than the one she'd had living with Lois. In the back right corner of the room, a crib was set up. It had taken Keeley the better part of a day to get it all put back together. Now, with Ollie in her arms, she knew every moment of effort was worth it.

She'd also picked up a changing table at the thrift shop and a few toys. There wasn't much else in the room, but once she had a job and childcare, and they were settled, she'd make sure he had the best room there was.

They were going to move back to the other side of the state once all the legal stuff was over. Lois, ecstatic about having them come home, was looking for a rent-to-own house that was big enough for all of them. Keeley would go back to work in the salon, and with some help from Jean and Ellis, they would arrange their schedules so Ollie didn't need daycare.

"This looks good," Ilene said. "You've got what you need, and I've brought his car seat in case you need it."

"Oh, good. I was going to take him to the park and then out for dinner," Keeley replied.

Ilene looked at the baby and put a hand on his shoulder. "I think you're all set here, Nathan. I'll see you tomorrow."

Keeley felt a wave of hurt hearing her call him Nathan. She knew that was the name his foster parents had given him, but hearing it was a reminder of all the time she'd already missed with him. It was a reminder that someone else had been taking care of her baby all these months instead of her.

Ilene stepped to the door. "I'll be by tomorrow around ten in the morning to pick him up."

Keeley's heart sank a little at the idea of sending him back to the foster home, but soon he'd be with her for good. She nodded. "I'll have him ready."

"Well, I hope your visit with him goes well." Ilene opened the door and stepped out. She waved at the baby and he raised a chubby hand to wave back.

"Bye, bye, Iean," he said.

Keeley struggled a little getting Ollie's car seat installed in her car. Ollie crawled around in the backseat of the car until she got it secured.

"There, I think I got it, Ollie. Come get in here and we'll go to the park," she said.

Ollie scowled at her for a moment, then broke into a smile. "Park!" he shouted, plopping down in his seat.

"That's right. We're gonna have some fun."

Arriving at the nearest park, Keeley lifted Ollie out of the car and carried him to the playground. As soon as his feet were on the ground, he ran to the slide and stood by the ladder, grunting.

"You want to slide?" Keeley asked, looking at the slide. It seemed too tall for such a little guy. "I don't know, buddy. Maybe I should go with you."

Ollie grunted again.

Picking him up, Keeley climbed up the ladder. She sat down and placed the baby on her lap. He bounced up and down. "Go!" he cried.

"Yes, sir. Here we go." Holding onto the baby with one arm, Keeley wiggled her hips and pushed off with the other arm. They started down and began to speed up. Ollie giggled with joy.

"G'in!" He said when they were at the bottom.

"You want to do it again, Ollie?"

He looked at her, scowling again. "Nae," he said and started walking back to the ladder when his feet were on the ground again.

They went down the slide two more times before Ollie ran to the baby swing and reached up to it. Keeley put him in the swing and pushed. She delighted in her son's joy as the swing went higher and higher. She was happier than she had dared imagine during the last year.

When Ollie was tired of swinging, Keeley lifted him from the swing and asked, "How about dinner now?"

The baby nodded vigorously. "Din!"

Keeley drove them to a nearby Wendy's and took the baby inside. She knew what she wanted to eat but wasn't sure what Ollie would like. She looked at him and made eye contact. "Would you like a burger or chicken, Ollie?"

Once again, he scowled at her. This time he patted his chest. "Nae," he said, louder than before.

Ignoring his apparent aversion to her calling him Ollie, Keeley decided to order the burger and hope for the best. She'd have to learn what he liked.

Looking down at him again she felt a wave of sadness at the idea that she didn't know what he liked to eat. Jillian was the one who knew all about him.

Pointing her chin back up, she pushed the sadness aside. She'd learn everything she needed to know about him. It would just take some time. And he was so little, he'd get used to being called by a different name. In time he wouldn't even remember being called Nathan.

After ordering and paying for their food, Keeley carefully balanced the tray in one hand and carried Ollie with the other. She put the tray down on a table and left it for a moment to quickly retrieve a highchair for the baby. Placing him in the seat, she sat across from him and began breaking his burger into small pieces and placing them in front of him. He picked up a bite and put it in his mouth. Almost immediately, he spat the bite of burger back out.

"Uck!" He said, making a face.

"You don't like the burger?" Keeley asked. She wondered if it was the burger or something on it. She should have ordered it plain until she knew more about his tastes. Oh well, she'd try the fries.

When a few bites of the fries were in front of him, Ollie snatched one up and ate it. He nodded. "Num!"

"Well, good. At least you like something I got for you."

While Ollie ate his fries, Keeley began to eat her burger, but after only a few fries, Ollie began to push his food around rather than eat it. Then he pushed all of it to the floor and began to whimper.

"You don't want to eat any more, buddy?" Keeley asked. "You should be hungry by now, but you only ate a few fries."

She tried to give him some more of the fries, but he shook his head and pushed them off the table, continuing to whimper.

"I guess you're done then. Mind if I finish mine?"

She started to eat again, but Ollie's whimpering kept getting louder.

"Home," he cried. "Nae home."

Keeley sighed. "Okay, we'll go home now."

Ollie met her eyes and looked hopeful, bouncing in his seat and reaching his arms up.

"Just a second. Let me throw all this trash away."

Ollie's impatience was growing rapidly, so Keeley hurried to clean up their mess and get him out of the highchair. Once he was back in his car seat, he was happy again. But when they arrived at her apartment, and she took him out of the car seat, he scowled at her again. "Home!"

"We are home, Ollie," Keeley told him.

He began to wail. Figuring he'd settle down after a while, Keeley carried him inside and set him down with some toys. He kept crying.

"Maybe there's something in your bag that will help." Keeley grabbed his bag and pulled a stuffed dog out.

"Oggie!" Ollie said, rushing over to snatch it up. He wrapped his arms around the stuffed animal as if it was a lifeline.

"This guy is special, huh? Does he have a name?"

"Oggie."

"Just doggie, huh? Okay. I'm glad he makes you feel better."

Ollie was content with the stuffed dog for about twenty minutes before he began to whimper again. Keeley looked at the clock. It was almost eight o'clock. "Maybe you're getting tired. How about we get your jammies on and read a story?"

The idea didn't do a thing to change Ollie's unhappiness, but Keeley picked him up and took him to his little room. She changed his diaper and put on his PJs. Picking up one of the few books she'd bought for him, she carried him back to the living room and sat down on the couch with him.

Ollie wasn't having it. He fussed and pushed the book away. "Mama," he cried over and over.

Giving up on the book, Keeley set it aside. "Mama's right here, Ollie. I'm your mama."

He shook his head vehemently and continued to cry mama and da-da over and over.

Keeley tried some other books and looked through his bag to see if there was anything else in there that might soothe him. Nothing helped. He cried and cried, his face red and wet with tears.

"Ollie, it's going to be okay," Keeley said.

For a split second, the crying stopped. *Did he believe me?*

Then, slapping his chest with one hand, he shouted, "Nae!" His eyes flashed with anger.

Keeley took a deep breath, a bit shocked by the intensity of his outburst. "You want me to call you Nathan?" she asked, knowing that he did.

The baby nodded, still patting his chest, but not as hard. "Nae," he said in a calmer tone.

"Okay, Nathan." Something inside Keeley broke as she gave in to calling him by this name. "It's going to be all right. I know you miss the mama and daddy you're used to, but I'm your mama too."

He looked at her closely, studying her. Then he shook his head. "No mama," he said.

Keeley's eyes welled with tears. "I am your mama," she said in a sad whisper.

Nathan began to cry again. "No mama."

He cried, and holding him against her chest, Keeley cried too.

Finally, after what seemed like hours, the baby fell asleep on Keeley's chest, exhausted from his crying. She carefully stretched out on the couch and let him stay where he was. As she stroked his soft hair, his chest continued to heave every once in a while with a sob.

Keeley thought about the day she'd left him in the church. She remembered praying for God to send someone to find him who would love him as she did. She knew God had done exactly that. Jillian and Wyatt did love him. That was obvious. And now, it was equally obvious that Nathan loved them just as much. Was it fair to pray that away? To ask God now to fix it so that her baby would give that love to her? Was it fair to Nathan?

She thought then about her mother again, the sadness in Greta's eyes the night she'd walked away. "Remember the butterfly," Keeley whispered to herself.

Closing her eyes and holding her child tightly, she let all her tears flow.

Keeley slept for a few hours with Nathan on her chest. When she awoke, it was close to three o'clock. Nathan was sleeping soundly, so Keeley carefully moved the both of them around until she was in a sitting position. She eased up to her feet and carried the baby to the room she'd set up for him, gently laying him down in the crib. She let out a breath of relief when she was sure the movement hadn't woken him.

After standing over the crib for several minutes trying to memorize every detail of her child's beautiful face, she went to her own bed and tried to sleep. Her efforts were useless. She could not fall asleep again with the heavy weight of the decision she'd made. With a long sigh, she crawled back out of the bed and went down the short hallway to her kitchen. She made herself a cup of coffee and took a pen and pad to the table where she began to write.

An hour later, with her cup empty and her hand sore from re-writing her letter several times, she folded up a sheet of paper and stuffed it in an envelope. Then she typed out a text to Ilene that read: WILL MEET YOU AT YOUR OFFICE INSTEAD OF YOU COMING HERE. HAVE THE GREENS MEET US THERE. I HAVE NEWS FOR YOU AND THEM.

After sending the message, Keeley turned her phone off and went back to Nathan's room. She would spend every second with him until the meeting with Ilene and the Greens, and she didn't want any interruptions or questions. They'd all know about her decision soon enough.

Chapter Thirty-nine

Jillian was surprised when her phone rang at seven o'clock in the morning and Ilene's name showed on the screen. Ilene was supposed to pick Nathan up at Keeley's apartment that morning at ten and bring him home. *Why was she calling so early? Was something wrong?*

Swiping the screen to answer the call, Jillian put the phone to her ear and said, "Ilene? It's early. Is something wrong?"

Ilene hesitated, making Jillian's heart race. *Was something wrong?*

"I don't know," Ilene said. "I got a text message just over an hour ago from Keeley. She says she'll meet me at my office instead of her apartment and she wants you and Wyatt there. She says she has something to tell us."

"Tell us?" Jillian said. *What else was there for her to tell them?* "Did you ask her what?"

"Yes, but she isn't answering and when I try to call her, the phone goes straight to voicemail."

Jillian felt a wave of fear run through her. "She has her phone off? Why? Doesn't she know it's important to be reachable during a visit?"

"Calm down, Jillian. I'm sure everything is fine. Maybe her battery died."

Ilene's tone was soothing, but Jillian was still worried. She chewed her pinky nail.

"Let's not jump to conclusions. I'm sure Nathan is fine. Just come to my office at ten, okay?" Ilene said.

Her mind still running through possibilities, Jillian nodded.

"Jillian? Did you hear me?"

"Huh?" Realizing she hadn't responded with any words, Jillian said, "Oh, yeah, sorry. We'll be there."

The next three hours ticked by excruciatingly slowly. Wyatt tried to reassure Jillian that everything was fine. After all, if Nathan were hurt or sick, Keeley would say so and take him to a doctor. So, that aside, what could be any worse than the fact that they were already about to lose the child they'd come to think of as theirs?

He was right, of course. Surely, Keeley would get the needed help if something was wrong with Nathan. Still, not knowing what was going on set Jillian's nerves on edge.

At nine-thirty, despite Wyatt's protests that they'd be too early, Jillian insisted they head on over to Ilene's office. She didn't care if they had to sit and wait. She wanted to be there the moment Keeley and Nathan arrived.

It took less than fifteen minutes to make the drive and they did end up sitting and waiting in the hall outside Ilene's office. A few minutes into the wait, Wyatt reached over and put his hand on top of Jillian's, stopping the nervous finger tapping she'd been doing. She glanced at him and sighed. In response, he squeezed her hand.

When Keeley came through the door, Jillian flew to her feet.

"Mama!" Nathan yelled as soon as he saw her. He strained against Keeley's hold, trying to reach Jillian's arms. She reached out and took him, surprised by the impassioned way he launched into her and held on.

Without thinking better of it, Jillian whispered into Nathan's ear, "Mama's here, sweet boy."

When she looked up, she saw the anguished look on Keeley's face and the tears welling in the young woman's eyes. Jillian wanted to apologize but wasn't sure how.

Keeley met Jillian's eyes. "Can you promise you'll always love him?"

Surprised by the question, Jillian furrowed her brow. "Yes, forever. Even if I never see him again. I'll never stop loving him."

Keeley glanced at Wyatt, who had one hand on Nathan's back and one on Jillian's, then she nodded and went to the door of Ilene's office. She poked her head in, then a moment later signaled for Jillian and Wyatt to follow her.

Once in Ilene's office, all attention was on Keeley.

"So, what's this big announcement?" Ilene asked, handing Keeley a tissue to wipe her face.

"I've decided that it would be better for Nathan to stay with the Greens," Keeley said with obvious difficulty.

The fact that Keeley called him Nathan and not Ollie grabbed Jillian's attention even more.

Ilene's eyebrows flew up. "What?"

Jillian sat stone still in shock. *Did I hear that right?* Though she wanted it to be true, she was afraid to let herself believe it. The last thing she needed was another heartbreak.

"It isn't that I don't want him," Keeley said quickly. "I want to be with him more than anything. But last night made it clear to me that he already has parents who love him, and he loves them.

"I can't regret leaving him in that church. It was the hardest thing in the world to do, but his life was on the line. I had to do it. Ripping him away from the life he has now and the parents who have loved him all this time is something I can choose not to do." Keeley's lips tightened and another tear escaped to roll down her face. "I know he'd adjust in time and forget all about the Greens and his life with them. He'd learn to call *me* mama." Her voice broke and she took a moment to regain control. "But the adjustment would take time and in that time he'd suffer. He'd have to lose the people he loves. I'd be putting him through the same thing I went through when I left him." Keeley looked at Jillian, then Wyatt. "The people who were there for him—and me—in the time we most needed would suffer too, and they wouldn't just forget."

Silence filled the room as they all tried to absorb what Keeley said. Jillian's heart pounded. *Is this real? Will I get to keep my baby?*

Breaking the silence, Keeley spoke again, "I've decided it isn't fair for me to show up now, after so much time has passed, and hurt three people so I can have what I want." She made eye contact with Jillian again. "In that church, I asked God to send someone who would love my baby the way I did." She sobbed and wiped at her eyes. "That prayer was answered. I'm thankful for that." She stepped close to Jillian and reached a hand out to rub Nathan's back, her lips trembling as she spoke again. "Take good care of him and," she pulled an envelope out of her purse and put it in Jillian's hand, "when he turns eighteen, give him this."

Jillian peeked at the envelope and saw Nathan's name written on it rather than Ollie. "I'll always love and care for him. And I'll make sure he knows you love him."

Keeley's composure broke. She kissed Nathan's head, then hurried out of the office

Jillian and Wyatt looked at Ilene. "Should we go after her?" Jillian asked.

Ilene stared at the doorway for a second, then brought her gaze to them. "No, she probably needs some time alone with this. I'll call her in a while and talk to her." Ilene let out a heavy breath. "I'm going to have to make very sure that she wants to give him up, and even then, she could still change her mind before an adoption finalizes and who knows what that would lead to."

Jillian's heart skipped a beat at Ilene's words. Another crushing blow was the last thing she and Wyatt needed. But at the same time, hope soared inside her, and along with that hope, sadness for what Keeley was going through.

"She sounded sincere, but I just want you to understand that nothing is final until the adoption is done," Ilene said.

"We understand," Wyatt said.

Jillian hugged Nathan close to her, kissing his head. He drew back and touched her face. "Love Mama," he said.

The only sound in the car on the way home was Nathan's happy babbling from the back seat. Jillian's emotions ran all over the place and she imagined Wyatt felt the same—excitement tempered by a self-protective fear, sadness for Keeley. No matter how this played out, someone had to be hurt.

When they arrived home, Nathan was joyful but clingy. He seemed determined to have either Jillian or Wyatt in sight at all times. They were happy to spend the day playing with him. It gave their nervous energy an outlet. They took the baby outside and helped him play ball with Dodger. Then they built a castle together with Nathan's blocks.

At the end of the day, when Jillian tried to put Nathan to bed, he cried desperately at being left alone in his room. Jillian picked him up and rocked him to sleep, happy to have him in her arms.

Leaving Nathan's room, she found Wyatt asleep in the living room recliner, Dodger on his lap. Since it was a Saturday night, she decided not to wake him. He'd probably wake in the middle of the night and come to bed, and if he didn't, it would be okay.

Jillian thought about getting ready for bed herself, but she still felt unsettled and emotional. She needed to talk to someone.

Taking a box of cheese crackers with her, she went to the bedroom, put on pajamas, and settled on her bed. She picked up her phone and dialed Layla's number.

"What's up?" Layla said when she answered.

"Plenty." Jillian paused, not sure how to tell Layla everything.

"Well, spill. It must be big. You don't usually call this late."

"Yeah, sorry about that." Jillian popped a cracker into her mouth.

"Don't worry about it. It's late for you, not me."

"Nathan came back from his overnight visit with Keeley this morning, and it didn't go the way we expected."

"What does that mean?" concern filled Layla's voice.

Not knowing how to explain it all, Jillian blurted out, "She says she wants to give him up again."

Layla began coughing loudly. Then she sputtered, "What! Are you serious?"

"I'm serious." Jillian fiddled with the lace on the edge of a pillow sham.

"Is she crazy? Or is this some kind of game to her?"

"No, it isn't like that, Layla. She was beside herself. She said she didn't want to hurt Nathan or us just to get what she wants."

After several seconds of silence, Layla said, "Does that mean you guys get to keep him?"

"As long as she doesn't change her mind."

"Change her mind again? Can she really keep doing that?" Layla was incredulous. She hadn't been there to see Keeley's pain.

"I guess it could happen, but she seemed sincere. Ilene said she'd have to talk to Keeley and make sure she really is sure about this new decision."

"You say she seemed sincere, but you don't sound happy," Layla said.

"I'm not sure what to feel. I think that's why I needed to talk to someone." Jillian paused and ate another cracker. "I want with all my heart to be Nathan's mother. I want him with us forever. But it breaks my heart to see Keeley's pain at giving him up because I know she loves him too … enough to give him up because she thinks it's what's best for him."

"Just like you were doing after reading her letter."

Jillian wasn't sure why Layla saying what she already knew to be true affected her so strongly, but at her cousin's words, her eyes flooded with tears and her throat clogged with emotion that erupted into sobs.

Layla waited quietly on the line until Jillian finished crying. "I'm sorry. I don't know what came over me," Jillian said.

"You love Nathan and Keeley loves Nathan. Her love for him gives you love for her, and you don't want to see anyone you care for hurting. And … maybe you feel guilty for wanting to be happy about keeping Nathan when you know it hurts her."

Jillian sniffed and wiped her face with a tissue. "Yeah, maybe that's it." She sighed. "Why does it have to be so complicated?"

"Why can't everyone win and be happy?" Layla carried on Jillian's thought.

"Yeah."

"I don't know, Jill. Life is complicated and it isn't fair."

"That's for sure."

Layla spoke again in a soft tone. "If you want to honor Keeley's sacrifice, do it by loving Nathan. I think that's the best you can do."

Jillian nodded. "That's what she asked me to do. And she didn't need to ask. I'll always love him."

"Then try to let go of the guilt."

"Yeah, I'll try. Thanks for the talk, Layla."

"Sure. Goodnight, Jill."

Jillian returned the goodnight with a yawn. The mixed-up feelings weren't gone, but she felt more settled and thought she'd be able to sleep.

That night, Jillian once again found herself dreaming about Natalie. But the dream didn't feel the way it usually did. This time the ominous feel wasn't there. Instead, peace filled Jillian's heart as she looked at her sister, standing outside the car, looking in the window at her. Natalie smiled, and Jillian's lips curved upward as well. Then Natalie's eyes turned to her left, drawing Jillian's gaze there as well. She found herself looking at a beautiful baby in Natalie's arms that looked like Wyatt only with strawberry blond hair that matched Natalie's.

That's my baby, Jillian thought, looking at the infant as Natalie placed a kiss on the child's head, *the one I lost*. Then Jillian followed her sister's eyes to the backseat of the car. Nathan sat there, only he was older, around five years old. He smiled at Jillian, and her heart soared with joy. He looked so happy.

Jillian turned her eyes back to Natalie. Her sister and the baby she held were bathed in light. Then they were gone, and the dream ended. Natalie didn't walk into the store and there was no gunshot, and Jillian awoke with a feeling of serenity. She was still sad for Keeley, but she felt settled and able to be happy that Nathan would stay with Wyatt and her. They would love him and do their very best for him as parents. They would honor Keeley's gift to them in that way.

And, somehow, Jillian knew she wouldn't have the dream again depicting her sister's death. Natalie was at peace and Jillian no longer felt guilty for being the one who lived. She looked forward to the day when she'd see her sister and her lost baby again in heaven. Until then, Jillian was going to throw her whole self into loving Wyatt, Nathan, and the rest of her family.

 # Epilogue

Seventeen years later

Nathan awoke to the sound of knocking. He groaned and held a pillow over his head.

The knocking came again.

"Go away!" Nathan called in a gravelly, sleepy voice.

"Not happening, birthday boy," Nathan's sister Angela called back. "Mom told me to make sure you got up and got your birthday boy butt downstairs." Angela giggled at her own words.

Nathan tossed the pillow at the door. It hit with a soft thunk and fell to the floor. "Okay, okay, I'm coming," he grumbled.

"Happy birthday!" Angela called.

Nathan smiled. He'd hoped to sleep at least until his alarm went off on his birthday, but he wasn't upset, certainly not at Angela. She was his best friend.

Angela and her biological sister, Terri, had come into the family as foster children when Nathan was five and were later adopted. Angela was only ten months younger than him and they'd become fast friends. Nathan couldn't imagine life without her as a sister.

He was just dragging himself out of bed when another knock sounded on his door.

"Cut it out, Angela! I said I'm coming," Nathan yelled.

"It's Dad, Nathan."

"Oh, sorry." Nathan trudged to the door and opened it for his father. "Hey, Dad."

Wyatt smiled. "Happy birthday!"

"Thanks." Nathan grinned.

"Your mom is making you a special breakfast and I've got something to give you."

"A present?" Nathan asked with surprise. Gifts were usually done at dinner on birthdays.

"Not exactly." Wyatt held out an envelope with Nathan's name on it.

Curious, Nathan took it.

"It's a letter from your birth mother. She asked us to give it to you on your eighteenth birthday." Wyatt paused. "Why don't you hold onto it and read it after the other kids go to school."

Nathan's face scrunched up in confusion. "Won't I be going to school with them?"

Wyatt squeezed Nathan's shoulder. "Not today. We have other plans ... if you agree to them."

Confused, Nathan furrowed his brow. But before he could formulate his questions, Wyatt slapped him on the back, said, "We better go get that breakfast while it's hot," and headed out the door.

After throwing on some clothes and combing his hair, Nathan made his way downstairs. A loud, "Happy birthday!" erupted from the group seated around the table when he reached the dining room. Grinning, Nathan let his eyes scan the room. They were quite a group with an array of appearances. They all looked different, but they were a family. Nathan loved how different they were. He loved Angela's sparkling blue eyes, Terri's red hair and freckles, and his little brother, Josiah's, head of close-cropped curls and dark skin. Terri found it uncomfortable when people asked how they could be siblings, but Nathan liked telling their story.

"Nathan, sit by me," Josiah said, patting the chair next to him.

Smiling at the eleven-year-old boy, Nathan sat down. Josiah held up a fist and Nathan bumped it with one of his own, remembering the way Josiah had shied away from almost all physical contact when he first came to them as a toddler. He'd been neglected and wasn't used to anyone touching him. Of course, that was nothing compared to the bruises and fear that accompanied Angela and Terri when they first arrived. Even though he was only five at the time, Nathan would always remember. They all still had their issues, but they were healthy and improving all the time with the love they got in this home.

Nathan's mother came in from the kitchen with a platter of pancakes. "I got the birthday boy's favorite!" She set the platter down in the middle of the table and smiled at Nathan with teary eyes. "I still can't believe you're eighteen."

"Believe it!" Nathan said, beaming, as he put two large pancakes on his plate.

When breakfast was over, Wyatt ushered the other three kids out to the car and drove them to school.

Jillian turned her attention to Nathan as he got up from the table, carrying several plates.

"I'll get these," Jillian said. "You go on and read your letter. Dad will be back soon, and we'll talk about our plans."

"Yeah, what are these plans?" Nathan asked, handing the plates over.

"The letter first, then we'll talk."

Nathan wasn't sure if his mother was happy about these secret plans or sad. Her eyes gleamed in a strange way.

He nodded and headed upstairs to his room.

Picking up the envelope, he slowly opened it. He'd already read one very long and very heartbreaking letter from his birth mother and heard the story of how that letter had affected his parents. He knew about his birth mother's return when he was a baby and everything that had happened back then.

So, what was this letter about?

He pulled the paper out, unfolded it, and began to read.

Dear Nathan,

It's been hard for me to learn to call you by that name, but you've made it clear to me that it is your name. You've also made it clear to me that coming back to get you isn't such a simple thing.

First and foremost, I love you. You are the most precious thing in the world to me and always have been. I hope your parents have told you about me and let you read the letter I wrote for you the first time I walked away from you. If so, you know I never wanted to leave you. And now that there isn't any threat to you, I thought I could come back for you. You're still so little, I thought it would be easy. But I was wrong.

I was wrong, but for the best possible reason. It's simple—you're already loved. I could see that quickly after I came back. It was obvious how much Wyatt and Jillian love you. I was glad to see that you were well cared for, but I still thought it was best for you to be with me. You've changed my mind.

Taking you away now would only serve me. I prayed for someone to come along and love you as much as I did. God answered that prayer. Now I see it would be wrong for me to wrench you away from that love. You're happy and healthy with parents that love you. And you love them.

I asked your parents to give you this letter when you turned eighteen because I hope that, as you are no longer a child, it might be possible for me to get to know you. I'll understand if you don't want that but know that I have no desire to change anything in your life. Your mom and dad will always be your parents. I don't expect you to call me Mom or change anything about your life. I only want some small part in it. I only hope to know you.

All my love,
Keeley

Nathan sighed as he put the letter back in the envelope. His birth mother wanted to meet him. Could that be what the secret plans were about?

He sat on his bed, thinking about his birth mother's words until he heard his mom call him. *Do I want to meet my birth mother?* He'd thought about it before, but he hadn't decided.

Standing up slowly, Nathan left the envelope on his bed and headed downstairs. When he reached the living room, where his parents waited, he asked, "Are we going to meet her? Is that what the secret plan is?"

"Only if you want to," Jillian said.

Nathan frowned, still unsure. "But you have a meeting planned? You know where she is?"

Jillian nodded and Wyatt said, "Yes, but if you don't want to, we can call it off. It's up to you."

Nathan shrugged. "I'm not sure if I want to. I'm curious, but what if it changes things?"

"It won't change anything with us," Jillian said. "And I don't believe Keeley wants anything from you except a chance to know you."

"It feels weird to think about it all." He scrunched up his nose. "I mean, do I have any sisters or brothers?" Nathan felt strange even asking. Angela, Terri, and Josiah were his siblings. Still, how could he not be curious about biological siblings? If he had any, would they look like him?

"Keeley has a daughter," Jillian said. "But you won't be meeting her today. Of course, if you want to meet her at a later time, I'm sure you could."

Nathan nodded thoughtfully. He didn't know what he thought or felt about all of this. It was so much to think about.

Wyatt stepped up to him and patted his shoulder. "Think it through for a few minutes, then let us know what you want to do. If you aren't ready, we can put it off. You're in charge of this."

Nathan met his father's eyes, then his mother's. "You'll both be with me?"

They nodded.

"Then let's do it," Nathan said, trying to sound more confident than he felt. In truth, he was filled with unease and uncertainty.

They climbed in the car and Nathan's head filled with questions. He sat in the middle of the backseat so he could see both of his parents. Leaning up between their seats, he asked, "Are we going to meet her at her house?"

"No," Wyatt said. "She lives on the other side of the state. We're going to meet her halfway at a park."

"Okay," Nathan said and fell silent. He let his mind drift with the vibrations of the road and before long, he was dozing off.

When the car hit a bump in the road, Nathan's eyes flew open. "Are we there?" he asked.

Jillian chuckled. "Do you think kids ever outgrow that question?" she asked, glancing at Wyatt.

"Probably not," Wyatt said with amusement.

Smiling at the joke, Nathan said, "Cut me some slack. I was asleep." He rubbed his eyes and let them scan the view out the window. "Is it okay to ask if we're close?"

"We'll be there in about thirty minutes," Wyatt said. "You took a pretty good snooze back there."

"Yeah, I guess so. Thirty minutes, huh?" Butterflies filled his stomach as the realization hit him that he'd soon be meeting his birth mother. "Do you think she'll like me?"

Jillian twisted around in her seat and regarded him with a soft expression. "Of course, she will. You're an amazing young man. And besides, she already loves you."

"I know she did. But it's been a long time." He paused, his stomach flipping more with the next thought on his mind. "I'm not a baby anymore and ... she has another kid now."

Jillian furrowed her brow at him. "You think that could change her love for you?"

He shrugged.

"Nathan," Wyatt spoke up, "did we love you less when Angela and Terri came into the family?"

Nathan shook his head. "No."

Jillian reached a hand back and took one of his. "Having another child doesn't diminish the love you have for the first." She squeezed his hand. "And, sweetheart, she loves you. I know she does."

Nathan nodded, and Jillian turned back to the front of the car.

"You know what I've had on my mind today?" Jillian asked.

"No, what?" Nathan said.

"I've wondered if you might like her better than me." A waver in her tone told Nathan his mother's feelings were nearly as raw as his.

"It won't matter how much I like her," Nathan said. "You'll always be my mom."

Jillian sniffed. "It means the world to hear you say that. Now, we all have our questions and fears. What do you think Keeley's are?"

Frowning, Nathan shrugged. "I don't know."

"Imagine being in her place as best you can for a moment. What do you think she feels?" Jillian asked.

Nathan thought for a minute. "Maybe she thinks I won't like her? Maybe she thinks I'll be angry with her for leaving me?"

Jillian met his eyes again, turning to the backseat. "Maybe she's just as nervous as you are."

"Maybe," Nathan said almost to himself.

"This is emotional for all of us," Wyatt said. "Try not to put any pressure on it. No matter what, you have us and your sisters and brother. But maybe soon you'll have that plus a relationship with your birth mother and sister. Just let her get to know you and try to get to know her."

"And no matter what, you'll always be our son," Jillian added.

Nathan nodded with a wan smile. He sat back against his seat and stayed quiet the rest of the way to the meeting site.

A short while later, they pulled up to a park and parked the car under a stand of trees. There was a red Chevy a few spaces away and, on a bench, not far into the park, a lovely Asian woman sat.

"We're here," Wyatt said. "And it looks like Keeley is waiting for you.

"That's her?" Nathan said as the woman on the bench stood up and looked toward the car.

"That's her," Jillian said.

They all got out of the car and Nathan wiped sweaty hands on his pant legs.

"You want us to walk over with you?" Wyatt asked.

Nathan let his eyes meet up with his birth mother's. She did look as nervous as he was, and somehow, that made him feel better. He turned to his parents. "No, I think I'll go alone."

With a nod from his parents, Nathan began walking toward Keeley, and when she smiled at him, a calm filled his heart. He could see the love in her eyes, and as he closed the distance between them, he found himself walking right into her arms. Words would come later.

ABOUT THE AUTHOR

Rebecca L. Marsh is an award-winning author of women's fiction and member of the Paulding County Writer's Guild. She grew up in the mountains of Western North Carolina, and now lives in Dallas, Georgia, with her husband and daughter.

When she isn't writing or taking care of her family (cats and dog included), she occasionally likes to make homemade candy and work on her scrapbooks (she is woefully behind).

She is the author of five novels: When the Storm Ends, The Rift Between Us, Where Hope is Found, Remember the Butterfly, and Summer's Runaway.

Visit her website at rebeccalmarsh.com

Or follow her on Facebook at

Author: Rebecca L. Marsh

ACKNOWLEDGMENTS

A special thanks to those who took the time to help me in any way—all my beta readers. Thank you to Maggie Brewer, my niece who does an often thankless job in social services and who helped me with the research for this book. She was kind enough to give me information and answer my many questions. Also to a friend and nurse, Angie Young, who is always willing to help me with the medical questions that crop up. Thank you to the Paulding County Writer's Guild who are both friends and support group for me, and especially Heather Trim who did such a nice job designing the cover for this book. Most of all, I want to thank my family—all of them. I also want to give a very special thanks to Joe and Maegan for being my support all along the way.

Note from the Author

Thank you for reading *Remember the Butterfly*. I value all my readers, and hope you have enjoyed it. Independent authors really depend on reader's support for their work. If you'd like to leave a review on Amazon or Goodreads, I would greatly appreciate it. You can also follow me on Facebook@ Author: Rebecca L. Marsh.

Leave a review on Amazon

Leave a review on Goodreads

Thanks for your support!

Made in the USA
Columbia, SC
15 March 2023